SOLO

Rana Dasgupta

HarperCollins *Publishers* India

First published in hardback in India in 2009 by
HarperCollins *Publishers* India

HarperCollins Publishers India, Cyber City, Building 10-A, Gurugram,
Haryana-122002, India

www.harpercollins.co.in

First published in paperback in 2011

ISBN: 978-93-5029-060-6

2 4 6 8 10 9 7 5 3

Typeset in Minion Pro
InoSoft Systems

Printed and bound at
MicroPrints India, New Delhi

MIX
Paper
FSC
FSC® C218906

This product is made of FSC®-certified and other controlled material.

HarperCollins Publishers, Macken House, 39/40 Mayor Street
Upper, Dublin 1, D01 C9W8, Ireland

RANA DASGUPTA was born in Canterbury in 1971. His first book, *Tokyo Cancelled* (2005), was shortlisted for the John Llewellyn Rhys Prize. He lives in Delhi.

From the reviews of *Solo*:

'Utterly unforgettable in its humanity. It hums with the inner and outer melodies of a life lived solo, until it becomes a discordant symphony of the human condition. The kind of 'philharmonic' novel that reminds us why we will always need to tell the extraordinary stories of people's ordinary lives' *Guardian*

'Dasgupta is an inventive, experimental writer, whose second novel is often meditative and sometimes witty; a finely wrought achievement' *Times Literary Supplement*

'This gloriously eccentric adventure through a century of Bulgarian history is so much fun to read you'll hardly realise how much you're learning ... Weird, wonderful and warmly wise stuff' *Daily Mail*

'In this deliriously sad, bewitching novel, the Delhi-based Dasgupta updates the magic realism of the subcontinent, and brings it fully formed into a new century' *Metro*

'*Solo* is beautifully symphonic – elegiac and prophetic, underpinned by intelligence, compassion and a wonderfully unfettered imagination. It's a necessary as well as a timely novel ... When I finished I wanted to go back to the beginning and read it all over again' *Sunday Business Post*

‘Dasgupta consistently provides flashes of brilliance and masterful descriptions … in this bold, stimulating, unclassifiable epic’
The Boston Globe

‘Dasgupta’s writing soars … [a] deeply empathetic and serious writer’
The New York Times

‘Utterly refreshing … Mr Dasgupta writes so silkily …’
The Wall Street Journal

‘*Solo* is bold in execution … Rana Dasgupta has created a work that is both literary and compelling’
The Globe and Mail

‘The novel’s eclectic mix of music and misery is fatally addictive. … one of the most energetic magic-realist novels in recent times … should be read not just for the brilliant story-telling, but also for the universal truths that it reflects and reiterates’
The New Indian Express

‘Dasgupta’s narrative is designed more like a jazz composition.… This is a beautiful book well worth the reading’
Hindustan Times

‘The writing is always compact … remarkable … images linger in the mind for some time after the pages are turned’
Elle

‘A journey of the soul, an exploration of grief’
The Statesman

for my darling Monica

FIRST MOVEMENT
'Life'

Magnesium

1

THE MAN HAS WOKEN SUDDENLY, in the dead zone of the night. It is unnaturally hot for the time of year; his throat is raw and there is sweat in all his creases.

He stumbles to the sink for water. Then he sits in his armchair, and snorts a few times to clear his nose.

The bus station outside his window is being modernised, and he can hear the drills screaming even at this hour.

In the interest of reducing crime, two blinding floodlights have been installed in the station forecourt. They seem to have deceived the local birds, which now begin their dawn chorus in the middle of the night, just as the man succeeds in dozing off. At this very moment, they are squawking as if possessed.

Breathing heavily in his chair, the man is scorched by a halogen glow from outside, though there is darkness in the room.

Unmindful of the time, the travellers in the bus station bring great ingenuity to the making of noise, shouting and clanging and revving their moribund cars, as if no one were trying to sleep.

The man is nearing the end of his life's tenth decade, and his apartment is on the fourth floor.

The main room measures four by three and a half metres. There is a bathroom to the side, and, at the end, an area for cooking. The window looks out on the stalls in front of the bus station, where people sell goods from China: alarm clocks, watch straps, plastic plants, batteries, T-shirts, souvenirs, and so on. There are also currency sellers who sit waiting to trade with those who arrive on buses from other countries.

There is a leak in one corner of the man's ceiling, which lets in water when it rains. This water has leached slowly into the plaster in a shape that resembles a map of Australia, causing paint to fall and a smell of cisterns to hang continually in the room.

The window faces west; so the apartment is brightest in the evening.

The government still sees fit to pay the man a pension every month in order to sustain him in his penury. When he retired, many years ago, this money was quite adequate: he lived alone and had few requirements. But with everything that has happened in the economy, his pension has become nearly worthless, and his savings have disappeared. If it were not for the generosity of his neighbours, who buy food and other supplies for him every month, he would now find himself in an alarming situation. They are good people: they pay for the man's television subscription, and the wife even cooks his meals, since he can no longer manage it himself.

But he does not like bothering them every time he needs more coffee or toilet paper. He has put in many years on this earth, and he feels he has a right to expect that such things will come to him unbidden.

Events have turned the man blind. But his hearing is quite intact, and his primary entertainment is still his television. He sits in front of beauty contests whose contestants he cannot see, infomercials, badly dubbed period dramas from England, travel shows, German pornography, and every other kind of modern wisdom.

Sometimes, late at night, when his television is turned off, he hears the interminable ring of a telephone somewhere below, and he lies awake wondering where in the world this yearning might be housed, and what it might seek so insistently in this building.

In the afternoons, the breeze brings with it a slight scent of old urine from the wall below his window. All the men who pass through the bus station duck behind that wall to relieve themselves against it. There are public toilets in the station, but they do not seem to be able to compete with the wall, which holds an uncanny attraction for any man with a full bladder. Even men who have never been there before, and do not realise it is already filled with the reeking sludge of twenty years, give not a second glance to the broken cubicles at the edge of the square. At any moment, two or three of them can be seen standing in the shelter of this wall, shaking out their last drops.

Women use the cubicles, broken as they are.

On hot days, the smells become overpowering, and rain comes as a relief, washing everything away. The blind man sits by the window when the rain is heavy and he can hear the patters of near and far: the silky spray in the trees, the heavy drumming on plastic water tanks, the hard scatter of roads and pavements, the different metallic pitches of car roofs and drain covers, the baritone trilling of tarpaulin, the sticky overflow of mud, the concentrated gushing of drainpipes – and, for a moment, the landscape springs forth, and he is reminded how it is to see.

With the exception of his back, which tortures him every morning, the man's health is still passable, and yet, by the sheer force of numbers, his death cannot be so far away.

As a child, the man watched his grandmother put up biographies of the dead on the trees outside their house. She had come from a village near the Black Sea – cut off, now, by the border – and it was the dead from this distant village whose accomplishments were listed on the trunks of those proud and equidistant plane trees. Every day, it seemed, was the death-day of someone or other from that remote place and his grandmother told him the stories over morning tea as she wrote out her obituaries. She tied them with string to the trees, where they decomposed gradually in the rain, to be renewed the following year.

'How do you remember?' he asked her again and again, for it seemed marvellous that the entire history of that lost dynasty could be preserved in her mind. But his father disapproved of the rural practice and her own life was never written up on a tree.

Sensitive, like all infants, to the beyond, the man had in those years a powerful sense of the infinitude of generations. He had seen people buried in the ground with their eyes closed; and in his mind he envisioned the earth in cutaway, with the stacked-up strata of sleeping bodies so vertiginous in their depth that it was simple to believe the lightness of life on the surface to be no more than their collective dream. For the dreamers, quiet and eternal in their moist refuge, greatly outnumbered those with open eyes.

These early intuitions returned to the man recently, when he listened to a television programme about a town that was buried under water after the construction of a dam. Eighty years later, the dam was decommissioned and dismantled. The lake subsided, the river resumed its previous route, and the town rose again into the sunlight.

There had been extensive damage, of course. Water had dissolved the plaster from walls, and roofs had caved in. Wooden buildings had floated away, bit by bit. Trees had died, and the whole town stank of dead fish and river weed for weeks after it was drained. But there were cars still parked on the streets – antique models, as the man remembered from his own youth. There were clocks arrested at different times, and a cinema with the titles of old films stuck up outside. Road signs had stood firm all this time, pointing the way to underwater destinations. In every house, things had been left behind. A man found a jar of pickles in a kitchen, and tasted them, and pronounced them still good. Some old people who had lived in the town before the deluge were taken to see it again – and it was for them as if they were transported back into a childhood fantasy.

These days, the man devotes himself to wading through the principal events of his life in order to discover what relics may lie submerged there. Of course, he has no family around him, his friends have all gone, and he knows that no living person is interested in his thoughts. But he has survived a long time, and he does not want it to end with a mindless falling-off.

Before the man lost his sight, he read this story in a magazine: a group of explorers came upon a community of parrots speaking the language of a society that had been wiped out in a recent catastrophe. Astonished by their discovery, they put the parrots in cages and sent them home so that linguists could record what remained of the lost language. But the parrots, already traumatised by the devastation they had witnessed, died on the way.

The man feels a great fraternity with those birds. He feels he carries, like them, a shredded inheritance, and he is too concussed to pass anything on.

That is why he is combing through his life again. He has no wealth and no heirs, and if he has anything at all to leave behind, it will be tangled deep, and difficult to find.

2

THE MAN IS CALLED ULRICH. The absurdity of this name can be blamed on his father, who had a love affair with all things German. Over the years, a lot of time has gone into explaining it.

Ulrich was born here in Sofia, in an imposing house on Dondukov Boulevard just opposite the Shumenska restaurant. Ulrich's father built the house in the Viennese style during his years of affluence: he employed an Austrian architect, and had the façade plastered with lyres, and urns overflowing with fruit, and the bold-faced year: 1901.

In those days, men like Ulrich's father, the men in suits and hats, were the minority in Sofia. They were outnumbered by the pigs and donkeys and the kerchiefed peasants driving poultry and pumpkins. They were outshone by the august Jewish and Armenian merchants who struck business deals amid scented smoke, silks and spittoons. They could barely understand the speech of the women at the market stalls, who sat jangling with iron hoops. The rhythms of commerce were supplied not by the opening times of their banks but by the gait of camels, which came in trains from all over the Ottoman Empire to provide carpets and gold to the Turkish traders around the Banya Bashi mosque. And they were powerless against the Gypsies who took over the city now and then, assembling in an afternoon a swarming settlement of skin tents and fires, filling the bazaars with curiosities from abroad and sowing restless thoughts among the children.

But the men in suits had plans for expansion. As the Ottoman Empire's tide retreated, Sofia found itself beached in Europe – and these men plotted to turn their provincial Turkish town into a new European capital city. They studied Berlin and Paris to find out what was required, and all of it – cathedral, tramway, university, royal palace, science museum, national theatre, national assembly – they re-created faithfully in Sofia. At the entrances to the future metropolis were haystacks piled up like mountains to sustain the multitudes of horses carrying stone and steel for the new constructions, and traders and labourers swarmed over the swampy void left by everything that had been torn down.

Ulrich's father was a railway engineer. He had had the good fortune, in his youth, to study engineering at the mining school at Freiberg in Moravia, and his career was begun on the Vienna–Constantinople railway line built by Baron de Hirsch. By the time of Ulrich's earliest memories, his father was engaged across Anatolia and Mesopotamia under Philipp Holzmann, the contractor for Deutsche Bank's enormous railway investments in the Ottoman Empire, who appointed him senior engineer on the new line from Berlin to Baghdad.

For Ulrich's father, there was no calling more noble, more *philosophical*, than the railways. As he dreamed, his moustache trembled with the snaking of glinting rails across continents. Next to the churches, synagogues and mosques he saw new edifices hatching roofs of steel and glass, and departure boards unfolding within, full of the promise of discovery. In the ecstasy of his reverie, he hovered above the cartoon face of the planet, now wrapped in twin lines of steel and given over, finally, to science and understanding.

When he took a journey, he travelled second class in order to encounter the awestruck families in traditional clothes who found themselves in a railway carriage for the very first time. He eavesdropped on their anxious commentaries, he grunted conspicuously and shook his head; and while Ulrich's mother gave her husband discouraging flicks with her gloves, he waited for the right moment to intervene.

'I beseech you all: fear not!' he began, grandiloquently. 'This is a scientific road, built according to the principles of Newton, and should we travel at triple this speed, still we would come to no harm!'

Having verified to his satisfaction that all mindless chatter had ceased, he stood up to address the company.

'You good and simple folk, who have never travelled faster than the poor horse could drag you through the mud, are lucky to see this day when suddenly you are plucked up and propelled as fast as thought! Treasure this moment, and think upon this speed which now sends your minds descending into chasms of terror; for this is the rumbling inside you of the new age.'

When some village woman drew her shawl around her and complained of the nausea that the flashing landscape produced in her stomach, he pointed at the horizon and adjured her:

'Do not look at the poppies outside your window, madam, for they race more rapidly than your senses can apprehend. Look instead at the church spires and mountains in the distance, whose movements are more steady. For this is the vision of our new times: we have been liberated from the myopia that kept human beings peering at their own miserable patch of earth, bound to proclaim with sword and drum its superiority to every other. From now on, they will see far, and look upon a common future!'

As the unfortunate target of this outburst withdrew farther under her wrappings, a meek husband would draw the fire gallantly to himself, asking some timid question about how rails were laid, or how signals operated – to which Ulrich's father gave long and ecstatic answers, gesticulating with the loftiness of the spirit within him, and drawing technical diagrams for the edification of his audience.

Whenever the newspaper arrived in the morning with the story of a railway accident, it would throw him into a temper for days. He cursed the drowsy signalmen or drunken drivers who betrayed the scientific age with idiocy, mutilations and death. 'These abominations will cease,' he would retort angrily when anyone chose to engage him on the subject. 'It is only a matter of time.'

Much of Ulrich's childhood was spent in train compartments and hotels, following his father's work. The entire household set out for weeks on end, journeying to where the tracks gave out. There were the armies of the workers, thousands of them, tented in the brushland under a dome of dust that signalled their labour for miles around: Italians, Greeks, Armenians, Turks, Arabs, Kurds, and others from all over the empire – hammering at the desert floor under the supervision of turbaned envoys from the Sublime Porte and handlebar-moustached German engineers. Crowds of cooks, doctors, prostitutes, fruit sellers, musicians, tobacco sellers and dancers advanced with them along the envisioned highway, and, as the daylight expired, an endless congregation of wood fires sprang to life under the stars, chickens and goats were thrust on spits, and great iron cauldrons were set upon the flames. Everywhere men were eating, joking, sleeping, arguing and pissing, while packs of camels and horses looked dispassionately on. This was the assembly that hauled the silver lines from the mouth of the metropolis across the scrub of Anatolia; and Ulrich's father could weep with the grandeur of it.

The earliest memory Ulrich still retains is this: he is lying alone at night under translucent canvass, a blanket folded carefully around him. At the edge of his hearing is the hubbub of the multitude, and he watches the twitching shape of a lizard on the roof above him, outlined by the lapping firelight. The brightness of his eyes comes not from these things, however, but from the sounds of the musicians. Even at this age, he does not need to see the dancing to know what reflexes the music induces in the men's bodies.

After so many years, the melodies have drained away, but he can still recall their effect on his tucked-up child flesh.

He stores another memory from that time, or shortly after: his father's temper in a café in Constantinople when politics interfered with his work. 'If the British Empire is so fragile that a pair of steel rails can bring it down – then let it fall! Will they threaten us, because we approach their routes, because we near their India, their precious Suez Canal? We are here to bring the peoples of the world together, and such a mission will stand before any rebuke!'

He stamped on the floor with the injustice of it, and Ulrich learned it was possible to be angry with people one did not know.

Ulrich's father's idealism proved to be a liability in the long run. When, during the Great War, the British destroyed the railway tracks he had helped to build, he took it as a personal calamity, as if the charges had been set at his own nerve junctions, and he fretted about it for the rest of his life. Trying to pull his country as fast as possible out of Asia, he never thought he would be razed by an excess of Europe.

Ulrich's mother's name was Elizaveta. Throughout Ulrich's life, whenever he has wished to picture her happy, he has returned to one memory. He wakes in his tent in the desert to find his parents already arisen. He crawls out into the dawn, fuddled by sleep: the fires are burning for breakfast, a camel coughs clouds in the chill, and the horizon is smooth and bichrome. His mother sits on a wooden stool sipping steaming tea, and she stares from under her shawl at the sun's bubble, ascending over the edge of the world and turning her smile orange.

She picked up Turkish and Arabic, and she loved to set out among the villages with a muleteer and pay visits to the local women. She made sketches for them of Bulgarian peasant costumes so they would have an idea of the place she had come from, and she kept notebooks full of observations about their beliefs and customs. Sometimes she stayed away for three days at a time, journeying with her young son through the Tigris valley with only her Bulgarian manservant and a Kurdish guide for company.

Is Ulrich deceiving himself when he imagines that he has stood with her in an ancient monastery carved entirely out of rock, somewhere on the way to Mosul, where the aged bishop has taken vows of silence and lives in solitude on the top of an inaccessible mountain? Surely not: for he remembers looking up to the astonishing incline where every day the man lowers a basket for his food – the basket in which, when his last mortal sickness comes upon him, he will send down a message so they may climb up to collect his body. Ulrich remembers eating mulberries and pomegranates plucked from trees by the Tigris, and all the flowers, and his mother laughing with her Kurdish guide, saying,

This is paradise. Another snatch of the past: Ulrich has been dressed in a red shirt (for the wearing of blue is offensive to Yezidi people, and how marvellous that there can be a prohibition on a colour!) and he sits in a dim room in a low-built house whose threshold is decorated with a painted snake. There is a woman seated on a mat who wears a flowing headdress (whose unfamiliar folds are disquieting to the young boy) and who cuts up into squares, with great delectation, a pulpy substance that is shiny on her fingers. She eyes him curiously and without warning she is possessed by the desire to stroke his cheeks with her sticky hands. He runs to take shelter behind his mother, who appals him by eating these syrupy squares and declaring her delight. On the journey home, she tells him these people have experienced violent raids and live in terror of a great massacre: their religion is an offence to the Musulmans who live in these parts and, now that the empire is breaking up, they are in perpetual peril. And with the narcissism of childhood he is filled with regret at having denied the woman his cheek when she was about to die.

Ulrich remembers his father's late-night fury at Elizaveta when she returned from one of those rural expeditions – and perhaps they were less numerous than he now imagines. For he also recalls the heavy tedium of big city hotels where the family stayed for weeks together, and restaurants where his mother sat in unending debates over politics. Elizaveta had a consuming passion for Ottoman affairs – she wrote about them regularly for the Bulgarian newspapers – and she was never so content as when exchanging political analyses with other informed observers. These conversations drove her young son to distraction. He hated the diplomats and businessmen whose arguments absorbed her so, and he tried to disrupt their speeches with tears and full-blown choking tantrums. He developed an array of ruses for prising Elizaveta's attentions away from them, and, though she held out for a while, his complaints of sickness, headaches and ringing in his ears would eventually force her to board a train with him back to Sofia.

He sang on the journey, happy to have her to himself again. He was joyful when they arrived back at home (the house cold and dim save for the small corner kept alive by his grandmother's movement) and he ran off to play with the children he knew in the houses round about. But each time he discovered that they had grown out of the games he had shared with them before he went away, and turned to others he did not know – ones that seemed calculated to exclude casual visitors such as he.

Perhaps this was why Ulrich became such a solitary child. The stuccoed cube of his bedroom, perched up in that big house, became the most dependable thing in his world, and he filled it with the ample emission of his daydreams.

His father was exasperated by his early signs of introversion.

'You are privileged enough, at a young age, to enjoy the society of talented and influential men – and all you can do is stammer and scratch, and hold your foot in your hand like a fool. You will not be a failure, my son. Whatever it takes, I will not allow it.'

3

BY WHAT ALCHEMY is an obsession kindled in a boy?

Another child who passed through Ulrich's early experiences might have emerged with a passion for machines. His father encouraged him in that direction, with his tender demonstrations of engines and the delightful way he simulated moving parts with his long white fingers. Or he might have conceived a fascination with exploration, or the study of peoples. But there was something Ulrich's early attentions found more marvellous.

One day, when Elizaveta was alone with Ulrich in the house, she heard him singing. Following the sound, she came upon him, not yet six years old, giving a solo performance in the middle of the lavish drawing room, where there hung a series of prints of the Ringstrasse that her husband had once purchased in Vienna. Ulrich produced from his boyish throat a passable imitation of a violin's whine, and he improvised a tune with such zeal that Elizaveta wondered where this spirit had come from to enter her son. He moved while he sang, a jerky child's version of a grown man's dance, and he clapped a drum here and there. His music became faster and more breathless, and, as he rolled into the last variation on his theme, his eyes widened and his head shook with what he felt inside – until the performance exploded in one final stamping flourish. Ulrich stood entirely still for a moment, the hiss of the fire the only sound in the room. Then he burst into his own applause and bowed low to an unseen audience, and his mother took her opportunity to withdraw.

Whenever news reached Ulrich that the Gypsies had come to Sofia, he would run through the streets to their encampment and beg the weary fiddlers to play for him, jumping on the spot with impatience until they gave in. As long as they were in the city, he would follow them wherever they went, capering on the street corners where they played, and imitating, with an imaginary violin under his chin, their sway, their foot-tap, and their bow.

The Gypsies always left without warning, so there would come a morning when he went out to find only a forlorn patch of ground, flattened and smoking, where dogs and pigs sniffed the leftovers. He would take out his handkerchief and wave it at the empty road – a gesture he had observed at railway stations and presumed grandiose.

Ulrich heard about gramophone records, in which men captured music and sealed it up, and he developed a fascination for them. The family did not possess a gramophone player, but this did not prevent him from demanding records, for it made him happy to arrange them around his room like talismans. In those days there were few gramophone records available in Sofia, and Elizaveta discovered therein a means of appeasing her son when they set off for journeys abroad. His favourite place on earth became Herr Stern's Odeon record shop on the Grande Rue de Pera in Constantinople, where it was possible to listen to records in an enchanted room festooned with rugs and paintings.

It was Herr Stern who introduced Ulrich to the music of Cemil Bey, the great Turkish tanbur player, and who expanded his tastes to include the Armenian and Greek musicians, and singers from Egypt. Together they discussed music, innovations in recording equipment, and news from the big companies that manufactured Ulrich's delights – Odeon from Germany, Gramco from England, Baidaphon from Lebanon and Victor from America.

'Is Odeon the *very* best company, Herr Stern?' he liked to ask.

'Odeon certainly has a very great range,' replied Herr Stern without condescension. 'In our part of the world, they have recorded many more musicians than the others. Many excellent masters who were only known in their own small towns until a few years ago – now Odeon has made them into celebrities that you and I can listen to in our homes.'

'But Odeon invented the double-sided record, and now all the others have copied them. So they must be the best!'

Herr Stern laughed.

'Perhaps you're right!'

'Will someone invent a triple-sided record some day, Herr Stern?'

Ulrich was full of questions, but he chose not to ask why his own family did not possess a gramophone player, when modern brass horns had begun to bloom proudly in all the other houses they visited in Sofia. There was an evening when his father, increasingly irritated by the piano exercises of the girl in the adjoining house, suddenly banged down his spoon and appealed furiously: 'Can that child not be made to stop?' Other things added up along the way: the absence of musical instruments and Sunday afternoon concerts. Ulrich noticed that his mother's singing voice fell silent when his father was around, and he began to sense in her a philharmonic sadness, looming like the outsized shadows in the modern paintings they saw on their visits to Vienna.

He was therefore surprised when his mother announced, during one of his father's absences, that she wished to buy him a violin. He knew it was an assault on the household's unspoken rules.

He went with her to the violin maker's shop, and of course it was the climax of all his hopes: the gloomy room where rows of ruddy instruments were hung, redolent of wood and varnish. The violin maker played on them so Ulrich could judge the tone, the children's half-size instruments tucked like toys under his enormous beard. Ulrich chose the one that was the most beautiful of all. Elizaveta was delighted, and she said to the violin maker, 'Please just show him how to put his hands. He doesn't have a teacher yet.' So the man crouched behind Ulrich and operated his hands like a puppeteer, supporting the instrument and moving the bow, and Ulrich felt it was all much more difficult than he had imagined.

He threw himself into his violin practice. Mealtimes and lessons became inconveniences, and all his other pursuits were forgotten. Lacking a teacher, he studied photographs of violinists to see how they positioned their fingers, and he invented exercises to make his movements more assured. When the Gypsies next came into town, Ulrich ran with his violin and pestered them for advice and demonstrations. He studied their performance with the attentiveness of a fellow musician. By the time they left, he was confident that the mysteries of music would not resist him, and he would play his violin as well as any human being. He told himself, 'I am one of them.'

'Do you think that Father will allow me to take lessons?' he asked his mother doubtfully.

'I think when he sees how much progress you have already made on your own, it will be impossible for him to refuse.'

'Really?' Ulrich asked, unconvinced.

'Why not?' she said, with a hint of evasion. 'Why don't you give a concert for him when he returns? He will be amazed at what you have achieved.'

Given his father's love of all things Viennese, Ulrich decided to prepare a waltz that was often performed by the orchestra in the Shumenska restaurant opposite their house. He listened at the restaurant window until he had memorised it, and then began to reproduce it on his own instrument. He practised it until every note was perfectly sculpted for his father's return.

On that evening, he set up the drawing room as a concert hall, with two armchairs for his parents and an upturned chest as a podium. He put on a little black suit and took a bow tie from his father's dressing room. When his preparations were complete, he summoned his audience and sat them down. After a few vigorous swipes of his bow in the empty air, he began.

Ulrich's eyes were set on his father, who sat folded in one half of his armchair. He saw the lines gathering on his father's forehead, and he watched the tips of his moustache rise to meet them. He thought of a stormy tangle of telegraph wires, and a flock of birds above the bars of lowered railway barriers. He thought of a set of photographs he had once seen in a bookshop, which showed the expressions induced in mental patients by the application of electric currents to the various muscles of the face. He thought of a day when he had posed for a photograph in front of the opera house in Vienna, the folds of his mother's parasol ticklish against his bare legs, and his father had said, 'If only we had been conquered by the Austrians, and not the Turks, we would have had some of this Enlightenment for ourselves,' and Ulrich had wondered if he was talking about a kind of cake. He thought of anything but the music, and, in the middle of the waltz, a great buzzing filled his ears, and his playing simply trailed off.

His bow caught a violin string awkwardly as he lowered it, and there was a catastrophic *plink*. And the family sat once again in a silence punctuated only by the funereal bark of the crows outside.

His father seized the violin from Ulrich's hand and brandished it at his wife like a meat cleaver.

'You bought this for him? Haven't we talked about this before?'

His anger raised him up, and he circled the room.

'You won't do this, my son! I won't have you waste your life. Musicians, artists, criminals, opium addicts… You'll end up poor and disgraced. I won't have it!'

As he threw the violin into the fire, Ulrich's mother was already sobbing, and, when the sparks flew up with the impact, she howled with grief and ran from the room.

Ulrich, still holding his listless violin bow, joined his father in contemplating the incendiary demise of his instrument. He noticed that the varnish burned differently from the wood underneath – more furious, and almost white – while the copper from the G string sent a streak of green through the conflagration. The ebony did not burn fully, and later, when the fire died down, a charred rack was left behind.

The next day, Ulrich had occasion to note that the shellac from which gramophone records were made burned differently again. A broad orange, with a diffuse, sooty, pungent flame.

Ulrich was too young to imagine that his father's opinions could be simply brushed aside. For a long time he bore a grudge against both father and music. But since the former would not be altered, he pushed the latter far down inside him where it could cause no more damage. Only in the concealed realm of his daydreams did it emerge again, inviolate.

In the rest of his life, Ulrich resolved to be more circumspect in his attachments, and to surrender them when necessary. Later on, when he saw what happened to people who refused to give up their convictions, he wondered if this is why he survived so long.

A curious thing: Ulrich's father made an exception, in his strenuous censorship of music, for the song of birds. In fact, he had an unusually passionate love of birdsong, and could recognise a hundred different species by their calls. He taught Ulrich how to imitate birdsong with whistles and throaty warbles. On such tender ground, Ulrich and his father found common cause; and his memories of the walks they took together to hear the dawn chorus remain some of the happiest of all his childhood.

4

One day, Ulrich's father came into his bedroom. He said, 'Remember everything.'

He was dressed as a soldier.

All at once, Ulrich's father stopped taking him for Sunday walks. His exercises. His excitement at new scientific discoveries. Buying pork at the market. He abandoned all this and became a soldier in a war.

He sat on Ulrich's bed in his improbable uniform. He looked at his son and said, 'Remember everything.' When Ulrich thinks back now, he feels that he was staring into the gas lamp to examine its glare. Was there also another boy with him, crouching by his side? It seems to him there was. It was so long ago: and as he pictures it now his father is but a military silhouette to his dazzled eyes.

He has forgotten.

Those were the days of his father's wealth, when he was admired in the city, and would strike out into the world with projects and opinions. He had travelled widely, and dressed in a way that made him seem idiosyncratic and cosmopolitan. He liked dogs and cameras. He was proud of his Russian samovar, and had many discussions with his servant about its use. He took Ulrich to the fair, and roared with delight as he soared on the swings. He attended lectures by famous scientists, and tried to reconstruct their arguments over the dinner table. He had a system of exercises to which he ascribed his vigour. He loved to travel by tram, even on the most crowded days. He saw signs in every morning's newspaper that the world was getting better. He stood rigid in church, and irritated Elizaveta with his devotions. He requested daily letters from Ulrich, even when they were in the same house, and insisted that he learn German and French. He took him to the opening of the first cinema in Sofia. He became a soldier in a war.

'I chose your name, Ulrich. I have always thought it sounded noble.' He said that, too; and then he left the room in a manner that indicated he had not got what he came for. He was gone for years.

Ulrich does not know which war his father was going to on that day, since there were several at that time. But he knows he fell sick with typhus while his father was away. It was the year of the epidemic, and the disease was all around. He had seen a dead woman by the side of the road, and while his mother had yanked his hand and said *Don't look, don't look!* he had turned back obstinately to stare at the unhappy corpse, and wondered whose job it was to clear such things away.

But typhus was not supposed to enter clean, well-aired houses such as theirs, and Elizaveta was terrified. She burned all his clothes and filled the closets with mothballs.

Ulrich cannot recall the feeling of typhus, only the effect it had on adult faces. His eyes are burning with formalin, and the doctor sits heavily by his bed. The stethoscope is great and cold on his chest, and the medical gaze is intent behind the pince-nez, in whose steady glass the reflection of the window is two bright dancing rectangles; and, as Ulrich lies motionless, searching in the doctor's eyes for the intuition of whether he will live or die, twin white feathers fall there, scything side to side in the miniature double sky.

When he recovered, his mother clasped him to her and said,

'My baby. Don't ever leave me!'

Some time after, on an evening when she had filled the Dondukov Boulevard mansion with guests, he remembers descending the broad staircase quite naked, and weaving unselfconsciously through the adult crush to find her. Seeing him so exposed, she hurried over, furious with shame, and sent him running back up the stairs.

At breakfast the next day, Ulrich had to listen to an indignant speech about how he should behave in public. His mother was too simple-minded to understand that his humiliating display was intended to prove that he was innocent of the knowledge that would turn him into an adult, and take him away.

With his father's absence came the end of their travels, and Ulrich began to attend the local school. He sat next to a boy named Boris, who had been born on the same date as he, a year before. Such a coincidence gave Ulrich a sense of predestination, which was redoubled when he discovered that his classmate played the violin.

Boris lived in a grand house where Ulrich loved to go. It had modern blinds that you raised with a cord, and a Blüthner grand piano, which Boris's little sister could play delightfully well. There was a tree house in the garden, where you could sit looking down on the breeze in the grass. Boris's mother was from Tbilisi in Georgia, and Ulrich thought her beautiful, with her blue eyes and black hair; she liked food, and she laughed often, and spoke with a rich accent.

In that house Ulrich discovered conversation. What he had thought to himself in his most obscure and original moments could be expressed there, for Boris was also filled up with thoughts.

One afternoon Boris took him to the attic. Up the steep wooden stairs hidden behind an upstairs door, all dim in the afternoon, and, at their summit, the highest door of all, which opened into exotic smells and great glass sculptures in the half-light.

'What is it?' asked Ulrich, and Boris replied that it was chemicals. There were rows of glass bottles with the emboss of skulls, as if good and evil struggled inside, and on a long bench was an assemblage of glass flasks and funnels joined with rubber tubing. *Mercury Bichloride*, read Ulrich to himself, and the name felt considerable.

Boris's father was interested in chemistry experimentation, though Boris could not say well what that meant.

The boys sat on the floor amid all these wonders, and Boris reported the news that his uncle had been killed in the war.

'He didn't look like the sort to die. If you saw him. He was always playing football with me, more like a friend.'

'Only old people are supposed to die,' said Ulrich. 'Maybe when they are fifty. Not people who can still play football.'

'He knew about every kind of animal. And now everything in his head has gone.'

Ulrich let it sink in.

'Why was he born? Just to die when he wasn't even married yet?'

Boris said,

'One day I will die. And you will die as well. All these thoughts in our heads will disappear.'

Such an idea had occurred to Ulrich before, but it had never been corroborated by anyone else. It was still difficult to appreciate fully.

'We're just boys. We can't die.'

'Those boys from school died of cholera. It could have been us. Many things could happen. We could fall out of a window.'

It took some time for Boris to add,

'We could be hit by a motor car.'

A big accident had happened the previous week in Sofia, when a speeding motor car had ploughed into a market and killed three people, and for a time no one could talk of anything else. The two boys sat in silence, imagining their tragic death under a gleaming motor car – and the thought was unutterably glamorous.

They talked on so long that they could no longer see each other's faces. It was secret and wonderful to be in the laboratory at that forbidden time, trying to find words together in the darkness. Ulrich felt as if the blinds had been raised on the world, for when you sat with another human being and launched out into new thoughts, there could be no end to it.

Boris introduced Ulrich to the fool, Misha, who was sometimes found at the tea stall near his house. Misha wore rags and sung them strange rhymes that he made up himself. There were stories about Misha: that he was actually a Turk who had committed a terrible crime, that he had once owned a famous perfumery where princesses and dignitaries went to shop. He had a way of imitating a machine, and asked people to pull his crooked forearm to turn on the motion, which sent his body juddering violently until Ulrich and Boris exploded with laughter. He always seemed to have marbles for them in his pocket which he reached for conspiratorially and pushed into their hands, two for each, saying,

Keep them on a slope
And say goodbye to your hope!

Ulrich's mother did not like him talking to Misha. She tolerated it until Ulrich told her that they had seen the fool tying the tails of two dogs together with rope. The dogs could go neither forward nor back, and barked in bewilderment, the bigger one dragging the smaller one behind, while Misha warmed his hands on his fire and laughed at the startled animals until the tears cut channels in the dust of his face. Boris protested the cruelty, and cut the animals apart, but it was enough for Elizaveta to forbid Ulrich ever to talk to Misha again.

On their voyages abroad, Ulrich's mother had always carried magnesium wire for lighting up the interiors of caves and ancient buildings. Her reserves now lay uselessly in a drawer in her study, and Ulrich would sometimes cut off a length with scissors to light up for his own amusement. He loved the white brilliance that left a black hole in his vision when he looked away, and the smoke that ribboned coolly from the ardour.

In the decades since then, Ulrich has tried to see his emerging interest in chemistry as the revisitation of his entombed love for music. It has struck him that the two have this thing in common: that an infinite range of expression can be generated from a finite number of elements. But this was not apparent to the boy who now began to quiz his friend's father on the nature of molecules and the meaning of alkalinity. Boris's father often answered these questions with an invitation to his laboratory, where substances were made to do startling things out of their obedience to laws. He decanted some copper sulphate solution into a small bottle for Ulrich to take home and grow blue crystals from, and he showed how you could plate steel with copper by putting electrodes in sulphuric acid. He told Ulrich affecting stories of Ernest Rutherford and Marie Curie, who had peered into the mists of the atom.

Those years all merge together in Ulrich's mind, so he cannot remember the sequence of events. But it was certainly while they were still living in the house on Dondukov Boulevard, and while his father was away in the army, that he first set up his chemistry laboratory.

The feeling of that laboratory comes back to Ulrich sometimes, in the moments before sleep, when the mind is unmoored. The wooden door, rotting at its bottom, could be locked from the inside. There was a large barrel in the corner which he kept filled with water for his experiments, and a table where his beakers and retorts were lined up. At that age he read biographies of inventors, and these books were collected here, as well as the adventures of Sherlock Holmes, who was a chemist and violinist as well as a detective.

The teenager who laboured there believed he would chance upon something that would change the world forever. Ulrich had read *The Time Machine* by the Englishman Wells, and many other such books, and he loved the descriptions in these stories of the rickety domestic workshops in which eccentric inventors tinkered uncertainly towards earth-shattering ideas. And though he knew little of the scientific breakthroughs that were then taking place in other parts of the world, his immature trials were not without success. His investigations of the chemical properties of discarded animal bones resulted in a powerful glue that his mother adopted, with no apparent dissatisfaction, as her sealant for letters. There was every reason to hope that in his dim shed he would one day have one of those historic moments of realisation that was the high point of all his scientists' biographies.

When Ulrich's classmates came to visit his laboratory, he would set up the right atmosphere by dripping sulphuric acid continually on to chalk so it bubbled and steamed. This simple magic was guaranteed to impress, and he kept his laboratory in a constant chemical haze until one winter's day, with the windows closed, he fainted from the carbon dioxide and was discovered just short of asphyxiation by his horrified mother. Boris was delighted when he heard the story, for Ulrich's gimmick had always seemed ridiculous to him.

When Ulrich's father arrived home from the war, his left trouser leg was rolled up and empty, and his ears were damaged by the shells. Ulrich watched with disbelief as his father was installed in the house like an incapable infant.

Elizaveta cleared out a disused room whose view of the garden recommended it for convalescence, and she arranged it with flower vases and ornaments. Though the family's finances were approaching a crisis – for the war had destroyed the economy, and her husband had been away for years – she made new purchases to diminish the impact of his injuries: a wheelchair from England, for instance, and an armchair with a folding table, where she encouraged him to read and write. But these acquisitions failed to penetrate the blankness into which her husband had retreated, and even her most inspiring speeches could extract nothing from him except complaints and wild accusations.

Ulrich knew he ought to feel pity for his father, but this emotion refused to come. In fact he found it hard not to blame him for having returned so unlike himself, and over time he began to punish him in countless insidious ways.

On one occasion, Boris came to dine with Ulrich's family. By that time it had become clear that Boris's musical talent was exceptional: he had been taken on at the Bulgarian State Music Academy by a famous teacher from Moravia, and had already given a number of well-received recitals around the city. As dinner was served, Ulrich chattered proudly about Boris's accomplishments, shouting for the benefit of his father, who sat at the head of the table with the morose air he kept in those days. Ulrich said,

'Boris is going to play the Mendelssohn concerto next week in the national theatre. His teacher has told him to give up everything else and devote his life to the violin!'

His father did not look up, but bellowed,

'No more of this talk! What are your parents thinking of? You'll fall in among criminals!'

Boris wrestled with confusion, but Ulrich looked triumphantly at him and smiled in happy complicity. In plotting this provocation, he had reasoned that what linked siblings was their sharing in the most irrational aspects of their parents' characters; and, having exposed Boris to his father's absurdity, he could now truly consider him a brother.

Ulrich remembers that he kept, for some years, a notebook about his friendship with Boris. He felt that their sentiments for each other were so noble, and their conversations so remarkable, that everything had to be preserved for posterity. In the inevitable way of things, this notebook has disappeared, and with it the detail of those adolescent feelings. Thinking back on Boris too many times has buried him with rememberings, and turned him into a shining icon that glides unblinking through the past without smell or voice.

There is one event he can still call to mind. He was sixteen, perhaps, when the two of them were invited by older friends on a foray to the brothels of Serdika. Ulrich had never been with a woman before, and was terrified; but he could not find an excuse that would pass in public, and he found himself carried along against his will to the streets of pacing men where whores beckoned from the windows. Once inside, a cudgel in his chest, there were women stacked up on the stairs, smoking and talking, their breasts peeking out, and Boris, pointing, said, 'You like the one in green?'

Ulrich was startled by his friend's self-possession, but the woman had already responded to the signal and led them away into a corridor with gold-framed mirrors, her pale behind clearly visible through her robe, and Boris went in ahead. Ulrich sat in an armchair outside, wretched at his own uselessness. The curtain over the doorway was inadequate to its function, and he could see the whole room through the chink, where his friend hopped on one foot then the other to pull off his boots. The woman sat on the bed, watching him coolly and removing her gown while Boris threw off his clothes. He stood naked in the lamplight, his penis tall, and the woman pulled him close. Boris lifted her up and fell with her fully on the bed, where he kissed the breasts she offered and moaned over them and suddenly, so expertly, entered her! And Ulrich's heart burned cold at the realisation that Boris had done this before without telling him. He stood up and ran from the brothel, not stopping till he reached home, and the refuge of his laboratory.

Perhaps that is the last memory, in fact, that Ulrich has retained from his garden laboratory, for it must have been immediately afterwards that the house on Dondukov Boulevard was sold. When it no longer belonged to his family, he would walk past it every day on his way to school. It was later destroyed in the bombings and now the site is occupied by a car showroom.

5

THE FAMILY MOVED INTO A HOUSE on Tsar Simeon Street. It was much smaller than the previous one, and built in the old style with clay and straw. It shared a courtyard at the back with several other houses.

A girl lived in one of these houses, whose name was Tatiana. After dinner, she used to take a lamp up to her bedroom so she could read novels, and Ulrich liked to sit at the top of the steps outside his house watching her. She spread out in a chair with her bare feet up on the windowsill, and, during the long hours when she read, Ulrich could follow the unfolding of the story in the splaying and clenching of her toes.

He decided he would make a photograph of her sitting there. He discovered the principles of glass-plate negatives, and he built a pinhole camera out of wood, sealed at the joins with tar. On one visit to Boris's house he made an excuse to go up to the laboratory alone, and, with beating heart, he sought out the bottle of silver nitrate and purloined enough for his secret project. He knew it was wrong, but he would neither compromise his experiment nor make it public.

One evening, he set up his camera on the steps. He estimated an exposure of twenty minutes in that darkness, and he waited for Tatiana to become comfortable in her seat before uncovering the tiny hole. But instead, to his alarm, she got up and came to the window, calling out to him,

'Why do you always sit there watching me?'

Ulrich was paralysed and could not reply.

'Wait,' she said 'I'm coming down.'

He waited for her to retreat into the house before snatching up his camera and running inside.

'What is the matter?' his mother asked, and Ulrich could see her suspicions were aroused. He shut himself up in his room.

Later on he tried to make a print from his negative. But there was hardly any exposure, and only Tatiana's lamp showed up, an almost indiscernible smudge in the night.

One night, when Ulrich was approaching his eighteenth birthday, Boris came to visit. Ulrich's mother opened the door and embraced him effusively. Boris was now fully a head taller than she. He wore his tie loose, like an artist, and there were dark circles under his eyes. Though it was quite dry, he carried an umbrella: it was his latest affectation, and he took it with him everywhere.

'You know our house is always open to you. Just because Ulrich is going away, you mustn't stop coming to see us. Come for dinner whenever you want. You're part of our family. You know how proud we are of you.'

Boris smiled at her, assenting, and murmured a greeting to Ulrich's father, who was staring in his armchair.

'Ulrich is out in the courtyard,' said Elizaveta. 'He doesn't like to sit with us in the evenings anymore.'

Boris went out of the back door and climbed up to where Ulrich was perched on the steps.

'So are you ready to leave?' he asked stiffly. They had recently got into an argument over Ulrich's departure, and had not spoken since. Down below, four young boys were kicking a small rubber ball around.

'I still have another week.'

'I suppose so.'

Boris offered a cigarette. Ulrich shook his head, and Boris lit one himself. He tried to lighten Ulrich's mood:

'When you come back, can you bring a chorus girl from the Admiralspalast? That can be your gift to me. I met a trumpet player who told me Berlin girls are like a more evolved species. They do things that Bulgarian girls won't be able to imagine for centuries.'

Ulrich said nothing. Sometimes Boris irritated him. The boys downstairs shrieked in dispute over a goal.

Boris sighed. He said,

'What are you going to do in Berlin? Day to day?'

'Study. Do my experiments. I'll go to lectures by Fritz Haber and Walther Nernst. I'll live and breathe chemistry. I want nothing else.'

'I still don't understand why you couldn't stay here and study.'

'I've already told you: there's no chemistry in Sofia. If you want to learn chemistry you have to go to Germany. They invented chemistry, and they lead the world.'

'They lead the world with oppression. Their chemical companies are great tentacled monsters, exploiting the poor of all nations and making fuel for wars.'

'You don't know what you're talking about. German chemical companies are saving lives every day with their new cures and treatments.'

'I know Bayer invented mustard gas. Is that the kind of cure you mean?'

'Why can't you see the good in anything?' exclaimed Ulrich. 'A great new age is being born through chemistry. Polymers. That's what they've discovered in Berlin: long carbon molecules they can use to make furniture, utensils and houses. It is all completely new, and society will be better for it. One day you'll understand.'

Their arguments were often like this. They were still young, and they spoke sententiously, reproducing opinions they had read or heard.

Boris was watching the sport in the courtyard, his long hair over his eyes, his cigarette burned down to his lips. He had his hand tucked in his belt, as he often did. He said nothing to Ulrich's outburst. He wanted to tell a story.

'Last night I went with Georgi to see this Yiddish theatre troupe from Prague. The story was absurd: people were beheaded and shot and set on fire, there were love affairs, and a scene with Lenin and Mussolini that had us shrieking on the floor. The female characters were played by men with enormous lipstick but there was one woman in the troupe, a beautiful Jewess, and the climax of the play comes when she is taking a bath in red wine: she's dragged naked from her bathtub and viciously raped by a group of marauders. But this Jewess was a magnificent presence and the other actors were too timid to touch her, so she just lay in her bath, waiting for them to rape her, and nothing happened! I've never laughed so much in all my life.

'After the play we went to the house of an artist named Mircho. He had a large collection of high-quality liquor, to which I paid due respect, and there was excellent gossip about society men. There was a little dog barking all night, which for some reason seemed hilarious, and the women were pretty, and a man recited Latin poems that were apparently very erotic. After a well-planned sequence of manoeuvres, I ended up sitting next to the Jewess: I was so close I could smell her washed-off make-up, and she touched my arm when she spoke. She was a jewel! She had dramatic gestures: she would spread a long-fingered hand with horror on her cheek, or cover her breasts with her handkerchief. She sang Bohemian love songs and told comic stories from her travels. Someone had a violin, so I played a folk dance for her, which she admired, though I'm sure by that time I had no control over my fingers. I offered to show her around Sofia, and she said, *Next time I come!* Then a photographer arrived, it was already the early hours, he had printed some photographs from the performance, exquisite ones of her under the lights, and I asked her for one, which she gave me and signed it on the back.'

He took the photograph out of his pocket.

'Look at this.'

'God,' said Ulrich. 'She is lovely.'

'Yes. And look.'

He turned the photograph over and read:

For Boris. Next time we make music together! Ida.

Ulrich contemplated the handwriting for a moment.

'She is much older than you,' he said.

‘I know,’ said Boris, joyous.

The stars were bright overhead, and fireflies glimmered.

‘Look what else is written there,’ said Ulrich bending close. He indicated with his finger where the photographic paper was embossed with the manufacturer’s name

‘Agfa,’ he said.

Boris sighed. He ran his hands through his hair. He said,

‘I have to tell you: I’ve given up playing music.’

Ulrich looked at him in disbelief.

‘Why?’

‘There’s no point anymore.’

‘What do you mean?’ demanded Ulrich. ‘Just last week you were so excited about your concert of Bach!’

‘I don’t know, Ulrich. You’re caught up in all your ideas about chemistry and I can’t talk to you about it. If you opened your eyes you’d see our society is destroying itself. Bulgaria has already lost the best of its men in the wars, and things are only getting worse. I can’t stand by and watch. Will I just throw in my lot with the nations, whose governments are more bloodthirsty with each passing day? They will end up killing us and each other. No: the only chance we have of surviving until we are old, you and I, is the international revolution. It has happened in Russia, it will come soon to Germany, and before long we will have no nations, only international socialism. Then there’ll be time for Bach. When there’s no more Bulgaria.’

Boris flicked his cigarette stub down into the courtyard. Ulrich watched the red glow skate across the paving in the breeze, and then die.

‘This is some insanity that’s got into you.’ His voice trembled. ‘It’s not even fifteen years since Bulgaria was independent, with so much joy, and now you want to destroy it?’

‘Joy?’ cried Boris with unpleasant emphasis. ‘You borrow everything you say from other people; you don’t see anything for yourself. Is your father joyful since he lost his leg and everything he worked for? Did the independent nation thank him after it had sucked out everything he had? The truth is there in your own household, and you cannot see it: nations are steel boilers pitching madly with our soft flesh inside. I cannot think of anything that was not much better when we were just a territory in the empire, scratching our backsides for entertainment. And it will not be better again until we have abolished this Bulgaria, and all the other killing machines.'

'And for this you'll give up your violin?' said Ulrich. 'You're an idiot. You could do much more for the world with your music.'

Down below a mother banged a spoon on her kitchen window to summon her sons in from their game. It was early in the year, and still cold outside, and her boiling pot had steamed up the window.

Boris took a magazine from inside his jacket. There was a bloated capitalist on the cover, stifling houses and factory chimneys in his enormous arms. There was jagged geometry, and words split up at different angles.

'Have you heard of Geo Milev?' Boris asked.

'I heard he's a dangerous man.'

'He's a genius! *A bloodstained lantern with shattered windows*. That's what he wrote after he lost an eye in the war. Half his skull was blown away and he's completely without fear. He's a true poet and revolutionary, and he's asked me to write for his magazine.'

'You'll be lucky if you don't get yourself killed.'

'We die anyway. At least this way there's hope.'

'These people have poisoned your mind,' said Ulrich. 'I couldn't stand it if you didn't play the violin. I only live it through you.'

'Oh, don't be such a child!'

Boris's face was contorted with anger.

'Damn you, Ulrich! Until you wake up and take a look at the world around you I have nothing to say to you.'

Boris stood up and went down to the courtyard below, step by step.

'I warn you: when you arrive in Berlin you'll find the crisis even more advanced than here.'

And with that, he walked out of the gate.

Ulrich sat for a while, watching candles illuminate the upper rooms around the courtyard. He did not call on Boris before his departure for Berlin.

His father had roused himself from his deafness to oppose it.

'What use is chemistry in this town?' he raged. 'Do you see any opportunities here? Our family will starve for this chemistry.'

But Elizaveta supported him. She shouted in her husband's ear, as she had to in those days,

'You must let him grow up in his times, my dear. How did your father make his money? With his pig farming! and look at you, an engineer, a railway builder, a man of the modern world. Have you lost your hope of the future? Look at Germany now with its chemical industry. Do you think things will not improve and it will not spread everywhere? He will be a pioneer in our country, as you were. You know his passion for the subject.'

Ulrich's father gave in. He sent his son off to the University of Berlin to study chemistry, and, with this last-ditch investment, hoped he might hold the old world together.

Carbon

6

ULRICH PREPARES TO FRY SOME POTATOES. Even without his eyes, he is capable of that much, and on this day, his neighbour has failed to come with food.

It is a long time since he has cooked anything. He puts his hand into the plastic bag, and withdraws it with a shock. It has been months, and the tubers have sprouted into a blind underworld tangle, which provokes disgust in him, unexpectedly intense.

He throws the bag out, and eats instead from a tin of beans, which he does not bother to heat.

Ulrich's kitchen activities are mostly restricted these days to the making of morning tea. It is a ritual he has stuck to for most of his life, and he still uses the same cup, only survivor of a once complete tea set. For as long as he can remember, he has held this hot cup in the morning, and it has become part of each day's resolve to put the night behind him.

He switches on his television for a bit of sound to eat his beans by.

He is irritated by the weather programmes that come on the international channels. Ignorant people judging the world's weather. *In that place it will be a nice day because there is pure sunshine.* They estimate a nice day as when you can sit outside in sunglasses and drink coffee that no normal person can afford. Their minds cannot consider that a place is full of people cursing because there is no rain. They say: *There it will be a nice sunny day today.* Or: *There they will have to suffer rain.* What do they drink, these people? he thinks.

And here there has not been rain for so long.

He hears explosions: there is another war in Iraq, and now Bulgaria is sending troops to assist the Americans in their occupation. He pictures the journeys of his childhood, when Baghdad was part of his family, when his father strove to connect that great city with silver rails to Berlin. He thinks of his dead mother, who would be driven mad if she knew of her country's assault on those places she loved so much. How time changes things, he thinks: making people forget who they were, and turning them against their own kind.

He switches the channel.

It is a science documentary, and Ulrich hears how the world has far more computing capacity than it needs. Most computers are idle for most of the time. He hears that when a modern computer is idle it switches into a reverie, and displays on the screen a meditative pattern, like swimming fishes, whizzing stars or geometric designs. At any one moment, most computers in the world are occupied in this way. They sit alone in dark, after-hour offices, considering the movement of fish or the emptiness of space.

Ulrich thinks about a planet full of computers with nothing to do except daydream.

In his own idle moments, Ulrich makes lists in his head. He makes lists of journeys he has made and animals he has eaten. Making lists gives him a sense that he is in command of his experiences. It helps him to feel he is real.

He makes lists of the pills he has to take each day, though in reality it is his neighbour who takes the responsibility. She draws up grids that she pins to the cupboard door to remind herself, and she walks back and forth to check them as she pours out the pills, because she is never sure. Her step is uneven as she goes, and the floor creaks with the heaviness of one side, the left or the right. She has referred before to problems with her legs, but Ulrich does not know exactly what is wrong.

He has a strong feeling about the calendars that she makes: they seem like divine plans, sustaining him in life.

'I cannot die yet,' he jokes with her as she draws them, 'or who will take all those pills?'

He has many more lists. He makes a list of activities that, when they have been proposed to him, have always triggered the thought *That is not for me*. A list of things he would tell his son about himself, if he ever saw him. A list of things he never enjoyed, though he always said he did. A list of things that comprise, in his view, the minimal requirements for a happy life. He makes a list of his possessions as if it were a will:

Item: One armchair.
Item: One television.
Item: One writing desk.
Item: Two photograph albums with photographs.
Item: Books, assorted.
Item: Gramophone records, assorted.
Item: Gramophone player.
Item: One bed.
Item: Kitchen utensils, various.
Item: Clothes, various.
Item: Tools, various.

There are several things he does not include. Paint, ashtrays, various kinds of string and sewing thread, medical supplies, writing ink, cleaning fluids, playing cards. There is a host of objects like this that seem too insignificant to be part of a list.

7

SOME DECADES BEFORE Ulrich arrived in Berlin, German scientists made a philosophical leap that would change history. They rejected the idea that life is a unique and mystical essence, with different qualities from everything else in the universe. They reasoned instead that living things were only chemical machines, and they speculated that with enough research, chemical laboratories could emulate life itself.

They began to experiment with making medicines, not merely from trees or plants, but from man-made chemicals. A triumph came in 1897, in the laboratories of the chemical company Bayer, when chemists observed several positive effects of the first synthetic drug: aspirin. Not long afterwards, the chemist Paul Ehrlich, who was seeking a cure for the sleeping sickness that devastated his compatriots in the German Congo, injected infected mice with hundreds of different chemicals until he found that an industrial dye cured the disease – and so discovered the first antibiotic. Ehrlich coined the term 'chemotherapy' to describe the great new work he had started.

German scientists also wanted to see whether chemical laboratories could make materials that were usually found only in nature. The world was running out of natural nitrogen deposits, for instance, and agriculturalists were concerned about how they would continue to fertilise crops. Populations were exploding. Doomsayers warned of imminent famine, and people dying off in swathes. The Berlin chemist Fritz Haber began to seek a chemical solution to this problem. He discovered a way of fixing the enormous supply of nitrogen in the air, and turning it into ammonia for fertilisers. He won a Nobel Prize for his discovery, and a large fortune, and the newspapers called him the saviour of the human race.

When its empire was taken away after the First World War, Germany was deprived of access to essential raw materials. It was set far behind Britain, which could take all the Malayan rubber it wanted, and Middle Eastern oil. Germany's chemical firms – BASF, Bayer, Agfa, Hoechst, Casella and the rest – were consolidated into a vast chemical cartel, I. G. Farben, whose objective was to produce chemical versions of these lacking natural resources.

Farben's synthetic rubber and oil technologies soon became the envy of the world. Within a few years, it was the largest corporation in Europe, with stakes in oil companies, steelworks, armaments manufacturers, banks and newspapers – in Germany and across the globe. It had its own mines for coal, magnesite, gypsum and salt, and cartel arrangements with leading American companies DuPont, Alcoa and Dow Chemical.

It was in Farben's laboratories that a chemist named Hermann Staudinger, while attempting to synthesise natural rubber, first hypothesised that there might exist molecules much more extensive than any hitherto imagined. These giant molecules, he suggested, would be arranged in mobile, chain-like structures, which explained the unusual flexibility of rubber. Staudinger's work on polymers won him a Nobel Prize, and set the course for a new direction in chemistry: the development of plastics.

This new area of innovation transformed the human environment. Until that era, every human being had lived among the same surfaces: wood, stone, iron, paper, glass. Now there emerged a host of extraterrestrial substances that produced bodily sensations that no one had ever experienced before.

This was the production of which Ulrich wished to be a part.

When Ulrich arrived in Berlin he realised immediately that he had walked in upon the wonder of his age. Berlin was the capital of world science, which lifted him on its tremendous current and made him certain of his own great future. But Berlin was also the studio of mighty artists and musicians. Bertolt Brecht was there, Marlene Dietrich and Fritz Lang. It was a carnival of boxing, jazz and cabaret.

Later on, after Ulrich left it, this miraculous metropolis ceased to exist. With the next war, old Berlin was gutted, tossed away and forgotten, and it sank into forgetful waters, until only a few bent tips were visible above the surface, twitching with the bad dreams below.

This has had a curious effect on Ulrich's memories of the time he spent in that city. They do not hang together, or fall into sequence, because they were later scattered like refugees, and were forced to take shelter in other times and places. Some of them were lost entirely in the great dispersal.

Ulrich tries to assemble the remnants into one place.

Item
How lovely was the Jewish girl, Clara Blum, who took notes in the chemistry lecture with her left hand.

Item
As a boy Ulrich had wandered so many times among the parasols and dogs of Unter den Linden, but now there were staring, mutilated soldiers and penniless refugees. The men in Berlin had lost more limbs than the men at home.

Item
He saw Fritz Haber and Walther Nernst. Their thought was so clear it was terrifying, and Ulrich felt reborn with every lecture he attended. He often struggled to follow their theories. But he loved them because they were also practical men who reminded him of the old-fashioned inventors he had read about as a child. In his spare time, Walther Nernst applied himself to such tasks as the invention of incandescent lamps and the development of an electric piano. Fritz Haber, whose chemical weapons had failed to achieve a German victory in the war, was looking for a method to pay off his country's war debts by distilling gold from the sea.

Item
Clara Blum had a habit of reading books as she walked in the street.

Item
Ulrich was afraid of spending money, for his father's wealth was already exhausted with his university fees. But there was an irresistible world of jazz in Berlin, and Ulrich fell in love with the new sounds as deeply as he had once fallen in love with Gypsy music. He could not keep himself out of debt.

Item

In one of Max Planck's lectures, he thought that his father, with his admiration of far sight, would have approved of all those eyes set on the remote country of atoms.

Item

He took Clara Blum to his room. He had set up a long glass tube with holes drilled along the top. He had removed the horn from a gramophone player and led a pipe from there into one end of the glass tube, while in the other end was a supply of methane. 'Watch,' he said, lighting the holes so there was an even line of flames. Then he set the record going and a Beethoven symphony was fed into the glass tube. The sound waves in the tube bunched the gas and the flames dancing on top were arranged as a graph of the symphony. And Clara Blum laughed gaily with his gimmick, and begged to see a hundred other pieces of music in fire.

Item

How curious it was for Ulrich to find his German name so commonplace.

Item

The rapturous crowd in the Admiralspalast shouted *Bis! Bis!* to the American Negroes playing jazz. The musicians exchanged frowns among themselves, hearing English words – *Beasts! Beasts!* – and within minutes they had packed themselves into cars and left Berlin. In their language they say not 'Bis' but 'Encore'.

Item

Clara Blum had a fascination for the new towers in New York. *When we go to New York*, they used to say, for all their fantasies. Ulrich once gave her a postcard of the Woolworth Building. *Tallest Man-made Structure in the World!*

Item

A man and a woman, refugees, frozen to death on the street, with an infant boy between them who was quite alive, and crying for food.

Item

Ulrich read that Fletcher Henderson had begun to play jazz only when America's oppression of the Negro made his further pursuit of chemistry impossible. He had a degree in chemistry and mathematics, but he was a Negro, so he became a bandleader.

Item

Almost every week, a shattering new scientific idea arrived from Rutherford in Cambridge, Bohr in Copenhagen or Curie in Paris. Someone would read the paper aloud, and young students would march madly around the laboratory, their bodies unable to absorb such news sitting down.

Item

The first time Ulrich laid eyes on Albert Einstein, he was in the circus, screaming with laughter at the antics of midgets.

Item

After the struggle, you could tell from the way the police slung the revolutionary into the ambulance that they knew he was already dead.

Item

Clara Blum loved the dark things that happened in Berlin. She kept Ulrich awake at night reading aloud newspaper articles about all the suicides and murders. For a long time afterwards his love for her would well up again whenever he read a crime report.

Item

His mother wrote solicitous letters every day, full of enquiries, advice and warnings about the consequences of romantic entanglements.

My dearest baby Ulrich, they began each time. This phrase returned to him like a maddening chaperone during his caresses with Clara Blum

Item
Walking on the street in the early evening, he saw a famous film actress get out of a limousine in front of the Savoy Hotel.

Item
Clara Blum helped Ulrich prepare for his examinations, for she was more accomplished in theory than he. 'I want to *make* stuff,' he protested when his throat went hard with academic frustration. 'I didn't come to study mathematics. I want to make plastic!'

Item
Watching the men pushing barges, Ulrich and Clara Blum walked by the canal and discussed chemistry, and he suddenly had the feeling that he would be a great man.

Item
There were many Bulgarians arriving in Berlin, and they used to get drunk together, and speak Bulgarian, and play silly pranks. They spent nights laughing in the steam baths, where men poured in from the brothels and refugees from Galicia got clean from the streets. When German women saw them together in the street they would run away. They called them *dark Balkan thugs*, and other such things.

Item
When Ulrich picked up the papers that Albert Einstein had dropped behind him in the corridor, the scientist looked him in the eye and said, 'I am nothing without you.' Ulrich managed to say 'Nor I, sir,' as Einstein turned his back and ambled on. Ulrich has thought back so many times to this moment that the figure in the corridor has transmuted into something more than a man. Now Einstein looks down on him with

eyes that scan like X-rays, and his speech comes not from his mouth but from somewhere invisible and oracular.

Item
The animated electric mannequin in the window of the optician's shop had spectacles as thick as paperweights, but still reminded him of Misha the fool.

When Ulrich made his abrupt departure from Berlin, the mighty German chemical industry was at its height. He believed afterwards that, if he had completed his degree and remained in Germany, his life might have been very different.

But while the big German companies triumphed through the hyperinflation, which wiped out all their debts, many ordinary investors were ruined. One of them was Ulrich's father, who, Germanophile to the end, had put the funds remaining from the sale of the old house into German investments. His mother held out for as long as she could, but at last the money dried up for Ulrich's fees, and for everything else too – and she wrote a desperate letter begging him to come home. Ulrich dropped everything and rushed to Sofia.

8

ULRICH FINDS THAT HE CAN ASSIGN dates to his life only through reference to the events recounted in newspapers. He wonders sometimes why it is not the other way around, and whether it signifies some weakness in him. Should a man not have fostered his own time by which other things could be measured? But he suspects it is the same for others too, and he concludes that the time inside a human is smooth and lobed like a polyp, and only history is striated with the usefulness of dates.

History allows Ulrich to date his return to Sofia with precision. April 1925: for it was only two days after he arrived that the bomb went off in the St Nedelya cathedral, dividing Bulgarian time into *before* and *after*. The bombers put their dynamite under the dome and detonated it during a state funeral, wiping out the country's elite. The city had never seen so many corpses. The king's was not among them: he was recovering from another assassination attempt, and did not make it to St Nedelya in time.

Sofia filled with foreign journalists. They called it 'the worst terrorist attack in history', they talked about 'the misery of defeat' and 'economic collapse' and 'more convulsions in the Balkans'. Ulrich took his father to see the damage, where crowds of onlookers and photographers looked up at the missing dome, and the surviving cupolas all askew. The interior of the grand church was filled with rubble, and the air was still hazy with dust. Ulrich's father said,

'Everything is fog. I cannot see.'

His mind had gone by that time, but even he was overcome.

Elizaveta wept often.

'See what has become of your father. He doesn't get up from that chair. He doesn't say anything. I have had to sell things to get by.'

She had begun sewing dresses for money, and she kept geese to supply the royal palace, where she knew people in the kitchen. She found many things to do like that.

She said,

'I've found you a job, Ulrich. Remember your father's friend Stefanov? I think he has something for you. Go and see him.'

She wept again.

'I'm trying to keep you out of harm. The king has decided he will tear this city apart and root out terrorists for good, and I don't want you getting caught up in it. Every young man is a suspect. It's so awful for a mother. Look how thin you are, after all that time away. Did you not eat?'

A note arrived from Ulrich's old friend, Boris. The two had not communicated for three years. It said, *I know you are back. Do not come to see me. Too dangerous now. Greetings.*

After days of uproar and terror, the army produced the men responsible for the bombing and hung them in the square. People climbed on each other's shoulders to see the gallows. The explosion had put their minds in a spin. They could not stop looking at the cathedral's open roof: it was like a festering cavity from which society's bad smells drifted up. They would not go to their homes, and the streets were full of crowds and fights and eruptions that the army had to quell.

Ulrich followed his mother's instructions, and went to see Mr Stefanov, who ran a leather company. The old man received him in a mighty drawing room. He was dressed in an immaculate suit and tie and he sat in a wheelchair.

'Your mother seemed desperate, so I agreed to see you. Your father and I were friends once, and I stay loyal to things like that. I need a bookkeeper.'

Ulrich began work at the leather company. He sat at a table facing rows of junior clerks, whose work he was supposed to supervise; but the table was not enclosed like a proper desk, and his legs were fully on display underneath, which he felt diminished his authority. High up on the wall opposite him was a mirror, angled down in such a manner as to allow him to monitor his subordinates' activities without leaving his chair. In the top of this mirror, his disembodied legs were also reflected.

He heard nothing more from Boris, and resolved finally to pay him a visit, in spite of the note he had sent.

The grand house looked exactly the same, and it was moving to ring the bell again after all these years. The woman who opened the door was an echo of someone lost, and he realised it was Boris's sister, Magdalena, grown up from a girl. She was wearing a short dress in the Paris fashion.

'Stop staring and come in off the street,' she said. 'You shouldn't be here. They've already come for him once. Every time the doorbell rings…'

She shut the door behind him, and they stood facing each other inside.

'How was Berlin?'

'Fine.'

She looked at him. His shirt, his hair. She said,

'You don't know what's been happening. Since the uprising, they've killed so many of our friends. Every day it's another pointless tragedy. I don't hold with this communism. I think all their dreams are absurd fantasies. *No unemployment, no hunger.* They are idiots, and they're dying for nothing.'

He agreed. She brightened.

'I still play the piano. When things have calmed down, I'll play for you.'

She went to fetch Boris from his room.

Disappointed as he had been to curtail his studies and return home, Ulrich had consoled himself with the idea that he had now seen everything the modern world could offer, and his prestige in this provincial city would be greatly enhanced. He looked forward to the gap being closed with Boris, who had been stuck in Sofia all this while. He pictured his friend sitting awestruck while he told him his stories of metropolitan life.

But as soon as Boris appeared in the hallway, Ulrich realised it would not be like that at all. Boris had become mature and imposing and evidently his character's growth was in full proportion to Ulrich's own. Ulrich fell back instantly into looking up to him.

Boris put his arms around him.

'Welcome back, my friend,' he said. 'What a time to come!'

He stepped back appraisingly.

'You've become thinner since I last saw you. But less fragile. It's good.'

Boris's hair was longer than before, and so uneven he must have cut it himself, but his tie was neater and he stood more erect. He and Magdalena were a handsome pair: tall, with the same blue eyes and dark hair from their Georgian mother.

Boris took his sister's hand.

'Have you seen Magda? How grown up she is these days!'

She fought her brother off, cheeks red and hair tossing.

'Don't talk about me like that!'

Boris took Ulrich's elbow and led him to his room. Books and paintings were stacked everywhere. It smelt of cigarette smoke, and the floor was covered with electrical components. There was another man sitting in the armchair.

'This is Georgi. He and I are trying to make a radio.'

Georgi was a big man with features that Ulrich found coarse. His smile uncovered broken teeth.

'We can't make it work,' said Boris. 'They send us instructions from Moscow but you can't get the parts in this damn city.' He moved a pile of books. 'You can sit here. How was Berlin?'

'Fine.'

Boris filled three glasses with vodka.

'Just when we're all trying to escape, you come back. I can't believe it. No one wants to be in Sofia. There aren't enough steamships for all the peasants who are running off to Argentina. Even Georgi and I are planning to go somewhere for a while. Paris or Moscow. There's no point waiting here to be killed. They killed Geo Milev last week, you know that?'

'No, I didn't.'

'As ever, Ulrich, you don't know anything. The police took him in and strangled him in a basement. That's how we treat our great men in Bulgaria. Did you get *any* news in Berlin? You know the Agrarian government was overthrown by the fascists? And now it's war?'

'I know all that.'

'In their immense wisdom, the Bulgarian Communist Party decided that their sibling feud with Stamboliiski and the Agrarians was more important than opposing the fascists. They didn't raise a fingernail to help Stamboliiski when the fascists took over. They bear a lot of the guilt for his murder. He was a decent man.'

'His head was sent to Sofia in a tin,' added Georgi.

'So then they realised – *quelle surprise!* – that things were much worse now than they had been before. With epic dullness they decided they needed some heroic offensive against the fascists – better late than never! – so they planned this bomb, which any fool could have seen was pure suicide. Now the government is purging the entire country. When they can't find the person they're looking for, they just destroy whole towns. Remember Petar, the one in your class who played football? Shot down yesterday in the street while he was out with his mother. Just like that.'

Boris's fingers moved as he talked, but his body remained still. He was in complete command of his words, which lay at rest until needed, then formed themselves into deadly beams of coherence. Ulrich realised he would go to great lengths to avoid an argument with him.

'On top of all this, the Macedonian revolutionaries are going crazy. Assassinations every week. We all sympathise with their cause but they're making things much worse.'

On the wall was a framed sketch of Boris. The artist had drawn only one continuous line, but in its charcoal loops and zigzags it captured exactly the way he looked. There were a number of photographs of Boris and friends in theatrical make-up.

'You saw this?' said Boris, noticing his gaze. He passed the photograph down to Ulrich. 'That's me playing a Balkan shepherd. I was acting in this theatre group until it became too dangerous. Geo Milev designed the stage set full of skyscrapers. The shepherd wanders in amid the colossal geometry with his stubble and his flute and the sky is the only thing he can recognise.'

In another part of the house, Magdalena began to play the piano.

'The prime minister has told the British, French and Americans that the whole problem is caused by communist terrorists, which is just what they want to hear. They've given him seven thousand extra troops to murder us with. I suppose we should be flattered, eh, Georgi? You see what firepower they need to defeat the thoughts in our heads?'

'How is it you don't know all this, Ulrich?' Georgi said, with a thin-lipped smile that Ulrich found condescending.

'He's been in Berlin for three years,' said Boris. 'Studying chemistry. He doesn't like politics.'

'Chemistry?' said Georgi. 'Do you know how to make bombs?

Boris glared.

'I said he doesn't like politics.'

'Your friend doesn't have that choice anymore', Georgi said, not looking at Ulrich. 'There is no life, now, outside politics.'

In the other room, Magdalena paused in her music. Boris said,

'She's playing for you, Ulrich. Ever since she heard you were back she's been asking me when you are coming to see us. We've talked about you often, these years.'

Ulrich considered Boris's face. He felt it had acquired new expressions since he last saw him, and at times it could look entirely unfamiliar.

Boris said,

'Georgi and I have been involved in several operations. He's a forger. He makes visas for people going abroad. They go to Paris to learn how to make bombs and they come back having learned only how to write poetry, which they think is more explosive. I write for some of the underground newspapers. I'll show you my articles some day. You'd be proud of me. Many important people have made it known that they admire my analyses!'

He laughed.

'But the imbalance of forces is too great at present. Everything is aligned against us. At this point, the greatest service I can render to the world is to stay alive. My parents are suffering with all this, and Magda too. It's time to get out and let someone else deal with these bastards.'

He drained his vodka.

'By the way – you'll like this story – my father sold an invention to your Germans. Have you heard of a company called BASF? They bought a compound he invented. You'll have to ask him – he loves talking about it.'

'What was it?'

'Some kind of resin. He's been messing around with trees for years, and we never took any notice, and finally he's come up with something that people want. It's a new material that's useful for electrical insulation, apparently. They paid him quite a lot of money for it.'

Georgi yawned inimically, showing his teeth.

'I should leave,' he said. 'Getting late.'

Boris thought for a moment.

'Let's *all* go,' he said. 'We'll have a drink to celebrate your return, Ulrich, and then I'll go home with Georgi. He has an apartment on his own; no one knows the address. I try not to sleep here, because they often come at night.'

They made to depart. Magdalena was still playing the piano, now some modern work that Ulrich did not know. It was strident and brave, and he looked towards the closed door. Boris smiled.

'Let me call her.'

She came out of the room, her shirtsleeves rolled up.

'Goodbye, Magdalena,' said Ulrich, and kissed her on the cheek.

'Goodbye!' she said. She went to the front door as they stepped out into the street, and she called after Ulrich,

'We are all so happy to have you back.'

They wandered through the square around the Alexander Nevski church, whose vastness made it tranquil in spite of the remaining trinket sellers and the packs of roaming youths. The golden domes were lit up, and the moon shone overhead, almost full.

'Do you remember this, Ulrich? Berlin hasn't crushed your memories?'

'It's coming back.'

Boris carried an umbrella, the same one from the old days.

'I haven't been to Berlin. Or anywhere very much. But I think nowhere else has this altitude. I still love the way you can look down our streets in the afternoon and see them walled off by cloud. That's when you feel that the city lives up to its name. A city called Wisdom should float on clouds.'

'What about a city called Murder?' offered Georgi. '*That* would need a veil around it.'

Boris sniggered boyishly.

'Georgi pretends he's a revolutionary,' he said. 'But look at the quality of his suit. His father owns coal mines: you should see the house they have. Even the flies wipe their feet before they go in there.'

Georgi scowled.

'Have you seen the police?' Boris asked. 'Lining every street? That must be new for you. Everywhere you go they're watching. You should see them when they give chase on horseback. I never realised what a powerful formation was a man on a horse until I saw a poor wretch being chased down in the street. Three hissing men on horses with pistols and raised batons – it was a terrifying sight. They beat him senseless.'

Boris led them down a narrow passageway and through a courtyard. They entered a grimy bar where the wall lights had red handkerchiefs tied around them for atmosphere. They sat down at a table, and Boris called for beer. He looked expectantly at Ulrich.

'So now. Tell us everything about Berlin.'

Ulrich had been looking forward to this moment, but did not know how to begin.

The sullen barmaid brought a tray of beer. At the next table the men played cards, roaring with victory and defeat. The barmaid said,

'I hope this time you have money to pay?'

'Don't worry about that,' Boris replied, grinning.

They raised glasses. Over the lip Ulrich watched Georgi, whose face became a sneer when he puckered to drink.

There was a loud exclamation at the door, and a large man came bellowing to their table, his arms theatrically spread. Boris gave a broad smile and stood for the embrace.

'You're here! You're back!' he cried.

The man shook hands with Georgi and Ulrich, and sat down. He was red faced and ebullient, and talked a lot about his journeys.

The air was thick with vapours: tobacco smoke, and the smoke from the paraffin lamps that had left such ancient black circles on the ceiling. An old man played an out-of-tune piano that had been wedged in behind the entrance so that the door hit it every time someone entered. The red-faced man was saying,

'Everywhere I went I saw him. First he was looking pointedly at me in a bar in Budapest. Then he was waiting when I came out of a meeting in Vienna. Then, a few days later, I spotted him at my elbow while I watched two men fighting in the street in Bucharest. And every time I caught sight of him, he looked away. I thought he was Secret Service: I couldn't understand how they'd got on to me.'

The man was entirely bald, and, as he talked, Ulrich wondered at how the mobility of his lined, arching forehead stopped suddenly and gave way to the utterly inexpressive smoothness of his pate.

'Then I saw the bastard here in Sofia, sitting calmly in a café, and for once he hadn't seen me. I listened in to his conversation and realised he was a revolutionary like me. He's from Plovdiv, would you believe? Now we're great friends. Turns out he was even more scared of me than I was of him!'

Two other men joined their table, and more beer arrived. The table was soaked with spilt drink. A large group of people, actors evidently, came into the bar and took over two more tables, and the noise of arguments and conversations became clamorous. One man brought out some dog-eared pages from his pocket, offering to read his poems, but everyone protested scornfully.

Boris's face was shiny in the close air. He asked Ulrich something inconsequential, and Ulrich soon found himself discoursing about music. He told him about jazz, which Boris had never seen; he described the shows in Berlin, and explained about Louis Armstrong and Fletcher Henderson. 'If only you could have been there,' Ulrich kept saying, because he could not find words to convey the music. He told him about the women who dressed as men and the men who dressed as women, and how Berliners took no notice when they saw lovers of the same sex, for everything was possible in that place. There were people from all over the world, and all they cared about was to do things as well as human beings could do them.

He said,

'I saw Leopold Godowsky play. I am convinced he is the most spectacular pianist in the world: he piled his own embellishments upon Liszt. He's a little man, with small hands. Albert Einstein was in the audience, just a few rows in front of me.'

Boris was impressed by Einstein, and Ulrich went on happily with other anecdotes about the scientist. In his gesticulations he sent flying a full glass of beer, and the man next to him had to mop his thighs. The group at the table was large by now, and the red-faced man was telling another story.

‘The whole Russian army comes through Sofia on its way to fight the Turks. And they see my father, a nine-year-old boy, and take him off with them to war. And they beat the Turks and they bring the boy back to Sofia and say, *Boy, you’ve served us well. Tell us what you’d like to be and we will help*. They expect him to say, *A general*, or something like that. But he says, *A cook*. And the men all laugh, but the boy sticks to his guns so the Russian soldiers, good as their word, take him to Petersburg to work in the tsar’s kitchen.’

More beer came, and the red light began to curdle: Georgi’s face looked almost green in the corner. Ulrich watched the woman behind the bar, who used it to rest her breasts on. She made evident her displeasure when a customer ordered a drink and obliged her to haul them away again.

‘My father works his way up over the years and becomes a great cook, and when our independence comes around, Tsar Nicholas wonders what he can give to the Bulgarian king in congratulation, remembers that my father is from Sofia, and sends him. So my father becomes the Bulgarian royal chef.’

A young woman sat down next to Ulrich and introduced herself as Else; they talked about why they both had German names. She was pretty, but he did not like the prominence of her gums. Her stockings were full of holes.

‘So – listen! – so the years go by. My brother and I grow up. My father makes good money and he builds himself a house in the Centrum, the first two-storey house on the street. The new king comes in, and hears rumours of his chef’s wayward sons. He says he would like to come and see the house. So my father brings the king to Ovche Pole Street and shows him, and the king asks him how much it cost. My father works in a good margin and says that all in all it cost around twenty-five gold napoleons, and the king takes the money from his purse and gives it to him. And it’s obvious what the money says: *You and I both know that no one can kill me more easily than you. So don’t forget it was I who bought you your house.*’

Amid the hubbub, Else smoked unhappy cigarettes and told Ulrich that the girl who used to work here was coming back and she, Else, would be out of a job. The other girl had a more attractive body than she, and this thought made Else melancholy. She asked Ulrich if he would go upstairs with her and he declined, so she slipped away to another table.

'My brother keeps company with revolutionaries and he's always falling into scrapes. The king covers it up each time, but he tells my father, *You have to control those boys because I can't protect them forever.* One night two foreigners come into a restaurant and start to harass the girl my brother is courting, who's having dinner with her mother. Word gets to him and he goes down and shoots both the foreigners dead. Everyone sees it, and most people support him, though it was an extreme response. But the king says, *This time you have to get that boy out of the country. Otherwise I'll have him killed.* My father sells some land, gives him the money, tells him to go to Paris, live a good life and never come back.'

Boris was talking to the people on his other side. There was a chorus of shouts at the other end of the bar, where an old singer was sitting. A crowd was pleading with her to perform. The red-faced man took a sip of beer and resumed his story.

'So last week – my brother's only been gone ten months, hasn't written a single letter since he left – last week he appears at the door, says he's spent everything and he's got nowhere else to go. I asked him a thousand times what he's done with the money but he couldn't account for it. Paris is full of Bulgarians, apparently, and he fell straight into a high life. His lover was a Romanian princess who loved gambling, and it all seems to have left him with a perpetual smile on his face. That's what sends my father close to apoplexy.'

There was laughter all round, and people raised glasses to the obstinate rake.

'So I tell this idiot he has to leave. Does he realise what he's doing, coming back here with things as they are? He takes no notice, he's out every night, and eventually he doesn't come home. They found him face-down in the river yesterday morning. The king was as good as his word.'

They fell silent. Someone murmured,

'Bastard.'

On the other side of the room the old folk singer had agreed to sing, and there was enthusiastic applause as she made her way to the piano. She had lost nearly all her teeth. Her companion tuned his violin. Ulrich had a glass wedged between his knees, and Boris clinked it to rouse him from his reverie. He said,

'Did you meet any girls?'

His eyes were velvet with drink, and a tinnitus started up in Ulrich's ears as he told the story of Clara Blum. Boris shook his head as he listened. He said,

'Why have you come back, Ulrich? You love this woman and you've left her there. You've sacrificed this chemistry degree, which was all you ever dreamed of. What are you thinking?'

'What could I do?' asked Ulrich fiercely. 'There's no more money to keep me there: that's the clear reality. You should have seen what my mother wrote to me. Surely you can imagine what it's like when you hear your mother in despair? I have no choice but to stay here and help her.'

'Reality is never clear,' said Boris. 'It's never final. You can always change it or see it a different way. If you'd asked me for money I would have given it to you. I want you to become a great chemist, not to sit around here in Sofia. This place is a disaster. You should have asked me, and my father would have sent you money. He's still got a lot left.'

Ulrich stopped short, for he had never considered such a thing. Boris said,

'You never once wrote to me from Berlin, as if you broke everything off as soon as you left. And now you've given up your degree and this wonderful woman. It's as if you're never truly attached to anything. Except your mother, perhaps.'

Ulrich felt foolish. He made a silent resolution to solve future dilemmas by imagining what Boris would say. He said weakly,

'Well, there's nothing I can do now.'

Boris drew curly lines with his finger in the beer on the table, extending the reflections of the lamps. The folk singer began to sing, and the bar became hushed. She had a deep, raspy voice, but sang with great sensitivity:

There sat three girls, three friends
Embroidering aprons and crying tiny tears,
And they asked each other who loved whom.

Boris said,

'What do you think of Georgi?'

'He has a vicious face.'

Boris laughed.

'I knew you wouldn't like him,' he said. 'The strange thing about Georgi is that he holds a devilish attraction for women. You and I would think, with those teeth and that face, he'd have to make a big effort. But Georgi treats women with contempt, and they still fall over themselves trying to get him. I can never understand it.'

The first said, 'I love a shepherd.'
The second one said, 'I love a villager.'

Boris said under the music:

'Do you remember the conversation we had before you left? When I came to your house?'

'Yes.'

'I've thought of it very often. I was wrong. You were right.'

Ulrich was taken aback. Boris added,

'I sometimes wonder if I should not just have carried on playing music.'

To Ulrich's astonishment, Boris's eyes began to overflow with tears.

'I'm sorry,' he whispered. He wiped his face

The third one said, 'I love a huge dragon.
He comes to me in the evening,
In the middle of the night.
He lightly knocks and he lightly enters
So that no one will hear him
So that no one will know.

'Things can't continue as they are,' said Ulrich, trying to help. Boris gave a doubtful smile.

This evening the dragon will come,
He will come to take me away.'

Georgi came over.

'Let's go,' he said to Boris. 'It's very late.'

Boris dropped an offering of coins among the glasses and shook a man whose head was collapsed upon the table. The man would not stir. They left the gathering, pushing through the crowd of people waiting for the musicians' next song, and made for the door. Outside, the night was cool, and with the air on their necks they realised how drunk they were.

'He wouldn't even wake up!' said Boris, who was suddenly overcome with giggles. 'He couldn't raise his head to say goodbye!'

Ulrich had no thought of returning home, and walked where they led him. Georgi said to Boris,

'He can't come with us.'

'Why not?'

'My room is secret. No one goes there.'

Boris put his arm around Ulrich.

'He *will* come with us!'

Georgi was unhappy, and walked ahead. Boris sang with drunken sentimentality,

This evening the dragon will come,
He will come to take me away.

The street was empty, and the echo of their footsteps ricocheted between the rows of houses. Men dozed under fruit barrows, and horses slumbered by a line of caravans. On the steps outside a church, a man was sitting patiently with wakeful eyes, and, seeing him, Ulrich felt a wave of happiness. He said to Boris,

'Soon we'll go for a long walk, and I'll tell you everything!'

There were bats overhead, and a sense of life pent up behind locked doors. Cats wailed.

Ulrich said,

'Did you ever see Ida? The Jewess?'

'No. I never heard from her again.' Boris laughed loudly. 'And you? Did you see the angels in the Admiralspalast?'

'I did. Everything you said was true.'

Boris screamed with joy. He called out to Georgi in the distance,

'Georgi! Let's all go away to the country! We'll find some pretty girls. We'll take books and keep some pigs. I'll get my violin out again!'

They came to a gate, which surrendered to their drunken rattling, and climbed two lurching flights of stairs. They arrived in Georgi's room, the ringing worse than ever in Ulrich's ears. Georgi lay straight down on one of the beds in his clothes and boots and went to sleep.

Ulrich had a belated realisation.

'That man we saw. Outside the church. It was Misha the fool.'

'I don't believe you.'

'I knew I recognised him. I'm sure of it.'

'I haven't seen him for years.'

Boris took a swig from a bottle of brandy.

'I'm sure of it,' Ulrich repeated, and they fell together on the narrow bunk in a dreamless embrace that lasted until the next afternoon.

9

TWO DAYS LATER, Boris was arrested for sedition, and executed. The police went out in force, with names and addresses, and many were taken in. Georgi was arrested too, and thrown into jail.

Afterwards, the police sent word to Boris's parents that his body was available for collection.

When the coffin was lowered into the earth, Magdalena and her mother collapsed simultaneously into their skirts.

Ulrich walked home afterwards with his parents. Elizaveta was disabled by what had happened.

'I loved that boy,' she kept saying. 'I loved that boy.'

She forbade Ulrich from going out, fearing that something might happen to him too. But when evening came he could not stay shut up anymore. He ran to Boris's house.

A storm had come up suddenly, and unfastened shutters banged. He battled through a wind so fierce that the entire sky was too small a pipe for it, and the air groaned in its confines.

Outside Boris's house was a crowd of street people. Magdalena stood in front, handing out clothes, while her mother wept on the steps. Boris's shrunken father watched from an upstairs window.

'Ulrich!' cried Magdalena when she saw him, and she threw herself at his chest.

'What's going on?' he asked.

'I'm giving away his clothes.'

She had brought everything out of the house. Jackets, shirts and sweaters flapped in the gale. Ulrich could not bear to see it all disappear.

'So his warmth stays alive,' she said. 'Look how many have come.'

Ulrich saw Misha in the crowd and, for the first time, burst into tears. The fool approached him. He secreted two cold marbles in Ulrich's hands.

'I did not know that fish could drown. Those marbles were his eyes.'

It began to rain. The people dispersed, only a scattering of unwanted shirt collars and neckties left on the ground. Magdalena went into the house and emerged with Boris's umbrella.

'Let's walk,' she said.

'But it's late.'

She ignored him.

The storm became stupendous. She led him, pulling his arm, and they found a place for sex. There were no lips, no hands, no hair: just genitals. In the tumult, the umbrella blew away and they were entirely exposed under the flashes. Her skirt was at her thighs and she screamed: not with the sex, but with its insufficiency. Over her shoulder, Ulrich saw a man watching them from his shelter in a doorway, and he felt ashamed. He sank to the floor, sobbing in the downpour.

'No,' he said.

She stared at him in disbelief, untrussing her skirt.

'You know how much I need you,' she shrieked into the tempest.

She beat his head with her fists and ran away, clacking and splashing on the street. He pulled up his trousers and retrieved the umbrella from the iron fence where it had lodged. When he reached the main road she had disappeared.

Disturbed crows wheeled overhead, their wet wings slapping ineffectually at the air.

He did not know where to escape to. The city was without dimension, like a whipped-up ocean, and the umbrella, in this horizontal torrent, a flailing superfluity. He arrived finally at the bar where they had been two nights earlier. He found Else, the guileless prostitute, and took her upstairs. She was alarmed at his inconsiderate, uncouth pounding, but he did not stop until the barmaid knocked angrily at the door, complaining of the noise and the hour, at which point he grabbed his clothes and went home.

For a long time, Ulrich avoided all places where he might run the risk of meeting any member of Boris's family.

Many years later, Ulrich heard a story about the great pianist, Leopold Godowsky, whom he had once seen in Berlin playing the music of Franz Liszt.

Godowsky was born in Lithuania but spent his life in Paris, Vienna, Berlin and then New York. He had a gift for friendship and hospitality, and, wherever he lived, his home became a centre for artists and thinkers. His friends included Caruso, Stravinsky, Gershwin, Chaplin, Diaghilev, Nijinsky, Gide, Matisse, Ravel – and Albert Einstein.

Godowsky was one of those people who are born to do one thing, and when a stroke rendered his right hand useless for piano playing, he fell into a deep depression. He never played in public again.

During his final unhappy years in New York, Godowsky saw Einstein frequently, as the scientist had moved from Berlin to nearby Princeton.

Leopold Godowsky had an Italian barber in New York, named Caruso. Caruso was a great follower of Einstein, and when he discovered that his customer, Godowsky, knew him personally, he begged him to bring the famous man to his shop. Each time Godowsky saw Einstein, he told him that Caruso the barber wanted to meet him, and Einstein each time agreed to go and see the man whenever he was next in the city. With one thing and another, however, the visit never took place.

Eventually, Godowsky died. When the news reached Einstein at Princeton he did not say a word. He immediately picked up his hat and coat, took the first train to New York, and went to visit Caruso at his barbershop.

Ulrich thinks back, sometimes, to the conversation he had with Boris in that attic laboratory so long ago, when they discussed the news of an uncle who had died. He feels that he did not ever progress far beyond his childhood bewilderment, and is ashamed of the inadequacy he always felt in the face of death. He has always been affected by stories of people who knew precisely how to respond when a person has died.

Perhaps it is because his behaviour after Boris's death fell so short of the mark that the terrible finality of it never truly settled.

Whenever he thinks back to his wedding day, he remembers the smile on Boris's face, and the way his hand was tucked in the belt of his green army uniform. But such a thing is impossible, for Boris had been dead for years by then, and he would never have worn such clothes. There are many other memories like that, which have all the flesh of terrestrial recollections but must have slipped in somehow from another world.

10

ULRICH THREW HIMSELF into his bookkeeping at the leather company. It was not the kind of work he had imagined for himself, but the sense of finitude he discovered there turned out to be a surprising relief. When he immersed himself in grids of numbers, every ache in his head went away. He developed a knack for spotting the errors in a page of figures with just a casual glance, and he traced several routes to every total to ensure the computation was robust. He became notorious among his subordinates for spotting even the most trivial lapse, and asking them to do the work again. He delivered the completed books at the same time every day to the office of Ivan Stefanov, the son of the owner, and, when his work was finished, he applied himself to the greater task of overhauling the bookkeeping systems to make them more accurate and efficient. Ivan Stefanov, who was bored by procedure, was delighted by Ulrich's devotion to it, and quickly promoted him to financial controller, a post that carried with it an office with his name on the door, and a fully enclosed desk.

When his thoughts were not occupied with bookkeeping, Ulrich could not prevent himself wondering how so much had been snatched away from him. He tried to deny it had happened: he played tricks on himself, marking time in Sofia by the timetable in his Berlin diary, full of far-off lectures and exams. He even chose to ask directions around his home town, and feigned gaps in his Bulgarian speech – as if he were an outsider here, who might be called away at any moment. He lay awake at night, completing in his head his thesis on plastic fibres in time for the deadline, which passed unobtrusively by.

In Sofia there was no one who understood the scientific wonder he had left behind, and it became like a heavy secret he could only dwell on alone. He maintained an archive of Berlin science, full of notes and news clippings about the people he had encountered there. Every year he added to the list he kept of all his Berlin teachers and colleagues who won the Nobel Prize – an award that always held enormous allure for him. But as time passed, his ponderous rehearsals became detached from any reality of Berlin, which had moved on without him. His peers graduated and advanced to greater things. New chemical discoveries were made every day, which Ulrich knew nothing of.

Clara Blum began to teach chemistry at the University of Berlin, and married one of her colleagues in the department. Ulrich had to hear it from someone else, for she had broken off all contact when she realised he was never coming back.

Meanwhile, in the cramped space of Ulrich's Sofia home, his father sat in his chair, showing fewer and fewer signs of life. His leg stump became regularly infected, and every few months a little bit more had to be shaved off the end. And his deafness became more pronounced with the years, until he was finally delivered from the music he disliked so much. When he could no longer hear at all, Elizaveta erupted into a festival of song, chanting arias from Verdi to *lah-lah-lah* as she worked.

Ulrich took advantage of his father's deafness too. He found perverse satisfaction in whispering insults in his ear:

'You whipped your son so hard into success, and look what he has become. He has come back to this godforsaken place, and now he will never be anything at all. Your son is a failure. How bitter your disappointment must be!'

His father looked at him in bewilderment, his eyes narrow under heavy brows, and he peeled off a ribbon from his tattered mind:

'Nothing can sing like the lyrebird. It can imitate the song of every other bird. It can make the sound of branches creaking in the wind.'

Ulrich was invited to a piano recital in the house of the well-known doctor, Ivan Karamihailov, who had once been an associate of his father's. Ulrich arrived directly from his work, and paid little attention to his surroundings. He waited distractedly in the audience, still preoccupied by the concerns of the day, eschewing the sociable gazes of people he knew.

He was snatched away from the accounting columns in his head when the pianist entered, and he realised that it was Magdalena. He was ashamed: he had not seen her since the night of Boris's death, and he had convinced himself she must despise him.

She had tied her black hair back, exaggerating the exoticism of her pale skin and blue eyes. She was now approaching the age that Boris had been when he died, and the resemblance was more striking than ever.

She wore a long dress of radiant blue.

In the centre of the room was a music stand, which Magdalena picked up and moved aside so she could deliver some words to her audience. The stand was wooden, and carved in the shape of a lyre.

Against one wall stood a magnificent long-case clock, whose pendulum had been stilled so the chimes would not disturb the performance. Hanging behind the piano was a painting of a solitary man contemplating an Alpine lake.

Magdalena said,

'I would like to dedicate my first public recital to the memory of my brother, Boris, who died two years ago on Saturday. I am delighted to see that some of his friends are here this evening.'

And Ulrich was carried away to see her smile at him, openly and without restraint. He has kept that smile with him ever since, even as it has become progressively detached from the time and the place, and, finally, from Magdalena herself.

She sat at the piano. Ulrich watched the tightly laced black shoes that reached below for the pedals, and the narrow band of her legs that was visible beneath the blue of her dress.

Ulrich was astonished by her performance. She had become an intent musician, and he watched her with every kind of yearning. As she played, her toes were on the pedals, and only the point of her shoes' long heels touched the floor. Ulrich found himself aroused by the click each time her soles made contact with the brass.

Afterwards, they walked in the garden together, and he told her about jazz. She told him she had fallen in love with him long ago.

'As a little girl I was always tender for you,' she said. 'And my brother told me such stories about you when you were away in Berlin. He knew you would do something wonderful. He knew he was less than you, and he put your ambition above his own. Since he's been gone I've not stopped thinking of those stories.'

11

THE FRICTION OF ULRICH'S MEMORY, moving back and forth over the surface of his life, wears away all the detail – and the story becomes more bland each time.

Nowadays, Ulrich finds it difficult to remember any happy moments from his marriage to Magdalena. Whenever he stumbles upon such a memory, he adds it to a list so it will not disappear.

Item
Magdalena's father paid for the newly wed couple to honeymoon in Georgia. She wanted Ulrich to see where her maternal family came from, and where she herself had spent many happy times. He loved Tbilisi, and her joy at showing it. Her cousins were eccentric, attentive hosts who woke them in the middle of the night to climb into horse carts and travel for hours along mud roads just to see an old church, or a beautiful hill. Ulrich took Magdalena to see *Tosca* in the arabesque opera house, and their happiness was absolute.

When they emerged from their room each morning, Magdalena's

uncle made gestures to Ulrich that would have been obscene if it were not for the great generosity with which he delivered them.

After this journey to Tbilisi, Ulrich never left Bulgaria again.

Item

Ivan Stefanov invited Ulrich and Magdalena to dinner to celebrate the couple's wedding. There was a strict dress code in the Stefanov mansion, and Magdalena wore her most sumptuous gown. Gloved waiters carried lobsters aloft, and each place had its own cascade of crystal glasses. Ivan was merry, and stood up to make a speech about the deep affection he had always held for Ulrich. His lugubrious aunts blinked behind diamond necklaces, and ate little. After dinner Ivan became drunk, and he kept his guests up with his ideas about the company, his gossip about his workers and his theories about life's various dissatisfactions. Magdalena signalled several times to Ulrich that she wished to leave but he could not find the appropriate break in his employer's monologue, and they did not make their exit until Ivan Stefanov fell asleep in his chair.

Item

Boris and Magdalena had grown up in luxurious surroundings, which Ulrich's bookkeeper salary did not allow him to match. They moved into a small house on Pop Bogomil Street, near the entrance to the city. But she liked the house very much, which was a relief to Ulrich. Every time he asked her, she said that she liked it.

Item

It became a tradition with them that Magdalena came to meet Ulrich after work every Friday, and they went to hold hands over the table in a nearby cake shop. He used to watch for her arrival by the upstairs window where he worked, and every week he had the same stirring of love when he saw her come round the corner, dressed up for him, and so small she fitted inside the eye on the casement handle.

Item

Ulrich surprised Magdalena with a chemistry trick. He put a glass vial in a bowl of water, and, calling her to watch, broke it open with pliers. The bowl erupted with boiling, and a pink flame hovered over the water. Magdalena started, while Ulrich looked between the bowl and her face, incandescent himself.

'Isn't it marvellous?' he said as the flame died down.

'It's very pretty. But what does it lead to?'

'Oh! Something will come of it one day.'

'It's childish, it seems to me.'

There was a coolness between them for the rest of the day. And yet it was on that night that their son was conceived.

Item

They were once invited to a wedding in the Jewish quarter. The guests spoke Ladino and Bulgarian both, mixed together. There was a klezmer brass orchestra, and Magdalena laughed with the music, and danced unrestrainedly with him, though she was exuberantly pregnant. She kissed him and said, *I hope our baby will be a Jew.*

Item

Faithful to her maternal tradition, Magdalena wanted to give their son a Georgian name. Before choosing, she called several names from the front door to see how they would sound when, in years to come, she summoned her boy from his play.

Item

Elizaveta loved Magdalena. *I never expected such a wonderful daughter-in-law*, she said. Her own situation was gloomy, with no money and her husband lost, and the life of the young couple gave her new joy. She went to the house on Pop Bogomil Street with gifts she could ill afford, yodelling and prancing to delight her grandson. Early one sunny morning, when she was drinking tea with Magdalena, Ulrich came back from a walk with his son and announced, 'Birds don't fly away from a man holding a baby!' and the two women burst into laughter at the expression of awe upon his face.

Item
An upright piano was brought into the house for Magdalena to continue her practice. Nothing gave Ulrich greater happiness than to sit behind her after dinner and request his favourite pieces, one after another.

As the months drew on, Magdalena ceased to find romance in their meagre situation, and she and Ulrich were led more and more frequently into arguments.

'When are you going to leave Ivan Stefanov and his leather company? It was supposed to be temporary, and now it's been years. And you're still earning the same as when you began.'

'Think of Einstein. While he was doing his routine job in the Swiss Patent Office he managed to come up with his greatest theories. Perhaps something like that will happen to me!'

He smiled bashfully, and she *tutted* with exasperation.

'You're no Einstein! And you have a wife and a son to take care of.'

At social gatherings he asked his acquaintances whether they knew of any jobs that would pay well. But his enquiries lacked conviction, and led to nothing. He said to Magdalena,

'Perhaps I could set up a little chemistry laboratory here. Investigate some compounds in the evenings. Your father made some money that way.'

She said,

'Ulrich! Face up to reality!'

He looked at her strangely, and exclaimed,

'What is reality? Is it this?' – and he banged the table excessively, then the wall – 'is it this?'

She waited, impassive before his outburst, and he said,

'Did your brother believe in *reality*? Didn't he spend his whole time thinking about how to overthrow it?'

'I am not my brother, Ulrich.'

One day, Ulrich arrived home with an old desk that had been discarded from the office. A colleague helped him cart it, and they carried it to the back of the house.

'This will be my workbench!' he announced happily to Magdalena.

'It's filthy,' she said.

'I'll clean it. Don't worry.'

'There isn't much room here. How much more junk will you bring?'.

He sighed gravely.

'Please, Magda. I need to do this.'

'I don't know what's happening to the man I married.'

Ulrich took her hands and comforted her. She studied him for a long time, until tenderness flowed back into her cheeks. She put her arms round him and inhaled from his hair.

'I don't like to see you living below yourself. You need a plan, Ulrich. Right now I don't think you have one. Soon all your intelligence will be accounted for in Ivan Stefanov's books, and you will have none left for yourself.'

He looked at the floor.

'Mr Stefanov is a decent man. I will talk to him about the salary. He is not a bad man, and I'm comfortable there.'

She put her hands over his ears and peered into his eyes as if they were dark shafts in the earth. She held his head tight and shook it back and forth.

'Comfortable?' she said, shaking him. 'Comfortable? Are you comfortable now?'

And she went on shaking him a bit too long.

They attended a lavish party at the house of her parents, who were celebrating their wedding anniversary. The preparations had been going on for a month. Ulrich surprised Magdalena with a new dress, and that night she was joyful among so many people she knew. Her father was tall and jovial, and he put his arm across Ulrich's shoulders and introduced him around, exaggerating his career: *He has a lucrative line in leather.*

At home afterwards, Magdalena seemed unusually subdued. They went to bed, but neither could sleep, and they lay side by side, looking at the ceiling.

He said,

'Why don't you play the piano anymore?'

She sighed with contempt, and turned her back.

Ulrich drifted into sleep. He dreamed of a stormy journey on a ship full of pigs, and a shipwreck, and standing tiptoe on the summit of the mountain of drowned, sunken hogs to keep his mouth above water. When he came to, later in the night, she was standing at the window.

'What's wrong?' he asked.

She scanned the street outside and said mournfully,

'I wish someone would come to take me away.'

He bought some supplies for his laboratory. He lined up the bottles on his bench while Magdalena was out.

He was polishing his shoes in the kitchen when she came in, brandishing a bottle embossed with a skull and crossbones. She shouted, 'What's this?' and before he could warn her, she hurled it against the wall. He leapt at her as it smoked, and ran her out of the room.

'What are you doing?' he cried. 'What are you doing?'

He was shaking with emotion.

'That's sulphuric acid. You could have killed yourself.'

She snarled at him,

'And you bring it into the house when we have a small boy running around?'

In her rage she twirled her fingers at her ears to show his insanity.

'You are crazy, crazy! Why don't you just throw him into acid right away? Be done with it!'

She ran away, inconsolable. While Ulrich looked for something to cover his face while he cleaned up the acid, he heard the *thrum* of bass strings as Magdalena kicked the piano in the other room.

One day, Ulrich came home to find that Magdalena had moved out with their son. Her family closed ranks around her, and Ulrich could not get to see either of them after that.

Their boy was nearly three years old, and Ulrich was used to taking him out for long weekend walks. He would tell him stories of the seasons, and his son would ask 'Why?' to every reason, to hear whether the world's explanation had an end. Ulrich had found peace and fulfilment in simple fatherhood, and now he suffered actual physical pain at his son's absence. He woke up in the night with the fantasy that the boy was crying in the room. In the morning he leaned over the abandoned little bed to inhale the vestiges of his scent.

Some time later, he read in a book of a Japanese word that described the unique pleasure of sleeping next to a young child. It spoke of a sensuality that was not erotic, but indecent, nevertheless, in its fervour. It captured the feeling of what tormented him so, in those days, by its absence.

Nowadays, that word dances just beyond his grasp.

Later on, Magdalena divorced him and married a Bible scholar from a well-to-do Protestant family. Ulrich went through extremes and did regrettable things. He drank on his own and made a nuisance of himself in bars.

One night he went to the big house on Krakra Street where his wife and son were now shut up. It was late, and he was incoherent with drink. There were no people in the street, though a dog pestered him, trying obstinately to lick his hand. A light was burning in an upstairs window. Ulrich saw a route up to the window by the roof of the outhouse.

In his stupor, he was intent on clear thought, and he climbed with excruciating slowness, monitoring the movements of each limb so it did not escape and set off the cymbals of the night. Silence returned his favours, and finally he crouched undetected beneath the lit window, and could lift his head to the view.

Ulrich had heard that Protestants kept their windows uncurtained in order to prove that nothing furtive ever happened inside; and somewhere he believed that they were truly unacquainted with secrecy and urge. Even at this hour, he imagined he might fall upon some scene of decorous domesticity: novel-reading, perhaps, or symmetrical bedtime prayer.

But when he looked inside, the man was fully inside her with his shirt still on, she crying *More!*, which Ulrich could hear through the glass. The room was scattered with objects he dimly recognised, though his attention was not there: for her mobile breasts shone under the electric lamp, her legs were open, and her face was transported no differently than once for him. The body pushing into her was thin and had a repulsive smoothness to it, as if it were without hair. As Ulrich squatted on the roof, his chin just clear of the windowsill, the sweat gushed from his armpits and his clothes stuck to his back. While the preacher's fishy foot soles flapped with his exertions, Ulrich became extravagantly aroused by the sight of Magdalena displayed luxuriant, so that he could not tear himself away even as the evangelist flurried his backside to a clench, and let himself collapse upon her, spent.

So it was that Ulrich's wide-eyed, jerking face, lit up by the room's blaze like a glossy mask in the night, still bobbed at the window when Magdalena's gaze came to rest there, and they locked eyes for a strange duration.

No longer fearing discovery, he gave up climbing down and let himself fall most of the way. He lay in the street for a while, his limbs gliding like the after-movements of a dead insect. When he pulled himself up, he saw Magdalena silhouetted in the front door, newly wrapped in a dressing gown. She beckoned to him.

She put her arms around him and clasped him to her, still ripe from the other man, and he let himself be held until she pulled herself away and shut the front door against him.

It was not long afterwards that Magdalena departed for America. Ulrich went to the railway station to watch the family board the train. Her husband extended his hand to cut the ceremony short, and Ulrich stared at its long thin fingers, which reminded him unpleasantly of those kicking feet. He felt vaguely nauseated at the thickness of the man's new wedding band and the neatness with which he clipped his fingernails, but he took the hand and shook it. Magdalena looked him in the eye, and he mumbled some empty words of good fortune, to which she nodded.

Ulrich wanted to embrace his son, asleep in her arms, but he felt unable to approach Magdalena, and the opportunity passed. The young family got on the train, and Ulrich thought with bitterness about the prehistoric bombast of his father, who pretended that the railways would unite what was split apart.

As far as he can remember now, he put his palms together in some perplexing gesture of prayerfulness, and turned to leave.

The Bible scholar took Magdalena and her son to Detroit, where he studied at a seminary for some years before going to serve as pastor to a Lutheran church somewhere in Texas. At that point, Magdalena broke off contact with Ulrich and his mother, and Ulrich never knew more about them.

For years afterwards, Ulrich remained convinced that the world was too systematic for a child to become lost to a father, and he continued to expect that his son would reappear at some point – if not in real life, then at least in the lists of names he sometimes read to this end. Lists of sports teams and prize winners, lists of committee members, lists of students sent on exchange visits, lists of convicts, lists of important poets, lists of patriots and botanists, lists of marriages, lists of academic appointments, lists of the approved, lists of the disgraced, and lists of the dead.

Radium

12

Whenever Ulrich's neighbour knocks at the door, he reaches for his pair of dark glasses. A residue of vanity.

She has seen them a thousand times before, but she chooses today to make a comment.

'They make you look funny, those sunglasses,' she says. 'They're small for you, and a bit lopsided.'

Ulrich explains that he fabricated them himself, and given the difficulty of shaping plastic by hand, he thought them quite good.

'I never heard of a person making sunglasses before,' she says. She sounds as if she does not believe him.

Ulrich says he copied them from a pair his mother had. She became extravagant towards the end of her life, and asked her friends to make unnecessary purchases for her in town. She bought this pair for a lot of money: they were made to look like tortoiseshell, and she found them glamorous. Ulrich told her he could make a pair just like it himself, without the expense. And he did it, too, but only after she died.

His neighbour is not interested in Ulrich's story, true or not, and concentrates on what she has come to do.

The shape of the world changed when Ulrich lost his sight. When he had relied on his eyes, everything was shaped in two great shining cone rays. Without them, he sank into the black continuum of hearing, which passed through doors and walls, and to which even the interior of his own body was not closed.

His hearing is still perfect – which is why he wakes up so often at night, cursing the bus station, or the eternal wailing of cats.

If cats were to make an atlas, he sometimes thinks as he lies awake in his sagging bed, Sofia would be a great metropolis of the world. It would be the legendary city of pleasure, he muses, so loud and ubiquitous is the nightly feline copulation.

The blackness of his obliterated vision has made a fertile screen for his daydreams, and they have intensified during the last years. There he finds treasured smells, and tunes he has whistled, and other remnants that are lustred, now, with the mauve of nostalgia. He pictures the strange offspring that might have grown out of a man like him, whose blurred faces float among rows of lamps strung like greenish pearls in the darkness. He forgets that his own son, if he is still alive, would now be over seventy, and he dreams of strong young people filled with the courage he never had. He pleasures himself with implausible tableaux of revenge, and sometimes he can see himself in the streets of New York, as clear as day.

His daydreams seem to come from without, like respiration, and they have the power to surprise him. They provide relief from the rest of his thought, which rarely brings up anything new.

Whenever he recalls any event involving a horse, for instance, he always asks himself the same question. *What happened to all the horses?*

He remembers the smell of them filling the streets, the lines by the river chewing in their nosebags, the constant sound of hoofs and shouting drivers. He thinks of the horses thronging in Berlin, hauling every kind of merchandise.

He does the same calculation every time he thinks of it: one horse for every twenty people, he estimates, making twenty million across Europe at that time, and still their numbers exploding with the population. Then, after the centuries of coexistence, humans turned away from horses and embraced machines. But he does not remember seeing how the surplus of horses was carried off.

He tries to visualise the volume of twenty million horses. *Did we eat them, without knowing?* he asks himself. The question irritates him because he has gone countless times through this sequence of thoughts, and he knows it does not produce any answers.

13

ULRICH MOVED BACK into his parents' house, where he watched his father die of chagrin.

The days were already running out when people could die of such things. Ulrich knows his own will be a modern death, and his death certificate will require a mechanical justification for it: for even at his excessive age, bureaucrats will see his demise as a suspicious error. It is no longer possible to say on a death certificate that a person died of old age.

But Ulrich's father died of chagrin. He sat in a chair for the better part of a decade, looking out of the window and growing deaf, and squawking, sometimes, with snatches of birdsong. The gap between his breaths became longer and longer, until finally, almost indiscernibly, they ceased.

While he was still alive, Elizaveta would say, 'All he ever does is sit in that chair and look out of the window.' It infuriated her to see him so inactive. But after he died she never said anything but, 'That was the chair he loved.' Or, 'How he loved sitting in that chair.' Or, 'They are spoiling the view your father loved so much.'

Ulrich had never played music again after his childhood violin was thrown into the fire. But his separation from chemistry was not so complete. It continued to seep back in, diverting him from his proper life, and prodding him, sometimes, to do puzzling things.

Though life had uprooted him from the pursuit of science, he continued to surround himself with chemical accoutrements, which acted as substitutes for the real thing. He fell into the routine of spending an hour or two after work in a scientific bookshop, which stocked some of the most reputed international publications about chemistry. He liked to look through the contents of the German journals – the *Zeitschrift für Angewandte Chemie*, the *Berichte der Deutschen Chemischen Gesellschaft*, the *Zeitschrift für Physikalische Chemie*, and *Liebigs Annalen* – and to pose questions to the shopowner, who knew something about recent developments in the field. Ulrich usually came away with some small purchase or other: manuals for practical experimentation, mostly, and biographies of scientists. These books and papers began to accumulate in every room of the house, filling corners and covering chairs.

'Are you trying to close up all the gaps?' his mother asked bitterly, staring at the piles. 'Make sure I never let down my hair?'

Elizaveta viewed Ulrich's return home as an admission of failure, and she no longer indulged his whims. In the past, she had supported him whenever her husband had stood in his way, but now she turned on him in just the same way – as if she were trying to preserve the dead man's memory by taking over his attitudes. She treated Ulrich's chemistry as if it were a form of onanism that had to be rooted out of him, and she forbade experiments in the house. She quizzed him about how he planned to get on in life, and cursed him for losing the daughter-in-law and grandson she loved so much. For years, she continued to write letters to the last address they had, which always found their way back to her, unopened.

Ulrich developed a routine. Every month, he delivered his salary to her, placing a pile of notes on the dresser, weighed down with a lead battleship that survived from his childhood. On Saturday mornings he set off with a shopping bag to the Ladies' Market, where he bought groceries for the week. Then he went to the library, where he read for a few hours. He purchased a gramophone player, which he listened to some evenings, with the volume down. After dinner on Sundays, he polished his shoes.

Ulrich had good features and bright, even teeth, and he could look distinguished in the glasses he now used for reading. But since the failure of his marriage he had lost his desire for communication, and even his old acquaintances seemed uneasy around him. He sat in his father's armchair, and made his displeasure felt when his mother invited guests to the house. On weekdays, he arrived home late in the evening and sat down to read at the kitchen table, and though Elizaveta offered a nightly monologue of thoughts and anecdotes, it did nothing to draw him out.

She exploded, sometimes, with the emptiness.

'I am full of thoughts, you know, full of feelings. Do you realise how lonely I am, living like this?'

She found things to occupy her. She stripped everything out of the house, and had the walls repainted. She organised old photographs, and resumed her dressmaking. She read every newspaper with close attention, and she began to write a series of memoirs about the travels she had made with her husband before the wars.

She bought a dog to keep her company. She called it Karim, and she took it for walks in the evenings, which gave her some release.

In the hour before they retired, the silence claimed his mother too, and Ulrich relaxed into contentment. While the ball of wool twitched with her knitting, his attention drifted from his books and spiralled into his own recesses, where old faces coasted past like comforting submarine monsters, and fine filaments lit up a route to the future. He came to find solace in these daydreams, and on the days when he did not have an opportunity to cultivate them, he went to bed quite unsatisfied.

After the fascist coup of 1934, democratic freedoms were cancelled, political parties abolished, and espionage and surveillance reigned in every sector of society. Elizaveta became the centre of a group of men and women who met regularly to discuss political affairs. Her ideals of democracy, commerce and freedom were being squeezed between the Bolsheviks and the fascists, who swept the country, recruiting new members under threat of death. She clung to the hope that earnest discussions between learned, reasonable people would somehow help to restore sanity and moderation.

Every Thursday, priests, lawyers, doctors and professors came to her house to debate the burden of war reparations and the rise of Macedonian terrorism, the oppression of Bulgarians in Yugoslavia and the problem of the refugees. They discussed the awakening in the East, and the rise of China. They argued about Spain and Abyssinia.

At one meeting Elizaveta gave an edifying lecture about the prospects of the new nation of Iraq, a land for which she still entertained an extravagant affection.

Above all, they discussed German politics, and the increasing hold of that country over their own. German industrialists now filled the hotels of Sofia, planning new mining ventures and chemical plants, and taking over the Bulgarian tobacco industry. When the king allied himself with Chancellor Hitler, and German industry began to supply the Bulgarian army with gleaming modern armaments, Elizaveta and her associates wrote a plea for political prudence that they circulated to the newspapers and to several thinking people in the city. It began thus:

> *WHILST IT IS TRUE that, since the independence of our nation, we have, by war and enforced treaty, lost great expanses of our territory to neighbouring countries, AND thousands of our fellow countrymen live under the daily oppression of foreign governments, AND our politics have descended frequently into violence and chaos which have resulted in terrible deprivations for our people, NEVERTHELESS, the decades have revealed that the Great Powers are not swayed by these sufferings, and every alliance with them has rebounded even more disastrously upon us. WE OPPOSE the alliance with Germany, whose might will never be employed to right the wrongs of our Bulgarian history, and whose use of us in the past has been responsible for many of our present ills.*

When Germany invaded Poland and the Great Powers went to war, the king tried valiantly to keep Bulgaria out of the conflict, but there was no way to hold off the inevitable. The Wehrmacht pushed through into the Balkans and overran the country, taking command of its army and industry – and humble Bulgaria found itself at war, against its will, with America, Britain and the Soviet Union.

Ulrich was sent to man an observation tower, scanning the night skies with binoculars for British and American aircraft, but the bombardment, when it arrived, was mighty and irresistible. He remembers looking up at the lines of planes, their bellies lit up theatrically with the explosions, the deep noise out of phase with the flashes because of the distance. He wondered how Sofia would look from so high, and thought it must seem unreal, like a toy, and incapable of pain.

One night, sheltering in the basement with his mother, though he had a blanket pressed to his ears to protect his hearing, he heard a terrible screeching outside, inhuman and uncouth, as if a savage and relentless giant were sawing steel. It went on and on, undaunted by the explosions, tearing at Ulrich's nerves, and all at once he went out to see what it was.

A house was hit near by, and flames sprang from the upper-storey windows, lighting up the street. In the gaps in the smoke he could see the domes of the Alexander Nevski church glinting in the flashes, and the red air shook with an overwhelming roar. Others were running to discover what the noise was. Someone brought a lantern, and soon they came upon a horse pinned down in the rubble, its raw flesh glistening in the lamplight, screaming as if it would wake the dead. In this pitch of war they could find no gun, and they had to dispatch it with an axe.

In the mornings, Ulrich wandered through the stench of quenched fire watching people digging corpses out of the wreckage, and he saw women writing the names of missing people on trees. He looked up through Doric windows that now housed nothing, and were only frames for the implacable sky.

With the military leadership absorbed by the war, the long-suppressed partisan communists, in concert with Moscow, saw their chance for a full-blown uprising, and the government's retaliations saw whole villages destroyed at a time. The country was ripped apart. Elizaveta honoured every side with obscenities that Ulrich had never before heard from her mouth.

'Bulgarian soldiers are cutting off the breasts of our young women,' she wailed. 'They are throwing young Bulgarian men into ovens! And who is benefiting? Only our enemies, who will come in and build cities over our dead.'

She was consumed by the horror of what was happening, and she became grim and dogged. When Hitler ordered the king to round up the Bulgarian Jews and send them to the labour camps, Elizaveta became an organiser for the protests. Her house served as a war office for the outraged teachers and lawyers who marched during the day and debated through the night. When the king finally announced he would not give up Bulgaria's Jews, Elizaveta was exultant, for it was apparently possible for decent people to make themselves heard. But after the war, all the Jews who had been saved departed for Israel and America, and the society she had fought to preserve was anyway broken up.

Ulrich saw her weeping every day, and he wished he could reach out and help her. But he felt inhibited around her suffering, and he could not bring himself to ask how she felt. It was a cowardice that he acknowledged in his character, but could not overcome. For all their life together, his mother's troubles made him panic, and he kept his distance from them – as if they contained a poison to which he was peculiarly vulnerable.

It was around that time that Ulrich glimpsed an aged vagrant in the street, and realised it was Misha the fool. Misha was filthy and carried a sack. He marched up and down Tsar Osvobiditel Place, where bureaucrats parked their limousines. When cars drew up there, he guided them in, flapping his arms and grimacing with his missing teeth. Then he wrote out parking tickets that he pressed upon the uniformed chauffeurs, who threw them away and took no notice.

Ulrich watched for some time, but he did not approach. It was the last time he ever saw Misha. During the communist years, they cleaned out people like him.

The Red Army marched into Sofia on 9 September 1944, and was met by frenzied crowds. Ulrich and his mother watched the tanks arrive, and they cheered with the rest of them, for now Hitler's hold was released. Bulgaria changed sides in the war, and fought with its Soviet liberators against Germany.

During those last months of fighting, Ulrich's thoughts were set upon distant Berlin. He read of the thousand American bombers flying over the city every night, and the million Russian soldiers encircling the city with their tanks. He saw pictures of wilderness where once he had sat in cafés, and he knew that the Berlin he remembered had already ceased to exist.

Albert Einstein had left for Princeton even before Hitler came to power, and, during the Nazi years, Berlin was emptied by a full-blown exodus.

His old teachers had gone. Walther Nernst had resigned over the anti-Jewish policies that had gutted his department. Fritz Haber an ardent German nationalist, who had been decorated by the Kaiser for his invention of chemical weapons and who wore Prussian military uniform on official occasions, was thrown out of the university because he was a Jew who had converted to Protestantism. He fled to Switzerland and died of chagrin.

Max Planck had visited Hitler to ask him to spare the scientific community from persecution. He remained in Berlin during the war to tend to its ruins. His house was destroyed in the Allied bombings, along with decades of his notes, and his son was tortured to death by the Gestapo for his role in a failed plot to assassinate the Führer. When the war came to an end, the eighty-seven-year-old Planck was discovered living with his wife in the forest.

Ulrich lay awake thinking about Clara Blum who was not mentioned in the newspapers. He did not know whether she had escaped. He wondered what the canals looked like now, where he and she used to walk.

14

THE RUSSIANS PARKED their tanks on the courts of Sofia's tennis club, and there was no doubt which way things were heading. So many were executed from the previous regime that the judge took days to read out the list of names. *In the name of the People: death.* Others were taken away and shot without any such performance, including those of Elizaveta's friends who had been most outspoken in their criticism of the communists. The fresh government was filled up with party activists from the villages and communist stalwarts fresh out of jail – and after what they had been through, they were in a vengeful mood.

The new society had already been formulated in Moscow, and it was unrolled here even as the war still raged. The Stefanovs' leather company was confiscated, and the scientific bookshop where Ulrich used to stop each day was closed. The newspapers he had grown up with disappeared. His family home was divided in half, and a party man from the countryside was installed upstairs with his wife and six children.

One afternoon, Ulrich opened the door to a delegation that had come to confiscate the remaining relics of his family's one-time prosperity: his mother's jewellery, an ancient crucifix with a gold figure of Christ that hung on the wall, and the framed prints of the Ringstrasse in Vienna.

Elizaveta turned apoplectic with these indignities, and never lost an opportunity to rant about them. She abused the policemen in the street who presumed to interfere with her, and she complained about the Russian tanks. Most of all, she seethed about the family who had taken over half her house, whose party membership earned them many privileges she did not enjoy.

'We don't even have flour or oil, and they have everything. People without a grain of civilisation who leave spit every day in the stairwell.

Your father bought this house with his last money, and look at us now, crouching here like vagrants!'

She shouted such diatribes at the ceiling, hoping they would hear, and she hissed when she saw them on the stairs. The man said to her,

'You should be more restrained in your expression, comrade. Your opinions don't matter anymore. They may land you in trouble.'

The war ended with one dictatorship crushing another. The exultant newspapers showed the Soviet flag raised over the Reichstag in Berlin.

A few months later, when America dropped atomic bombs on Hiroshima and Nagasaki, the front pages were strangely mute, and Ulrich searched in vain for details of how it had happened. It seemed Einstein had started off the bomb with a letter to Roosevelt, and other scientists from Berlin had been involved in building it. But already the books from England and Germany had disappeared, and it was difficult to get reports from the West. He was left troubled and bewildered. *What happened to those beautiful scientists when they got to America?*

Now, in his blindness, his imagination of it has become more vivid. Two infernal flashes, immense shadows clutching for an instant at the earth, and survivors stumbling in the dust, their retinas burned.

The bombing of Sofia, just a year and a half old, already seemed quaint and remote. The bombs that dropped on Dondukov Boulevard were mechanical and comprehensible. You could imagine how they might look the moment they came through the ceiling. With these two white-outs in Japan, everyone knew that humans had become entirely without substance, and henceforth there was only abject obedience.

Ulrich received a letter summoning him to the offices of the Council for Industry and Construction at 3.15 on a Thursday afternoon.

He was led through modern corridors, glimpsing men poring over tiny columns of numbers. Every closed door bore a name. He was brought to one inscribed *I. Popov*.

Popov sat at his desk looking at photographs. He glanced at Ulrich as he entered, not bothering with greetings. He placed one of the images in front of him.

'Can you tell me what this is?'

Ulrich looked at the photograph.

'It seems to be a factory,' he said.

'Continue.'

'A chemical factory. This is a kiln, and there's the reactor vessel. It would be used for making some kind of heavy metal salt.'

'Good. Good,' said Popov.

He turned his attention to the typewritten pages in front of him. He smoked curious yellow cigarettes, and left long gaps between his sentences.

'You studied chemistry?'

'Yes.'

'University of Berlin?'

'Yes.'

Popov looked at him quizzically, as if wanting more.

'My teachers were Fritz Haber and Walther Nernst,' Ulrich offered.

Popov nodded impatiently.

'You've been supervising a leather factory for some years.'

'No,' replied Ulrich. 'I was in the Accounting Department. I was not connected to the factory.'

'And yet it says here—'

Popov stared for a moment. 'No damage done,' he said lightly. 'None at all.'

He stubbed out his cigarette and took up a pencil. He crossed out a line from his notes, and wrote in an amendment.

'I am an admirer of bourgeois science,' he said magnanimously, making abstract diagrams on his paper. 'In their day, the bourgeois scientists achieved some useful things.'

His diagrams followed the rise and fall of his speech, as if they were musical notation.

'We have been a rural economy for many centuries, and it is difficult to put that behind us. But our leadership is strong, and the people are invigorated. Next year, our industrial sector will grow by sixteen per cent.'

The sharp tip of Popov's pencil hovered.

'Chemistry. Nothing will be more important than chemistry.'

He smiled at Ulrich.

'It has been decided at the highest levels: Bulgaria will be the chemical engine of the socialist countries. We have ore, we have rivers, we have land and good climate. We have workers who will soon forget cattle and crude village dances and fill their minds with modern things. What we lack is chemists. We are training them: soon we will have world-class chemists in the thousands. But for now, everyone with even basic chemical knowledge has to do their part.'

The telephone rang.

'Three million seven hundred thousand last year,' Popov said immediately into the receiver. He wrote that number down absent-mindedly as he listened to the commentary on the other end. Ulrich studied the sheet of paper to see whether he could decode Popov's thoughts from his outlines.

Popov put the phone down. He looked into Ulrich's face.

'What are you thinking?'

There was a long silence. Ulrich said slowly,

'Perhaps I could have some position at the university? I would like that very much. I could get back to my experimentation.'

Popov was unimpressed.

'It's many years since you studied chemistry, and science has moved a very long way since then. Moreover, your ideological credentials are unclear. No one knows where your loyalties lie. What kind of name is *Ulrich*?'

'It's a German name, comrade. My father chose it.'

Popov took a long time to consider.

'I don't even know how to say it properly,' he said. 'It does you no favours, holding on to a name like that. If I were a suspicious man I would see a reactionary statement there. You could easily have changed it to something more patriotic and revolutionary. Ilyich, for instance, after our beloved Lenin. You should consider it.'

He looked over his papers.

'Your mother's opinions are particularly disheartening.'

'My mother?' echoed Ulrich.

Popov skimmed through his notes.

'She continues to dwell under the influence of bourgeois-fascist propaganda. She praises bourgeois society. She said she would kill herself if the Russians did not leave. Blah blah blah. It leaves a nasty taste.'

He returned to his photograph.

'This factory was built by Germans. Now they have gone, we are looking for someone to get it running again. I thought such a task would fall within your capabilities.'

Ulrich nodded, not able to look Popov in the eye. He kept his eyes on the notepad, where Popov had made a sketch of a bird perched on a lamp-post.

A week later, Ulrich took a bus to the factory, which was thirty kilometres outside Sofia. He was the only passenger, and he sat on the back seat. The sun was just rising, and the land was dewy, unlit and desolate. Old bomb craters in the fields had filled with water, and the wind whipped through the naked window frames of the bus. It made slow progress: the road became muddy, and the gears whinnied. The driver honked the horn to the rhythm of some tune in his head.

Ulrich saw pylons rising above the green bar of the horizon, and then the factory appeared, its smokestack frigid, its steel reactor rosy in the dawn sky. The bus dropped Ulrich off and drove away, and he stood by the roadside, turning around to take in the scene.

On the other side of the valley were barite mines, where the ore came from. Cables ran overhead from the mines to the factory, but everything was dead for now, and the lines of buckets hung empty, squeaking in the breeze. The town was quiet, and shaggy pigs ran in the streets.

Ulrich climbed through a hole in the wire fence and walked on to the factory forecourt. Bracken had taken there, and the pipes were damaged in places. From high up, the chimneys whistled with the wind on their lips. Ladders went to the very top, one missing a rung, and

Ulrich thought of what he would find when he climbed up there and looked down into the shafts.

He walked around the installation, studying how it was set out. The kiln was mighty, a ribbed steel tower laid out on its side. Spindly conveyor belts fed it at one end, where sparrows lined up chattering. He looked over the leaching tanks and the reactor vessel, where moss had started to grow. The mills looked run down and exhausted.

The former owners had taken everyone out in a hurry, and the debris of departure lay all around: discarded overalls and tin lunch boxes, a pair of broken spectacles and, in the office, a dusty scattering of old invoices and cigarette ends. People had written on the wall in childish German. On a bench, a plant had shrivelled in its pot.

The logic of the plant was gratifyingly simple. It was built for the production of barium chloride, and its design was an architectural expression of the chemical process:

1. $BaSO_4 + 4C \rightarrow BaS + 4CO$
2. $BaS + CaCl_2 \rightarrow BaCl_2 + CaS$

Ulrich checked the state of the pipework, following the lines on his knees, tapping a steady *chink-chink* against the wind's commotion outside, and noting the dimensions of sections that needed to be replaced. He opened every valve wheel, checking the seals. Corrosion had worn the reactor walls too thin for continued use, and he made recommendations for a new vessel.

In the office he found volumes of the old logs, and he set to calculating the factory's capacity, and the volumes of raw materials it could consume. He worked out what labour would be required. He inspected the town, and described the provisions for worker housing.

After the first few days he took to spending his nights in the factory in order to assess it more intimately. He brought the gramophone player with him on the lurching bus, and he spent obscure hours lying by the kiln, wrapped in blankets, with the valves and pressure gauges just above his head, and the brassy sounds of Louis Armstrong and Fletcher

Henderson echoing in the expanse. He woke up stiff every morning, lit a fire for tea, and looked beyond the enclosure fence, where crested larks dipped over the straining grass – and he was absolutely content.

His report was later typed up and ran to sixty pages. The report was given to I. Popov for him to add his comments. He in turn handed it upwards, and it arrived, ultimately, in the lofty corridors of the Supreme Economic Council, where invisible experts of almost unimaginable intelligence performed the devilish calculations required to coordinate the production of barium chloride with the million other items necessary for the well-being of the Bulgarian People.

For months, iron balls swung against Sofia's empty façades, watched by murmuring crowds, who could still remember dimly what had once been inside. No matter how many times he saw the buildings come down, it was never enough for Ulrich to believe it.

He watched the cranes demolish the house he had lived in as a child. The neighbouring building had been directly hit, and his father's Viennese fantasy had been blown wide open. The flues connecting the fireplaces to the chimney were now a gaping lattice on the outside of the building, and a wooden door opened into the void. The walls of Ulrich's childhood bedroom were exposed to the sky, though the wallpaper had been changed since then. As they pummelled the stone, it was like a series of concussions, and the final dusty surrender came as a relief.

The intense new men who arrived in Sofia at that time to build a replica of Moscow made the men from Ulrich's childhood, the men in suits who had tried to emulate Vienna, look infantile. Vast, wedge-shaped meteors were chiselled for party offices, with steel windows arrayed back towards the vanishing point. They made meticulous restorations of the bombed-out churches, and they put up angular memorials to stirring ideals. They liked neat flowerbeds, grand spaces, clear numbering, railings, scientific design, well-laid pavements, and clearings for flags. They liked culture and conversation to happen in the appointed places, and in the street they liked human figures to be evenly distributed, with ample space between them.

Outside the cities they built mighty factories and power plants. They had no affection for villages, where it was impossible to know what people believed; they confiscated animals, equipment and land, and sent everyone to live in the cities. The destruction of the farms and villages took less than five years, and everything that was ancient was cleared away to make room for a scientific nation. Fruit and vegetables, for instance, once the best in Europe, now disappeared from Sofia's markets, leading to scuffles and queues.

Housing projects were built for all the peasants who arrived in the city, still stupefied from the confiscation of their sheep and cows. Some came with every brick and beam of their old house loaded on a donkey cart, vainly imagining they might recreate it in the capital. But there was no space amid the blossoming offices and schools and hospitals. In the new playgrounds, rocket-shaped climbing frames gave children an early passion for the future.

The former villains were cast in bronze and put up in the parks, and all the stories changed. The paintings of Geo Milev, who had been executed as a traitor, were now put on the postage stamps, and his poetry was taught in schools, while the old murdered prime minister, Stamboliiski, was given a statue outside the opera house. The newspapers claimed it was the Communist Party that had saved the Jews from the fascists, and everyone was speechless with the audacity of it – when it was still so recent and everyone could remember how it really was – but memories altered to fit the books, and many things passed into silence.

Prohibitions stamped out the music. Jazz became illegal – and Turkish music, Gypsy music, Arabic music, and most of the other kinds Ulrich had listened to as a child. Only classical music remained – and the folk music of Bulgarian villages, which Paris-trained composers rewrote for the concert hall, removing all the vulgarity and noise. Ulrich hid away his illegal records, and most of his last musical pleasures with them.

An eerie calm descended over Sofia. The trams ran on time, and things were fixed before they were broken. The disdainful glide of Volga limousines was smooth over the gold cobblestones of the official quarter, the branches of willow trees fell just so in the parks, and the military-green uniforms of the traffic police were unthinkingly pristine. Beggars, eccentrics and delinquents were deported to labour camps, and even on the busiest streets the crowds were somehow well rehearsed.

Ulrich's factory was restored to operational order. It started up again, and the emptiness was filled with noise and invigorating smells. Ulrich was appointed Technical Director and he settled into a new rhythm, taking the bus to the plant from his mother's house early every morning. It was a more arduous life than he was used to, but it afforded him a modicum of chemical authority, and he became more relaxed.

One evening, he paid a visit to Ivan Stefanov, who had been given work as a driver. The mansion had been confiscated, and the family was allotted a cramped attic for its nine members. Ivan insisted that Ulrich dine with them, and they sat around a long table with their heads banging on the rafters. The family emerged one by one from behind a curtain, where they had stooped in turn to don evening suits and dresses for dinner – though there was nothing except bread, cheese and tomatoes on the table. Old Stefanov was senile in his wheelchair, and dribbled through the meal. Having noticed how Ivan was surreptitiously chided by his wife when he made to serve himself with cheese, Ulrich also refrained from eating, claiming he was full.

15

THEY CAME AT FOUR O'CLOCK in the morning to arrest Elizaveta, and they gave her five minutes to dress. When Ulrich launched himself at them, they beat him with metal bars. There were four of them, in black leather jackets and helmets, and they used the time they were waiting to smash the bookshelves. They kept repeating *Fascist!* as if it had become a reflex.

'My mother is not a fascist,' said Ulrich, trying to keep control of his voice. He was lying on the floor with one of the men standing over him. 'She *hated* the fascists. She wrote articles against them in the newspapers!'

'Don't lie to us.'

'I've met fascists before,' said one of the men, so young he still had spots on his face. 'Their houses always look like this.'

They called out to Elizaveta and opened the door to her room. She was standing in her dress. They pulled her out and marched her to the door.

'I love you, Ulrich,' she said. The expression on her face was terrifying.

He ran to embrace her, but they pushed him back.

'Take *me*!' he cried. 'Take *me*!'

They had a jeep outside. They put her in and drove away.

The communist leader, Georgi Dimitrov, executed his former allies, and the one-party state was complete. The purges were felt in families across the country, and the waiting rooms of police stations were packed with distressed folk searching for the disappeared.

Ulrich does not care to remember the experiences he went through at that time. He did not know where they were holding his mother. He haunted the Ministry of the Interior at 5 Moskovska Street, where the interrogations happened. He circled the central prison. He went to the State Security headquarters, where the colonel in charge of deportations threatened the desperate families with arrest if they did not have authorisation to sit there. Ulrich carried a file of his mother's anti-fascist newspaper articles, which no one was interested in seeing. He grew sick with the uncertainty. He wandered the streets for days, and when he returned home he found Elizaveta's dog lying dead in her bedroom.

One evening, he received a telephone call from the police telling him that his mother had been sent to the Bosna concentration camp near the Danube.

It was an eleven-hour train ride to Ruse. He arrived in darkness and waited through the night for the local train, cradling the food and clothes he had packed for her.

The road from the train station to the camp was surmounted by signs saying 'Hail to the Soviet Communist Party!' and 'Long Live the Bulgarian Communist Party!'

Ulrich reached the gate and waited by a small window. A man inside was trying to thread a needle so he could sew a button on his uniform. He was startled to see Ulrich.

'Who told you to come here?' he said.

'I have come to see my mother.'

'Who are you?'

'I am … the son of a prisoner.'

'Have you lost your mind? Get the hell out of here!'

'Is my mother in this camp?'

The man summoned a guard, who seized Ulrich and led him away.

'I've brought food,' cried Ulrich over his shoulder. 'Will you give it to her?' He struggled against the guard. 'Leave me alone for one minute!'

An arm was extended through the window, and Ulrich handed over his bag of food and clothes.

The man rifled through the bag. He took out sweaters and threw them back at Ulrich.

'Comrade, she is old,' said Ulrich. 'She will not survive hard labour. Please let her go.'

The man found the letter that Ulrich had written on the way, ripped it into small pieces, and flung them at him.

'These things don't go inside,' he said.

Ulrich picked up the remnants, and got back on the train to Sofia.

He clung to his daily schedule as if it were a raft. Every morning, he cut through to his desk, ignoring the others' tea and chat. The previous day's logs were waiting for him, and he scanned the numbers with his ruler, checking they were correctly behaved. Then he retired to the laboratory, where assays of the previous day's production were waiting, and tested their purity. After that, he poured some tea from his flask and walked the factory floor, always inhaling the acrid odour of chlorides with the same feeling of reassuring repulsion, looking over the gauges for temperatures and flow rates. By lunchtime he had checked the factory's stocks of raw materials, dealt with his correspondence, and made a report to Comrade Denov, the factory director.

Comrade Denov was an amiable man who was fond of hard work and long speeches. The factory was not merely a production unit for him: it was like a mission, and he introduced a great array of activities there. There were picnics and outings to the zoo. He hosted an evening reading group in Marxist theory. There were visits to the opera, for which he entertained a particular love. His wife often sent him to work with a cake.

One evening, he called Ulrich into the tiny cabin he called his office. Portraits of Marx and Lenin hung on the wall.

'I've been watching you, Comrade Ulrich. You're a curious individual.'

Comrade Denov had a tragicomic face that was prone to absurd grimaces even in his most serious moments.

'You know the other workers make fun of you? They gossip about the lectures you give about chemical theories. They imitate the way you talk, staring at the sky over their heads. Did you know?'

'No,' replied Ulrich.

'Well, it's true.'

The monthly production figures lay on the director's desk. All the graphs were rising. But they still fell short of the official quotes, which rose much faster.

'But it's not malicious. They find you odd, but they can recognise you have a precious bond with this factory. Your affection is a strong thing. It commands respect.'

'Thank you, comrade,' said Ulrich uncertainly.

'I'm a party man,' said Denov. 'I've believed in socialism all my life. You don't know how poor my family was under the king, how desperately poor. I grew up with nothing – and now look at me. I'm running a factory and my sons are studying medicine at university. I owe everything to socialism.'

Ulrich found himself wondering where all the barium chloride went.

It was strange he had not ever thought about this before. The factory was a logical universe whose processes came to an end when the finished barrels were loaded into a truck – and Ulrich's thought stopped there too. But now he had visions of these barrels dispersing into every country of the Soviet bloc, and tried to imagine how they could all be used up.

'They warned me about you, Comrade Ulrich. They said you're a dangerous eccentric. But I've been watching you, and I like you. I want you to help me build a great factory. I'm not like others. I don't care what your private opinions are. Is that understood?'

'Yes,' replied Ulrich.

Comrade Denov gave a jocular grimace again, and Ulrich suddenly felt a great loyalty to him.

Whenever the economic plans were announced, Comrade Denov summoned all the workers together for a speech.

'These targets seem unattainable. But they have been calculated on the basis of the strength that each of you carries inside him. Strength you may not even know yourself. When it's all over you will feel grateful that you have been tested like this.

'The tales of your labour will be told far away! In Poland and Yugoslavia the workers will look jealously at the socialist Bulgaria you have created, and wish they had worked as hard as you. In the Soviet Union they will say, *They have out-Moscowed Moscow!*'

But the Five-Year Plans necessitated almost inconceivable leaps in production, and even the director fell prey to the general anxiety and depression. Crippling work schedules were insufficient to lift output to the required levels, and for months the factory was *underperforming*. There was hardship and misery all round, and no money for anything except essential supplies.

Ulrich could recall moments when he had fervently wished to be delivered from his mother. Her presence had tired him, and he had imagined that his energies would be released only when she was no longer around. But now that she was gone, he found he had nothing left. He was empty, and traversed only by ghosts and shadows.

His daydreams turned morbid. He invented damning reports against himself, which he would submit to the police in return for his mother's release.

Item

I complained on many occasions about the poor supply of bread in Sofia, and expressed aloud the belief that senior party members did not have to undergo such hardships. I allowed such delusions to lead me into public approbations of imperialist societies.

Item

I owned a number of recordings of Western music which I played at licentious gatherings at my house in order to corrupt the aesthetic taste of those around me. These included a large selection of American jazz of the most indecent variety. I liked to encourage women to imitate Western dancing at these gatherings for my own entertainment. I drank heavily, and, in my intoxication, I uttered obscenities against the party and against Our Friend, the Soviet Union.

Item

I harboured a dream of escaping across the border and making my way, finally, to New York. I boasted that many of my acquaintances had already made this journey, and they had told me of the tall buildings they had discovered there, and the wonderful life.

16

ONE SUNDAY AFTERNOON, Ulrich encountered Boris's old friend, Georgi, in the street. It was twenty years since he had last seen him, and he had grown stout and bald, but Ulrich recognised him immediately.

Georgi had spent years in prison for his revolutionary activities, and now he found himself showered with honours. He had become a colonel in the State Security, and he walked expansively, as if to allow room for his new aura. He seemed strangely happy to see Ulrich, and led him away to an expensive café with flowers and bow-tied waiters. Sitting down, he displayed his large stomach with a sensuousness that made Ulrich feel muddled. Georgi talked incessantly.

'In the last years I shared a cell with another revolutionary, Atanas. He was married to a woman called Maria. Maria's father was as rich as Rothschild: he was a big industrialist with several mansions, and factories all over the Balkans. So Maria was from one of Bulgaria's leading families, she was closely connected to the king and the entire fascist government – and she had staked everything on her love for a scruffy communist revolutionary. Her parents disowned her, so she joined the party and came every day to the jail to see Atanas. She brought fruit and biscuits, and told us news from the world outside.'

He ordered wine.

'So what happened? She began to bring me gifts too, and after a while she hid letters in them, full-blown declarations. *I cannot think for love of you, I am dead not having you with me.*'

Georgi raised his eyebrows to insinuate more. Man to man.

'Can you imagine? In the beginning I tried to stay aloof, but I'd been stuck in jail for more than ten years, and here was a soft-skinned young woman making offers. What choice did I have?'

Ulrich could muster no more affection for Georgi than the first time he had met him. His face was sour, and his teeth as broken as before, and Ulrich tried in vain to picture what this woman had seen in him, lying like a dog in a cell.

'Obviously Atanas wasn't happy. He and I went to war. Sometimes we beat each other through the night, until we had no more strength, and when Maria came in the morning our eyes were swollen like footballs. But after a while he realised he had lost her. He gave up hope in everything, and became like a pathetic animal. He slunk away to his corner when she came so we could have space for ourselves. In a while he grew sick and died. Maria and I had our wedding in the prison. We have two little boys.'

He smiled fondly. He wore an impressive suit and the kind of steel glasses that were in fashion then.

'Now her mother, who used to wear fur coats and drive sports cars, is getting a taste of how her workers lived. She comes to our front door to beg for cooking oil. A few years ago she was too good to even talk to her daughter. Now she begs us for soap.'

He exuded contentment.

'Nineteen years in jail,' he said, 'and now I have to make up the time. We're going to drive this country into socialism in twenty years, so it arrives while you and I have eyes to see it. You can already see the dams and factories we're building. Todor Zhivkov is more ambitious than Georgi Dimitrov, and there will be no compromises. One day you'll see the paradise we'll make, and you'll understand what all the fervour was for.'

The café was full of people, but the voices were measured and subdued. The laughter was appropriate. Every table had its maroon tablecloth and its starched white napkins.

'You don't know the challenges we face. People don't want to work. Unfortunately, there are many who become sick and envious. They see beauty and achievement as black spots.'

He threw up his shoulders resignedly and sighed, taking a gulp of wine.

'Anyway. What have you been up to?'

Ulrich told him about the factory. Georgi nodded distractedly. Ulrich felt out of place in this café, this conversation.

'My mother,' he began. 'My mother was taken to Bosna. I don't even know if she's alive.'

'Your mother?' Georgi's eyes narrowed.

'She's innocent!' said Ulrich urgently. 'She always had an amateur interest in politics. She mixed with the wrong people, she was confused, she didn't know what she was saying. But she always opposed the fascists. She always wanted what was best for Bulgaria. She loved Boris. She never stopped cursing the king for what he did to him.'

Georgi observed Ulrich wrestling with himself. He said,

'There are many enemies of the Fatherland. You don't know how riddled this country is. We've been forced to send out a clear message.'

Ulrich whispered,

'I have heard about the labour camps. She is old. She cannot survive it. She cannot break stones. She will die.'

Georgi continued to watch him, unblinking. Suddenly Ulrich flung himself on the floor, and held Georgi's knee to his cheek.

'I beg you. Find out what has happened to her!' He did not dare look up at Georgi's face. 'She is an old woman. What harm can she do?'

There was a lull in the café while people looked on. Ulrich kept his arms clutched tightly around Georgi's leg. Georgi tried to retain his dignity.

'There is nothing I can do.'

'I beg you,' said Ulrich, still on the floor. 'In the name of our friend. I will do anything in return. Anything. If you want me to take her place.'

Georgi mopped his mouth with his linen napkin.

'In the name of our friend,' Ulrich repeated.

Later, he heard the rumours about Georgi: that he had been exceptionally vicious in his revenges. It was said that he had hunted down his old enemies and shot them with his own hand. But there were many rumours like that during those times, and it was not easy to pick out the truth.

17

LATE ONE NIGHT, Ulrich's mother appeared at the front door.

Ulrich did not recognise her at first. She was half her previous size, and her hair was white stubble. She had terrible rashes on her face.

'Ulrich?' she said, hiding behind her hands. She seemed terrified of him.

He let out a cry and pulled her to his chest, his sobs erupting. She fainted in his arms, and he carried her inside. She was dressed in peasant clothes, and she was weightless, like a woman of straw. He roused her with water.

He brought her bread to eat. She took two mouthfuls and collapsed, clutching her stomach. She writhed with the pain and he massaged her hollowed abdomen, weeping with fear.

When the agony had passed, he went to bring a shawl, for she was shivering. By the time he returned she had fallen into a dead sleep.

Ulrich stayed at home to take care of her. Elizaveta lay on the sofa, watching him moving about the house, and covering her swollen face for shame. It was two days before she could speak.

She said,

'Where is Karim?'

'He's dead.'

She nodded, as if she had known it.

'Anyway, I have grown afraid of dogs.'

She had been plucked out of the fields and released from the camp, without any forewarning. They had told her that the public prosecutor had intervened on her behalf, and they had left her by the side of the road.

'I would have died if it weren't for the peasants who helped me. The people in the town threw stones at me.' She was weeping. 'In our country, only the ignorant still know how to be human and decent. They were saints. They saved my life.'

Ulrich could not look at his mother while she said these things. He did not sit down, but paced between the walls.

'Someone should pay for this,' he said.

'I am here with you,' she said. 'We should be grateful for that.'

His face was baleful. She said gently,

'You can't ask anyone to pay back the life they have taken. Neither kings nor dictators have that power.'

She was silent for a long time.

'I didn't speak while I was away,' she said. 'All the trouble was caused by words. The best chance I had of seeing your face again was to say nothing at all.'

They were gentler with each other than before. It came to each of them to wake up, sometimes, screaming in the night, and these submerged terrors were a form of silent compact. There were things they could never share with anyone else. Elizaveta had become politically contagious, and old friends now crossed the street to avoid her. She often mused about the ones who had fled to the refugee camps in Austria and Italy after the war, and now were in America.

'We should have gone as well. We could have made another life. We could have found your son. I was too proud, and I thought there would always be time.'

Their upstairs neighbour dropped enough comments to ensure their fear did not subside too far. He knocked on the door of an evening to observe how they were occupied, and to offer his advice.

'Yesterday I noticed you had a letter returned from America? Some of your phrases were hardly complimentary to our socialist nation. We all have to decide which side we are on.'

He spoke sententiously, and took the liberty of lifting up a book from the table to glance over the papers piled underneath. Ulrich did not speak to him, but stared at the door with hatred until he had closed it behind him.

One day, Elizaveta asked Ulrich to join the Party.

'I will not,' he said grimly.

It was a Sunday afternoon, and they were walking in the park.

'You must protect yourself,' she said. 'Your mother is an enemy of the state. There's no place for subtle considerations.'

Ulrich signalled to her to keep her voice down, as if someone were listening. He said,

'I don't want to discuss it. After everything they have done to you, Mother.'

They walked on, her arm through his. She said,

'You mustn't think about the other people's pain. It will never end. Look at the people you know, how much they have suffered, and multiply it by the population of the world. You could never imagine the volume of that suffering. It would destroy your own significance, and there's no point in it.'

The matinee had ended at the theatre, and people filed out into the square. It was a beautiful day in early summer, and cherry blossom drifted in the breeze.

'You should take better care of yourself,' she continued. 'I won't be with you forever.'

'Don't say such things.'

'Isn't it true? I am old, and soon I'll die. It would make me so happy to see you married again.'

He did not answer her. She was tired, and they headed for a bench. They watched the dressed-up children, and the red flags hanging on the war memorial. Elizaveta said,

'You travel so far to that factory, and you spend every day in that noise and heat. Your clothes stink when you come home. If you joined the party you could have an easier life. You would have comforts and promotions.'

She leaned her head against his shoulder, looking up at the sky and the tips of the poplars.

'Isn't there anything you'd like to do? What do you think about? You're always thinking. I wish you would tell me about it. I don't know what happens in your head.'

Soldiers were relaxing on a bench under the willow trees. There were wreaths around the war memorial from a few days before, and people strolled in Sunday clothes, their cigarette smoke luminous in the sun.

A few days later, Ulrich looked up from his evening reading and said,

'Did I ever tell you my theories about the baths at Carlsbad?'

'No.'

Ulrich told his mother about Pierre and Marie Curie, the pioneers of radioactivity. He told her how the Austrian government had presented them with a ton of uranium ore – pitchblende – that was dug up from the enormous silver mines of Joachimsthal in Bohemia. The precious gift arrived on a horse-drawn cart, still matted with Bohemian earth and pine needles, and the Curies set to work. They discovered that the ore was emitting very high levels of radiation, far higher than uranium, and they realised another substance must be present. After two years of work, they isolated from this ton of pitchblende one tenth of a gram of a new element. Radium.

'Pierre Curie's mother had died of cancer a few years before,' said Ulrich, 'and he and Marie started to experiment with the effects of radium on tumours. They achieved positive results. They thought it would soon be possible to destroy cancer forever. And that was the beginning of radiotherapy.'

Elizaveta settled back in her chair, happy to hear her son talking about something he loved.

Ulrich related how the rumours of radioactivity's life-giving power began to circulate among the public at large. It was assumed that the new force of nature must be invigorating for the body, and popular magazines were suddenly filled with advertisements for radium compresses, radium bath salts, radium implants, radium chocolate and radioactive inhalations.

'Can you imagine?' Ulrich exclaimed.

He told her about the fashionable spas of Carlsbad, which were close to the Joachimsthal mines. Carlsbad had already been an elegant summer resort of the European elites for a century or more, but now the sudden popularity of radium gave an additional boost to its prestige. Carlsbad boasted of the *tonic radioactivity* of its waters. And in 1906, a new 'radioactive spa' was built even closer to the mines, in Jáchymov.

'I've always been struck,' said Ulrich, 'by all the famous people who went to those spas and later died of cancer. There were so many musicians. Johannes Brahms, the composer, and Niccolò Paganini, the most famous violinist who ever lived.'

Later on, the harmful effects of exposure to radiation became well known. Marie Curie herself was covered with terrible welts from her laboratory work, and died a painful death as a result. But none of this stopped Leopold Godowsky, a pianist friend of Albert Einstein, from visiting the spas of Carlsbad in the hope that the special waters might reanimate his right arm, which had become useless after a stroke. Not long after that, he died of stomach cancer.

'My goodness,' said Elizaveta coolly. 'What things you carry in your head.'

'Soon after,' said Ulrich, 'Carlsbad and the mines were occupied by Nazi Germany. The Germans wanted the uranium for an atomic bomb, and they set up a labour camp in Joachimsthal, where non-Aryans were sent into the ground to pull out the pitchblende. Then, in the war, the territory passed to the Soviet Union, which did exactly the same thing. Enemies of the state were forced to dig uranium for the Soviet nuclear arsenal. Every day we have new stories about the Soviet Union's glorious nuclear might. Well, this is how it happens. Can you imagine those people? Can you imagine the cancer?'

After a while, Elizaveta said,

'I don't know why you would tell me something like that.'

She began to cry and Ulrich stiffened, as he always did.

'You just have no sense of things,' she said behind her hands.

He did not look at her. He said,

'A long time ago, Boris and I had a debate about chemistry. I said it was the science of life, and he said it brought only death. Now I see that our views were simply two halves of the same thing.'

But Elizaveta did not reply.

Barium

18

ULRICH'S NEIGHBOUR IS IRRITATED, and her limp sounds worse than usual.

'Water is still pouring through our ceiling,' she says bitterly. The man who lives above her has not been seen for months, and no one has the key to his apartment.

'I don't know what's going on up there. If he left a tap on or if his pipes have burst. It must be like a swimming pool, because our ceiling is completely sodden. We need an umbrella to go into the toilet.'

She has come to give him his pills. She smells musty.

'That man, he's better off than a politician. He's made so much money in a few years that he doesn't even bother to sell his old apartment. He's just locked it and gone: no one knows where he is. My husband's looking for a crowbar to break it open. Who knows what he'll find inside?'

Ulrich sometimes thinks that his neighbour talks too much.

'This building is slowly falling down,' she continues. 'I'm scared to walk in the stairwell! It's dark as hell and so filthy you could catch a disease. When I open the front door at night there are cockroaches in the hallway, running from the light outside.'

She sighs as she speaks, to make the point.

'I don't know,' she says. 'At least in the old days we didn't have all this. Now everything is shit. Excuse me, but it is. Did you hear about the rabies? The streets are full of dogs now, biting people, and we've just had another case. Who ever heard of rabies in Sofia? That's capitalism, I suppose. You must have heard that Ilia Pavlov has been shot?'

Ulrich has heard the news reports, but he is not sure who Ilia Pavlov is.

'You don't know? Don't you use that television? Every month I go to deliver the money. It's no use if you don't ever watch it.'

Ulrich thinks, *Yes, I turn it on every evening*, but he does not say it to her. He does not see why he should justify himself. He hopes she will live to a hundred so she can see how difficult it is to adapt to the new names.

She has gone to fetch today's newspaper, which has a big article about Ilia Pavlov's life. She reads to Ulrich.

> *Mr Pavlov, who died Bulgaria's richest man, began his rise to power in the 1980s as head of the Bulgarian wrestling team.*

This triggers something in Ulrich. He says he thinks he remembers, but he cannot be sure.

'You must remember,' she says. 'He had a big shaggy mane in those days. When he competed in the Olympics his picture was plastered everywhere.'

> *His sports career put Mr Pavlov in touch with high-level party members and brawny men looking for jobs. He set up a number of gang operations, starting with extortion and protection, moving into gambling, drugs and prostitution, and expanding into hotels, real estate and construction. When the Bulgarian government began its privatisation drive in the early '90s, he had become powerful enough to grab substantial chunks of industry for himself.*

She sits back on a chair and lights a cigarette. Ulrich doesn't like her smoking in his apartment, but he finds it difficult to say so. He'll ask her to open the window on her way out.

> *Mr Pavlov had the wisdom to choose for his first wife the daughter of the chief of the Committee for State Security, which*

gave him access to the vast amounts of communist state capital that his father-in-law had transferred to his personal accounts after 1989. In collaboration with Andrei Lukanov, the former prime minister, Mr Pavlov siphoned money from state coffers to fund a conglomerate called Multigroup, which acquired hundreds of companies, including former state assets such as the flagship Kremikovtzi steelworks outside Sofia. Multigroup became the biggest business conglomerate in Bulgaria, running everything from food processing to gas and quickly drew complaints from Bulgarian rivals and foreign governments for the violence of its practices. Though it has never been proved that Mr Pavlov was responsible for the assassination of Andrei Lukanov, he seized sole control of Multigroup immediately afterwards.

Ilia Pavlov divorced his first wife and married the owner of a modelling agency that supplied contestants to the Miss World and Miss Universe contests. His friendship with Miss Bulgaria 2001 added glamour and popular appeal to his image, as did his presidency of football clubs CSKA and Cherno More.

A bomb exploded under Mr Pavlov's car in 1999, and he made attempts thereafter to improve his image. Multigroup withdrew from some illegal sectors and focused on tourism. Mr Pavlov gave money to restore old monasteries, and his wife suddenly became upset by the poor, and the plight of orphans.

Mr Pavlov was shot yesterday afternoon as he was leaving the Multigroup headquarters. The sniper found a gap between the four bodyguards and shot him once through the heart. His body has been laid out in the St Nedelya cathedral.

'If you turn on your TV you'll hear his whole life story again and again,' the neighbour says. 'The journalists are all tearful. They say the next Miss Bulgaria contest will be devoted to his memory. People really loved Ilia Pavlov.'

Ulrich says he cannot understand this.

'People need saints,' she responds.

'But he was an appalling man!'

'Our saints have always been thieves and murderers. That's the proof of the loftiness of their hearts.'

He can hear her stubbing out her cigarette. He asks her to open the window, hoping she will take it as a hint. But she carries on talking gaily.

'When they brought in communism it was for the people, so they killed the people. Now they've brought in capitalism, which is for the rich, so they only kill the rich. This time you and I have nothing to worry about.'

She asks if he needs anything else. He says no, wanting to be alone to reflect.

He has become completely absorbed in thinking back over his life. Remembering, Ulrich realises, has its own pleasure, like spreading wings. The mind unfurls and proclaims its own sensuality – and sometimes it does not matter if the memory is bleak.

'I'll go and check upstairs,' she says. 'See if they've managed to break into the swimming pool. It's so ironic, you see. Outside it hasn't rained for weeks. But in our bathroom it's raining day and night.'

19

THE THINGS THAT HAPPENED to Ulrich after his mother's return from the camp are recorded in his memory differently from everything that went before.

He feels, in fact, that the environment turned hostile to the laying down of memories. Such slow sediment required a soft and stable bed, and he was too shaken up in those days by statistics, the roar of crowds, and bomb tests on the Kazakh steppe.

Ulrich remembers how he produced barium chloride in greater and greater quantities. That part is preserved. For everything around him had turned to chemistry, and his own production was part of something far more significant than he. Bulgaria had become a chemical state: in the streets there were posters of the nation's chemical factories smoking in formation, like synchronised swimmers. The government issued chemical challenges to the workers, and the newspapers gloated over the achievements of famous Bulgarian chemists.

This development might have been Ulrich's vindication, but it served instead to devalue the secrets he carried inside. Everything he had cherished as his own was taken away and turned into slogans.

It was the era of launching spacecraft, and when he thinks back, Ulrich sees himself as if from orbit. He can remember government statistics and the unveiling of new monuments, but he has trouble picking out what happened to him. His own figure is dwarfed amid the vaster wreckage: power plants and Georgi Dimitrov's mausoleum. The might of Olympic wrestlers and Todor Zhivkov's smile.

Sections of his life went missing, and there are decades he can hardly account for.

He remembers how a Soviet dyeing company wanted to obtain enormous quantities of barium chloride. Ulrich's factory did not have spare capacity, and the Soviet company sent a delegation to discuss the plant's expansion.

Ulrich went with Comrade Denov to the airport, and they waited on the tarmac. They saw the Aeroflot Tupolev touch down in the distance and taxi slowly to its place. A stairway was pushed against it, and the hatch popped open. The band began to play, and the Soviet visitors waited on the top steps to appreciate the coordinated kicking of the folk dancers.

Ulrich studied the distant faces of the Russians to see how it felt coming out of a plane, for he had never flown.

They descended with political smiles, and groups of dancers approached them with gifts of bread and salt while they shook hands with Comrade Denov and then with Ulrich. A young soprano from the conservatory sang a song of gratitude to Russian liberators.

The next day was a Sunday, and Ulrich had the responsibility of taking the Russians on an outing to Vitosha Mountain. *Give them whatever they ask for*, Comrade Denov had said. *Don't let them say a word against us.* Ulrich arrived at the Pliska Hotel with a chauffeured car, and found them lively after their breakfast. The car drove them out of the city, up the wooded roads towards Kopitoto. The Russians were bureaucrats, not scientists, and, to Ulrich's disappointment, they could not bring news of chemistry. They seemed distracted, and Ulrich had the sense they were mocking him.

They stood in a line looking down on Sofia from the mountain. In the foreground were rows of birch trees, leafless at this time of year. Down below, the city was like a brittle ivory star, with points spreading along the highways, and Ulrich had to suppress the desire to reach out and smash it.

He asked the Russians why they were laughing.

'Everything is so small here,' they said. 'Your city is like a village. And your mountain is just a hill.'

Over lunch, they asked what Bulgarians thought about Nikita Khrushchev and Dinamo Moscow, the football team, and Ulrich said he did not know what Bulgarians thought. The Russians ordered a succession of vodkas, and Ulrich grew worried about the bill he would present the next day to Comrade Denov. They went on asking him what Bulgarians thought about many other Russian things, and Ulrich realised that all questions had begun to sound to him like interrogation.

In the car on the way back, they listened to a monologue by the leader of the Russian delegation. He had Tatar features and thick limbs, and alcohol made him joyful.

'Your country is such a simple problem,' he said. 'The Soviet Union: twelve time zones. How can you ever solve such a thing? Bulgaria is so small, and your weather is gentle. That's why your socialism has much better alcohol than ours, and your women look so modern.'

Ulrich was silent, looking forward to the moment when he would drop them at their hotel and his responsibilities would be over. But when they arrived, the Russians were adamant that he should not leave.

'Will you make us drink alone? We have no new jokes to tell each other!'

Reluctantly, Ulrich let the chauffeur go, anxious about what the rest of the night would hold. In the hotel room, the Russians pulled off their shoes and called for expensive vodka. They poured for him too, though he protested.

'I don't drink,' he said. 'I don't like alcohol.'

They roared with laughter, as if it were a joke.

Ulrich began to drink out of conformity, while the leader told stories of his childhood in Minsk. The corners of his tales were jabbed out with cigarettes that he held between his fingers for a long time before he lit them. The others clapped around him and kept the glasses full. Ulrich felt the blood rise in his ears and allowed himself to sink into the cushions. He watched the indefatigable storyteller, who drummed his fingers on his belly, shook his head insanely into his enormous handkerchief, and sighed *Ah!* when others spoke.

He talked about old films, and how he had kept bees when he was young. He told stories about his first job in a factory, above the Arctic Circle, where he lived in a tunnel underground whose entrance he could never find for snow and the darkness that came for months at a time. At length he broke into verse:

My uncle, in the best tradition
By falling dangerously sick
Won universal recognition
And could devise no better trick.

The wingtips of his cheeks were raised in rapture like the roped peaks of a tent, and his cigarette left an aerobatic trail in the air.

How base to pamper grossly
And entertain the nearly dead
Fluffing pillows for his head
And passing medicines morosely –

While thinking under every sigh
The devil take you, Uncle. Die!

They laughed and clapped, and the leader got up from his recline, backslapping and hugging round the room, seizing Ulrich with his powerful arms and holding him for a long while. Then he sat down and stared open mouthed into his vodka as if it were a miracle.

'When we got permission to visit your factory, we knew we would drink a lot,' he said happily.

'Enough Pushkin,' said one of the others, his socked feet resting on the wall. 'We should have Bulgarian poetry!'

'Geo Milev! The great one-eyed Bulgarian. Give us one of his!'

'I don't know any poetry,' said Ulrich weakly.

They did not believe him, and took him for shy.

'Drink more!' they said. 'You are far behind.'

Ulrich was already drunk, and in the clarity of vodka he felt his usual aloofness collapsing He looked at these men, men he would normally despise for their drink and their uncouth dissipation, and this evening he felt ashamed before their cheer. He wondered what he carried inside him that could compare to such exuberance. He became despondent, wishing he were other than what he was.

He made a forced attempt at abandon.

'Shall I call some girls?'

The three men roared in unison. The Tatar raconteur screwed his face into love-agony at the ceiling, and froze for a second as if he might topple backwards with joy.

The old tinnitus struck up in Ulrich's ears, and he wondered how he would deliver what he offered. But his companions had already moved on to an exchange of jokes, the girls forgotten, as if all possible pleasure had been won from the mere suggestion.

'They wanted to open a striptease club in the Kremlin Palace. The applications were made, permission was granted, billboards were put up around Moscow. But no one showed up.'

Ulrich ordered more vodka.

'Central Committee called up in the morning. Why had the project failed? Telephones rang across Moscow. The report came back: the organisers were bewildered. The striptease club was well organised and all the striptease artists had a solid party record. In fact most of them were Bolsheviks from 1905 and some were even personal friends of Lenin!'

They seemed to have an endless supply of jokes, and the banter went back and forth. The hotel ran out of vodka, and they ordered rakia instead.

'... so Stalin opens the door and catches the couple *in flagrante* and he says to the man, I am very attached to my pipe, but sometimes I take it out of its hole!'

As the night wore on, Ulrich became so awash with drink that his gloom dissolved, and he grew happy on his companions' cheer. He felt confident, and proposed an anecdote of his own. He told a story about a young man who had to slaughter a pig in a small Bulgarian town. It had an uncanny ending. He talked with some power, and they all listened.

'Did that happen to you?'

'No,' said Ulrich. 'It's something I dreamed up.'

'He is a poet!' they said. 'No wonder he is so quiet!'

'The quiet ones are the most dangerous!'

The night expired somewhere there, and when Ulrich woke up he was still lying in his place on the cushions. He slipped out, unnoticed by the snoring Russians, and went home to clean himself up. He met the men at the factory later, and looked at them remorsefully, as if he were a guilty lover.

In their official conversations, the Russians showed themselves in a very different light, and as the week drew on Ulrich found it difficult to believe he had shared such a time with them. They were hard nosed and inflexible, and they rarely smiled.

Their approach to technical problems was crude. To increase the factory's productivity they wanted simply to build more of the same, cramming three more gigantic kilns alongside the existing one, lined up together like the microphones under Todor Zhivkov's chin. They did not give scientific justifications for their ideas, and when they were challenged they only repeated them more gruffly, with added ideological weight:

'Worldwide capitalist enterprise will be run into the ground!'

On the first day, Ulrich listened silently to what they had to say, but then he became more bold. He said this factory was built in the 1930s, and many new production methods had come in since then. He said they could achieve a substantial increase in production simply by replacing the coal-fired kiln with a new fluidised bed reactor that would run on gas. Natural gas had become very cheap, and the new technique gave a more efficient reaction.

The Soviet experts were uncertain about Ulrich's proposal, but Comrade Denov praised it in such a way that it soon seemed as if it had originated with them, and not with Ulrich.

The Russians condescended, happy to have been of service. They seemed never to take off their thick coats, though it was spring, and hot enough for ceiling fans.

A deal was struck, and Comrade Denov was delighted. He said to Ulrich, *You have worked a revolution in our factory*, and he forgave him the tremendous cost of his entertainment. A Bulgarian–Russian Friendship Party was held on the last night. But Ulrich did not try again to find his way into the Russians' conviviality.

The ancient kiln was lifted out with cranes onto a long truck. The new, modern reactor was much smaller, and after it was installed the factory looked strangely vacant.

Somewhere, Ulrich still has a photograph from the day when the new reactor was installed. An official from the ministry came to inaugurate the new machinery, and a photograph was taken to commemorate the occasion. Ulrich is in a row with four other men, all in slightly irregular suits, standing awkwardly because of the strong wind. Five shadows with ballooning trousers stretch behind them on the concrete.

When the economic impact of the new process became apparent, Ulrich was singled out for considerable felicitation. Comrade Denov presented him with a gold watch in front of all the workers, and a medal embossed with the heads of Lenin and Zhivkov. He said,

'If ever a man has given his love to a factory, it must be him.'

Ulrich was asked to go to the studios of Radio Sofia to record an interview with a smiling official from the Internal Information Department. The man asked him how he came to think of installing this new reactor, how he felt about the astonishing improvements in productivity, what these would mean for the Bulgarian people, and why he was inspired to work so tirelessly and selflessly for the nation.

The interview was broadcast in the evening, and several of Ulrich's colleagues, including Comrade Denov, came to his house to listen. They broke into applause when his name was mentioned, and gazed at each other in awe as the details of their small universe were broadcast to the nation. The programme called Ulrich an 'ordinary hero'.

Comrade Denov congratulated Ulrich's mother, and said she must be very proud. She held her vodka close, and smiled.

The photograph of the inauguration of the new reactor was displayed on Ulrich's wall for many years, next to that of Einstein with his violin. In the background of the photograph was the concrete water tower that once supplied the small town.

Shortly after the photograph was taken, this tower collapsed, without any warning. Ulrich remembers arriving at work the next morning and seeing the entire town flooded. The savagery of the debacle rendered everyone speechless, and all they could do was stare. It took days to pump the water out of the mine.

Ulrich recalls that as he stood with the crowds at the edge of the water, he was intensely moved by this mysterious eruption of forces. To this day, he wishes it could be given to him again to set eyes on that spectacle.

20

Elizaveta asked him to get her a typewriter, and he brought home a cast-off from the factory, which she banged on night and day. For years he woke up to that sound.

She opened and closed her mouth in those years, and sound came out, but Ulrich paid little attention. She wept in the house and complained about her life, and Ulrich withdrew into his thoughts.

He became subject to obsessions.

Todor Zhivkov announced that he would build the biggest steel combine anywhere in the Balkans, and Ulrich was preoccupied with it for years.

'The Germans wanted to make steel here during the war,' he ranted to anyone who would listen. 'But they couldn't make it from Bulgarian ore. Our ore is of the lowest grade. Has the government not done any research? Do they not realise?'

He wrote letters to the newspapers and the ministry, laying out his arguments in a numbered list. As soon as these arguments were seen and acknowledged, he felt, this vast and foolish project would be abandoned immediately.

But no one took any notice. The Gypsy labour gangs kept working on the site, and, after three years of construction, the vast Kremikovtzi Steel Works was opened near Sofia. Songs and poems were composed to the factory, and special coins were issued with a heroic engraving of it, but it was never able to squeeze any steel out of Bulgarian ore. They had to import the ore from Russia to keep the works going.

'They built one of the most expensive factories in the entire Soviet bloc,' Ulrich said to Comrade Denov, 'on the basis of an ore they could not use. Where is the logic?'

'Perhaps the logic was simply to build one of the most expensive factories in the Soviet bloc. Here in Bulgaria.'

Ulrich looked at him, appalled.

'But no one could do such a thing. It's completely unscientific. It's impossible to believe.'

And he never stopped going back over the story, telling people how he had warned the government about it before the factory even opened, and they had taken no notice.

He used to dream, in those days, of his mother's death, which also seemed to happen in a factory.

The machines churn, and he sees her suspended in the glowing tunnel: the burning sparks flying off her, her limp head thrown side to side in the force field, some last animal reserve keeping her righted, head-on to the slipstream, before the vibrations become too violent to withstand, and suddenly the turbulence catches her, the roar lets up, and he sees her whole for the last time, jackknifing, white hot, flipping like a rag doll, and then there is a giant shower as she explodes, slow motion, among the stars, and bright lights disperse into the endless silence, from whose remoteness the thunder will take years to arrive.

When Ulrich awoke from this dream he would come down and find his mother already hammering at the typewriter and feel relieved that nothing had happened to her. But he never asked her what she was writing. He had a suspicion it was her memoir of the camp, because he knew she carried heavy things inside her that she had not told, and he had made it clear that he would never hear them.

When Sviatoslav Richter, the great Soviet pianist, came to play a week of recitals in Sofia, Elizaveta begged Ulrich to take her. Richter was a wild-looking man, even in his suit, and he tamed the piano monster with the mere application of his fingertips. Ulrich was terrified to see the speed at which he played Chopin, for no one could sustain such a fury. When he finished it with such a contemptuous flourish, the tears ran down Ulrich's face.

It was the period when he had strong physical reactions if he witnessed some form of surpassing human achievement. He wept at athletes breaking records. He trembled when he saw a standing ovation in the theatre. When Albert Einstein died, he read his words in the newspaper, which made him weep too:

> *The years of anxious searching in the dark for a truth that one feels but cannot express, the intense desire and the alternations of confidence and misgiving, and the final emergence into light – only those who have experienced it can appreciate it.*

At the time of Richter's visit, there was an influenza epidemic in Sofia, and Elizaveta was one of those who coughed uncontrollably through the music. Her nose ran continually, and her constant wiping irritated Ulrich during the performance.

Many years later after her death, Ulrich heard a recording of those recitals on the radio and he could identify his mother's cough, preserved during the long note that Richter held at the beginning of 'Catacombs', near the end of Mussorgsky's *Pictures at an Exhibition*.

He can remember attending a funeral. It was his father's sister, who was over ninety. The blue veins around her face were sunk in skin like candle wax, her closed eyelids were violet at the edges. There were red carnations all around.

After the coffin was lowered into the ground, the mourners walked slowly to a rented hall, old relatives supported on many arms. The day was bright and cold, and their breath clouded in the air. The sharp wind carried the smell of mothballs rising from their clothes. Newly fallen oak leaves crackled, and a track of solid footprints was pressed in the frost. At the graveside the funeral band packed up their instruments.

The meal was already laid out, and people made for the soup, which was good and hot. A photograph of the departed woman was displayed and garlanded on a table, and the bare planks of the walls were newly covered over with pleated cotton panels, pinned at top and bottom. Ulrich found himself seated between the priest and an unknown cousin of the deceased. Her face was a force field of wrinkles, and she eyed him between mouthfuls.

'You have the eyes of your father,' she said. 'I would recognise you anywhere.'

Ulrich nodded politely. She said,

'He went years ago. Isn't that right?'

'Yes.'

She asked about it and Ulrich told her what he remembered. Tears came into her eyes as he spoke.

'We lost so many men,' she said. 'And many of the ones who remained were lost, if you understand me.'

'He wasn't himself in his last years. He was deaf and withdrawn. He didn't know what was going on around him. The day my son was born, we smoked a cigar together outside the hospital, and he asked me who was sick.'

She said gently,

'At least he was there. Somewhere, he must have understood.'

She looked into the distance, lost in her own thoughts. Then she said,

'When he was a boy, he was a miracle. We all admired him. We were just kids from the village – our parents were all pig farmers. But he was always reading, he knew about lots of things we had never heard of. I listened to him for hours, talking about this and that. He used to love birds, I remember, and could whistle just like them.'

Ulrich's father had rarely spoken about his childhood.

'He made the decision all on his own to go away to Sofia for school. You youngsters can't imagine what that meant. We were village people, we wore the kind of village clothes you only see nowadays in the museum. We were completely ignorant of other places. When Bulgaria became independent, we didn't even know. It took weeks for the news to reach us that they had made a country for the Bulgarians, and our village was not in it. We packed everything up, took all the pigs, crossed into Bulgaria and made a new village.'

She had cloudless blue eyes that seemed to open on to those distant times. Her head had a shake, and her earrings chimed.

'When your father came to Sofia he was just a peasant boy. He didn't have clothes or anything for school. Your grandparents had money but they weren't that kind of people, if you understand me. He found himself a place to stay with some merchants they knew, and of course he became the best student in the school. That was his independence of spirit. He never had a violin teacher – did you know that? He taught himself to play completely on his own.'

'My father? Are you sure you're talking about my father?'

'He was the one who introduced us to piano music, and orchestras, and classical violin. When we first came to Sofia we had never heard those things, and he took us to concerts. He played his violin in the evenings, and we thought he was a genius. Later he went to study in Freiberg, if you remember, and he heard every kind of music there. He taught himself to play the Mendelssohn concerto.'

The wine was served, and the dead woman's son stood up to say some words. His face was deformed by grief, and there were sniffles around the room. Ulrich whispered urgently under the speech,

'But my father hated music.'

'Oh, your father was a true musician! But of course he got into engineering, and his railways, and I suppose he didn't have time after that.'

She shrugged her shoulders.

'I don't know what happens to us. It's difficult to sustain our passions through life, and we become mournful for what we've given up.'

The speech was still going on, and suddenly Ulrich was seized by a mutiny within, which broke out in wild and foolish laughter. He was forced to leave the room and walk in circles among the gravestones for his seizure to subside. It was a light-headed laughter, like falling through time.

21

Two Secret Service men came to the door and asked to speak to Ulrich.

Elizaveta tried to tell them he was not at home, her old fears creeping back. They looked at her coldly and waited for Ulrich to emerge from his room.

'Let's go for a walk,' they said to him, a hand on his shoulder.

'No need to worry,' they reassured his mother. 'We'll have him back in a short while.'

They went downstairs, saying nothing. The two men sat on a bench in the courtyard, and Ulrich stood before them. A mother hurried her children inside from their games.

'You work in that factory in Vakarel,' said one of the men, and it was not a question. 'Doing quite well, isn't it?'

'Thank you, comrade.'

The men seemed to expect more, and Ulrich said,

'We have received our quotas under the fifth Five-Year Plan. We're working out the best way to fulfil them.'

'You're working very hard,' said the man soothingly. 'Everyone in that factory is working hard.'

'It doesn't go unnoticed,' said his companion.

'Denov,' said the first man. 'That's the name of the director, isn't it? What kind of a man is he?'

'He's honest,' said Ulrich hesitatingly. 'He does what's best for the factory.'

'You're close to him, aren't you? You've been to his house several times?'

'*Close* is not the word. But he has been good to me.'

'Has he? You haven't been promoted all these years. You were even in the newspapers some years back for your achievements in the factory, but he didn't put your name forward for advancement.'

Ulrich said nothing. The men continued.

'Comrade Denov has had several encounters with foreign businessmen over the past two years. Chemical industrialists from Yugoslavia and even France. Can you explain why he might meet such people?'

'No,' said Ulrich truthfully. 'I can't.'

'No idea at all?'

'No.'

The two men looked at each other, as if consenting to let Ulrich in on a confidence.

'Clerks in the Planning Committee have come across discrepancies in the numbers coming from your factory. What goes in is greater than what comes out. Isn't that strange?'

'It's impossible,' said Ulrich.

'Why?'

'There's no spare capacity in our factory. Sometimes we work for a month at a time without a break, until the workers collapse at their machines. We are constantly behind our quotas. There is no spare barium chloride for anyone to conceal from the authorities.'

'It's because you're all working so hard that this seems so unfair.'

'I can tell you a hundred stories,' said Ulrich, 'of Comrade Denov's commitment to this factory. And to his country.'

'Are you saying we're lying?'

'I think there must be a mistake.'

The men studied him.

'That's why we've come to you. We need more reliable information. You see him every day – tell us what you find out. Strangers he talks to on the phone, things on his desk that have no right to be there. Jot them down. We'll be in touch to find out what you've learned.'

'Comrade Denov has been kind to me. As I just told you.'

'You believe that because you don't know the whole story.'

'I've known him for a long time. He's not that sort of man.'

'You know, many things are opening up just now in our country.

Wouldn't you like to be part of them? So many new opportunities in chemicals. Look at your house, the state it's in. We could get you on the list for the modern housing blocks they're building. Imagine that.'

'Just so you know who your friends are. After all, we only want the truth. If he's doing nothing wrong, he has nothing to fear.'

They left him without farewells, and Ulrich began to shake. He sat down to steady himself.

When he went back upstairs, his mother was gulping vodka.

'What did they want?' she asked.

He stared at her and felt a sudden distaste. He realised he could not remember the last evening she had been sober.

Ulrich began to wait behind in the evening for Comrade Denov to leave the factory so he could look through the accounts in his office. The ledgers were piled up on a shelf behind the bust of Todor Zhivkov, where anyone could find them.

The gaps between the pages were stuffed with receipts and torn-off notes, and Ulrich frowned with disapproval. It was difficult to make sense of the hastily written columns of numbers. It took him several evenings to build up a full financial picture of the factory.

He had not lost the talent he had developed during his accounting days, and when he opened the page in the ledger where the discrepancies were revealed, he knew it instantly. The grids, the column headings, the underlined totals – all spoke clearly to him, and he knew that everyone in the factory was labouring under a fiction. He trembled as he looked through the pages, for he realised that most of their hard-won barium chloride went missing every month. The enormous sacrifices they made to fulfil the official quotas were directed to some quite different end. Comrade Denov had deceived them all.

Ulrich began to file weekly reports about Comrade Denov to State Security. He did so without hesitation or doubt. He wrote his reports carefully, giving evidence for each of his assertions, and footnoting every number and quotation as if it were a thesis. Every week, when he set out to deliver his envelope, he held his head high with conviction.

22

Ulrich and his mother were selected for an apartment in Zapaden Park, the miraculous new scientific housing project in the west of the city. Elizaveta was baffled as to how it could have happened to a political outcast like her.

The mighty development was not even complete when they moved in. The forest had been cleared, and the towers rose out of a swamp: white, and repeating endlessly to the sky. The roads were still just sketches in the mud, and the grind of great machines became a roar whenever a window was opened, even from their tenth floor. New turf was already laid in places, like felt over the wasteland, and naked twigs were propped up in the expectation, one day, of trees.

Journalists visited to report on the modern living, and famous artists came to prepare paintings of the fury from which peace and harmony are born.

Ulrich was not happy with the new communal living, where there was no escape from talking, prying people. He walked down the stairs to avoid the lift, but on his ascent he regularly found himself confined with neighbours, whose sociability he tried to repel by counting the passing floors through the ribbed glass, or concentrating on the spoiled shine of his shoes. He closed the curtains at home, preferring twilight, for he could not bear the pressure of the thousand panes of glass peering in.

Elizaveta followed him around, letting the day in again, for the sparkling altitude made her gleeful. She sat on the balcony on sunny afternoons: she liked the views of children playing on the swings, the people coming and going, and the interiors of the opposite apartments. She bought a reproduction of Leonardo's *Last Supper* to hang above the dining table, lined the windows with potted plants, and hung up a birdcage. She became a propagandist for *modern facilities*, commenting joyfully on the hospital downstairs, and the pharmacy, and all the other new things she found such a comfort in her old age.

Zapaden Park seemed ignorant of Elizaveta's compromised past, and at this late stage in her life she seemed suddenly unburdened. She sat in her headscarf chatting on the benches that lined the paths downstairs, and when she was in her kitchen she left the front door ajar, so that visitors could walk in whenever they wished. She was always surrounded by people drinking and laughing, and Ulrich returned home with trepidation.

When he bought a stereophonic record player, which cost him months of savings, she invited an artistic neighbour to give his opinion of the sound, and he came with his friends, the kind of people Ulrich hated, who had gathered at the Café Bulgaria and written revolutionary poetry when they were young, and now were comfortable and arrogant, and gave meaningless speeches at the Writers' Union that were printed in the newspaper. They inspected the new acquisition without emotion, and one of them, who was a decorated poet, said to him gravely,

'No one needs stereophonic sound in Bulgaria, my friend.'

And Ulrich said *Why?*, already dreading the answer, and the poet said,

'Because we already hear the same information from every side!'

They all laughed at the joke, one woman coughing on her cigarette, but Ulrich did not find it funny. These people had their fashionable suits, and sunglasses as big as welders' masks, and they affected this revolutionary cynicism when in fact they had ceased to be revolutionaries years ago, and loved their established positions.

His mother had given up her typing – or perhaps she had finished what she was writing. Ulrich did not know. Now she hosted parties at night, where her acquaintances came to drink and gamble, and she talked of nothing except entertainments. She began to brew brandy, and she made garish, extravagant clothes to wear. She bought a pair of sunglasses in imitation tortoiseshell that cost half their monthly rent, and she wore them indoors when her friends came to visit. She spent Ulrich's money on foolish things, though she had always been prudent before; she played Pasha Hristova hits very loud on his stereo. She kept rearranging the furniture, so that nothing was in the right place when he came home, and it drove him to fury.

'Are you a blind man?' she taunted him, 'that you are scared of bumping into things?'

With her nightly drinking, she began to lose the mornings, and Ulrich emerged from his dreams to find an empty room. He squatted on a stool in the grey hour and remembered how terrible was solitude.

Ulrich developed a friendship, without expecting it, with a woman who lived nearby.

She sat next to him on the bus one day, saying she had seen him coming and going. She was not much younger than Ulrich, and had her husband and her life. She worked in a printing press, and her name was Diana.

He made her curious, she said, for he seemed so private. She spoke about the way she felt and how she saw things. Ulrich talked about chemistry, telling her stories of what was now possible. She listened to him while the bus growled between stops.

He was walking home one evening when she saw him on the path and called out.

'I have something for you. Can you wait? It's upstairs.'

He watched her walk back to her block, where the fluorescent lamps set her off for a moment before she disappeared inside. Ulrich surveyed the mute concrete, imagining the elevator passing up through the building, the equidistant lights in the corridor, the key in the lock. She came down. She wore a long coat for the weather and carried a plastic bag.

Inside was a magnifying glass.

'I don't know if it's useful for your chemistry,' she said. 'But I never use it myself.'

Whenever they met, they walked together, and it became a routine. Talking to Diana was a relief from the trials of Ulrich's home. He was growing old himself, and mostly he found it difficult to concentrate on other people's conversation. But with her he found himself absorbed again. Though he told himself that their friendship meant little, he could feel his anticipation rise each time their rendezvous approached.

They met at two o'clock on Saturday afternoons, as if by repeated accident. Ulrich assumed her husband was not around at that time, though she did not say so.

She loved architecture, and took Ulrich to see buildings she found interesting, so they could discuss them together. Her sister was a famous architect who won the Red Banner of Labour and was sent on a trip to Italy once as a reward for her work. Later she designed hotels on the Black Sea, and something in Cuba.

A sanatorium, Ulrich thinks.

Diana thought the Moscow styles were not suited to the Bulgarian climate, and decried the new apartments with their thick walls and small windows. She had ideas about how a building should respond to the shape of a human. She took him to the massive Rila Hotel, and they walked all around it, discussing how it felt and trying to remember what stood there before. She was unafraid: she took him into the lobby and pointed out the features, and they sat there for a cup of tea.

She talked about her children, grown up and married, and her husband, who was somebody in the party. He was involved in planning, and Diana asked Ulrich about his views on the economy. They talked about the Kremikovtzi steel plant, just then opened. Ulrich said,

'There is no viable ore in Bulgaria. They have built the mightiest steel plant of all the socialist countries, and there is no ore. They have lost their minds!'

She nodded, but made no comment.

She wished she could have been a cabaret singer. She laughed like a girl when she said it: how she would have liked to have legs like Marlene Dietrich and to sing love songs to an audience every evening. He brought her a gift of a jazz record he still had from Berlin, which she gently refused.

Occasionally she ran across him and said, *I can't see you this Saturday*, and he felt as if his treasure had been snatched away.

He did not tell his mother about Diana, and never invited her to his home. It was an indefinable thing, only slightly beyond what would bear scrutiny by the world. Sometimes they just wandered along the grassy railway tracks, so they could be together. But they never called each other by their first names.

One day they went to the St Nedelya cathedral. Ulrich had not been inside it since just after the 1925 bombing, when he had visited it in ruins with his father. Now it was perfectly restored, and their footsteps echoed through the calm interior. They leaned backwards to look up into the dome, and their heads touched. He became talkative as they left. He told her about his father.

'He loved God. I never understood anything about religion, but my father loved churches and God. He was very quiet about it. I think there were a lot of things he did in silence. When he was younger he talked a lot, but it was not necessarily about the things that were most important to him.'

He told her about Boris, whose death followed on from this building's destruction.

She took him to a café and ordered Coca-Cola, which had come into Bulgaria. She offered it to Ulrich and he said,

'I don't like alcohol.'

'It isn't alcohol!' She laughed. 'All those films we saw, where American soldiers drank Coca-Cola to put themselves in a drunken fury before battle – they were all lies!'

Ulrich sipped it and told her he liked it. He gave the glass back to her, and watched the way she drank. He said,

'I care very much about these times we spend together.'

She smiled, and took his arm. They walked outside, where there was a crowd watching a dancing bear. The bear towered over its two minders, lumbering to the beat of a drum. There was a chain through its nose.

'You know how they train them?' she said. 'They bang a drum and set the cubs on hot coals, so they jump from one foot to the other to relieve the pain. After a while, they don't need the coals anymore. Just banging the drum is enough.'

The hopping bear looked inexpressively around the audience, its eyes like small buttons in its enormous head. The two men chanted to the crowd, tweaking children's noses, trying to keep it festive.

'It looks like dancing,' Diana concluded. 'But it's not.'

She kissed Ulrich lingeringly on the cheek, though there were people all around.

It was the next weekend that she said,

'I don't think I can go out with you anymore. My husband is jealous.'

Ulrich said,

'You told your husband?'

'Of course. He is my husband.'

Their meetings stopped at once, and then they saw each other only in passing. Once, Ulrich encountered her with her husband, carrying home a child's tricycle, and she introduced them, and the man was very affable.

She was not yet old when she died. A kidney infection killed her. Ulrich found out only a long time later.

23

ONCE A YEAR, there was a maintenance shutdown at the factory. The entire system was drained and broken down for repairs.

Ulrich still remembers the astonishing silence of those intervals, and the echo of human voices in the metallic expanse.

One worker liked to sing in the factory at those times. She was a small woman with a nimble soprano voice, and she loved the factory acoustics, which made the sound swell around her. She had a place where she used to stand, and she sang in all the breaks, not caring who listened: folk songs, arias and whatever else she liked.

One day, during one of these shutdowns, this woman was singing an old drinking song from her part of the country. It was lunchtime, and people were playing cards, talking and smoking. The day was mild, and Ulrich stood outside, watching the machines chewing in the open mines below.

Comrade Denov came over, his shirtsleeves rolled up. He leaned against the wall, mirroring Ulrich's own pose.

'Isn't it beautiful?' he said warmly.

Ulrich was not sure what he meant. The day? The singing? The factory parts laid out on the concrete? But he did not ask. Whenever he met Denov he was gripped with a feeling of culpability. He could not banish it, even though he was in the right.

They stood for a moment, not speaking. The song *was* beautiful. Comrade Denov said,

'You were always a faithful colleague.'

And he gave one of his odd grimaces, which could be humour or gall.

Ulrich was thrown into confusion. Why did Denov speak in the past tense? Did he know what Ulrich was doing behind his back?

Ulrich could not summon so much as a grunt in response. The song ended in the factory and, humming it over the mining noise, Denov walked away.

Elizaveta burst into Ulrich's room one night while her friends were drinking round the table. The door slammed into the wall.

'Come and join us,' she cried. 'Come and have a drink!'

She stood unsteadily in the doorway in a tiger-print dress. He had been trying to sleep.

'You look disgusting.'

She stared at him.

'What did you say?'

She anchored herself with the door handle. He did not repeat himself. She said angrily,

'One day I'll tell you exactly what happened to me when I was in the camp. Exactly what I had to do to survive till I saw your face again. That will stop you saying dirty things to me just because I want to drink and enjoy myself.'

To his consternation, she began to weep.

'You won't talk to me,' she wailed. 'You don't like me talking to other people. You won't so much as have a drink with your own mother.'

She sat on his bed and looked at him, her tears flowing. Her bones protruded, and she smelled strongly of alcohol.

'You're impossible to live with.'

She let herself down heavily beside him, forgetting her guests, and drew her feet onto the bed. They lay together in silence while the party continued in the other room.

'I'm sorry,' he said vaguely.

Soon afterwards, she began to snore, and he did not know whether she had heard him.

He put an arm around her. The noise outside no longer seemed to interfere, and he drifted into sleep himself.

It was announced in the factory that Comrade Denov's duties had been curtailed. Ulrich rushed to his office, and found him packing up his things. Denov did not stop what he was doing, but asked him simply,

'What did you tell them, comrade?'

'What do you mean?'

Denov shook his head significantly, and Ulrich's pent-up resentment poured out.

'How can you look me in the eye after everything you've done? All the people you've betrayed with your stealing. We worked like animals for all these years to meet our quotas, and you sold our barium chloride to foreign companies! You hoarded raw materials and sold them on the black market. You see: I know everything. How much money you must have piled up!'

'You've been to my house many times. Did you see me lining my pockets? Did you see cars or jewellery? No. Do you know where that money went? With all your accounting genius, did you ever ask yourself where the money came from for your new baths, your new reactors? *Comrade Denov, we need a heating system so the pipes don't freeze in the winter. We need new pumps. We need this, we need that.* It was *you* who spent that money and you did it without a care in the world. What did you think: that I built up all that surplus by obeying the rules?'

Ulrich sat down.

'You should have come to me,' continued Denov. 'You understand accounting ledgers well enough, like you understand chemical reactions. But human behaviour is much more complicated.'

'But it was not right, what you did.' Ulrich struggled. 'Even if it wasn't for yourself.'

Denov spoke without emotion.

'Do you know how this system works? The numbers they come up with in the Planning Committee are pure fiction. When they say a ton of barium chloride will sell for so many leva, do you think that number has any significance? A bureaucrat comes to work on his mother's eightieth birthday and he thinks, *Eighty is a good number*, so he writes it in a column, and forever afterward we are forced to sell the product of our factory at eighty leva a ton, though it may cost three hundred to produce. This system is fatal. If you don't have the ingenuity to invent another one, you die. And for this you inform on me to the police. I hope they rewarded you well, Comrade Ulrich.'

Ulrich was dazzled by the sun on the floor. He imagined himself jumping through the glass of Denov's study window, out into the light, where the scattered words of this conversation would be no more than distant tremors on a clear day. He imagined falling into the mine pit and smashing on the rocks, and what a release that would be.

He imagined himself standing far away, as if the whole world were no more than a small band of horses tossing their heads in a far-off field, and he could let the nearby vastness of the wind in the grass take him over, sweeping him this way and that.

He asked thinly,

'What will you do now?'

'What do you think I will do?' said Denov, standing on a chair and lifting dusty volumes down from the top shelf. 'I have been appointed to run a much bigger factory near Varna. I will make coatings for satellites. I will have a big house and a driver, and my wife will be happy that I do not smell when I come home from work.'

Denov put the last of the books in a box and sat behind his desk.

'They wanted information about me. They always want information. But they didn't want to destroy me. They wanted to *use* me. People like me who supply the energy to our socialism. Do you think they value idiots who follow all the rules? They like people who can take a hopeless project, like this factory, and turn it into a success. Even if it means exporting to France.'

Ulrich stood up weakly. He wanted to leave. Denov reached out for the hand at the end of his limp arm and shook it.

'Good bye, comrade.'

Ulrich remembers that the factory began to make the wrong sounds, and he developed headaches when at work.

The mills where the ores were ground became deafening, the smell of chlorides suddenly unbearable. The slurry heap was like a mountain after twenty years.

Denov's young replacement did not consult Ulrich about technical decisions. When Ulrich complained, the new director explained that he did not think he was competent to oversee a modern factory of this scale.

Ulrich went to work every day but did nothing. He was not asked to attend discussions, nor consulted on any issue, and he was prevented from intervening in the factory's routine. He walked around giving advice and approvals, but it was like a man conducting an orchestra heard on the radio.

Idle, he devised a rhapsody of chemicals for the worker who sang in the shutdowns, a scientific spectacle full of mystery and delight. He approached her at her station and invited her to take a walk with him to an abandoned place where he could set it up. Up close, her youth made him conscious of his thinning hair, and his sagging neck. She looked at him with alarm, and refused.

He began to steal regularly from the factory's small laboratory. Mostly little things, here and there. Old valves from gas canisters. Rubber tubing. Every kind of safety equipment: goggles, gloves, breathing masks. He stole an old microscope that had lain unused for years. He told himself there was no dishonour in such behaviour. These objects, he felt, were owed to him.

Ulrich was presented with a date for his retirement. When the day came, the director called him into his office and thanked him for all his work. He told him they were increasing security at the factory and that if Ulrich were to present himself there after that day, he would not be able to gain entry. Afterwards there was a quick ceremony in the forecourt of the factory, where the director presented him with a bottle of rakia and spoke to him as if he were a sick person. Several people came up to Ulrich and shook his hand. Then they escorted him to the bus.

24

THE LAST OF ULRICH'S contemporaries from Berlin, some of whom had long since become world famous, died.

Bulgaria built its own oil refineries in Pleven and Bourgas.

The economy began to fail in conspicuous ways, and the shops ran empty.

In those years, the Sunny Beach resort was opened on the Black Sea coast, and foreign tourists came to lie in the Bulgarian sun. The East Germans covered the costs of their vacations by selling jeans and Nivea cream to Bulgarians, proving that years of communism had done little to stifle the love of trade.

It was the era when the Ilyushins and Tupolevs flown by Balkan Bulgarian Airlines never stopped falling out of the sky, and when Bulgaria took the Olympic medals for weightlifting and wrestling.

Khrushchev, Stravinsky and Louis Armstrong died in a cluster, and Duke Ellington soon after. Shostakovich died too.

Pasha Hristova, whose pop songs drove Ulrich crazy in the house, came down in an aeroplane crash.

Ulrich's former employer Ivan Stefanov died. Boris's old friend Georgi died of a heart attack while leaving a banquet for party officials. He was sixty-eight years old.

Ulrich's appearance drew away from all the old photographs, and he began to look more like his elderly father than himself. And Elizaveta was diagnosed with cancer of the lung.

Suddenly their remaining time together seemed short, though she was anyway approaching ninety years of age.

On her birthday, Ulrich proposed a surprise expedition. He prepared some food early in the morning, and helped her brush her hair. He borrowed a car from a man he knew and drove out of Sofia along the E81.

'It's a new place, Mother. I think you'll like it.'

She was very weak by then, but she was enlivened by the plan, and told stories from the old days.

'Do you remember the Yezidi priest we met that time, near Mosul? What a beautiful place it was, deep grass, rice fields, and everywhere oleander. Storks wading in the rice.'

She was tiny in her seat, her head wobbling with the motion of the car. She looked out of the window, away from Ulrich, across the flat fields. Her sunglasses looked too big for her now.

'They had this idea that human beings would become smaller and smaller. Each generation smaller than the last, until they turned into tiny, insignificant creatures. Do you remember? What a fantastic mythology they had! Then a giant would come at the end of time and drink all the seas and rivers until he was full of water and unable to move. And a mighty worm would come and eat him. Then the whole universe would be flooded and cleansed, and it would be time for judgement.'

'That's what he said?'

'Yes. I remember it like yesterday.'

Her voice was almost gone, and she rasped through her words. It was Sunday, and the road was abandoned. Black factories went by, and orange housing blocks, and flocks of goats. Thistles sparked purple by the side of the road. Up the distant hills was a padding of clumpy forest.

'We are so lucky in Bulgaria,' she said. 'We have the best yogurt and the best countryside.'

He had heard her say this so many times before.

'Do you remember the picnics we used to have around here? When you were a child? I think about them so often. What times they were! We drank from pure rivers, and you could cry at the wealth in the trees. Do you remember?'

Ulrich inclined his head in a way that said neither yes nor no. It was a gesture he used often with her. But she was dying, and they had these two hours in the car. It gave her an autobiographical zeal.

'Before I die,' she said, 'I want to confess something. I have no one else to tell it to but you.'

Ulrich's forearms thobbed on the wheel. She said,

'Long ago, when we were in Baghdad, I had an affair with a man. He was a Kurd who worked for us sometimes as a guide. His name was Karim. It's wonderful to say it out loud. Even now.'

She was looking away from him, out of the window. She said,

'He came on a journey with me. You were with us too, but you were very small; you were always needing attention, and he was so perfect with you. We visited enchanting places and everything we did together seemed like a miracle. When we got back to Baghdad, I was pregnant with his child. I never told anyone, not even Karim. I didn't know how to contact him. I managed to get rid of it – I had to do that, for your sake – but I've never stopped thinking about what might have been. Karim was perhaps the most beautiful thing that ever happened to me. I loved him. When I was in the camp I kept myself alive with that feeling from so long ago – for what did your father ever give me to draw on?'

She wept silently. She said,

'I'm sorry, Ulrich. You were a beautiful thing too. I don't want you to think…'

But Ulrich was cynical.

'I always wondered why you talked so endlessly about that part of our lives. And all along, it was only because of a man.'

'No, I loved those places,' she said. 'With all my heart. We've been trapped so long in this accursed country.'

She gave way to a fit of coughing.

'I always hoped,' she said, wiping the saliva from around her mouth, 'you would find more love in your life.'

The seal around the car windows was broken, and the air was loud. Ulrich saw a formation of military jets flying overhead. He caught something in the distance.

'We've arrived,' he said.

Steel chimneys slashed the horizon, and white reactors clambered over it like domed pastries. In the distance, the ground gave way to a sea of mercurial piping. Vast clouds drifted from the coolers, white like dough stretched across the sky.

'What is it?' said Ulrich's mother.

'We're near Kozloduy. Nearly at the border – the Danube is just ahead, and then Romania. And this is a miracle of our times, Mother. The first nuclear power plant in our country.'

'*That's* what you've brought me to see?'

He parked the car, and lifted her out into her wheelchair. The land was very flat, and monumentally empty. While he walked around the car shutting the doors, the wheelchair stood in the road. She had a blanket on her knees, battling the rushing air.

He wheeled her as close as possible, but he was unable to get her up the steep grass embankment surrounding the enclosure, so they saw what they could from below. The fence was topped with barbed wire, and plastic bags were caught there, thundering in the wind. They were a long way from the installation itself, but the basic structures were visible, and Ulrich explained how the system worked. His mother listened with her tortoiseshell sunglasses on. Her white hair, so thin by then, was all blown to one side.

Ulrich took out their lunch, because she had to eat regularly. He knelt on the grass, feeding her with a spoon. The skies were grey, but beams of intense sunlight occasionally broke through, shining in their eyes. Elizaveta's face was expressionless as she ate. Ulrich said,

'Happy birthday, Mother.'

She looked at him, forlorn.

'How could you ever think I would want to come here?' It took a long time for her to chew with her gums. 'I am a nineteenth-century woman with cancer. And this is where you bring me?'

'I thought you'd appreciate a day out of Sofia,' he said.

When she had finished eating, he wiped her mouth, and tried again to push the wheelchair up the incline, but it was too much for him. He left her sitting in a clearing by the side of the road as occasional cars shook the ground, and he climbed up to the fence to examine the power plant, shielding his eyes, and shouting descriptions and explanations to her down below.

She was put into hospital.

She was too old to withstand chemotherapy, so it was only a matter of time. She was allergic to morphine, and in her last days she could not sleep with the pain. After she died he found in her hospital bed some pages she had scribbled during the nights, while he slept in a chair. She had made plans for her funeral: she wanted roses to be given to all the mourners.

Once, she opened her eyes and said to him,

'Have you heard the latest joke?'

'No.'

'A woman goes into a store and asks for six eggs. The shopkeeper says, *You're in the wrong store. Here we have no meat. You have to go next door if you want no eggs.*'

He tried to smile.

'The doctor told me that,' she said.

She was no bigger than a child under the bedclothes.

'You're allowed to laugh,' she said. 'There's nothing tragic about disease, or age, or empty shops. It's time for me to die. The tragedy is when people don't feel around you, and never laugh. I hope you laugh some more when I'm gone. Look into the eyes of others, Ulrich, and you'll see there's still a field of life there.'

Her hair was limp and greasy, and her plait kept falling open. She asked him to tie it up again.

He propped her up and sat behind her.

'Mother,' he said.

He was nearly seventy years old, plaiting his mother's wispy hair. He broke down weeping.

'I can't live without you.'

He curled himself around her, sobbing. She put her hand on his head.

'Don't be afraid,' she said. 'Just remember everything we did.'

When her body gave out, he went back home. The house was cold.

It was as if all her possessions had died with her, for they were noticeably less animated than before. He touched her glasses, her knitting, her lifeless books. He overturned her shoes to contemplate the soles' wear. He found the enormous pile of papers she had typed over the years, and, for the first time, he allowed his curiosity out. He flicked slowly through this thing she had made, seeing the curlicue script down the left-hand margin, inked in by hand.

It was a dictionary. All those years she had been writing a dictionary. A Bulgarian–Arabic dictionary, which she had left piled in neat bundles secured with rubber bands.

25

SOON AFTER HIS MOTHER'S DEATH, Ulrich converted her bedroom into a chemistry laboratory.

He moved her bed out into the corridor, where it stood on its side for years before he finally chopped it up for firewood.

He set up a workbench and laid out all the equipment he had stolen from the factory. He installed an extractor fan that propelled effluent gases through a length of corrugated piping hanging out of the window. He brought in barrels of petroleum and canisters of chlorine. He erected a small oven.

Ulrich set out to discover plastic.

The 1970s were already well advanced. The shops downstairs from Ulrich's apartment used plastic cups and trays, polystyrene packaging and polythene bags. His own house was full of plastic pens and vinyl flooring, and even the clothes he wore were polyester. His sofa was stuffed with plastic foam. The casing of his television was plastic, and a plastic clock hung on the wall.

But Ulrich's knowledge of polymers dated from his time in Berlin, half a century before, when these materials were still unknown. The intervening time had added little to his theoretical understanding, for he had been cut away from the world of research. He had only vague ideas as to how nylon might be made, or even vinyl. In his scientific world, the entire empire of plastics had yet to be invented – and he set out as a late-coming pioneer.

He devoted several years to fundamental experiments, and taught himself many of the principles of polymer science. He developed a range of materials with different properties, and he began to test how they responded under various conditions. He learned how to adjust hardness, plasticity and heat resistance.

He drew his plastic curtains on the world outside. There was a plastic lamp on the bench, in whose bright circle he lived, day and night.

There were occasional accidents and his neighbours sometimes came to complain about the smells and the explosions. They were suspicious of his perpetual confinement.

There were days of euphoria, the ethylene gas coming off in a hot polymer slurry and drying solid. He gazed at glistening blobs of virgin plastic, and he felt the satisfaction of having planted himself in something outside himself.

His inner thoughts from those days are mostly sealed off to him now. When he remembers what he did, he is reminded of a monkey he once saw in the Sofia zoo, beating its head rhythmically in its cage.

The police came to the apartment. It was after his remaining hair had turned grey, because they remarked on it. They seemed alarmed at the conditions he was living in. They took him to the station for questioning.

Ulrich had lost the habit of conversation, and was intimidated by the interrogation room. His eyes were wide with confusion, and the interrogator had to steady him.

'There is nothing to worry about,' he said. 'We're not trying to scare you. We just want to understand what you're doing. Your neighbours are concerned.'

There was a lamp in Ulrich's eyes, which released glowing spores in front of the interrogator's face.

'When did you last take a bath, comrade?' the interrogator asked.

The question seemed easy, but Ulrich's mind had become a vacuum. There were three men gathered around him who seemed to think there was a truth inside him that they would persuade him to part with. But inside him was nothing. He could not tell them when he last had a bath.

'What is the purpose of the experiments you are conducting in your apartment?'

This, too, was impossible. Ulrich foundered on *purpose*. The interrogator tried to simplify his approach.

'Are you making something?'

'Yes,' replied Ulrich.

'Well, what are you making?'

'Plastics. Various kinds of plastics.'

'Plastic. Like this, you mean?'

He knocked his knuckle against the plastic clock that stood on the table between them. Ulrich picked up the clock and examined it.

'No, not like this,' he said at length. 'This is made of polycarbonate. I don't know how to make that.'

'So what do you make?' asked the interrogator patiently.

'My experiments are at an early stage, and I don't know where they will lead. At present I am trying to develop some transparent materials using acetone and hydrogen cyanide. I may succeed, I may fail.'

'Hydrogen cyanide. That sounds dangerous.'

'I wear a gas mask,' said Ulrich. His nerves had stilled.

The interrogator asked,

'What do you intend to do with these transparent materials, supposing you succeed?'

'I don't know.'

'Let me ask you this. Are you running an illegal business? Are you trying to undermine our socialist economy?'

'No.'

'You don't intend to sell what you make?'

'No.'

'How can you afford to buy your supplies?'

'From my pension. I have no other expenses. And I have some savings.'

The interrogator was silent. Ulrich said,

'If someone wanted me to make plastic things for them I might be able to do so. I think I could make buttons for a suit.'

'But it is easy to get buttons for a suit!'

Ulrich picked up the clock and looked at it again. The interrogator continued,

'Why do you do this, comrade? You are behaving like an eccentric and making people nervous. If it continues we will have to confiscate your equipment. And who would suffer from that? You are using dangerous chemicals in a residential building. There are several chemistry clubs you could belong to, where everything would be above-board.'

'No,' said Ulrich. 'I want to do it in the proper way.'

'What does that mean?'

'The proper way. The authentic way.'

Ulrich remembers that his door wore padlocks like so many earrings, and it was reinforced with steel. He plugged his keyhole and kept his curtains drawn.

He began to manufacture plastic objects. He made plastic dolls and animals. He sculpted a plastic comb, painstakingly, tooth by tooth. He did not have moulds, and everything he made looked like craftwork: irregular and roughly shaped.

He conducted some experiments with colouring, and set himself the task of producing a replica of his mother's imitation tortoiseshell sunglasses, which had sat on a sideboard in the main room all this time.

He had to construct his own equipment: a reactor loop made of two new car exhausts he found, and a pump he had stolen from the factory. He used a chromium catalyst that he powdered himself. He needed high temperatures, and the apartment sweated. He used phthalic anhydride to make the frames more flexible, which he produced on his own, from naphthalene.

How many years of work did it take him to produce the material for the lenses? He remembers the first successful sheet, pressed between sheets of aluminium foil under a pile of heavy books. When he drew it out it was unintentionally embossed with the words *Dictionary of the Bulgarian Language*, and the seal of the Bulgarian Academy of Sciences.

He made moulds out of concrete, lined with aluminium foil. He used his own weight to hold the moulds closed while he injected the plastic with a hand pump, and he crouched there, on the mould, until it had cooled. He lifted off the top, pulled out the foil, and peeled it away carefully from the plastic. Glistening, and still warm.

He was unable to make hinges for the glasses, and he could not find out where to buy them. He was therefore obliged to go to the market and buy another pair of sunglasses to take the hinges from. That pair cost four leva. Over the years he had invested hundreds, if not thousands, of leva in his own production.

The police took years to return, but when they did they asked no questions. They simply dismantled his laboratory so that he could not continue his work any more.

Uranium

26

Today, Ulrich's neighbour is preoccupied by the recent arrival of two more Gypsy families in the building.

'They're taking over,' she says as she unloads Ulrich's laundry. 'These days I'm scared to come home after dark. Their young men stare at me while I walk to the lift.'

She has brought hot sausages, which Ulrich can smell. She puts a new packet of tea bags in the cupboard, and disappears into the bathroom with toilet paper.

In this weather, everything is storing heat. When there is absolute quiet, Ulrich can hear the wood of the window frame creaking with desiccation.

He hears his neighbour tidying up in the bathroom. She flushes the toilet and emerges again.

'You know they steal the electricity?' she says. 'Their children are electrical wizards: they disconnect their meters and connect their supply to the meters of hard-working Bulgarians. That's why our bills have been rising so much. The Gypsies don't pay one stotinka. They spend it all on dancing and weddings. And if you try and confront them ...'

She leaves Ulrich to picture the consequences. He feels he should show more concern, since she also pays his own electricity bill, but he can think of nothing to say.

'You'd imagine they'd become more civilised, living among Bulgarians.

But it's quite the opposite! They have marble floors and satellite dishes, they mint money like the National Bank – and still they steal from us!'

And with a sigh she said,

'God save Bulgaria!'

Ulrich has his own pet hatred. A man living on the ground floor collects bits of old wood and iron and covers them in gold spray paint. He picks up a rusty plaque with a lion on it, or a wreath, sands the rust off and sprays it gold, and sells it as a decoration for someone's house. He stores all his junk in the common garden downstairs, though Ulrich is certain that none of the other residents has agreed to this. On windy days the man applies his spray paint inside, in the hallway, and the entire building smells of acetone.

These proceedings incite inexplicable fury in Ulrich. His mind dwells on this man for much longer than it should, and whenever his neighbour is counting out his pills, Ulrich asks whether she has news of the man, to feed his irritation.

In the extreme of his life, Ulrich's emotions have begun to pitch and toss on their own, with no proportion to what caused them. He no longer laughs at jokes, or weeps at things that are sad, but he finds himself weeping and laughing at other times, for no obvious reason. Nothing flows when expected, and then an entirely simple thing – the sun on his face in the morning, or the feel of a spoon in the hand – punctures an escape route, and a torrent bubbles out, erotic and sickly, of grief, or anger, or mirth.

Earlier today, the excited voice of a football commentator activated in Ulrich a sharp happiness that seemed to have been laid down decades ago.

Ulrich has come to enjoy this unpredictability of his emotions. He feels as if something new is happening to him, even at his age.

'You know what we found in the flooded apartment upstairs?' his neighbour says as she opens the door. 'Beetles.'

Ulrich nods, imagining the scene. But that is not what she meant.

'He had them on the wall, in wooden cases. Must have been at least twenty wooden frames full of different beetles. Beautiful things, they were: iridescent green, some of them as big as your fist. There was nothing else in the house: the place was emptied out. A radiator pipe had burst, that's why we had all that water, and the floor was completely rotten. Don't know who's going to pay for the repairs. My husband's going to see if he can get some money for those beetles, but that won't begin to cover it.'

Ulrich asks if the owner of the flat was an entomologist.

'I don't know,' she says. 'I never met him. But I have to get home and take the weight off these legs. They're killing me.'

Ulrich takes the opportunity to ask what exactly is wrong with her legs.

She blows out her air.

'There's nothing wrong with my legs as such. I don't have any. Didn't you ever notice? I lost them years back.'

Ulrich does not feel he can ask how it happened, since she has not volunteered it. She shuts the door, and he hears her limping hurriedly along the corridor. He feels a little guilty that he takes her so for granted.

It is the most beautiful moment in the day, and though Ulrich can no longer see it, he has lived in this room for long enough to sense when it is beginning. In the middle of the morning, the sun shines through his window on to the mirror, and the room glows joyfully for a few minutes with the travelling rectangle of light on the opposite wall. Even without his eyes, he feels the fleeting transfiguration

27

RELEASED FROM HIS OWN CHEMISTRY, Ulrich realised that Bulgaria had become a chemical disaster. The rivers ran with mercury and lead, and hummed with radioactivity. Fishing had dried up on the Black Sea coast, and every year more fields and forests were lost.

The Kremikovtzi steelworks and the Bukhovo uranium mine flooded Sofia with lead, sulphur dioxide, hydrogen sulphide, ethanol and mercury. Radioactive sludge from Bukhovo was dumped in an open forest, contaminating water and land for miles around.

The copper mines in Pirdop devastated everything around them. Arsenic flowed straight into the Pirdopska River, and dead fish piled up downstream in enormous stinking banks. Nylon stockings melted on contact with the air.

Bulgarian sheep had miscarriages and died, and the cows went mad. Children were born with cancers and deformities. Like all his compatriots, Ulrich had become chemical himself, his blood a solution of cadmium, lead, zinc and copper.

Reactor 4 of the nuclear power plant in Chernobyl blew up, and the atmosphere altered. The undead leaders clung to office and alcohol, but they had lost the power to stop talk. Intellectuals denounced the chlorine pollution from the chemical plant across the river in Romania, which poisoned the Rousse air. They criticised industry and the socialist ideal. They made films against chemical contamination, and demonstrated in the streets. They spoke with impunity, and it was clear that Zhivkov had lost his mastery.

The Turks protested the treatment they had received: their ghettos, their labour, the forced change of their names. The old factories churned but the shops were empty, and even a child could see that the eternal system was only propped up with contraband and rust. The Gypsies worked on trucks and trains, and made money moving things from here to there. People said it rained banknotes at their weddings.

The forbidden music returned.

Ulrich watched his television, not really understanding what was going on. People said, *Communism is no more!* and, after forty years, Zhivkov stepped down from his height, and became subject to human things. His arrest and trial were shown to the world. He sweated in the courtroom, he was nervous and made mistakes, and it was no longer possible to believe in his divinity. Secrets were laid bare, and everything collapsed like a public demolition.

It was amazing how fast the old order was swept away. People told stories about their previous crimes and punishments as if they were rumours from another place. The State Security archives were opened, and people could see the transcripts of their old phone calls and the reports their friends had filed against them. Ulrich watched a documentary on television about the labour camps, and howled for what his dead mother had kept inside her.

He never had an instinct for politics, and now he could not even tell what kind of world he was in. They said, *Now we are capitalist!* but all Ulrich could see was criminality raised to a principle. Murderers and thieves took over and called themselves *businessmen*, and kept the people happy with pornography. The United Nations cut off supplies to Milošević's Serbia, and gleeful thick-necked Bulgarian toughs stepped in to supply the food and oil, becoming billionaires overnight. They bought TV stations, hotels and football clubs, and they adorned those necks with gold crosses the size of dinner plates.

They were former sportsmen and State Security men, and they had manoeuvred well through the debacle, but even they could not believe how many millions they had managed to steal. For a time they lived out in the open, and everyone could see their incredulous carnival; but then they began to die in daylight assassinations, and they retreated behind walls.

Bulgaria became Asiatic again, as it had been when Ulrich was born. Big-breasted Bulgarian singers embraced the long-suppressed Turkish and Arabic music and turned it into anthems for the new gangster society. Heroin poured in from Afghanistan. Criminal syndicates selected the best-looking Bulgarian girls to work in brothels in Dubai.

The world returned to war. Armenia and Azerbaijan fought. Yugoslavia fell apart. Russia razed Chechnya, trying to hold on to it. There was civil war in Georgia, with tanks firing in front of the Tbilisi opera house, where Ulrich had gone to see *Tosca* with Magdalena on their honeymoon so long ago. The Americans bombed Baghdad, which his father had tried to link harmoniously to Europe with his Berlin-Baghdad railway line. People said, *Now our country is open!* But even if it had been possible for Ulrich to journey to the places of his life, they all seemed to be in flames. America bombed Yugoslavia, and chemicals flowed down the river into Bulgaria from the destroyed factories, and bloated corpses too.

Ulrich was reduced to absolute poverty. He could not afford the electricity in Zapaden Park, and nearly froze in the winter. He moved into a run-down building near the bus station, whose hollow partitions were built against the grain, so that the windows stood half in one apartment, half in another.

He left behind many of his possessions. He could not transport the great number of his chemistry books.

He brought some paving slabs into the new place, and built a fireplace under the chimney. In the winter, he collected bits of packing crate from the street to make a fire with, which blazed up in an instant, searing the room, and burned out without leaving any warmth.

He began to forage for food, but he moved slowly, and the competitive hordes were energetic and desperate. Even the young could not make it, and many of them left the city in the hope of sustaining themselves on a bit of chemical land. Ulrich sat in doorways, trying to preserve his energy, and he watched the drunk children and the women praying for miracles. There were stains on the pavements from where people slept at night, and sometimes there were corpses in the morning.

One afternoon, Ulrich collapsed while trying to open his front door, and was taken in by his neighbours. That was when they began to give him money.

For weeks afterwards, he lay curled up on his bed, unable to think or move. He spent all night trying to sleep, and groaned when he heard the first clatter of morning water in the pipes.

He leaned his head against the wall, which was like a great membrane capturing the sounds of the building. Conversations in other apartments came through as indistinct reverberation. Music, sometimes, and telephone rings. It was rainy, and at night the wall groaned with damp distension. Wet patches spread with clicks as molecules found new space, and the plaster ballooned.

In the afternoons the air warmed up. The damp paint, hanging off in curled butterfly wings, dried out with the sun, crackled, and fell, finally, to the floor.

Ulrich's heartbeat slowed, and his pressure dropped inside. He was tired, and his daydreams were not enough to keep out the news stories.

Balkan Bulgarian Airlines sent its air hostesses to pose nude for *Playboy* in order to save itself from bankruptcy. The Kremikovtzi steelworks was sold to an American company for one dollar.

The new leaders incinerated the communist mummy of Georgi Dimitrov, and decided to demolish his tomb, which had become a glowering affront to the nobility of their new capitalism. Great crowds came to watch the mausoleum come down, while the prime minister surveyed the solemn proceedings from behind his office curtains. The country's leading explosives experts came in clean uniforms to lay down their dynamite. With a magnificent lack of humour, they signalled their readiness, and everyone prepared themselves for the house of spirits to evaporate.

The explosion was so massive that the speakers crackled on Ulrich's rickety television. People ducked and covered their eyes; the surrounding windows were blown out, and great cracks streaked across the stone square. But as the smoke cleared, the crowds burst into laughter – and even Ulrich laughed in his solitude. For the mausoleum stood indifferent, entirely unharmed. The experienced experts set more explosives, and still nothing happened. They claimed a technical hitch, and tried a third time. But it would not fall. They packed up and went home, and returned with pickaxes after dark. That was what it was to live in flimsier times, with the past simply too well made.

There was a knock at Ulrich's door one day and government agents asked for Elizaveta, who was twenty years dead. They carried a parcel containing her jewellery, a gold crucifix, an oil painting of the Blue Mosque in Tabriz and a series of framed prints of the Ringstrasse in Vienna. These objects had been held in a vault for close on half a century, and now they were fastidiously returned.

This miraculous event contradicted everything Ulrich thought he knew, and he felt he had lived too long. He had seen the statues pulled down again and again – this time they were putting up shrines to Ronald Reagan – and everyone around him had passed away. He was living in the aftertimes, whose rules he did not understand. Forty or fifty years, he thought, were enough for a modern life, for the human frame could not hold up if the world was destroyed too many times and made again.

He was forced to sell all his mother's valuables, and his gold watch too. He resented the smugness of the owner of the antique shop, who accepted these things with so little emotion. The shop was piled high with painted wooden icons, china horses, military decorations, sports trophies, stamp collections and old spectacles. There were boxes full of yellowed postcards sent from the Black Sea. The place swelled with the lives that were deposited there.

Till the very end, Ulrich had sustained the hope that there would be someone for him to bequeath his gold watch to.

Ulrich's life had become minimal. He rarely left his tiny apartment and he had little to do. There was no telephone in his apartment, and the list of his possessions was short. He no longer cooked his meals. He produced nothing at all. He spent some time every day making lists of the things he threw out. He listed toothpaste tubes, exhausted pens and sachets of coffee, and he found there some signature of his remaining significance.

One day, Ulrich decided to throw out two old canisters of sulphuric acid that were left over from his days of experimentation. He had kept them with the vague idea that they might come in useful for stripping electrical wire or something of the sort, but he had not touched them in many years. He took them down from the shelf, and, out of some inexplicable desire to see what state the contents were in after all this time, he tried to open one of them. It was sealed tightly shut. After several minutes of wrestling, holding the canister between his knees to keep it steady, the seal broke and the acid burst in his face. He ran to the kitchen to plunge his head in the sink, still full of dishwashing water, but the pain remained intense. When finally he could open his eyes, everything was dark.

His neighbours took him to the hospital, where the skin of his nose and forehead was treated for burns, but there was nothing they could do about his eyes. His corneas were destroyed.

28

THIS MORNING, ULRICH sensed a new, ripe feeling in the air, and now, in the afternoon, the storm is being prepared.

Just a succession of pinpricks at the beginning, but swelling to a single sighing sheet: a sonic layer over everything. The breeze in the window – *thank God!* – and the smell of dust flowing off the roof and dripping from the tree leaves. Ulrich can hear his neighbour's hurried limp next door as she rushes between windows, throwing them open. It's an even downpour, and he sees everything in fine grain: the cars are spraying now, the back-hiss of radials, and there is the bus station laid out, the long steel roofs resounding like tin drums. Figures caught unprepared: the street pours its people into the doorways, and somebody runs with a polythene bag held tutting overhead. Plastic takes on more of the roar as the stalls are quickly covered across the street. The windowsill is a delicate pattering bar.

Underneath, directly below, is an umbrella open wide, where the sill's globules bomb. Silver drops swell on the rib tips till they break and fall, smattering the ground plumply amid the slender rain. They burst on the paving and scatter into spray; and, caught in the flare – is he being fanciful? – is something too large to be one person, a dark doublemass absorbing the sibilance. Two hidden lovers holding each other close under the awning, a huddled shadow in sound.

By now, Ulrich has reconciled himself to the loss of his vision. In the beginning he was terribly shaken, and for months afterwards he mourned the sense he had lost. But his system gradually regenerated itself, and now he does not feel inconvenienced without his eyes. In fact, his gaze turned inward, he has become rejuvenated. Little disturbed by sensory impressions, his mind generates its own material, which absorbs him completely, and he finds his days are full.

Thinking back, he realises how much has slipped through the fingers of his memory. Everything he still retains could be told in an afternoon, and yet there is so much more. The substance of all those days, which has entirely escaped.

The days of dust drifting in the light shafts. Tea bags put out to dry. Listless newspapers with new dates on them every day. The pipes of grubby gloss that turn from the back of the radiator along the wall. The gradual death of things: plants and machines and animals, furniture and friends. Twisted hairs trapped in a hairbrush. The seasons, and their increasing irrelevance, even if there is still a sense of eternity about the clouds. Cracks in walls, and the refusal of windows to close properly after too many coats of paint. Filling in forms. New buildings whose purpose is unclear. Things that have not been seen for some time: a good pen, a souvenir key ring. Lying in bed, and ceilings. Surprises, such as window glass blown in by the wind. Small changes that appear in routes walked often: a new fence post, or a sawn-off tree. The shocking breathlessness of climbing just a few stairs, and shaving in the morning. Thoughts in the background: concerns about money, and whether he can still be considered good looking. The cleaning of things just cleaned: cups, plates, bathtubs, cookers, hands and all the other parts of the body. Old-style banknotes discovered in jacket pockets, and the recollection of facts when the need for them has passed. The relief of television, and its futility. The persistence of shit, and its undue hold on the mind. The stuff that passes through the days: empty food cans, old batteries, rotten fruit and notepaper.

It has all slipped away.

Ulrich has sometimes wondered whether his life has been a failure. Once he would have looked at all this and said, Yes. But now he does not know what it means for a life to succeed or fail. How can a dog fail its life, or a tree? A life is just a quantity; and he can no more see failure in it than he can see failure in a pile of earth, or a bucket of water. Failure and success are foreign terms to such blind matter.

Ulrich's spirit has expanded in these last days, and he is no longer bereft. Einstein said, considering his death, *I feel such solidarity with all things, that it does not matter where the individual begins and ends.* When his mind is particularly aware, Ulrich can sense the great black ocean of forgotten things, and, ignoring his beginning and end, he casts off into it. Everything he has known has drained over time, from the actual world into this ocean, and he is blissful in the endless oblivion. Only when his surroundings insist – when the electric drill whirs downstairs, and the walls start with that powdery vibration, so unique to this place – does he alight again, reluctantly, in the narrow confines of his room.

In his childhood, Ulrich's parents were often invited to evening parties. His father would come down first, his velvet coat resplendent and his moustaches waxed to dagger tips, and he admired himself in the fireplace mirror, saying, *Look at your handsome old man!* Then his mother, whose heart-shaped diamond necklace shone in the firelight, who leaned over the flurries of her sapphire dress while he begged her not to go, and kissed him *goodnight* in a gust of perfume. Ulrich watched their departure from the window: the coachman's whips and cries as the horses strained against the carriage's inertia, and he sat back down, barefooted, with toys and books.

His grandmother enjoyed these moments when she had him to herself. She sat with him, and told him stories. Over the hours, the oil lamps burned out, until they were left only with the glow of the fire, which Ulrich prodded now and then.

It is a feeling that Ulrich has sought again and again throughout his life.

Thinking back, he is surprised at the quantity of time he spent in daydreams. His private fictions have sustained him from one day to the next, even as the world itself has become nonsense. It never occurred to him to consider that the greatest portion of his spirit might have been poured into this creation. But it is not a despairing conclusion. His daydreams were a life's endeavour of sorts, and now, when everything else is cast off, they are still at hand.

SECOND MOVEMENT
'Daydreams'

Narwhal

1

IN A SMALL INDUSTRIAL TOWN some two hundred kilometres from the Bulgarian city of Rousse lived a youth named Petar, who was looking to prove his manhood.

Petar was small and spindly, and could not attract the girls, while his father was a bull of a man whose feats of strength were talked about even in the next town.

Old Petar never stopped remarking on it.

'Don't know what games your old mother must have played to bring out a gimp like you.'

Petar felt it was time to show everyone what he could do. He was twenty-one: he worked as hard as anyone else in the factory, and, if you did not take his size into account, he could look quite striking.

His opportunity came when the mayor announced a party for his wedding anniversary. Old Petar was the mayor's brother, and naturally it would fall to him to slaughter the pig. He was famous for it: he could slice a jugular in an instant, and with his bulk he pinned down the largest animals and held them as they died.

'Pigs are sensitive beasts,' he would say as he got up from his exertions and acknowledged the crowd's approval. 'You can't let them suffer.'

On the morning of the mayor's party, Petar approached his father and said,

'Today *I* am going to slaughter the pig.'

Old Petar burst out laughing.

'You? You wouldn't have the first idea. It takes skill to kill a pig. Can you imagine what kind of beast my brother will have stored up for a day like this? It will weigh twice as much as me! How could you keep it down?'

'I've watched you all my life, and I know how it's done. As for my size – I'll make up for it with ingenuity.'

The argument went on until his father gave in.

'But you're on your own. I'll have nothing to do with it.'

Around midday, people began to gather at the hall where the mayor was having his party. Water was already heating in a steel bathtub on the fire, for them to dunk the pig in afterwards and remove the hair.

Old Petar arrived, his son in tow. Everyone knew what his arrival portended; they greeted him excitedly and walked with him in a jubilant crowd to where the pig was penned. Old Petar opened the gate of the enclosure while everyone else climbed onto the fence and sat there to watch. The pig was sleeping inside a wooden hut with its head resting in the mud outside. The sudden commotion roused it, and it blinked drowsily.

Old Petar stood in the middle of the enclosure and took his knife out of his belt. He raised it above his head, and everyone cheered. He spoke:

'I'm not slaughtering the pig today. My son here thinks he can do it better. So see him try.'

There was general surprise. Old Petar walked out of the pen and handed the knife to his son. Then he turned his back on the crowd and set off down the street towards home.

Petar jumped down from the fence into the enclosure. Everyone was watching. The mayor and all his friends. The young men who had mocked Petar when they were at school. All the prettiest girls in the town were there. They were all sitting on the fence watching how Petar would fare with the pig.

The mayor was a little nervous.

'Are you sure about this, young Petar? I have a lot of guests to feed today and I don't want anything to go wrong. That pig's been waiting a long time for this day.'

Petar had brought three long pieces of rope. He tied them to sturdy posts on different sides of the pen, and laid the three loose ends together in the middle.

The mayor said,

'Do you want some men to hold him down? You're just a snip of a thing yourself.'

Petar approached the pig, which eyed him lazily. He took its ear and tried to pull it to its feet. The pig did not move. He seized both ears and leaned backwards, pulling as hard as he could. The pig was oblivious, and the girls began to snigger. Petar took a sharp stick and began to poke the pig in the neck. It still did not react: its skin was as tough as bark. Finally, he threw himself into the ripe darkness of the sty, wriggled along the length of the pig's warm flank, and prodded it vigorously in the backside. The pig snorted and flicked its tail in his face, and, as Petar dug in harder, it whined irritably and struggled to its feet. Finally, it stumbled out of the sty and into the open. Petar crawled after it, covered in filth.

The pig stood under the hot sun, drowsy and bewildered. It was the mayor's prize boar, and the largest Petar had ever seen. Its head was larger than his torso. Its body was a long pink mountain of muscle and fat, and its legs were as thick as pillars. Its eyes were moist and human, with a thatch of stiff gold lashes.

Petar coaxed the pig into the middle of the enclosure. He stroked it to keep it calm, and pushed it gently ahead of him. The pig was in no mood for an argument. When Petar had it where he wanted it, he began to stroke its snout and speak soothingly in its ear, until the pig folded its forelegs and lay down on the ground. Petar pulled the ropes taut and tied them firmly around the pig's ankles.

Everyone was still. The mayor said quietly,

'You're sure you're all right, boy?'

Petar nodded.

He took the knife his father had given him and held it ready. He lay down gently on the broad surface of the pig's back, speaking softly in its ear, his arms around either side of its head. Suddenly, and so violently that even his expectant audience was taken by surprise, Petar thrust the knife into the pig's throat.

The pig let out a scream that split their heads like the screech of an electric drill; it staggered to its feet, eyes flung wide. Petar gripped its head and tried to push his knife in farther, but the pig started to run. The two posts at the far end of the enclosure were pulled clean out of the ground, and spectators fell into the mud as the fence collapsed. The pig lowered its head and broke through the barrier at the other end; the crowd scattered in all directions as Petar gripped the pig's back with his knees as best he could and sawed at its windpipe, opening a hole that gushed blood in the wind. The third rope tautened, and once again the post was ripped out – and now there were three fence posts bouncing on the end of ropes as the pig ran screaming down the hill, its eyes rolling in its sockets and Petar hanging on for dear life.

Behind them ran the party guests, calling and screaming and grabbing at the flying ropes, but none of them could stall the careering pig.

Ahead of them, Petar could see the main road coming close, where cars flashed by on their way to Rousse or the Black Sea, and still the pig charged pell-mell, hoofs a-clatter on tarmac and piston legs accelerating with the incline; and just as the road broadened out into a junction, still bucking and lurching, Petar managed to cut through the pig's windpipe. Its shriek dried up in its throat and he felt it flag. Its giant lungs heaved, sucking impotently at the air.

The pig came to a halt. The running crowd caught up and watched as the big eyes turned white, saliva coursed from pig lips, the legs buckled – and the huge animal rolled over, its nostrils still whistling. Petar did not loosen his grip but clung on as if in his own rigor mortis. People formed a circle around the dying pig. It was covered in sweat, and blood was pumping out on to the street. Its eyes opened wide and its back legs kicked once, twice, three times times. It took a long time to die. No one spoke.

The mayor marched after them. He was red with rage.

'A fine mess, young Petar. What a way to kill a pig. The whole meal will taste of this. And now we have to carry a quarter-ton beast back up the hill. A big fucking mess. I should have just put a bullet in its head.'

Petar got off the pig. He was covered in blood from head to toe. Someone brought a tractor, and everyone heaved the dead pig onto the trailer. They walked behind it up the hill.

Petar went home. His father was sawing wood.

'Did you kill it?'

'Yes.'

His father smirked.

'Looks like it put up quite a fight. You'd better get washed.'

Petar took a shower. His hair was matted with blood and pig shit. He felt depressed. He watched the brown water go down the plug hole and vomited suddenly, holding in the noise.

In the evening, he put on a new shirt and set out with his father for the party.

The men gathered round as they arrived.

'Never seen a pig killed like that, Old Petar! Your son did it bareback! Did well to keep his focus, he did.'

Old Petar gave a half-smile. The men pressed rakia into their hands.

'You'll need a drink after that, boy.'

The pig had been roasting for hours on a spit, and the aroma displaced everything else. Women were peeling vegetables and chopping onions and herbs. It was a beautiful autumn night, and the men talked in lazy groups, smoking and drinking.

The mayor came over with more rakia.

'Your son told you how he ruined my pig? Big mess. Big fucking mess. I saved that boar a long time.'

Old Petar did not look up. There was music coming from inside the hall, too loud for him to think straight, and he said,

'My brother has rented a Japanese stereo from the Gypsies, with speakers as tall as me. He thinks it will make the young people like him. Meanwhile we can't even hear what we're saying.'

The stars grew bright, and the mayor announced dinner. They went inside to take their places. A life-size photograph of the mayor and his wife on their wedding day had been pasted on one wall. The stereo was blaring pop music and the worldlier girls were singing along. The tables were piled with food, and people began to eat hungrily. The mayor sat at the head table with his family, glaring all the time at his brother. He shouted through the music,

'Can you taste it, Petko? Can you taste the upset your son made? The meat is ruined.'

Old Petar laid an arm across his son's shoulders and said,

'It tastes fine to me. At least he had the courage to try. You should have taken the pig on yourself. Then we could have laughed good and proper.'

The girls got up to dance between the tables. It was raucous music that Petar did not know. Several babies started crying at the same time. The mayor continued to complain about the pig.

Somebody came and hovered over Petar.

Petar had always loved Irina, but only from afar. He had loitered outside the bakery where she worked. He had seen her at weddings, singing songs until the old men cried. She had never sent a single glance in his direction, so she couldn't know what she was to him: an insouciant flock of laughter, a tumbling-sycamore girl, a bliss of damask roses.

'Why don't you ever dance?' she asked.

'I'm not very good. I prefer to watch.'

'Why don't you try?'

She held out her hand and he took it. Standing next to her, he was half a head shorter. She led him into the middle of the room and succumbed to an energetic dance which was a perfect translation of the wild sounds into flesh. He tried to follow, awkwardly. She smiled at him.

'That was the worst slaughter I ever saw!'

She laughed loudly.

'It was a big pig,' he said, not sure what she meant.

The dance was not working. She said,

'Let's go.'

They went outside and walked idly.

'Don't you like music?'

'I don't know much about it.'

'You're missing out. Music is the reason to be young!'

And then she said,

'The Gypsies bring in music from England and Germany. I can teach you everything. In England there's a style called punk, and there's another kind called heavy metal. Motörhead, Iron Maiden – have you heard of them? I have headphones at home: you put those pads on your ears and hear the guitars groaning behind your eyelids, your brain melts and it's crazy.'

Petar looked at the ground while they walked, thinking, *She is amazing.*

'Let's face it,' she said, 'the world is shit and full of lies. You need music. Then you understand that none of this matters – this punishment, this stupid Bulgaria.'

The factory had stayed closed that day, and the air was clear. She said,

'I'm going to join a band some day. Get out of this town.'

'You'll be a great singer,' said Petar.

'What do you know? What have you heard, except for the stuff they play on Radio Sofia? The songs I write would scare you.'

Petar smiled. He said,

'I know *you* well enough. I know we'll switch on the television one day and see you on the big shows from Moscow. And we'll still be here, living like we do. We'll say, *Once we knew her – she grew up here!*'

He was wistful. He said,

'It will make me happy. To know you did what you dreamed of.'

She thought about it.

'They'll never play my music on those stuffy shows.'

They had arrived at her house.

'Come in. Everyone's at the party. We can drink on our own.'

They went into the house. He sat down at the kitchen table. She took some vodka down from a shelf and poured it into two glasses.

Nine months later, Irina gave birth to a baby boy. She and her new husband, Petar, named him Boris.

They had moved into a small apartment in an old tower block, but Petar was making plans for them to move to Sofia so that Irina could pursue her musical dreams.

The new baby was tiny and frail. Boris breathed with difficulty and seemed to be in continual discomfort. The doctor warned that he might not live. He advised that the baby sleep with an oxygen mask, since his lungs were not yet fully developed.

The worried parents laid their baby between them each night and stayed awake for hours, watching every breath going into his lungs and every exhalation misting the mask. Finally, exhausted by the anxiety, they fell asleep. Long after they had drifted off, the cylinder of oxygen stood like a sentinel by the bed, its rubber tube looping over one parent and blowing gently into baby Boris's mouth and nose.

And so it was, on a cold night in November, when a spiteful water leak caused the flame to go out on the young family's gas heater, when gas started to fill the bedroom (whose windows had been closed against drafts), when all the oxygen was expelled from the air and a deathly heaviness began to descend – that only little Boris, out of all his family, survived.

2

AFTER THE DEATHS OF PETAR AND IRINA, Old Petar collapsed into incapacity and fell away from the life of the town. Orphan Boris was taken in by Irina's mother, Stoyana, who was the accountant in the local post office.

Stoyana considered her grandson's preservation to be nothing short of a miracle. She loved him to distraction, and his infant antics were her cardinal joy.

When Boris was two years old she heard him singing a tune to himself. She recognised the melody, but could not recall where she had heard it. Boris continued to sing the same tune every evening, until Stoyana remembered it was a lullaby that Irina had written for her unborn son, and sung to him in the womb.

The town had seen better times. Money did not do what it once had done, and people began to suffer. The old housing blocks were damp and crumbling, and light bulbs had become so scarce they were pilfered from every corridor and elevator. Half the factory buses had stopped working. Broken windows and balconies were mended with corrugated iron, and there was nothing in the shops. Outside the factory, the mountain of slurry had collapsed into the river, and people blamed it for their cancers. Every morning there was a repulsive scattering of syringes around the bus shelter.

The Gypsies made money, which only increased the general plight. No one had ever liked Gypsies, but things were easy while they were poor and their children safely stowed in a school for the mad. Now they were lording it around with second-hand Volga sedans, illegal satellite dishes and sparkling new façades on their shabby houses – and it seemed as though their years of exile were bringing rewards. The socialist economy, which gave jobs to all the Bulgarians, had seized up, and now the only money was in contraband.

Another person who seemed to do well was the mayor. He was an exuberant character who was appreciated as much for his dancing and his erotic novels as for his political opinions, and he had been a well-loved fixture for many years. But behind his jovial exterior he evidently had operations that no one surmised, for even in this dark era he had managed to buy himself a new villa by the Black Sea. So when it was time for his daughter to marry, everyone looked forward to an extravagant feast at which to drink away their privations.

Boris was seven years old. On the morning of the wedding, Stoyana took him to the mayor's house to wait with the bridal party, where he sat uncomfortably in his new suit and observed the goings-on. Two girls, hardly older than he, ran around with some unaccountable glee. The mayor, dressed up like a battleship coming into port, banged repeatedly on his daughter's door – *Fifteen minutes! Ten minutes!* – while his wife packed bottles of rakia into a box for the party later, weeping all the time and mopping her nose.

The bride's door opened a crack, the bridesmaid's head peeking through it, mouthing some secret need to another woman outside; behind her Boris glimpsed the bride in the mirror, still getting dressed.

A rooster scrabbled in a crate in the corner. Boris knelt by it, his only ally. Its wings were tied and it seemed enraged. Boris put his head close. Its eyes were stupid, with only a dot of presence. He took the bird's beak in his teeth and held it stiffly closed, eye to twitching orange eye, until its stifled struggling pulled it free.

An old lady said,

'I will bring roses for all the guests!'

She grinned at the ceiling.

'The flowers are arranged, Mother. We've already talked about this.'

Boris wondered what you might carry so many roses in. A wheelbarrow? Perhaps you would need a whole truck. But if there were that many, the ones at the bottom—

'They are coming! They are here!'

The girls ran to open the window, and music drifted in from the road. Boris heard it and ran too. *What sounds!* Somebody played clarinet like a painted spinning-top tripping and skipping on the uneven ground of the beating tapan, with kaval and violin leaping overhead. *They have brought Petko Spassov to play at the wedding!* He began to dance like a seven-year-old at the window as the musicians turned the corner and the sounds became louder: he could see the party approaching down below, the bridegroom looking even glummer than usual because of his shaved head, and Petko Spassov himself with black flowing hair holding high his clarinet as he walked.

The mayor banged again at the door.

'They're already here! What's going on?'

Slowly, the door opened. Out came his daughter, stooped, her face behind a veil. The room went limp.

'Oh, my darling girl!'

The mayor looked at her tearfully, his urgency forgotten. He kissed her on the head through the gauze.

'What a day, what a day!' he said.

His wife rushed out of the kitchen, shaking dry her hands, and her tears flowed again at the sight of her daughter in white. The two girls smashed a glass thing with their running round the house.

The bridegroom's party arrived at the foot of the apartment block. There was already a crowd outside, listening and laughing, and the music continued, loud and muffled, up the staircase, the tapan still banging though there was little room for it around the corners. The mayor and his family could hear people opening their doors and clapping on the floors below, while they had fallen silent and stood transfixed by their own front door, shut solid in its frame. The music ascended slowly: there was a long way to climb, and those who played wind instruments blew less vigorously. Then they could hear the crowd on the landing outside, and the music finished, and there were three loud knocks on the door. The mayor began an argument with the party outside, winking at his family with each witticism, *Begone with you! Unless you're a millionaire! She won't go for less!*, with so much laughter, and Boris wishing he were not shut up in this crush.

'He's not only rich, he's handsome. Open the door and see for yourself!'

As soon as the door was ajar, Boris forced himself between the mayor's legs, through the doorway and out into the crowded stairwell.

The musicians waited a few steps down, big Petko Spassov sweating and panting from his climb and the man on the tapan smoking a cigarette.

The violin was held easily like a giant would hold a woman, looking like music already, and deeply wood. Boris looked at it with longing.

'Can I hold it?' he asked.

The man frowned.

'I don't think so, boy. If anyone's going to break it, it should be me.'

Boris clasped his hands behind his back and stared avidly. The strings were like silver electricity lines arching between pylons, and the sky behind.

'It looks old.'

'Eighty years. Look here. *Mihály Reményi, Budapest, 1909*. The best violins were made there.'

'What's your name?'

'I'm Slavo. This is Petko Spassov, the famous clarinettist.'

'I know! I knew who you were as soon as I heard you from the window!'

Boris sang the rushing clarinet line from a cassette someone had made of a Petko Spassov concert. His grandmother loved music, and played these things all the time in the house. The musicians laughed, and Slavo joined in lightly on the violin, his bow bouncing on the strings, Petko clapping and bear-dancing on the spot – but quietly so as not to disturb the merriment of the wedding crowd above: their mock, their hoots, their disputation. The rooster crowed through the middle of it all. Boris finished. Slavo said,

'You sing well. What's your name, boy?'

'Boris.'

The tapan player threw his cigarette butt on to the concrete.

'Come on. Let's go down.'

They set off down the stairs with their instruments, and Boris followed, saying,

'I can sing the whole concert if you like!'

It was a sunny morning. The mayor's Lada was polished and decorated with roses. A few people were waiting for the wedding party to come down. Boris sang more tunes to impress the big musicians.

'Shouldn't you be upstairs with the wedding?'

'I want to stay with you.'

'He *is* one of us,' said Slavo the violinist.

A cart came up the hill, piled high with hay, and Boris read *Yamaha* from the barrel of Petko's clarinet. Birds soared high. The yellow cloud rose from the chemical plant like a ponderous genie.

The wedding party started to emerge from the building. The tapan player banged out a rhythm that fired Petko's instrument into the air, followed behind by the soaring kaval. Slavo joined in.

The guests gathered downstairs, with whistles and mirth. Boris hid while they all got into cars. The mayor directed things, six or eight to a vehicle; doors slammed, neighbours threw flowers, there was a great cheer as the bridal Lada started up, and one by one the cars drove away to the town hall. The remaining neighbours returned to their apartments.

Petko stopped playing, mid-phrase, and wiped his mouth, and once again there was just the sound of the street and the birds. Slavo put his instrument in its case. The musicians had sandwiches and beer. Boris sat down meekly with them.

'Still here, I see,' said Slavo. 'Do you want a sandwich?'

Boris shook his head. He watched them eat. He watched how they were: their beards and the way they talked.

'Does anyone know you're with us?' asked Petko.

'No.'

Boris hummed his own improvisation on an old song, as if he were not aware of it.

They finished eating and packed everything into their van.

'Come on.'

Boris climbed in, and they drove to the hall where the evening party was happening. In the back of the van were their speakers which they carried inside, and Boris followed behind with Slavo's violin, which he held as if it were a fledgling bird fallen from a nest. Some men were laying food out on the tables, and there were decorations on the ceiling. The musicians set up amplifiers and stands and plugged cables into sockets that set off electronic screams. Petko warmed up on his clarinet. Boris sat on the stage kicking his feet. They had offered him a sandwich. He had ridden in their van.

The kaval player stood at the back semaphoring while they adjusted sound levels. There was a lot of time before everyone arrived from the wedding.

A woman put out flowers on the tables. Petko tossed his song with a honey tone, and the fluorescent lights went on. The tapan was like the pounding of the earth through the speakers – it was a beating and a life!

– and there were trestles all along one wall that made a great corridor underneath where a boy could hide away from everything, under the tablecloths, under the dishes and the cakes that the guests would eat; then the kaval player took up his flute and began to play, and all of them joined in the tune, the whole band playing in this empty hall, the arabesque jaunt, the newcomer's flaunt – and he, Boris, in the offbeat, in the heartbeat. The clarinet sang *nar-whal nar-whal* with its elbow-vowels like treasured smells, and over it the silvery lattice of the violin. And Boris thought, *He* is *one of us*.

Boris's grandmother was at first indulgent towards his sudden involvement with the Gypsy musicians. *He is young, and it will pass*, she thought; and she did not prevent him from going every day to that part of town. She did not object to the old violin the Gypsy gave to her grandson, and she listened patiently to his tales of music and learning. She even spoke to others of the remarkable aptitude he showed for his instrument.

But Boris's enthusiasm for the Gypsies began to extend too far. He started to use slang and mannerisms that appalled her. He played nothing but Gypsy music. She said,

'You should spend less time with Slavo. The music you play is all illegal – where will it get you?'

But Boris loved his new teacher, and nothing could keep him away.

Slavo said,

'Now we'll play an hour of our lives.'

He raised his violin and played the things of sixty minutes. The colours, the thought. The unclipped nails, the oval pool of vision. The time, the need, and the sounds that break through from beyond. The book on the fence post. The other person drawing close. The normal emotions, the thing-at-hand, the body's suck and pump.

He did it in a couple of moments, which was another part of the feat.

Boris tried too. To play an hour of his life on his own violin. But he did not know how, and his sound spoke of nothing at all.

Boris was intimidated by Slavo, who was a man where he was only a boy. In the cleft of Slavo's open shirt was a chest of hair hung with chains, and he had manly concerns that sometimes kept him silent and thoughtful for minutes on end. Next to him, Boris felt he did not occupy space adequately or well. While Slavo did other things – while he spoke on the phone, or discussed business with his brother, or simply looked meditatively out into the street – Boris was not sure how to be. He was certain of himself only when he was playing.

Slavo said,

'Let's play a person who looks at an angry crowd. I will play the crowd. You play the person who looks into all the furious eyes.'

At such moments, both of them were entirely involved, and happy.

One day, the chemical plant shut down. Almost everyone worked there. Boris's own father had been a hand there, and most of the men he knew. The plant set the rhythms: the buses came in the mornings to pick people up and drop off those who had worked through the night. And suddenly it closed: the gates were padlocked, the yellow plume disappeared, and with it that omnipresent, tangy smell.

It was remarkable how quickly the town emptied. As it was, people were already on the edge, for wages had not come for months. With the factory gone, the economy immediately seized up: shopkeepers could not buy in supplies, there was no petrol, no beer, no bread. So people locked up their houses, piled together in clanking cars, and set out for the cities. Every evening the diminishing bar talk was of those who had gone and those who had yet to go.

In their frustration, they pulled down the statue of Lenin in the town square. Boris was shocked, for the old man had always pointed to the future, and with his other hand he had gripped his lapel in a permanent way. Now his outstretched arm had broken off, and it was hollow inside, and he lay unclaimed on the ground. Boris wondered whose job it was to clear fallen statues away.

The mayor was among the last to go. All the remaining townsfolk went to the big house to help load trunks and paintings and squawking chickens into his car. The mayor's wife came out first, leading his unhinged brother: Old Petar. Everyone was appalled to see him, the man whom everyone could remember for his feats of physical strength now shuffling like a vacant idiot and leaning on his brother's wife for support.

She sat him in the back of the car among the coats and photographs. The mayor wore his best suit, and shook with grief.

'Goodbye to you all!' he cried. 'Goodbye to our beloved town! Goodbye to these streets!'

He looked around him mightily.

'Fate has spoken, and we have no choice but to bend. I loved you all! I hope you find a place in this godforsaken future! Forgive me! Goodbye to you all!'

He got into the car, wiping his eyes with a handkerchief. The engine jerked to life, and the laden vehicle moved slowly away. Everyone waved. Still driving, the mayor leaned out of his open window, clutching the air and shouting into the wind, 'Farewell! May we meet again!'

Boris's school gathered its eight remaining pupils together for an official closing day. The petrol station closed, the pharmacy, all the restaurants. His last friends departed, and all the faces that had made up his childhood.

Boris went to Slavo's house and found it empty. The whole Gypsy precinct had emptied, in fact, without anyone seeing them go. He broke a window of the house and climbed in; he sat in Slavo's room and sobbed. The man had gone with no acknowledgement or sign. The house was a scene of hurried departure: dirty plates lying on the table, unwanted clothes abandoned on the bedroom floor, an overturned chair, and posters that had been ripped away from the ghost line of their four pinned corners. Slavo had left some records which Boris claimed and took away.

He walked back home through the empty streets, and ran upstairs. He climbed out of his bedroom window, up the drainpipe and onto the sloping, red-tiled roof. Steadying himself against the chimney, he took the records out of their sleeves and spun them angrily into the distance. One by one he flung them, black glinting circles against the sky, spinning too fast for music, and crashing, finally, into pig troughs and lamp-posts and chimneys, all of which had lost their own voices, and made no protest.

Boris's grandmother chose not to leave. 'What will I do in a strange city?' she asked as she paced in the house. 'It's all very well for those who have sons and daughters to show them the way. But my daughter is gone. At least here I know how to survive. I grew up on what I planted and tended, and I can die that way too.'

A few months were enough to clear the place of everyone else, and Boris grew up with Stoyana in the empty town. They cultivated pumpkins and turnips together, and beans and herbs.

Boris looked after the pigs himself, for he enjoyed their company. The sows were tender and knowing, and it was a quiet rapture to share their pregnancy with them every season. He slaughtered the young boars when they reached a year; he cured the meat, and made shoes from the skin. He used the fat for candles and soap.

Stoyana turned quiet. She thought about the dead: for according to the custom, obituaries were put up in the bus shelter on the anniversary of every death; and with the town empty, she assumed this responsibility for all its deceased. In the mornings she wrote out a little account of some departed life or other, and pinned it up – even though there were no longer any buses, or people to wait for them, and her tributes went unseen by human eyes.

She continued to love Boris as before, but her speech had turned inward, and when their work was finished at the end of the day, they sat on the earth together, gazing at the distant hills, and saying nothing.

Boris roamed the strange museum that his town had become. He went into all the houses, and searched through their contents with no sense of trespass, for the lives had been withdrawn that once gave these things their secret pique, and now they lay flagrant and matter-of-fact. He went through drawers of old coins and certificates. He read diaries and letters with innocent curiosity, intrigued, merely by the variety of life. He lay on the double beds of the town's absent couples to see what they had seen as they awoke in the mornings.

The old bookshop became his library, and even as the years curled the pages of its volumes and condemned their facts and opinions to obsolescence, he continued to return there, seeking hopeful pleasures in books he had previously rejected.

Buildings crumbled and grew wind-prone. Trees and animals made their own adaptations to houses. Two trains had stopped in the railway station: they were loaded with steel barrels stencilled with skulls and crossbones, which corroded over the years, and grew over with moss.

Boris became a young man. He masturbated in overgrown gardens or rusting bathtubs looking at pages ripped from histories of art and medical textbooks.

He did not abandon his music.

The chemical factory became his studio. The bare walls and steel surfaces gave his instrument a broad sound, and every day he took his violin there to try new improvisations. In the early days he played cassettes in there, too, listening for inspiration as he lay on the concrete floor looking up at the ranks of pipes – but after some time the town ran out of batteries and surrendered all music except his own. So Boris made his own tunes and styles, angling his mind askew to the world as his Gypsy master had taught him.

Year after year, he sat in the factory playing music. On the vast concrete floor there were smudges where Boris cleared out his ambit in the dust – and in the gloom his violin bow flashed like a sewing machine, steadily stitching his youth.

Beluga

3

IN TBILISI, THE PICTURESQUE CAPITAL of the Georgian Soviet Socialist Republic, it is a cloudless evening near the end of May 1981. Dignitaries are assembled in the banquet hall of the Hotel Iveria, talking light and smoking heavy, collecting in corners in twos and threes, abandoning wives who whisper together and adjust hair. Out of the windows, the Mtkvari River gleams under the sunset, cars circulate idly, ordinary people sit on balconies in the last warmth: and generally the world is lowly, and insensitive to the momentousness of the night. For Leonid Brezhnev is in Tbilisi, and behind these closed doors there is to be a parade of political tenterhooks.

The table is decked with place names as big as licence plates, but no one sits yet, for the guest of honour is not here. And since the room is heavily populated by local party members, the time is given over to mutterings of ill-controlled glee that have little to do with matters of state: for Tbilisi's victory in the UEFA Cup Winners' Cup is not two weeks' old and the memory of those two winning goals sits recent even in party minds. *Dinamo Tbilisi* is still the chant around town, and Gutsaev and Daraselia are national heroes.

There are those who stand at the window above Rustaveli Avenue watching for the limousines of the Moscow contingent, and now they signal the arrival. Ties are straightened and expressions banished. The room holds its pose for an awkward length of time, for the old man is sick and his ascent arduous to this lofty room. At last he arrives, in a party of five, accompanied by the First Secretary of the Georgian Communist Party, Eduard Shevardnadze. He delivers a half-smile to the assembled guests and takes his seat.

Four waiters pour wine. There is a very long silence, embellished only by the trickle of Georgia's finest vintage and the inattentive shuffle of the chief guest, who is looking under the table for a place to comfortably rest his feet.

When all the guests are served, First Secretary Shevardnadze raises his glass and offers a toast. All stand.

'The Georgian Communist Party is honoured to welcome you, Commander Brezhnev, and all the members of the Central Committee. We lay before you all the hospitality our country can offer. Raise your glasses to Commander Brezhnev and to the glorious Communist Party of the Soviet Union!'

The General Secretary drinks falteringly from his glass. He offers some words in response, which fail to rise. 'Invitation' is there, and 'productive'. He is heard to say 'sporting success'; and there is applause from the Georgian nomenklatura.

The waiters begin to bring food. There is every kind of roasted meat, cold chicken and ham, pork shashlik, baked aubergines, garlic potatoes, khajapuri, breads, cheeses, plates of dill and parsley, pickled vegetables, khinkali – and now plates are piled upon plates and others are coming and already there is not one patch of tablecloth visible through the feast that has been stacked up. People begin to eat loudly and with gusto. Toasts are drunk to Georgia and to Comrade Shevardnadze, and wine is flowing freely. The blandness of party members becomes more ardent. After all, Brezhnev is a man assailed by crisis and every grey suit conceals a human chest throbbing with questions. *What will happen?* They bring up Poland – in entirely proper tones, of course – how is the threat being addressed, whether it will be possible to retain the country as a member of the Warsaw (yes) Pact… Other conversations give way to the actual question:

'We would be honoured to hear, Commander Brezhnev, your learned opinion as to the glorious future of socialism.'

Brezhnev is tired and his eyes are full of water. He murmurs a prearranged instruction to a young man at his left, and sucks some wine to clear the dill from his teeth. The young man stands, earnestly impersonal and impeccably suited, with a smile like an American president's. His eyes are grey like the northern sky.

'We have been demanding for several months that the authorities in Poland declare martial law in order to stamp out the counter-revolutionary menace. We have lost much time. The government has been too lenient towards Solidarity, and now has a serious situation on its hands. The lengthy legal procedures for introducing martial law are finally being completed, and I believe that the tide will now turn. But damage has been done among all our neighbours, and we must learn from these events. The Polish people have had too much contact with the West, and from it they have learned the evils of self-interest. It is a salutary lesson for us all.'

There is more than a hint of sadism in the curiosity that stalks the chatter; there are those present who in the excitement of the evening have surrendered themselves to an inconceivable temptation, who have edged beyond the landmass of political prudence in order to prod the fantasy – incredible as it seems – of seeing the leader squirm. They ask about the implications of the bad harvest, the second in a row, and surely a challenge for the entire bloc? There is talk of the cutbacks in oil exports and the resulting disaffection in East Germany, Hungary, Czechoslovakia … A toast to Comrade Chernenko … They discuss the hijacking in Bulgaria, the French election, the Afghan war. *Willi* Brandt and *Ronni* Reagan. They move on to the troubling issue of Romanian debt.

Everything is observed with a combination of disdain and reluctant excitement by a woman with onyx hair who smokes her cigarettes through a holder. She is the wife of a prominent young party member who is currently exchanging glances with her every time Comrade Brezhnev opens his mouth. She claims descent from one of Georgia's ancient royal families and has been known to sign 'Princess' before her name; she admires spirit and excess, and harbours only contempt for the cheap suits, the sycophantism and the cult of impersonality around her.

But this is not like other party gatherings: tonight she senses something unfamiliar that arouses her interest. There is Brezhnev, of course: pathetic absence of a man whose astonishing position in the world is somehow (she has drunk not a little) beautiful and tragic – how can one not be moved by the discrepancy between this wilted figure and his epic office? There is his grey-eyed apprentice, whose razor youth eclipses every other man in the room with body and poise. But there is something else as well. She drinks more, the better to sense it. There is the romance of chaos. The delight of seeing petty men panic over the crisis of their *system*. The tremulous voices that understate cataclysmic things in the name of decorum. But there is still something more, something she has never realised before tonight, something new in the eyes of the party men who now hang on Brezhnev's words with a heady mixture of public fear and private ambition. For the first time, she has seen bloodlust in these bloodless men. It is a revelation. Her spirit rises and she is glad; and there are bloodwings beating in her own organs. While they talk with concerned faces about the spread of the Polish counter-revolutionary contagion, while they drink with unusual gusto out of respect for their Russian guests, she smokes greedily and allows her mind to conjure scenes of stubbled heads banging on the glass wall of the future, giant fronds waving against the sky, and underground seas of lava heaving with grandiose slowness on a fantastic vortex.

Brezhnev announces his departure. It is still early, but the old man needs his rest. The woman is only vaguely aware of the Russians' exit, and yet it is now that the night spills forth. The Georgians drink toasts to their guests in absentia, and review the highlights of the evening's conversation. There are sweaty moustaches still constrained by neckties, and there are the beautiful necks of women. One man sings and another seeks to recruit the gathering to his chant of *Dinamo Tbilisi* and then there is a joke not for the ladies: the men huddle, crouch-headed and wheezy, with the voices low and the sniggers premature, and the story proceeds in fits and starts till he gets to the punch; he stands up broad-faced, shouting, *If I were a gentleman I would marry her!*, laughing laughing crying with cheeks upon the table and even the ebony-haired woman's husband is doubled up, his vodka glass the only vertical part of him. She watches him as time sweeps them into oblong orbits and the senior party members begin to depart. She can drink no more and wants to escape these insignificant men; she demands her coat and wrestles her husband from his stupidity, *Let's go! Let's go!*, and though he is reluctant he hurries after her, grabbing some last ham from the table, wrong-footing down the corridor to the elevator whose attendant smiles, closing the grille, and in the mirror they are green night creatures with shining pitted faces and her folded arms find her own skin above her skirt. They land weightlessly and the grille crashes open and the evening breeze is in the lobby the smell of the river and the city and they flow liquid into the limousine. The night is shut out with the car door and there is only her jealous tussle. She does not even like to make love to this man who is so unromantic in his soul but now, now! she pulls it from him and he is drunk, lost to it, holding the back of the seat fucking on cobbled streets and they are turning corners driver grabbing mirror glances she deep in herself, his tie swinging pestilence in her eyes headlights in his face laughing red in the night city thrusting into the corner and things turn breathing matter circumference diving axis she sees houses shapes depth out of the window they are reaching home now, now! the car stops and stills with engine silent and night seeping into the car and the driver sits endless immobile looking straight ahead as if the loud fucking is not behind his very head and she shouts out,

'Keep driving, you imbecile!'

Nine months later, the woman gave birth to a baby girl, and named her Khatuna.

4

As a young girl, Khatuna loved secret things. She had a secret name for herself that no one else knew. Her mother called her *my treasure*, and she smiled at the notion of a hidden wealth whose value is only to itself. For special occasions she donned outfits that had once belonged to great characters from literature, but she did not reveal their provenance. She liked the secret her mother had told her, that deep down she was a princess.

There was in the house an old box with a lock, which she took for herself. Accessible only with her key, her personal relics could breathe there safely and in silence. The box was of her, yet outside her, and so it offered the prospect of solemn reunions.

When she turned the lock and lifted the lid, the spirits of this box flowed into her. She fingered the objects entombed there: two glass marbles given to her by an important man; an ivory crucifix she had stolen from her mother's bedroom; a picture of a beautiful woman, cut from a magazine; a lock of her own hair, tied up with silk; an instruction booklet for a radio which looked impressively official, like a passport; and a dead beetle of stunning iridescent green, mounted on a glass slide, which she had once asked her father to buy for her in an antique shop.

When she was four years old she gained a baby brother named Irakli. She loved him immediately, and, far from jeopardising her realm of secrets, his arrival promised to double its size and appeal. As he grew old enough to understand, she drew him in under the mantle of her world, revealing to him her secret name and showing off her box of relics. He responded fervently, full of admiration for everything she had worked out during her short head start on earth. He fancied she was another half of himself, carelessly separated before birth, and he plotted how they would be joined again.

She had a blue cloak she sometimes wore that made her walk very upright, with her lips pursed to look like a princess. She also had a blue teddy bear that she endlessly stroked and cuddled. And there was another thing: the pen around which she clenched her early, gawky writing hand was blue.

Observing all this, the young Irakli one day took a brush and painted blue over his penis, in the hope it would become another of her playthings. He ran into her bedroom naked, glistening blue paint daubed even on his stomach and thighs, his blue child's penis wagging with expectation.

Khatuna burst out laughing at the sight; she summoned her mother and the two of them cried with mirth at what he had done, sitting and pointing and saying it again and again. He was ashamed, and hoped they had not uncovered his motives. He relegated the incident to his own realm of secrets, which in his case was not shared with anyone.

Change was overtaking the country, and even their solid family home could not keep it out for ever. There were phone calls late at night, and guns in the house, and groups of men who arrived at odd hours to talk business. On certain days there was nothing to eat. Khatuna's school was destroyed in the civil war, and the city became overrun with beggars and refugees. Until then, she had only read about poor people in books.

Her father took her to a factory. They drove out of Tbilisi with a convoy of men and guns. Her father was the one in charge of these other men: they all looked to him. Guards held the gates open and the cars roared through and skidded to a halt. The factory was silent – and disappointingly small, Khatuna thought, for a factory. Her father stood before the men and made a speech. The men leaned on machine guns for the style of it. The speech was about milk. The applause was thin in this desolate air. They opened champagne and passed around plastic cups for a toast. They went on a tour of the site, Khatuna's father pointing out condensers and explaining freeze-drying, resplendent in the Red Army uniform he had bought for the occasion.

They drove back to Tbilisi. Khatuna said to her father,

'I thought you worked in politics.'

He said,

'Now I make milk. Powdered milk for people to buy. And that's only the beginning.'

Khatuna was impressed. She knew how undependable the world had become, and she admired her father for knowing what to do.

He began to think only about foodstuffs. He read the ingredients on packets and talked about how various things were made, and where, and by whom. He was going to buy more factories: a vegetable canning facility and a plant for bottling water.

There were armed guards at the house, and everywhere they went. The stories Khatuna heard took on a wild edge. Communism had collapsed, and people were selling off the government's chemical weapons on the street. There was a wave of suicides and murders. The electricity would go off for days at a time, and there was no water.

Her father unveiled his new company, which he named after himself. It was a *diversified foods conglomerate*. He carried business cards with his own logo. He invited men to the house who seemed no better than thugs, and whose speech he was forced to censor: *Not in front of my family*. He looked at maps and reports like an anxious general.

But he did not live to see the fulfilment of his plans. Unwittingly, he carried a congenital tissue disease, and he died one afternoon while climbing up to the roof of a building he hoped to acquire; his wasting heart burst from the exertions. His death certificate explained: *Aortic rupture arising from Marfan's Syndrome.*

Khatuna's box of secrets began to look bankrupt. Though she had always kept it locked, something essential had slipped out, and she no longer understood why she saved these things. Why this doubling up? – she had hair on her head, and had no need to hoard it in a box. The beautiful woman from the magazine now looked like a prostitute. The marbles reminded her of dead fish eyes.

She threw everything out – except the crucifix, which belonged to her mother.

She began to keep a diary. Whenever she felt something out of the ordinary, she wrote it down: an account of her eyes in the mirror, a description of a mad old woman shitting proudly in the street, a poem about an uncle she found particularly handsome.

One morning, her periods came. Her mother inspected the situation and marched out of her room proclaiming balefully, *Welcome to the world of women!* Khatuna lay in bed, sticky between her legs, helplessly indignant that her mother might understand her in ways she as yet did not herself.

In his own room, Irakli was also lying in bed. He was awakened by his mother's epochal chant, and, though he did not know what it meant, he felt an icy pain in his throat, and the foreboding that his sister would never again belong to him as she had before.

Khatuna's mother tried to keep control of the freeze-drying plant and all her husband's other ventures, but she was outmanoeuvred by his rivals, who sent a band of nineteen-year-olds with AK-47s to surround the plant.

Her savings vanished rapidly in the inflation. She began to sell things. She had a house full of heirlooms, and though the prices she obtained were derisory, this store of wealth saw her a reasonable way. An antique dealer with international connections had set up in town especially to provide for people like her. She went every week with a ruby necklace or an ancient icon, and he paid her in the new currency.

Then one night five men broke into the house and stole everything she had left. They did not even bother to cover their faces, so she knew who they were. They had come from that same antique shop, whose owner had no doubt grown impatient with buying up her treasure one item at a time.

They herded the family into the corner of the room; they removed paintings and ornaments and stacked them in a van outside. Khatuna's mother was delirious with rage and impotence: she shrieked at them, and spat and flailed.

'Where's the jewellery?' one of them said to Khatuna, ignoring her mother.

'Find it yourself.'

He looked at her, trembling in the corner.

'You're not so young, you know. I can do you right now in front of your mother and brother. So just tell me what I need to know.'

'You don't frighten me.'

He punched her in the face, and her mother screamed.

'Shall I show your little brother how he came into the world? Then I'll send him out of it again with a bullet in his head.'

Khatuna glared at him.

'The chest under my mother's bed.'

Her mother let out an infernal howl while they brought out the chest.

Khatuna said,

'One day you'll regret you ever came here.'

The man looked at her.

'And what? And what?' He put his hand up her nightshirt. 'Shall I take this too?'

She looked defiantly into his eyes. A long moment passed before he removed his hand from between her legs.

The men left the house and started the van, offensively loud in the silent street.

After the losses of that night, Khatuna's mother had to sell the house, and they moved into a single room.

'How do people survive?' cried Khatuna's mother. 'How are they surviving? They should all be dead!'

She began to rely on drink.

Girls followed Khatuna at school, and admired her. She dressed outlandishly, with no respect for fashion, and she led bands of youths to late-night bars, where they ordered one mint water between them. She drank anaemic toasts to her own memories, and described the extravagant scenes of her future, and cackled, and mocked them for their meekness, and told them that everything was illusion.

They listened.

One time she looked at them all in dismay. She said to them,

'You are all so fucking boring.'

Late one winter night, Khatuna walked home through the darkness of another night without power. Shapes clenched and tossed under street-side blankets, too cold for sleep, and occasional cars juddered over the cobbles, cutting brief swaths of rickety light. She pissed in a gutter before entering the building, for inside the toilets were frozen.

In their room, a single candle was burning.

Her mother had passed out with vodka, and snored in her stupor. Her brother's bed shook with agitation. She brought the candle close, and he was shiny with sweaty sleep; his lips looked blue. She desperately shook him awake and wrapped a blanket around him; she broke ice from a bucket and warmed it on the stove. He drank fitfully, and she wiped his face and neck. She gave him some bread. She wept.

'Please get well. I'm sorry for leaving you. Please get well.'

He smiled at her wanly and lay back under the blanket. She stroked his wet hair, and sobbed. Her mother was roused by the commotion.

'What's going on?' she murmured.

Khatuna leapt up, beside herself.

'Your son is delirious from fever! And look at you, knocked out with drink. He could die and you wouldn't even know it!'

Khatuna took a swig from the vodka bottle and emptied the rest in the fireplace.

'You're a worthless woman,' she said. 'You should die.'

Her mother began to cry.

'What can I do? There's no money. I've sold everything. I'm miserable, Khatuna. Be nice to me.'

Khatuna seized her relic box from the corner and unlocked it with the key she still kept around her neck. She took out the ivory crucifix and threw it at her mother.

'Why don't you sell this?'

Her mother fingered it blankly.

'I thought I had lost it.'

'No. I took it from you. That's why it isn't sold yet.'

Her mother moaned into the pillows.

'Stop it!' cried Khatuna. 'This self-pity. Find yourself a man like everyone else. Someone to pay for your vodka and your son's medicine.'

She stared at her mother.

'Don't worry yourself about us anymore. I'll take responsibility for Irakli and me. You just look after yourself. See if you can.'

After that, Khatuna burned all her diaries. She had written regularly, and had filled a large stack of notebooks. She put them on the fire one by one, her mind becoming strangely void.

She got a promotional job with a foreign tobacco company. They gave her an outfit in the colours of a cigarette brand, and she stood by the Philharmonia in the evenings offering free cigarettes to passers-by. She was attractive and flirtatious, and people liked to take her cigarettes: she promised 'Best Brand in the World!' as she exhaled gaily.

Men stopped to talk, and she moved them on. 'Take another for your girlfriend!' she shouted after them.

The job did not interfere with school, and gave her a little money to stave off disasters. The company was satisfied with her performance.

Her mother sold her long black hair to a wig maker. Khatuna thought it was a bid for sympathy, and offered no reaction when she saw her mother's shaved head. Instead she asked,

'Did you sell that crucifix?'

'Yes.'

'How much did you get?'

'Three bottles of vodka.'

Khatuna spat in her mother's face.

One spring evening, Khatuna was standing with her tray of cigarettes outside a bar on Perovskaya Street. The bar was named Beluga. Young playboys were out, with Gucci sunglasses for the darkness and models for each arm. There were man-hugs and back-slaps, and car keys rapped on glass when bouncers took too long to unlock doors. Eye make-up sparkled in the nightlights, and men dealt kisses on practised cheeks. A taxi clattered around the potholes, and three girls climbed out, singing together,

You're just too good to be true.
Can't take my eyes off of you.
You'd be like Heaven to touch.
I wanna hold you so much…

A black Mercedes drew up, spilling bodyguards. A man got out with velvety movements, lithe in a suit and T-shirt, and Khatuna was surprised to see that it was Kakha Sabadze, the footballer-turned-tycoon. He was unmistakable, for his face was disfigured by a wine-red birthmark in the shape of Australia.

'What's he doing in a place like this?' she wondered.

Kakha Sabadze was one of Georgia's richest men. Before Khatuna was born he had already been a famous footballer who had played for Dinamo Tbilisi, and for the USSR in the World Cup. They used to call him *legendary*, when the word still had a depth of meaning. When communism fell, Sabadze became Minister for Sports, and made himself rich selling Georgian football players to foreign clubs. He left behind politics for business. Now he owned an oil company, several mines and a chain of hotels, and he had a monopoly on the import of Mercedes cars into Georgia. He was chairman of the national airline. His nephew ran a television company and his daughter was the country's leading model.

Kakha Sabadze walked past Khatuna with his men all around and she held out a cigarette.

'Would you like to improve your life, Mr Sabadze?'

He stopped.

'My life is already perfect. What can you offer?'

'Marlboro. Best cigarette in the world.'

'I don't smoke. I take care of my health.'

Khatuna looked at him patiently.

'I know how rich you are. But at your age, youth must be more exciting than money. Every time you talk to a woman as young as me, you must think of what you can never buy.'

'I'm not so old!' He laughed for his men. 'And I know a lot of women as young as you.'

'Passing through your life, in and out of your bed. Do you remember it after it's over, Mr Sabadze?'

'What does that mean?'

'Look into my eyes. The moon is full tonight, and you have met a beautiful Georgian woman. Wouldn't you like to remember how it feels? Smoke one of these world-famous cigarettes and you can inhale this moment so it will never go away. It will stay with you and keep you young.'

Kakha Sabadze laughed again.

'Do they tell you to say these things?'

He took a business card from his pocket.

'I don't want your world-famous cigarette. But here is my card. You can call me and we'll talk.'

'I'm very disappointed.'

'What's your name?'

'Khatuna.'

'Khatuna. Call me.'

And he disappeared into Beluga with his bodyguards, while Khatuna stood on the sidewalk staring at the business card in her hand. A little paper miracle.

5

KAKHA'S HOUSE WAS LARGE AND NEW, and set back from the street. When Khatuna arrived there, she found him in the kitchen, talking on the phone.

His movements were easy, and his birthmark less ruddy up close. She appreciated the smooth economy of his kitchen, the steely surfaces opening onto dishwashers and ovens.

She wandered out into the hallway. A bodyguard sat there reading a paperback. There was a giant framed photograph of Kakha Sabadze from the football days, standing with a trophy, a mass of tousled hair and a blue-eyed gleam of boyish achievement. Pairs of shoes were lined up neatly; in the corner stood a small tree planted in a yellow oil drum. A staircase wound up out of sight.

She heard the end of Kakha's conversation.

'Step outside your house in three minutes. A black Audi will come to pick you up.'

She went back into the kitchen and found him sitting at the table with two glasses of beer. She sat down with him.

'You're still selling cigarettes?' he said.

'World-famous. Yes.'

'Are you going to do that all your life?'

'I'm going to travel all over the world. I'll have a big house and another for my brother too, so he doesn't get into trouble. I'll drive a Mercedes and wear big diamonds on my finger.'

'How are you going to make all that money?'

'Business. I'll make loads of money in business. When I'm really rich I'll study architecture and rebuild Tbilisi.'

'What *is* this fabulous business of yours?'

Kakha spoke lightly, with a smile on his face.

Khatuna said,

'I'm still working it out. I haven't got all the answers yet.'

'Do you think today's your lucky day?'

She glanced at him severely.

'I'm not here to sleep with you,' she said. 'With that stain on your face you won't seduce me, no matter how rich you are.'

They drank their beer, and he said,

'Come on. I want to show you something.'

They got into the car. Bodyguards fanned out around the entrance while they reversed into the street.

'Where are we going?' asked Khatuna.

'My house.'

'I thought *this* was your house?'

He laughed. 'This is just for storage. It's temporary, while my house is being built.'

They drove up into the hills behind the old city, nearly to the television tower. Khatuna loved his car, which took no account of how steep the roads were. On top of a generous outcrop were the dilapidated outer walls of an old castle.

'*This* is my house'

He called from his phone. The gate opened, and they drove through into a courtyard.

Inside the ancient walls, the main building stood straight and thickset. There was a massive front door and windows with steel shutters.

'The building is completely new. We pulled down the old fort and saved the bricks. We built the most advanced security installation in Georgia, then we put the medieval bricks on the façade so it looks just like it always did.'

There was a tower on one side of the house, with a steep conical roof like on the old churches.

'The doors are explosive-proof steel, and there'll be a new perimeter wall, four metres high, with electric fencing, cameras, the lot. It will be totally secure. I have a shipment of Rottweilers arriving soon from Russia. There's a man called Sergei in a shitty small town outside Moscow who trains the best guard dogs in the world.'

They walked around the building. From inside came the sound of saws and drills. They ran into two men smoking together; Kakha introduced them.

'This is my cousin, Vakhtang. And our architect from Moscow Vladimir.'

The ground was wet and hacked. Hundreds of Corinthian pillars were piled up on tarpaulins.

'We'll clean all this up,' said Kakha. 'We'll landscape everything, put in trees and grass, make it look really good.'

'It will look really good,' confirmed Vakhtang, who had the build of a weightlifter.

'Vladimir is the best there is,' said Kakha, putting his hand on the architect's shoulder. 'Ask him to tell you all the things he's done. He's just built that new casino everyone's talking about. My young friend here, Khatuna, she's interested in architecture.'

Vladimir bowed. He said,

'What do you think of our castle?'

'It's beautiful. It's like old Tbilisi.'

'It's *just* like old Tbilisi. Mr Sabadze was very clear on this point. The proportions, the materials, the mouldings, the angles of the arches – they've all been taken from medieval Georgian architecture. Have you seen the interior?'

'No.'

'Let me show you. Come.'

Inside, men were laying a marble floor, and the place was raw and empty. A mosaic portrait of Kakha Sabadze had already been set into one wall of the main room – the backdrop, it appeared, to a future waterfall. Chandeliers hung prematurely from the ceiling, their wires trailing to the floor. Vladimir walked in front, commenting on the construction-in-progress, while Kakha Sabadze followed on, speaking on the phone.

'This room has been designed to show off Mr Sabadze's art collection. You probably read about the two Warhols he just bought. We'll hang them here. Over there is the gym. Then the billiard room and bar. The other side: the study. Gold walls and leather floor. Completely soundproof.'

'Amazing,' said Khatuna.

'The entire installation is served with custom internet and phone lines directly from the backbone. The lines come in underground to a bunker in the basement. The place has its own water reservoir and electricity generator. Mr Sabadze wanted to make something that would last a thousand years.'

They went upstairs. Vakhtang, was running madly through the bare corridors, dribbling a football. He scored a goal against the wall and exploded with his own awe, like eighty thousand people.

'Master bedroom,' Vladimir indicated.

Inside, workmen were fixing gold pillars into the four corners of the room. In the middle of the main wall was a tall window surrounded by a border of stained glass. It had been designed to frame the enormous aluminium statue of the Mother of Georgia higher up on the hill.

'Every morning, that statue will be the first thing Mr Sabadze sees. He has a strong affection for her. He feels she is a personal talisman.'

Khatuna went close to the window and looked down. She saw a muddy hole the size of a small house. There was a length of hose pipe in the bottom, and a rainbow of oil slick, and two crows pecking at a plastic bag. The future swimming pool.

'Khatuna. Come here.' Kakha Sabadze was standing in the doorway. 'Come with me.'

She followed him down the corridor, which opened out into a large hall. The outer wall was a sweeping semicircular window as if for air traffic control, and there, spread out below, was the city.

'This is what I wanted you to see,' he said.

'All Tbilisi,' she murmured.

She tapped the glass absent-mindedly with her knuckle.

'Bulletproof,' he said softly.

Just below them were the tiled roofs, ornate balconies and winding streets of the old city, sloping down towards the river. She could see into ramshackle courtyards, where boys and girls kicked footballs and washing hung low between the houses. Far away she could see groups of apartment towers, flecked with the royal blue of tarpaulin.

'When I was at school,' said Kakha Sabadze, 'we were taught the general story of the world: feudalism is replaced by capitalism, and capitalism is replaced by socialism, and then history ends. And look at this: socialism has gone, and here is Kakha Sabadze standing in his castle looking down on all the peasants.'

He seemed to find it very amusing. He said,

'Come to Moscow with me next week.'

'Why?'

'You speak nicely, you look good. I'm sure there are things you could do for me.'

'Are you offering me a job?'

'If that's how you'd like to see it.'

'It has to be something real. I'm not going to be your mistress.'

Kakha looked at her appraisingly.

'Why don't you start by furnishing my house? You like buildings: get the plans from Vladimir and take charge of the interior. Since you want a challenge, I'll give you the whole job. Let me see how capable you are, behind all that talk.'

During the five days she spent in Moscow, Khatuna put somewhere close to thirty-nine million roubles on Kakha Sabadze's credit cards.

On her last night in the city, he took her for a drink in a bar behind Novy Arbat, not far from the Kremlin. Bodyguards waited outside, their bulging jackets zipped to their chins. The waitress who led them to their table was the whitest woman Khatuna had ever seen, her pallor accentuated with dark pink lipstick and an immense black wig with ringlets.

They talked about the things Khatuna had purchased for Kakha Sabadze's house. He quizzed her about each item, and she explained how she had arrived at her decisions. She described the antique Turkish rug she had found for his study, and the crystal chandelier she was putting in the reception room.

He nodded approvingly.

'You've thought of everything.'

Her face shone with excitement. She had put on heavy make-up, a 'K' written in eyeliner on her cheek.

The bar was maroon and gold, and there was a florid painting on the ceiling, showing palaces, clouds and angels. Businessmen and politicians mingled with models and film stars, and the air swirled with church incense and cigar smoke.

Their wine arrived with caviar. She clinked his glass with her own.

'To Georgia,' she said.

He smiled and drank.

'To women,' he proposed, raising his glass.

'To feelings.'

'To God.'

'To Stalin.'

Khatuna held out her glass for more wine, and said,

'To secret dreams.'

Fashion TV was showing on the walls, and the latest Russian club hits played just loud enough to ruffle the atmosphere. She smoked her slim cigarettes, and everything felt perfect. She liked being with this strong man.

'What do you do, Mr Sabadze? I can't imagine how you spend each day.'

He talked about his business. He had just returned from a military trade fair in Johannesburg, and he talked about strongrooms, interrogation aids and perimeter protection systems. He described the latest innovations in armoured vehicles and surveillance. He spoke easily, but without giving anything away.

Khatuna said,

'I heard you like art.'

Kakha's face lit up.

'Fantastic,' he said. 'There are these new artists who totally mess up your head. I have a woman in New York who buys for me and educates me bit by bit; you have no idea how sophisticated these people are. I wish some of our Georgians would understand: they're like children, drinking and squabbling all the time. They don't know what it means to do something well. I'm just a dumb sportsman myself, but I want to learn about everything.'

Khatuna said,

'You're more serious than people think. You remind me of my father. He died when I was a child. He was a bit like you.'

A waiter brought more caviar. The DJ nodded in a glass booth, headphones against one ear. There was a mezzanine for models, and Khatuna gazed up at a woman on display there, admiring her breasts, her gestures, her dramatic make-up.

'Look at her. She's so beautiful!' Khatuna said.

Kakha Sabadze glanced up neutrally.

'She's a TV hostess. Her father's a general in the army.'

The ceiling spotlights pricked Khatuna's retinas, and black patches swam over Kakha Sabadze's face as she watched him. She said,

'I'm so happy tonight. But happiness isn't real. Don't you think? Happiness is fleeting. When I'm unhappy I want to be happy, but when I'm happy I get tired of this happiness because it is only illusion.'

She was feeling drunk, and the obsequious waiter made her laugh. She said,

'I used to take heroin. When you take it you have everything: you have wife, husband, lover – you are king and queen. But it's a mirage, and it vanishes.'

'There are some things that are real, Khatuna. Land is real. Loyalty is real.'

She sighed. She said,

'One day I will make a perfect bar like this, with perfect design and Fashion TV on every wall. Beauty gives you harmony. It makes you a perfect person.'

This was the mood she was looking for in her life. This security. She felt as if she were in a luxurious, velvet bomb shelter. She looked down at her own legs under the table, and she wished others could see how sexy they were, crossed like that with her shoe swinging from her toes.

‘Dying for another person, that is real,’ said Kakha Sabadze. ‘Would you ever die for someone?’

‘Of course,’ she said. ‘I’m the most loyal person you will ever meet. I will do anything for the people I love.’

He sipped his wine, watching her. She said,

‘You and I are real, Mr Sabadze. The emotion we have at this moment is real. Everything else is just footnotes. If you cannot generate emotion you are just a big hole. Don’t you agree?’

He said quietly,

‘Don’t call me *Mr Sabadze*.’

The bar was decorated like a fantasy from tsarist times. The mezzanine was gilt, like an old theatre balcony, and the walls were ornamented with plaster lyres, and urns overflowing with fruit. There was a frenzy to the laughter, and the beat of the music was remote.

‘This place is like the end of the world,’ said Khatuna. ‘You could slit a waiter’s throat and he would thank you for it. Then apologise for the mess.’

‘It’s a millionaire’s club.’

Khatuna said,

‘I’ve always been surrounded by juveniles. Teenagers without a car between them. I didn’t realise how sick of it I was until now.’

She told him stories of her friends. A good-looking boy who played in a band but had no ambition. Her friend Tako, who slept with older men in return for clothes and parties, and always talked about the same things. Kakha was staring at her, and he said,

‘Your eyes are so blue.’

The models on Fashion TV walked up and down, up and down. Khatuna leaned towards Kakha.

‘When I want to learn something about myself I look at my eyes in the mirror. I always discover something new.’

The candlelight showed up the fingerprints on their wineglasses. Their faces were close together.

‘With all this wine I’ve drunk,’ said Khatuna, ‘I don’t even notice your wine-coloured stain. You look almost handsome.’

She felt Kakha's foot against hers under the table, but she could not be sure: perhaps it was an accident.

'I always see the hidden meaning in things. I'm very sensitive. If someone is not aware of those things I break off contact with them.'

He was talking too, but she did not know what he was saying any more. She watched his expensive suit, how it clung to his shoulders, and the rings flitting on his fingers. Sometimes he left such great silences between his sentences that she wanted to dive in there and thrash about, blowing herds of bubbles.

Kakha's inexpressive face was not so at all. It was just restrained. If you focused on it too much, the other conversations became an unbearable din.

The night wheeled, and she hardly noticed him pay the bill. He was standing up, putting her coat around her shoulders. At another table, a man looked at her lustfully, and Khatuna realised it was somebody she had seen in the newspapers.

'I love this song,' she said as they left. 'You listen to this track at seven in the morning when you have no energy and you feel connected to the world. You can estimate the pleasure.'

Kakha's Moscow apartment was not far away, and the trip took only a few minutes. Khatuna fell asleep in the car. Upstairs, Kakha pulled off her shoes and she said dreamily,

'I'll introduce you to my brother. He's a lovely boy.'

He locked the door of the bedroom and turned off the light. She heard him undressing, and he lay down next to her.

'I had the best evening,' she said.

The wine was rushing in her ears.

He tried to kiss her, but she said, 'You're crazy' and turned away.

6

IRAKLI REMEMBERED THE BABY SPARROW he had found when he and Khatuna were children.

It fell out of a nest onto the pavement outside their house, and he picked it up and fed it. When Khatuna saw what he was doing, he said,

'If I take care of it, it will grow feathers and sing like all the other sparrows.'

'You can see red veins through its skin. It's disgusting.'

When it was time for the evening meal, Irakli took the bird to show his mother. She said,

'Leave that thing outside. And wash your hands!'

He tried to reason with her. It was getting cold, and the bird needed constant feeding. But she would not let him bring it in the house, and it was locked out for the night.

In the morning, the bird was stiff and dry. There was a drop of blood under its beak and, as Irakli watched, an ant scurried out from under a stubby wing.

Irakli might have blamed his mother for the bird's death, but he realised she was only the instrument. His true resentment was reserved for the order of things, which made the divisions between sleep and wake, human and animal, inside and outside – divisions through which a defenceless bird might fall to its death.

Irakli never ceased to find it strange that he should be stuck in *this* place, with *these* people, when there were a million other ways it could have been. Why had he been born now, and not in another era? By what chance had he come to be poor and not rich, a man and not a woman? Life seemed nothing more than a series of improbable accidents, and yet everyone had a sense – didn't they? – that there was something else, deeper and prior, to which they had to return.

Irakli chose for his associates people who set no store by the way the world had fallen out. He sought a truer place, and he paid little attention to his body, or his food, or anything else that was merely accidental. He harboured an unhappiness about reality – and he wrote poetry, because straight talk could not capture what he meant.

Khatuna was in Kakha's Mercedes, returning from a meeting, when she saw Irakli out of the window.

'Stop the car!' she said. 'That's my brother!'

The car stopped and her bodyguard jumped out warily. Khatuna opened the window and called to Irakli.

'Let me give you a ride!' she said. 'Where are you going?'

'Nowhere,' he said. He didn't get in the car. He looked thin and scruffy and had a newspaper under his arm.

The afternoon was warm – hot, even, for autumn – but Khatuna's bare arm on the sill had goose pimples from the car's air conditioning.

'Get in!' she said, and he did so. The car moved away. Irakli said,

'Is that a new haircut?'

'Do you like it?'

'You look like a gangster's girlfriend.'

Khatuna was irritated. They drove up Rustaveli Avenue, and she directed the driver to pull up in front of the old Marriott.

'I'm not going in there,' said Irakli. 'We can go somewhere else. We can go for a walk if you like.'

He set off along the street.

'What's wrong with you?' she called. 'Why do you want to traipse around out here?'

'I can't afford to go into places like that.'

'If you earned some money, you wouldn't have to worry.'

'I have money. You give me enough money. What else do I need? All I need is to think and write my poetry. I don't need to go to places where you pay a month's salary for a coffee.'

‘*Poetry*.’ Khatuna scowled. ‘Where’s your self-respect? Look at your clothes. Look at the state of your hands. I feel sick looking at them.’

‘You and I are exactly the same, it’s just that you get handouts from a gangster.’

‘I work hard for my money. And he’s not a gangster.’

‘There are thousands of Georgian women in other countries who pay for your coffees with their legs in the air.’

‘Don’t be gross, Irakli. Have some respect. All your money comes from Kakha.’

‘Everything he has, he’s stolen. That money was never his in the first place. Do you think I should be grateful?’

‘Kakha is a businessman. He loves this country, and he loves Georgians. He’s a role model. He has the best security forces. Without him there’d be no law and order in this place. There would be pure chaos.’

‘You’d better be careful. People like Kakha kill each other for no reason at all. Think about what you’re doing. You’re becoming frantic: you go from one thing to the next, and you never stop to think.’

A girl approached them selling roses, and Irakli bought two for his sister. They crossed Freedom Square and headed down Leselidze Street. Khatuna said,

‘One day I’d like to sit down and read lots of books. When I’ve lived this life and come back in another era I’ll teach myself a lot of things. I’ll learn about anthropology and economics. History, literature, philosophy, politics. Science. But how would that help me now?’

Irakli was studying her.

‘Your list,’ he said, ‘was in alphabetical order. Anthropology, economics, history… What are the chances of that? Every new word you added I was waiting for you to spoil it.’

Khatuna said,

‘Don’t you have a girlfriend to give roses to?’

He led her into a shop. A naked bulb hung down, illuminated for the late afternoon gloom.

‘No. A lot of girls like me, though.’

There was barely space to stand between the sacks of onions and potatoes on the floor. The shopkeeper was adding up a bill on an abacus. Irakli said,

'Do you want some coffee?'

She shook her head, and he picked out a single sachet of Nescafé. She said,

'Why can't you buy a whole jar like everyone else?'

They passed a couple of collapsed buildings, the gutted interiors piled high with fallen roof tiles.

'A jar is a long-term investment. You never know what will happen tomorrow.'

She looked sullen.

'I wish you would live better.'

'If I had ten million lari I would still live like this.'

He became inexplicably joyful, and Khatuna let herself relax. When he was happy he could make her laugh like no one else. They walked for a long time, crossing a bridge and coming down on the opposite bank of the river. She told him stories of Kakha, and people she had met. They passed a band of young men who were burning rubber to light up the encroaching evening. They had tied the tails of two dogs together, and were watching them for their entertainment.

Darkness came, and they walked on. Old people were begging in the shadowy doorways, or peeling sunflower seeds to sell. There were shops of second-hand clothes, old theatres converted into antique stores, and stalls for currency trading. They came to a freight depot where policemen inspected the contents of trucks, and men queued at the side of the highway waiting for night labour. There were stalls set up, lit by bulbs wired to car batteries, where people sold electrical components and construction materials, sinks, piping and cleaning fluids. Cabbages and potatoes were sold out of oil drums standing in the mud. A man gave his chickens water to drink out of a jam jar. Children chased each other around the stalls, and taxi drivers killed time by their line of Ladas, shaking their heads at the young man who was trying to sell a Coke bottle full of diesel fuel. Families were leaving at the end of the day, parents and children, their possessions piled up in old baby carriages.

Irakli and Khatuna arrived at a damp huddle of apartment blocks. The children's swings had lost their chains, and were just a skeleton of rusted poles where a group of teenagers were nevertheless gathered, burning polystyrene with bitter, lung-stopping smoke. It was dark now, and the green of the flame tinged their pale skin.

'Where have you brought me?' Khatuna asked.

'I've come to see some friends,' Irakli said.

Khatuna looked uneasy.

'I left the driver outside the Marriott. I didn't even tell him where I was going.'

'You can call him later.'

They entered an apartment block and started up the stairs.

'Can you see?' asked Irakli.

It was pitch dark, and Khatuna didn't like to touch the handrail.

'Just stick behind me,' said Irakli. He climbed quickly.

'How much further?' Khatuna asked.

'They're on the twelfth floor.'

They climbed until Khatuna was out of breath. Irakli stopped on a landing and lit a match.

'Two more,' he said, setting off again.

A door opened to a strip of candlelight, and a man threw his arms around Irakli, cigarette glowing in his mouth. Inside, the room was crowded, people sitting where they could.

'This is my sister, Khatuna,' announced Irakli.

In the middle of the room were two low candles, which threw their glow over a cluster of empty beer cans and bottles.

'She's good looking, your sister. And well dressed.'

'Are you sure she's your sister?'

'She's a rich girl who pays Irakli for sex.'

'She'll never use him again after he's brought her here.'

Someone got off the only chair and offered it to Khatuna, laughing.

'So many of us are living here, and we only have two rooms. We take turns with the love room. Sometimes we have to wait all night.'

'Have something to drink.'

'We're not used to chic people. We're all bums.'

'Give us more light! I want to see Irakli's sister.'

They lit more candles. Above their heads was a clothes line, where underwear hung. Firewood was piled in the corner. There was a television on a plastic stool and an Uzbek carpet hanging on the wall. In one corner, the ceiling had collapsed, and the beams were propped up by the wardrobe. Someone handed Khatuna a bottle.

'Give her a glass, you bum.'

Khatuna sat down in her coat, her arms crossed defensively.

'You must be proud of your brother,' someone said. 'He's so talented.'

'We all admire him.'

'We carry his poetry around with us.'

'Someone just gave me that poem with the long title. "The eloquence of a drunkard's hands when his mouth has stopped producing speech." I read it yesterday. It's beautiful.'

'I like to read your poems at night, Irakli, so my mind subsides.'

'At night you're so drunk, my friend,' said Irakli. 'You could read Shevardnadze's speeches and your mind would subside.'

'I love Irakli's poems. They remind me of feelings I've forgotten.'

'Stop it,' said Irakli. 'I feel ashamed you've read those terrible old poems. I get a cold sweat when I think of them.'

They drank. They talked about the taxi driver who had just been caught trying to cross the border into Turkey with a lead box full of enriched uranium. The female doctors who made up their income by sleeping with their patients. The twenty-year-olds driving million-lari Maybach cars. The rise of prayer and miracles, now that everything else was exhausted.

'How about you, Khatuna? Where do you steal clothes like that?'

'I don't steal. I work for Kakha Sabadze.'

There was a moment of silence.

'What does that mean? Have you met him?'

'Almost every day.'

'What's he like?'

'Is it true he never sleeps?'

Everyone was looking at Khatuna except for Irakli, who was lying on the floor with his eyes closed.

'He's the most wonderful man I've ever met.'

'He's the biggest criminal in Georgia. How can you work for him?'

Khatuna gave an exasperated sigh.

Someone said,

'Half the Georgian women in foreign brothels, Kakha Sabadze has sold them. Don't you feel ashamed?'

'How can you go near a man like that?'

'You should take advantage of your situation. Put poison in his drink.'

Khatuna retorted,

'Look at you all, living in this cesspit! At least Kakha Sabadze can hold his head up. He's a Georgian who works hard and doesn't just sit all day playing video games in the arcades. You're all losers – that's why you hate him.'

'Why is there nothing to do in our country except play video games? It's because of criminals like Kakha Sabadze who suck everything out of this place and leave nothing for anyone else.'

Khatuna said,

'There are some people who have to do a thing perfectly; it's an obsession with them. They may do it five times, ten times, it doesn't matter. In the end they set the standard so high that no one else can come close. Kakha Sabadze is like that.'

'Does he line the people up against a wall? So he can kill them five times, ten times?'

Khatuna snorted contemptuously.

'If you're ambitious you have to offend others. Sometimes you have to kill. That's life. In Georgia, if you don't fight for what you want, you won't get anything.'

There was silence. Irakli still lay with his eyes closed, and a woman studiously tore her cigarette packet into little squares. Breeze made the candles shiver, and someone quoted an old Russian poem:

That was when the ones who smiled
Were the dead, glad to be at rest.

Khatuna was frustrated. She said,

'Where's the bathroom?'

'It's there,' someone said, pointing. 'You can't use the toilet because the plumbing doesn't work. Use the bowl on the ground if you want.'

'Every morning we have to carry that thing down twelve floors to empty it.'

Everyone was staring expectantly at Khatuna. She said to Irakli,

'Get me out of here.'

He opened his eyes and looked at her.

'We have to leave,' she said.

The taxi rattled over the cobbles, and Khatuna was shouting.

'Are these the people you spend your time with? Infected losers floating in their own shit? Stealing whatever they have? It's disgusting that you're around those people.'

'Calm down, for God's sake. They're just ordinary people, like you and me.'

He sat forward in his seat, staring into the dim horizon of the car's headlights. The two men in front were silent. A few nightclubs were still running, but most of the city was shut up. Khatuna said,

'Our family was rich! We had everything taken away, we were humiliated, Irakli, do you remember that? – and now you're wallowing in poverty and dirt as if you loved it. I won't let you. I'm going to set us right again.'

In the distance Irakli saw a white horse lying by the side of the road, its head erect, watching the traffic. He squinted through the night: it was a glorious, miraculous beast, its coat as bright as cocaine, its mane billowing in the breeze. Then, as the car drew close, Irakli realised it was no horse, just a man in white overalls lying on his back by the side of the road, one knee crooked, which had made the head.

They arrived home.

Inside, their mother was asleep in an armchair. A candle was burning but the lights and television were all on, for the power had come back since she passed out. The room smelled bad.

'Do you want anything to drink?' asked Irakli, putting water on the stove.

'No.'

Khatuna switched off the television and stood looking at her mother. She had become painfully thin, and her face had gone slack.

Irakli brought a bowl of steaming water, took his Nescafé sachet from his pocket, and stirred it in.

'Did you see what I did?' He pointed to the ceiling, where he had hung a string of plastic ivy. 'Doesn't the room look better?'

She sat down on the mattress, her hands between her thighs for warmth. She said more calmly,

'I worry about you. That's why I get worked up.'

'Mother is the one you should be worried about.'

Irakli sipped his coffee in silence. Khatuna looked out of the window at the web of washing lines criss-crossing the courtyard, where shirts waved dimly in the night. Two pigeons were nestled close on the windowsill. She said,

'You know something strange about Moscow? The pigeons are twice the size of ours. The sparrows too. They're fat like you can't believe.'

There was no reply, and she turned away from the window. He seemed so alone on the sofa, so unprotected. She got up and put her arms around him, and held him for a long time.

7

THE YEAR WAS CHANGING to the next millennium, and Kakha organised a party in his new house.

Khatuna arrived early. A DJ was testing the sound in the bar, and disco lights were laid out on the floor. Security guards searched the bags of the women who had been hired for the evening.

Vakhtang, Kakha's cousin, was already dressed up, his hair slicked back, head-jerking to every ten-second burst of music coming from the sound check. He was short and had enormous muscles. He said to Khatuna,

'Have you seen the size of those speakers? This party is going to make some *noise!*'

And he raised his hands above his head and twisted his face into a silent scream of dance-floor ecstasy.

Then he remembered something serious.

'There's no sauna in this house. I thought you would have put one in.'

'No,' she replied. 'That was never in the plan.'

'Oh.' He looked crestfallen. 'When you have as much money as Kakha your house should have a sauna.'

He did some heavy hip hop moves which ended with a mock punch to Khatuna's jaw. He asked,

'So are you his girlfriend now?'

'No.'

'But you *do*—'

He simulated sex with his fingers.

Khatuna did not respond. Vakhtang pursued it.

'He really likes you, right?'

'I guess.'

Vakhtang said solemnly,

'You should get together with him. It would be an achievement for you.'

Khatuna went up to Kakha's bedroom. He had just arrived back from a trip to London, and was unpacking. He smelled of perfume, and his hair was wet. A big Rottweiler sat in the corner, eyeing Khatuna with a low growl.

'Don't worry,' Kakha said. 'He'll get used to you.'

He stroked the dog's head reassuringly.

'It's such a pleasure having him around. I've got fifteen of them, but this one stood out from all the rest. You should see him run.'

She sat on the bed. She was touched by how neatly he had folded his clothes. On the wall he had mounted an icon of Mary, and a football in a glass case. Above the bed were two modern paintings of medicine cabinets and skulls.

'Was it nice?' she asked, lying back and looking up at the seashell chandelier. 'In England?'

'They love meeting me,' he said. 'It's very exciting for them. They're all so bored in that country.'

He gave her a Gucci shopping bag, full of tissue paper.

'I got this for you.'

She took out the tissue and found a blue dress with a low-cut bodice and an extravagant crepe skirt.

'These shoes go with it,' he said, handing her another bag. 'I thought you could wear them for the party.'

She took them into the bathroom. The air was steamy, and the gold jacuzzi still pebble-glassed with water. There were mirrors on the ceiling and all four walls, and as she changed there were countless other Khatunas putting on Gucci dresses and shoes. She went back out into the bedroom.

'Fantastic,' said Kakha.

She kissed him on the cheek.

She said,

'Mostly I influence other people: my friends always told me I was a big influence on them. But you have influenced me. You've shown me what it is to be ambitious.'

She sat back on the bed.

'All this time you've been away, I see other men and they're nothing more than a cupboard or a chair.'

He looked at her for a while. He said,

'You have to understand: my life is different. Tonight my house is full of people I can't trust, and any of them could kill me. That's how it is.'

She was drinking Nemiroff from the bottle by his bed.

'I know you're brave,' she said.

'No. The reason I'm still alive is because I'm constantly afraid. I'm afraid of everyone – I'm afraid of you. I analyse everything. *Why did she come half an hour early? Why did he stop for petrol?*'

He took the bottle from her and had a swig.

'The moment I stop being afraid, it's over.'

He chose a suit from the closet and laid it on the bed.

'You haven't been exposed to this. If you get involved with me I won't be able to shield you anymore. You'll need protection, surveillance, all kinds of inconvenience. Not every young woman wants that.'

His phone was ringing, but he ignored it. He said,

'I can't stop thinking about you, Khatuna. I've not stopped thinking about you all the time I've been away. I want to have you near me. But it would mean a lot of changes for you.'

He was pacing in the room. The party music had started downstairs, and a regular beat came through the floor. Through the window, laser lights reached towards the stars, and the illuminated statue of the Mother of Georgia was like a smudge in the night.

'Anyone can see how much you love your brother, and that would become a weak spot for me. People could put pressure on you by threatening him. We might need to have him watched. Do you see?'

She suddenly felt sick.

'He would never accept it,' she said.

Khatuna was breathing deeply, and she was aware of a sweet and reassuring smell, like crude oil.

Then there was a knock at the door, and the dog stiffened.

'Who is it?' asked Kakha.

'It's me,' came the voice. 'Nata.'

Kakha opened the door to his daughter, and commotion flooded in from downstairs. Khatuna found it strange to see someone like Natalia Sabadze standing there, whom she had seen so many times on TV. She was a famous model, and she had recently launched a pop album called *Nata 2000* that was better than anyone expected. You could see her in the music videos that played in all the bars, singing her songs in the back of limousines, cute and self-absorbed, kissing lollipops and balloons behind the security of machine guns.

In reality she was not so good looking.

Natalia hesitated only for the briefest moment when she saw Khatuna sitting on the bed. She looked at the Gucci bag.

'This is who you were talking about?'

He nodded. Natalia said stiffly to Khatuna,

'Pleased to meet you.'

Natalia was in charge of the party, and she began to discuss arrangements with her father. She whispered so Khatuna could not hear, and as the conversation went on, she retreated into the hallway. Kakha closed the door behind them, and in the last crack Khatuna caught sight of the enormous steel heel of Natalia's leather boots.

Khatuna lay back in her blue dress. She let her eyelids drop, and looked at the chandelier through the thick pulp of her lashes. She thought of a bunch of roses she had seen that afternoon discarded in a trash bin.

She thought of her brother with his books and poetry. She thought of him dead, and how it would be impossible to bear.

She could hear the noise swelling downstairs, as guests arrived and the racket of conversation overtook the music. She pictured the glamorous people who might be coming, but she did not wish to leave Kakha's bed.

He came back in and put on his jacket.

'Come on,' he said.

He looked at her, lying there. She was still gazing at the ceiling. She said sadly,

'In ten years' time I'll be an old woman.'

'You will never be old,' he said.

He leaned over the bed and kissed her: it was the first time. He lifted her up, and she felt as if a winged horse were in her groin. They walked together down the stairs, the dog running ahead, and the house had filled with people. There was a queue at the main entrance, where guns were checked. A waiter handed out champagne.

Then the throng engulfed Kakha, and Khatuna left him.

She wandered around inspecting the new things put up for the party: champagne fountains and rotating video walls showing clips of Kakha's life. She saw politicians, beauty queens and famous assassins. She watched the musicians for a while – a turbofolk band that had been flown in from Serbia. She saw Vakhtang, who said to her,

'Wow, Khatuna, you look like a model.'

She took him in her arms and danced against his bulk. In her heels she was much taller than he. She began to sing into his ear the sugary love lyrics of a Russian song. Vakhtang remained stiff.

'Have you seen the women they've got here tonight?' he said.

'They look expensive.'

Vakhtang sniggered.

'On the house, sister.'

His face was pudgy, his mouth filled with gold teeth. He pointed with his eyes.

'I'm going to have me that one over there. Have you seen the tits she's got?'

He left her. Khatuna sidled through the perfume and clamour, looking for a place to be alone. In the billiard room she found an empty armchair, and she sat down and lit a Trussardi. There were men around her, arguing. A man in dark glasses said,

'There are colleagues in this room who have invested good money in oil pipelines and they are losing their investments because the government wishes to interfere where it has no business to interfere.'

'But Mr Maisaia has not invested anything! He set up a fictitious company overnight and he stole the money intended for that pipeline! He may be my friend, but friendship is friendship and activity is activity!'

'Mr Kenchosvili, may I ask you to cast a veil of discretion over your lips when you speak of these things in public? There are some things that are known but not said.'

When she finished her cigarette, Khatuna got up and wandered away. She had Kakha's kiss still on her lips, and her new dress felt like angel hands around her legs. People were dancing together: the party was whirlpooling, it was rearing up against the high walls, and she wanted to ride on top of it. Waiters brought in bowls of cocaine, and Khatuna took a couple of lines. She saw a pale man in foreign clothes who was discreetly taking photographs of the models. She saw TV personalities and businessmen on the dance floor. The Serbian turbofolk singer sang Turkish tunes while a rapper in mirrored glasses cut in with Russian and English rhymes. *Motherfuckin' Tbilisi.* A big gangster called the Raven walked in with his girlfriend, a porn star.

Khatuna went to the bathroom. An open toilet door was banging noisily where Natalia Sabadze was having sex with a male model. Khatuna checked herself in the mirror. She was amazed by herself. She went into a cubicle and locked herself in. She leaned back against the dim wall, closed her eyes and gave way to the luxurious feeling that she was many metres tall, and so was everyone around her.

She returned to the party, which extended outside and round the pool, for the night was not cold. She made deliberate sine waves through the crush, heading for the door, wanting to see the moon – and she almost collided with the foreign man who had been taking photographs. He stepped back to let her pass, and she said in English,

'Such a gentleman.'

He grinned and walked with her out into the darkness. They stood looking at the moon, blurred through the clouds. She said,

'What are you doing here?'

'I met Kakha Sabadze a few times in New York and he asked me to pay him a visit. I'm in construction, he likes buildings. You know him?'

'Yes.'

‘He’s a classy guy. Very smart. I understand he’s big in these parts.’

‘He used to be a famous footballer.’

Faces were blue in the light of the swimming pool. Out here the music was fainter.

‘Amazing party,’ said the American.

‘I saw you taking pictures of that girl on the sofa.’

‘Oh.’ He laughed sheepishly. ‘We don’t have girls like that where I come from.’

‘I thought you had everything in America.’

‘Well. Yes. In a different sense. How come you speak such good English?’

‘I speak four languages,’ she said. ‘It’s nothing. Do you know I designed Kakha’s house? He came to me and said, *Make me a futuristic Georgian castle that will last a thousand years*.’

She felt she could tell this man anything and he would believe it. If she wanted she could make him fall in love with her, *like that*.

‘Really?’ he said. He looked at the house with renewed interest. ‘It seems like a high-tech stronghold. Looks like it has every kind of security system on the planet.’

She said solemnly,

‘The only way to survive is to be afraid.’

He nodded earnestly. She was entertained.

They had left the rest of the party behind, and could see the lights spread out. Her blue dress brushed his legs, and he was slowing the pace.

‘What’s your name?’ he asked softly.

‘Khatuna.’

‘I’m Charles.’

‘What a fancy name.’

‘I guess so.’

‘And nice to look at too.’

He smiled, and stopped walking. He turned to look at her. He put his arm around her waist and leaned to kiss her. She avoided his lips, and for a moment they stood looking at each other, nose to nose. His hand loosened, and he stepped back, uncertain.

'You're lucky no one saw you,' she said. 'You could have been out in the street with a broken nose by now. Or worse.'

'I'm sorry,' he said. 'I didn't mean—'

'Of course you meant.'

'I'm very sorry.'

'You're funny.'

For a moment they looked with parallel gazes back to the house, and the shrieks of the party flickered over their silence.

'Shall we go back?' she proposed.

They started to walk. He said,

'If you ever come to New York, please give me a call. If you want to talk about architecture. I have lots of contacts. This is my card.'

She took it.

CHARLES HAHN
CEO

Struction Enterprises, Inc.
Building the twenty-first century

'Still a couple of hours before it starts,' she said. 'The twenty-first century.'

'No. It's nearly midnight.'

Inside, Natalia Sabadze had taken the stage and was performing some of the songs from her new album. Her voice was breathy, as if she were whispering in your ear, and she kept her eyes half closed as she sang. When her performance was over, Kakha led the applause, and the crowd clapped for a full five minutes while Nata walked slowly down the steps of the stage and kissed her father ceremonially on the cheek. Then a prominent businessman grabbed the microphone and gave a long speech in praise of Kakha. He proposed toasts to Kakha and his family. He listed Kakha's achievements and the many qualities of his character. He flattered for a long time. He said,

'I would like to present Kakha Sabadze with a special millennium prize for his contribution to Georgian business!'

A young woman proffered a velvet case to Kakha, who opened it and took out a gold medallion on a chain. He nodded graciously, and the guests applauded. The businessman said into the microphone,

'If you look at it carefully, Mr Sabadze, you'll see your own portrait engraved into the gold. You'll see we've given you something very special.'

There were cheers, and then the DJ pushed the volume towards the mythic. Fat, breathless men in suits left behind political debate to sing old socialist anthems and dance with the end-time. Here and there models in G-strings performed mannered lesbian acts on raised platforms. The room was hot, and there was hardly place to stand amid the swaying people. On the sofa, Vakhtang leered ecstatically over the exposed breasts of the woman he had singled out hours before, on whose satin surfaces he had just arranged stripes of coke. In the doorways, impassive security guards stood watching the writhing gathering, glancing coldly at each other across the room.

Khatuna was dancing gently on her own when Kakha appeared by her side.

'Where have you been?' he asked. 'I've been looking for you everywhere.'

She put her arms around him. He said,

'I saw you with that American. Was he disturbing you?'

'No.' She laughed.

'You realise there's only ten minutes left?'

Khatuna was laughing long and hard. She said,

'Nothing can ever harm me now.'

'Come and see the fireworks.'

They walked out together into the fresh air, and he put his jacket around her shoulders. Natalia Sabadze staggered out of the house, her arm around a friend, the two of them shouting, *Millennium!* The first rockets went off, a few minutes premature. Charles Hahn was there watching, and two men were pushed into the pool, coming up shining and breaking into a fist-fight. A countdown gathered pace in the crowd, starting from sixty and soon losing all relationship to actual seconds – and before it was over there was an enormous explosion of coloured light, and *2000* was written in fire above their heads. Kakha held Khatuna tightly against him, and guards let off machine guns into the air to show appreciation. The sky boiled with red and green, and from this high point they could see chemical bursts glinting over the rest of the city.

'It's so beautiful,' said Khatuna. 'It's so lovely.'

Tears flooded over her cheeks, but she did not know why. She wondered where all the festive bullets would land, and if the century would begin with incomprehensible deaths across the city. She had not expected the new time to be so urgent, and wished she were not apart from her brother. She whispered his name to the gunpowder galaxies, and even the word 'Mother'. She said to Kakha,

'Make love to me.'

They slipped away, Khatuna whispering,

'When you understand me it is like the best wine.'

They lay next to each other, and Khatuna undid the buttons of his shirt. His chest was covered in tattoos.

They made love. The incessant thud from downstairs filled her reeling brain with the dark pleasure of ducts, the moist embrace of membranes.

Afterwards, she did not move, so she could rock in the continuation. Her thoughts drifted on thermals to the ceiling.

He got up and put on his shirt. She had been asleep. She asked him,

'Where are you going?'

'Back to the party,' he said. 'You stay here. I like to think of you in my bed.'

He tucked a blanket around her and she smiled drowsily. He opened the door.

'Kakha.'

He turned back.

'Yes?'

Her make-up was smudged across her face.

'I have a favour to ask you.'

Khatuna did not go home for four days. When finally she turned the key in the lock and opened the door, she found Irakli roasting aubergines. The room seemed newly bright and clean, and her mother was dressed and sitting at the table. Khatuna kissed her silently on the cheek.

'Long time, sister,' said Irakli, sprinkling pepper.

Khatuna's mother inspected her stonily.

Irakli laid out three plates and served the food. He sat down and looked appreciatively at his cooking.

'This aubergine is from the twentieth century,' he said, holding a piece up on a fork. 'It was kept in a fridge from that century to this. Cryogenic.'

'It tastes good,' said Khatuna. 'Even now.'

'I feel weightless in this new time,' declared Irakli. 'I love this emptiness. We have no idea what twenty-first-century music sounds like, because we have never heard it.'

He ate with gusto.

'When the year ended, I realised: this is the century I'll die in. I feel protective about it. The last century was fucked up by other people. But this one is ours. This is the century when I'll write all my books.'

Khatuna could hardly eat. Her stomach was tense and twisted. She said,

'What the hell are you going on about?'

Irakli smiled indulgently.

'Khatuna. How are you? How did you celebrate the dawning of the new millennium?'

She glared at him. Her mother burst from her silence:

'Where have you been, for God's sake? It's been four days!'

Khatuna concentrated on placing her knife and fork parallel on her plate.

'I've had some merry conversations with the police,' said Irakli. 'They told me you were probably sold by now, and far away.'

'You couldn't call? What has happened to you? Is this how you treat your old mother?'

'You're not old,' Khatuna said. 'I hate it when you say that. You're not even fifty.'

Her mother began to cry. Khatuna kept on:

'What do you do for this household? Everything comes from me. If you want me to earn all the money, you let me live my way.'

Her mother was shaking, and Khatuna watched her with contempt. It was an attitude that made a lot of life's troubles easier, she found. She left the table and picked up her bag. Irakli said,

'You're tied up with bad people. It's not unreasonable for us to get worried.'

'Shut your mouth, Irakli.'

'Will you just stay for one moment?' wailed her mother. 'Where are you going?'

'Goodbye,' she said tersely, and slammed the door.

'Where are you going?' her mother cried again.

Khatuna moved in to Kakha's house, and Kakha made good on his favour. He asked his best men to take care of it.

It was only days later when a black car quietly pulled up near an antique shop in old Tbilisi. Khatuna sat in the front seat. With her were four men with guns. One of them was Vakhtang.

It was a gloomy afternoon and the lights were on in the shops.

'That's him,' she said, pointing. 'The young one on the stool. The man behind the counter is his father.'

The men got out of the car and ran across the street. In the shop, Khatuna saw the younger man leap towards the door, trying to lock it against them, but he was too late. She checked her hair in the car mirror and lit a cigarette. The smoke's twist was slow and feline against the windscreen.

She was aware of how she walked, careful strides across the street. A bell rang with the door's opening, and what she was most conscious of was how the shop was completely bare, with just a couple of painted icons, modern reproductions, propped up on cheap shelving, a few glass vases and a telephone, and the owner and his son held down on the floor.

'The shop is empty,' she said to Vakhtang.

'Money laundering,' he said. 'That's all they do.'

She lifted the chin of the younger man.

'Do you remember me?' she said.

'No,' he said.

She nodded to Vakhtang who smashed his rifle butt against the side of his head.

'Do you remember me now?' asked Khatuna while the father stammered entreaties.

The man groaned. Khatuna said,

'Put a bullet in his leg.'

Vakhtang aimed his gun and the man writhed and cried out.

'I remember! I remember!'

'What do you remember?' asked Khatuna.

'A few years back. I remember going to your mother's house.'

'Yes?'

'We stole some stuff. Paintings, I think.'

Khatuna was still smoking her cigarette.

'Hit him again.'

Vakhtang hit him. The impact of wood on skull was deep and sublime. Khatuna said,

'My mother came here to sell her antiques. She was miserable and ruined, and all she could do was turn to you. Every few days she came to hand over part of our family's history. Did you know she is a princess?'

There was no one on the road outside, no traffic, no evening sounds, just Khatuna standing over the man in her long black coat.

'You threatened to kill my brother. I told you that day I would come for you, and I have come.'

The father could not breathe properly with the muzzle of a gun in the back of his neck, and was dribbling saliva on the floor. The young man was dazed from the blows. He said,

'I'll repay you. In full. I'll get everything back.'

'I'm not here to bargain,' said Khatuna.

'There must be something I can do,' whimpered the man.

'No,' replied Khatuna.

She nodded to Vakhtang. The gun had a silencer, and the only sound was a brief sucking of air. The man slumped as if death had come from within. The father screamed hoarsely.

'As for you,' Khatuna said coldly, 'I have nothing to say because you are old and ugly. You can have one last moment to think of everything you did to my family.'

Crows were cawing with the end of the day, and the old man choked. Everyone watched Khatuna, who gave the signal, and he fell forward too.

She wandered around the shop. Her heartbeat was out of control. She was shaking and unslaked. She wished she had pulled the trigger. Her voice wavered.

'There's nothing here to break.'

'Break the window,' suggested Vakhtang simply.

She took his gun, went out of the shop, the bell tinkling again, and swung at the plate glass with all her strength.

The glitter-crash went on for an age. She watched it all: the subdivision of crystal, and the shards' rebound. It was a drastic cascade, and it did not touch her in the least.

She had waited years for this moment. She had expected, when it came, she would feel everything shift back into its rightful place. She had expected to feel reborn: she had expected that the spider-clutch of memory would be released, and the treasure of her tenderness exhumed. But she could detect none of these things. Her chemistry had not altered, and the sky looked exactly the same.

The noise had brought people into the street, and she was aware of them grouped behind her, watching.

'Burn it,' she ordered, through the broken glass.

She turned around to get back in the car, while the men emptied petrol canisters over the bodies, over the walls and shelves, over the telephone – and as they drove away she watched the cloud of oil smoke until it was hidden by the buildings, and she could see it no more.

Ichthyosaur

8

HIS CHAIR WAS AN EXPENSIVE OBJET D'ART that he'd picked out from a store in SoHo. Early Meiji, with gold dragons and cranes flying over Mount Fuji against a background of black lacquer, painted layer upon painstaking layer. Signed *Tokyo: Shibayama.*

A man who made his money from trends and cycles, predictions and futures, needed to seat himself on the firmness of the past, lest he become light headed and float away.

In the middle of his office stood an imposing pair of antique globes from Germany. They were his talking piece when people came. Engraved in Berlin, he told them, and manufactured in Nuremberg, the centre of eighteenth-century German globe making. He took his time, pointing out, on the celestial globe, the late addition of Uranus, just then discovered by William Herschel and, on its terrestrial twin, the brand-new Pacific coastlines mapped out by James Cook.

The office was on 53rd Street, on the forty-first floor, and the window faced south towards the midday sun and the financial district's hazy bar graph. Plastic was pacing up and down, poring over a sheet of paper. He had printed out an email in order to consider it better.

For the past month, Plastic Munari had been producing a band of mystic musicians from Morocco. It was a challenge, trying to focus the wailing *rhaita* into a regular lounge beat and still preserve the purity. He did it small: he had the bass and a woman on tabla holding it together, but he kept the instruments up front. There were moments when the beat disappeared entirely and you were thrown into that hectic infinity, speaking for itself.

Plastic had rented a big apartment on the Upper West Side for the musicians to stay in: they didn't want to be split up. They were a sight in the streets, fifteen Moroccan tribesmen in robes marching to the studio, and Plastic took a few photos for himself. Before they flew out from JFK they went to Bloomingdale's and bought up the entire stock of three-hundred-dollar cast-iron Le Creuset casseroles.

The record was finished now, and Plastic could think about other things. The email came at a good time.

There was a mirror on the wall of his office, set up so he could see the back of his guests' heads as they faced him at his desk. He stood close to it now.

Plastic had that enviable aura of a man whose inner obsessions have captured the imagination of millions, and so brought him, without obvious strain or compromise, enormous earthly rewards. He had hung on to all his hair and, as he approached the end of his forties, he slept with the kinds of young women who would have been unattainable when he was their age.

His suit was cashmere and his tan real. He worked out several times a week, and he'd never looked better in his life.

He stood up when the two men were shown in. The younger one was all smiles.

'I am Bozhidar Markov. This is my superior, Mr Gospodinov. He is Deputy Minister for Culture of the Republic of Bulgaria.'

Plastic's secretary hung the men's overcoats in the corner and they sat down, taking in the framed awards and the Manhattan view. They wore ties under their leather jackets. Plastic sensed that they didn't have the least idea of how the music business worked. Sometimes a good thing, sometimes not.

Plastic turned off his cell phones and studied the two men. Bozhidar Markov seemed earnest and hopeful. Gospodinov was older, with sunken eyes. Plastic said to him good-naturedly,

'You look rather tired, if you don't mind me saying.'

Gospodinov did not return Plastic's gaze. He looked away and surveyed the office. He let his eyes run over the furniture and the paintings while he reached absentmindedly inside his jacket and pulled out three packets of cigarettes. He turned back and said,

'So you believe the world is round?'

'I'm sorry?'

Gospodinov smirked. He motioned with his eyes towards the globes.

'It's a joke,' he said obscurely, piling his cigarette packets up on the edge of Plastic's desk. The brand name was *Smith & Wesson*.

Plastic passed it off with a nod. He said,

'You can't smoke in here.'

Gospodinov smiled sourly, but did not remove the packets.

'I think you understand from our email,' said Bozhidar, 'why we wanted to meet you.'

'More or less,' said Plastic. 'But I'd like to hear it directly from you.'

Bozhidar invited his boss to speak, but Gospodinov screwed up his face. Bozhidar said,

'For the underline of our discussion, Mr Muneri, it is necessary for you to understand the economic scene of Bulgaria.'

Bozhidar launched into an excessively detailed presentation of Bulgaria's economic break-down after the end of communism. As he listened, Plastic fingered the custom-made penknife he had recently bought from a boutique in Stockholm.

He noticed steam rising from the men's wet coats in the corner. He hated this weather.

'Five hundred thousand people left Bulgaria to become housemaids and construction workers ...'

Most people in the city complained about the summer, but Plastic loved the heat. He would die if he didn't have a job that took him frequently to hot places.

'Our university-educated women went to work as nannies in Greece ...'

Plastic don't melt, as someone put it once.

Bozhidar ran off statistics with a bureaucrat's ease. Gospodinov's phone rang silently in his shirt pocket. He took it out, inspected the screen with distaste, and put it back. He interjected,

'Mr Munari is here to do a job for us. Why are we giving him a history lesson?'

His caller persisted, but he ignored it, and through his shirt, where his heart was, came a blue flashing light.

Bozhidar pressed on.

'Nowadays it is absolutely fashionable to say, *In communist times everything was good! And now wild dogs are scaring people in the city and the roads are getting holes!*'

Plastic stole a glance at the clock. He was supposed to leave in forty-five minutes to attend the premiere of a biopic about a rapper he had worked with in the early days, when he ran a hip-hop label. An incredible talent who had died of an overdose.

'But there is no going back, Mr Munari. The past is a disaster. We have to make the future ...'

Plastic was still wondering whether or not to subject himself to the movie. The singer had been a collaborator and a friend, and Plastic didn't know if he wanted to watch his death again on the big screen.

He, Plastic, was portrayed in the movie by a scrawny twenty-something no-name actor.

'The Ministry of Culture has employed an American PR firm to send out positive images of Bulgaria. We pay CNN and BBC to make nice articles about Bulgarian wine and sunshine destinations ...'

The actor had come to meet him over a year ago. *So you're the real Plastic Munari!* Plastic was so depressed at the guy's ugly face he'd kicked him straight out.

His secretary came in with a tray of martinis. The room was turning dark in the winter afternoon, and she put on the lights. Gospodinov looked suspiciously into his cocktail glass. Plastic said,

'I'm a little pressed for time, gentlemen. Perhaps you should tell me what it is you want?'

'I want to smoke a cigarette,' said Gospodinov, taking one from the packet and holding it between his fingers.

Plastic called his secretary.

'Would you mind showing Mr Gospodinov to the fire escape? He would like to light a cigarette.'

Gospodinov took all three packets with him.

Bozhidar said,

'We want you to make a *global music superstar* from Bulgaria.'

He watched Plastic carefully.

'The people who run this world, Mr Munari, are not well informed. They have no patience to learn our history. We cannot attract them with rational arguments. They understand only celebrity.'

'Do you have any specific musicians in mind? Because without that, it's all academic.'

Bozhidar said,

'Listen to me. For five centuries our country was part of the Turkish Empire, full of every kind of music. Turkish, Arabic, Greek, Serbian, Gypsy. Then the communists banned everything. They sent expert musicologists to make police reports about musicians who used un-Bulgarian chords. Pop stars adored all over Bulgaria were taken to the camps for singing American songs…'

The truth was, Plastic had wanted for a long time to find a big musician from that region. That was why he had agreed to this meeting.

'The old music was suppressed, and we did not even hum it in our heads…'

Plastic was known in the industry for the originality of his ear. Back when no one had thought of it, he had found big audiences for klezmer music and remixed Arab devotional chants for New York bars. He had turned small-time Pakistani *qawwali* singers and Cuban *son* pianists into huge recording properties. But he had never found a musician from the Balkans, where they had some of the most exciting music in the world.

Bozhidar was saying,

'Pirate cassettes broke the stranglehold. I was a teenager when the Gypsies started to smuggle in cassettes and I can tell you, it electrocuted our brains! We heard heavy metal! Absolutely real music! We were bored of the hollow idealism going on for forty years, we wanted music from the heart. We wanted pain music! Teenagers in Bulgaria were pumping feelings: it was crazy times in our country and we were already old when we were twenty years.'

Plastic was enjoying Bozhidar's sudden verve.

'Illegal Gypsy musicians became so famous that the communist state didn't know what to do. Everything that was silenced came out again in joy, and the musicians walked like emperors. Music brought down the communist government, Mr Munari, because it showed clearly that everything illegal was beautiful and sophisticated and everything legal was shit.'

The door opened, and Plastic's secretary showed in Gospodinov. He smelled as if he had bathed in nicotine. He looked from Bozhidar to Plastic. He sat down.

'So when can you begin?' he asked.

Plastic eyed him coldly.

'So far, I've not heard you make any proposal.'

'Well: can you do it or not?'

Plastic gave a smile of finality. He said,

'I thank you, gentlemen, for your interesting presentation. But this is not how music is made. I need to start with talent, with artists. Great music doesn't come about because there is a government strategy.'

'That is *exactly* how it comes about,' retorted Gospodinov.

Plastic folded his hands.

'It has been an interesting conversation. But now—'

Bozhidar spread his hands to slow things down.

'My superior is a little impatient,' he said. 'Don't be offended. I ask you just one thing: come to Bulgaria. We will organise for you to hear every kind of Bulgarian music. You will find incredible artists. You will not regret it.'

Plastic took his time. He said,

'Let me give you some background, gentlemen. The record company I founded in the Bronx in the late 70s launched the brightest lights of hip-hop, and when I sold it to Universal, I became a very wealthy man. I left hip-hop behind and started this label. I invented what everyone now calls world music. I have an instinct for talent, and when I find an artist I want, I'll get him if I have to kill my own mother – and that's why this label is bigger and better than anything else in the field. I have a seat on the board of Universal Music Group. Do you see what I'm getting at? My inner life is secure. I have no interest in the Bulgarian government or its objectives.'

Bozhidar was sweating. He said,

'I would like to say this to you, Mr Munari. Do not talk as if we are idiots. If we did not know who you are, we would not be here. We know all about you and your country; it is you who know nothing about us. Try for one minute to imagine our perspective. You live in the richest nation on earth, and yet you speak as if you have acquired all your power with just your own abilities. In Bulgaria we are surrounded by people as talented as you, but their abilities go to waste. That is what we are here to change.'

It was true that Plastic could not think of a single fact he knew about Bulgaria. He had a vague sense that it wasn't much fun to live there, and Bozhidar's speeches had done little to change that. And yet the man was convinced his obscure little country would have its fortunes transformed if people could only hear its music. *Bulgaria grabs a chunk of the global pie with unique thirteen-time rhythms*. There was something endearing about it.

He suddenly remembered that there had been a record of Bulgarian folk music that had sold in the millions some years ago. He tried to think of the title.

'I wasn't trying to imply that you are idiots,' he said.

'Come to Sofia,' said the young bureaucrat more amiably. 'I'll take you to hear things you never imagined. And I'll give you nice warm weather, not like here.'

Looking into his cocktail, Plastic saw a tiny bubble escape from under the olive and surrender to the surface. He said,

'Get in touch with my secretary about dates, and send me a plan.'

9

PLASTIC WAS IN A HOTEL ROOM in Sofia, staring at the winged statue in the square outside.

Bozhidar said,

'I'm afraid the prime minister cannot meet you. He is away on official business.'

He appeared very regretful, and Plastic had the annoying feeling he was trying to show the level of his influence.

He was waiting for Bozhidar to leave his room so he could take a shower and freshen up from his journey. He had no patience just then for the twelve-page itinerary Bozhidar had prepared.

Plastic picked up his shampoo by way of a hint, but Bozhidar continued to read out the list of appointments. Plastic noted that two afternoons had been set aside for interviews with journalists, which he would cancel as soon as he could. It was not his style. He liked to go low-key, his ears unburdened.

Bozhidar was saying,

'Tomorrow you will meet Daniela Ivanova. She is talented and beautiful, with a recent big hit for the Bulgarian version of "Eye of the Tiger". In Bulgaria we are very obsessed with her breasts.'

Later that day, Plastic was taken to attend the opening of a new business park. An official delegation thanked him for everything he was doing for the country.

He said to Bozhidar,

'Do these people understand why I'm here? I've come on my own account. What are they expecting from me?'

Bozhidar waved it away. He took Plastic to the opening of the Leonardo da Vinci exhibition at the Sofia Art Gallery, which his ministry had been planning for a year. There were speeches and self-satisfied toasts, and the city's elite stood around drinking wine. Though they laughed among themselves, Plastic did not manage to get beyond formalities with anyone. He looked at the paintings and was astonished to see they were all paper facsimiles, and bad ones at that.

The next two days passed slowly. He heard several mediocre bands. He had lunch with overeager teenage guitarists. A musicologist gave a lecture.

Plastic was discouraged by Bozhidar's behaviour. He had liked him in New York, but in his own environment, Bozhidar appeared humourless and excessively preoccupied with etiquette, and Plastic found his presence burdensome. Over dinner he gave the same speech about heavy metal he had given in New York, almost word for word, and Plastic felt he had exhausted the young man's spontaneity in that first encounter.

Gospodinov was nowhere to be seen.

Plastic escaped for a couple of hours, eager to be alone. He wandered through old residential streets where the shutters were all fastened. He peered through the opaque glass of defunct shops. He looked at the rows of buzzers outside the houses, and the graffiti whose lettering he could not read.

He admired the Alexander Nevski church, and browsed the flea market in the square outside. The bric-a-brac calmed him down. He bought himself a presentation medal embossed with the heads of Lenin and Todor Zhivkov. It was very cheap, and probably fake, but that only made it more exotic.

That night, Plastic resisted Bozhidar's invitation to after-dinner drinks, and went back early to his hotel. He sat and listened to the excellent ensemble playing in the lobby, and had a long conversation with the violinist, a Gypsy named Slavo. Early the next morning, Plastic gave Bozhidar the slip. He packed his bag at six A.M., paid his bill and left the hotel.

It was only April, but as he walked to the bus station with his bags the morning sun was warm, and post-coital cats lay out in the shafts. Traffic was sparse at this hour, flashing double in the windows of the new boutiques. Plastic arrived at the bus station and read the timetable of departures for Belgrade, Bucharest and Istanbul. He conferred with a taxi driver, who had no problem taking him where he wanted to go.

'How long will it take?' asked Plastic.

'Four hours,' said the driver. 'Maybe five.'

'Great,' said Plastic. 'Give me a minute.'

He went off in search of a toilet. At the edge of the forecourt was a broken hut with the sign of the minimum man. Plastic stuck his head in, and immediately withdrew. There was an inch of water on the floor, and his entrance triggered a jazz-cloud of mosquitoes.

He was thinking of braving it on tiptoe when he spotted in the distance a friendly wall, and a secluded alley behind. He ran over gratefully and set down his bags.

He was not the first to have discovered this spot. In fact there were two other men standing there now, and Plastic had to walk down to find a place. The wall was black with ancient urine, and Plastic held his breath against the stench while he added another layer.

Still pissing, he felt an unaccountable need to turn around. He craned his neck and looked up at the dilapidated building behind him. There was nothing there. Nothing but rows of empty windows, old and blind.

The driver turns off the engine, and car doors slam. Such sounds are authoritative in this silence. Plastic stands for several moments in the expanse, motionless and uncertain, for the empty town is eerie, and he has impressions of ghosts.

The wind gusts now and then, and there are many butterflies, but he is unprepared for the pig that emerges from behind a sagging truck, snorting unrestrainedly. He is quite embarrassed at the strength of his reaction. He watches the pig amble for a moment and sees it is tied with a long rope.

He walks towards the building – which is a grand word for this flapping pile of corrugated iron. A conveyer belt, which once carried material from the ground level up to a hatch near the top of the factory, has collapsed, and lies shattered where it fell.

He calls out *Boris!* and larks take off from the trees. The silence does not alter, and he tries again.

A young man appears in an entrance. He cannot be more than twenty years old. He is taken aback to be summoned by name.

Plastic approaches, but not too close.

'You're Boris?' he calls across the gap.

The young man gives a nod.

'Slavo sent me. He said you would be here. He said you play violin.'

The young man stares for a long while. Then he disappears inside, and Plastic follows. The place is a death trap, with rusting tanks burst open and great pipes ready to fall from the ceiling. There is a bed here, and several books, and it smells of rat piss and cooking.

'You live alone?'

Boris nods.

'My grandmother was with me,' he says. 'She died a while ago.'

He has his violin in his hand. It is strung with wires he must have made himself. He plays a slow and enigmatic air.

Hearing the music, Plastic pictures himself walking along an empty road. Far ahead he sees people running towards him. When they draw close, they gesticulate fearfully to where they have come from, warning him against going there. They have no time to stop, and continue frantically on their way.

More people come, and more – and the line of people fleeing soon becomes so dense that Plastic is forced to walk by the side of the road so they may pass. He shields his eyes to look at the horizon ahead, but he can see nothing: no smoke, no flames, no dust. 'What are you running from?' he asks the crowd, but there is no answer.

Plastic says, 'You composed that yourself?'

The question is superfluous, and Boris does not expend effort on it. From outside comes the mahogany call of a woodpecker, which he answers on his instrument.

There is an elastic energy in Plastic's inner thighs: this is not some fake thing he has just heard. His senses are sharpened. Some nameless gratitude has descended on him and made his head light.

He takes a CD player from his bag and puts the headphones over Boris's ears. He reads the boy's face, watches his eyes widen. It is one of Plastic's old recordings. The best he has ever done.

Boris has to sort a few things out before he leaves. He goes into a house and comes out with his violin case and a few possessions tied up in a sheet. He sets his pigs loose and speaks to them roughly. He touches his forehead to the earth and tastes the air with his tongue. Then he gets in the car.

10

KHATUNA WAS READING *The Fountainhead* and humming along to the song in her headphones. Her cigarette tasted extra good this morning.

Her phone flashed. She put down the book. The message invited her to a dance party hosted by a foreign vodka company. A DJ was flying in from Paris.

Somewhere between deleting the message and picking up her book again, Khatuna realised she was pregnant with Kakha's child.

Kakha wanted their wedding to be the biggest celebration in Georgia since old King David won Tbilisi, but Khatuna bargained him down to a private affair in the mountains. She was becoming wary of the dangers that lurked in crowds.

Kakha spent the morning with the priest, walking out along a rocky path, and returning after several hours to pray in the church, the priest whispering in his ear while he knelt on the stone floor.

The couple were married in the afternoon. Irakli had refused to go to a *gangster wedding*, so the guests were all from Kakha's side.

'I will follow you forever,' said Khatuna into Kakha's ear. 'I will be a woman in a veil in the desert, following you.'

The crowd became drunk and festive. There were village musicians, and enormous piles of country khinkali, and the men danced boisterously. Kakha disappeared, and Nata talked to Khatuna about fame, and parties, and her fashion line, which was debuting in London. Her leg was in plaster because she had recently driven her Porsche into a wall.

Khatuna savoured her own feelings. She thought about Kakha. She pictured him looking at a waste patch of earth and imagining what he could build there. In the small of her back she had tattooed a great eye, so there would never be a time she was not looking at him.

There were moments when she was terrified by the emotions that would be unleashed when her baby came into the world. The agonies she went through for her brother were already bad enough. In her pregnancy, she had stopped going anywhere without bodyguards. Her child would never be vulnerable to the dangers she had suffered: she would build defences so formidable that nothing could ever come close.

She had moved her mother and brother into a bigger apartment with better security. She had her brother under surveillance now, but it was discreet, so he would not know.

She left Nata talking and went to find Kakha. He was leaning against a wall outside listening to Vakhtang, who paced around him, ranting.

'I'm your *cousin*. I'm *family*. Have you got so big you've forgotten your values?'

'Who takes care of you, Vakhtang? I pay for your cars and your women, and you don't do a stroke of work.'

'I *want* to work! You give everything to her! People come and you only introduce them to her. You sent her to those meetings in Dubai. You buy her diamonds. And now you've married her. What will happen to me? She doesn't like me. She'll kick me out of the house. You give her all the power.'

'She's a good businesswoman. She says she'll do something and it's done. Do you think you could ever have pulled off the deal she did with the Armenians? You're erratic. You leave me in the dark about what you're doing. You steal my friends' cars and leave me to deal with the mess. You seem to think it's only about dressing up. We're running a big business. It's no joke.'

'I was managing the hotels just fine. Everything was fine until you pulled me out.'

'Because you don't understand politics, Vakhtang. You just keep on blindly doing what you know and you don't realise that everything else has turned round a hundred and eighty degrees. Our situation is delicate now. You don't realise what a fucking range of things I have to think about since those towers came down in New York. There's a war in Afghanistan, the whole world is suddenly on our doorstep. The Americans are coming in here, muscling in on my oil, because they don't want to depend on the Middle East anymore. I have to think fast. You don't understand these things. You don't understand the big picture.'

'I can learn,' said Vakhtang. 'I'm not an idiot.'

'Don't push me to say things I don't want to say.'

Vakhtang started kicking the wall.

'I worship you, Kakha. Since I was a kid, I've always worshipped you.'

'A lot of people worship me. Do I put them in charge of my business?'

Later on, Kakha joined Khatuna in their bedroom. Khatuna smiled and said,

'Our wedding night.'

Kakha pushed the covers away and looked down at her body.

'A man can never compare to the beauty of a woman,' he said. 'There's always that basic inequality.'

'Wait till I get really fat.'

'I can't even tell you're pregnant. The only change is *here*.'

He gave zealous kisses to her breasts. He said,

'Can we tell people about our son yet?'

'It may be a *girl*.' She hit him playfully. 'No. It's still early. I want to be sure.'

Kakha put his arms around Khatuna and held her against his body. He said,

'I keep having this dream. I get up in the middle of the night and that statue, the Mother of Georgia, is calling to me. I open the window and float out into the night, far above the ground. I drift over Tbilisi, and my eyes are like floodlights, and there's nothing I cannot see.'

'That's it?'

'Yes.'

'What do you think it means?'

He shrugged. He kissed her ear. He said,

'I got a phone call this evening. Some of our men were attacked in the lobby of the Sheraton. Four men came out of nowhere. We lost two of our own guys, and we killed three of theirs.'

'Oh my God,' said Khatuna, her hand moving involuntarily to her stomach.

'It was a mess,' said Kakha. He sighed helplessly.

'Listen: I want to take you on a little drive,' he said. 'Now we're married, there's something I want to show you.'

They sped out of town in a procession of white Toyota Land Cruisers, taking no notice of the roadblocks where policemen collected bribes.

'You and I need a proper army now,' said Kakha. 'That's what keeps me awake at night. With the Americans coming in, our stability's falling apart.'

The road was empty, and they cut quickly through the hills. The driver peered through the arcs carved by the wipers from the windscreen's mud.

'All these smugglers and terrorists in the Georgian mountains, running from the war in Afghanistan –the Americans are going to come in and get them. The Americans will come in, the Russians will come in, and between one and the other, Shevardnadze will go down. Then all hell will break loose. Every vulture in the Caucasus will descend to tear up his corpse, and the country with it. Shevardnadze's a bastard but at least he's held things together.'

They climbed higher, and the valleys were hazy below. There was snow on the ground and patches of ice in the shadows. In the back of the car, Kakha's dog sat watching the flashing landscape, front paws spread against the bumps.

'The big powers need Georgia to be weak,' said Kakha. 'Do you think the Americans could just march armies in here to guard their pipelines if we were a normal, stable country? They keep us on the brink of crisis, so there's always an excuse to come in. That's why people in our country are so insane: they know they're only raw material.'

'But that's why we're stronger than everyone else. We know how the world is. We know the fairytales aren't real.'

Kakha said,

'There are many who are resentful that we own the borders, and they'll use the chaos to try and take that away. That's when we need an army. Our oil, our mines, our drugs – they all need proper military protection.'

The rolling hills were becoming more icy and rugged, and the pylons more precarious in their perch. They passed an occasional corrugated-iron village.

'The site is up there,' said Kakha, pointing as the car turned off the road. 'It used to be a Soviet training base. It's a natural fortress. Look at the visibility it has.'

They drove up the slope to a barbed-wire entrance. Armed guards opened the gates, and the Land Cruisers drove through. In the distance were two helicopters, their blades collapsed, graceful in a dusting of snow. There was a generator building and soaring military radar dishes. There were half-buried armoured vehicles and a series of pitted walls.

They got out of the car. Kakha opened the back and the dog bounded into the distance. The men in the other cars spread out to guard the site. The surrounding peaks were vast and silent, and the place was utterly alone.

'Watch the dog run,' Kakha said.

Khatuna sighed. 'Nothing else is real when you see a mountain.'

'If you carry on up the road you get to Mount Kazbek,' said Kakha. 'Chechnya and Dagestan are right over there. You are standing in a secure site in the middle of a massive war zone. That's why I grabbed this place as soon as the USSR moved out.'

He inhaled deeply and kicked an old mortar shell sunk in the grass.

'It's the most beautiful place I've ever seen,' said Khatuna.

'Those are the firing ranges,' Kakha said, pointing. 'They're derelict. We need to take them down. Probably the whole thing will come down.'

They wandered slowly around the site, enjoying the feeling of clean, cold air in their lungs. Kakha made for the entrance of the main building, a huge box-like concrete structure. Inside, a light bulb was smashed on the floor, and sections of the ceiling had collapsed, leaving spewing wires. Fires had left sooty stains up the walls. The torso of an anatomical model was propped against a pillar, its ruddy tendons dulled with dust. On the blackboards there were diagrams from ancient seminars, and vast crinkled maps showed the world as it had been thirty years earlier.

They went up the stairs, which opened out into a concrete expanse, walled on one side with glass. Rows of welded seats with numbers painted on the backs were scattered haphazardly, and a giant hammer and sickle, cut crudely from steel, hung askew on one wall.

They stood at the glass looking over the plateau below them, flecked with thistles and rusting metal, and surrounded by a high wall. Beyond, the mountains shone through the mist.

'No government will interfere with us here,' said Kakha. 'It's easy to guard. I've got rocket launchers stored here, and surface-to-air missiles. I've got small arms and chemical weapons. There's no problem with men: this region is crawling with soldiers who want to make money. I've hired top-class instructors from South Africa and England. They've been in Angola and Congo. They trained both sides in the Yugoslav war. You see? All the pieces are in place. We're talking about the most advanced private army on the continent.'

'You've been planning this for a while,' said Khatuna.

'I didn't want to tell you before. Now you know everything.'

The dog appeared at the top of the stairs and ran over to Kakha, panting and dribbling on the floor.

'If it's all as you say,' she said, 'we can hire this army out. It will pay for itself.'

'It will do more than that! Just think about it. We have America, Russia and China building pipelines and nuclear installations with totally inadequate military back-up. We have – what? – forty conflicts in the region, many of them already armed. We have bankrupt national armies, twenty years out of date – the men don't even have uniforms. You see what I mean? If you can't make money from a situation like that you're a fool. Our army will be equipped and trained for next-generation warfare, and governments and corporations will be queuing up to use it. This is business.'

Khatuna leaned her head on his shoulder. They looked out together at the mountains and the Land Cruisers parked below. The peaks were turning apricot in the late-afternoon light. Khatuna said,

'I feel better, coming here.'

Kakha put his arm around her.

'I've been so worried,' she said. 'With the baby on the way, I think all the time about security. I never cared so much before.'

'Look around you,' said Kakha. 'There is nothing to be afraid of anymore.'

For a while they stood there, close together, looking out at the Caucasus Mountains. The Rottweiler sat alert by their side, starting at the lines of birds flying towards the golden horizon.

11

SITTING IN THE BACK SEAT of her Mercedes, Khatuna saw a flock of pigeons take off from the roof of a building and wheel dizzyingly in the sky above.

The car swept past a big poster of Nata Sabadze, an advertisement for her upcoming concert. It showed her walking in the rain on a bridge in Moscow, intense against the romance of the old Stalinist buildings.

Khatuna was coming from a meeting with an arms dealer.

People were strolling in the streets as usual: groups of young men in leather jackets whiling away their unemployment, wrinkled women selling sweets and soft drinks by the side of the road, people queuing conversationally for the baker, whose shop was marked by an old loaf hung on a string outside. But it all seemed different today. She felt she was seeing her city like a surveillance satellite, with eyes that had no feeling. The clouds above had shaggy claws.

'Drive quickly,' she said to the driver.

The powerful Mercedes screamed past the other traffic and up the hill road that led up to the house. Something was indeed unusual, for there were cars parked haphazardly outside the gates, and here too pigeons were flying in great, agitated circles. The car raced into the compound and Khatuna jumped out while it was still moving. She ran into the house and the first thing she saw was Vakhtang.

'They shot Kakha! Kakha is dead!'

Vakhtang buried his head in her neck, howling.

'Kakha is dead!'

There was a great commotion outside, cars braking and everyone shouting directions, and four puffing men carried Kakha in and laid him on the floor. His head was bundled in his raincoat, which they unwrapped to show his face, and the pooled blood ran out over the floor. The shot had hit him in the forehead and most of the back of his head was missing. Vakhtang threw himself on the body, screaming. Every mobile phone was ringing, and Khatuna thought, *Who are all these people?*

She knelt beside Kakha, and wiped his face with her sleeve. She whispered in his harrowed ear,

'Couldn't you wait to see your baby?'

Kakha's Rottweiler galloped into the house, skidding on the marble. The circle of people parted to let him in. His nose bobbed against Kakha's motionless hand. He whined and paced around the body. He sniffed Kakha's face and began to lick at the brains on the floor.

Vakhtang bellowed,

'Fucking dog!'

He kicked the animal in the jaw. The dog turned on him, but Vakhtang flailed at the animal until it ran away.

Khatuna wondered where Nata was. She was aware there were people in the house she did not know, come to ransack its secrets. She felt an urgent need to escape.

She was in a daze as she ran upstairs to gather her things. She did not even know what documents she was flinging into her bag, and she hurried downstairs, passing men going up. She heard a man on his mobile phone whispering, 'Wineface has been shot.' She took a final look at Kakha laid out, put her hand on his stagnant chest.

She made for the front door, and Vakhtang flung his arms around her, sobbing.

'Where are you going?'

'I have to leave,' she said.

'Take me with you.'

'I'll call you soon.'

Her driver was standing by the door.

'Take me to town,' she said to him.

He stared at her with a new defiance. He was a big man, and he did not move. He simply leaned against the pillar, took a slow drag of his cigarette, and drew his finger like a knife across his throat.

Khatuna ran out of the house alone, carrying her bag; she walked out of the gates and down the hill until she found a church. She called her brother and asked him to meet her there. Irakli arrived twenty minutes later and found her inside, rocking on a stone step, her arms clasped round her knees.

When she saw him she collapsed into his arms, baying like a terrified animal. Her convulsions did not cease, and there was nothing he could offer to staunch her grief. She screamed in the empty church, she was impossibly heavy in his arms, she was like a paralysed woman who could not support her limbs. He tried to soothe her, reciting her secret name. She made bestial sounds and he shouted at her to bring her back.

She said she would die here. She wanted only to die Irakli said,

'You will survive this.'

The church was silent, and no one came in. The saints shone in the afternoon sun.

She stroked his face. She said,

'I have to leave the country. I promised him I would.'

She struggled with herself. *He is here. I cannot leave him.* Then she took the other side. *They will kill me if I stay. I won't let them put me on TV crying at his funeral.*

She said she was not strong enough.

'You have to come with me,' she said.

'What about Mother?'

She began crying again. *Will she die without you? I will die. I will die if you don't come.*

He nodded. He said,

'I don't have a passport.'

'I have it all. I've got papers for you. Passport, visa, everything. I've had them for months, for just this situation. You'll have to travel under a different name.'

They took a taxi to the airline office. Khatuna looked out at the city, trying to comprehend that Kakha was not part of it. They drove past the street where he had been gunned down, and she fancied there was something festive in the way the people walked there. A young man stuck his head out of a speeding car and yelled into the wind.

There was only one flight that evening, going to Vienna. The man behind the desk made a couple of phone calls and printed their tickets. Khatuna looked blankly at the bright tourist posters of Amsterdam and Jerusalem. She had the sense that the objects in the room were not fixed, as they appeared, but floated an imperceptible distance above the floor.

They set out for the airport. Khatuna murmured, *You haven't even met him*, and this thought made her weep again. *You don't know anything*, she said, for she had not told Irakli about her unborn baby.

Irakli laid his head on the back of the seat. He thought of his mother and all the things he would leave behind. He watched the sky through the back window, where pigeons had settled on the lamp-posts. He counted four on the first, three on the second, then two, then one, then zero. *A countdown of pigeons*, he thought.

They arrived at the ramshackle airport, apartment towers falling on every side and UN jets bristling on the runways. Inside the terminal, posters warned women not to sell themselves into prostitution.

Irakli called his mother. He wandered away for the conversation, and Khatuna could not hear.

They arrived in Vienna late at night. Irakli fell asleep in the hotel. Khatuna left him and walked around the city in her fur coat, the one Kakha had bought her.

She walked round the Ringstrasse, where cars droned indifferently past the mournful opera house and the Burgtheater, filling the night with the vinegar smell of burnt diesel. The place seemed to be astonishingly full of antique shops. The streets were desolate. She saw a man standing alone, in the middle of the night, watching silent football replays on a television in a shop window.

She returned to the hotel after sunrise and slept through the next day: a leaden, frozen sleep from which Irakli could not wake her. He sat by the bed and began a poem. The title was 'Looking for a place to lie down in secret, we crawled beneath a table and discovered, on its underside, the scrawls we had made together as children.'

Khatuna awoke in the evening to discover that her mobile phone had been cut off and all her credit cards cancelled.

She called Vakhtang from the hotel phone.

'What's the story?'

'They're saying he stopped to buy milk. When he came out of the store they were waiting for him with guns.'

'Can you imagine Kakha going to buy milk?'

'Not really.'

'So why are you giving me this bullshit? I thought you might have found something out. Where are you now?'

'I'm in the house. Nata has moved in here.'

'I'm sure she has.'

'They gave her Kakha's job. They made her head of the national airline. She's inherited his football club.'

'They must have made a bargain deal with her: we have to kill your father, but in return we'll take care of you.'

'There were speeches in parliament. They want to name a road after Kakha.'

'All right. Take care, Vakhtang.'

'Can I come and visit you? It's terrible here.'

'You should think about getting a job. Taking care of yourself.'

'I don't know what to do.'

'Bye, Vakhtang.'

She lay on the bed and stared at the ceiling for so many hours that Irakli got worried. He sat next to her.

'Are you all right?'

She whined in the darkness,

'I already lost my father, and now *he* is gone too.'

He moaned with her and held her tight, and she said,

'I am bad luck for men.'

She lay awake after he fell asleep, and her body began to tremble. The crisis swelled within her until she had to leap up and run to the bathroom. It was a miscarriage. She was nearly three months pregnant, and there was a lot of blood. Weak and dizzy, she cleaned every last trace off the surfaces, not wanting Irakli to know. She went back to bed, and held herself under the sheets, sobbing.

When she awoke in the morning she was coldly focused. She went to the phone and called Charles Hahn, the CEO of the construction company whom she had met at Kakha's millennium party. She said,

'Do you remember me?'

'Of course I remember. But it's three o'clock in the morning.'

'You told me to call you if I was ever coming to New York.'

'Right.'

'I'm coming and I need a job.'

'Right.'

'And I need you to wire me five thousand dollars.'

'You want me to wire you five thousand dollars!'

'Yes. I'm in Vienna at the Holiday Inn.'

'I see.' He paused. 'I'll see what I can do.'

'Thank you.'

Irakli was awake now, watching her gravely. As she put down the phone, he said,

'I don't think I know who you really are.'

The money arrived the next day, and Khatuna bought tickets to New York.

Charles met them at the airport, and was dismayed to discover he was taking charge not only of Khatuna but also of her dishevelled younger brother.

From the taxi, Irakli gazed up at the skyscrapers, which looked old and scaled like a prehistoric fish. *Ichthyosaur*, he thought.

The three of them went out to dinner. Irakli said nothing to Charles all evening, and Khatuna drank two bottles of wine. Charles thought, *All along, she was just a Third World girl. Give them an inch, they take a mile.*

Afterwards he took her home and fucked her, while Irakli, on the couch outside, pressed cushions against his ears.

Khatuna had only just stopped bleeding from her miscarriage. But her screams came not from the sex, but from its insufficiency.

Dugong

12

THERE IS AN INCANDESCENT GAP between the buildings, and Ulrich realises he is close to Times Square. He wears a maroon tie and a blazer beneath his overcoat, which give him a distinguished air, even if they hang a little loose on his elderly frame. He wanders towards the light.

In his daydreams, Ulrich is somewhat altered from real life. The gold watch he was forced to sell glints once more on his wrist, and his blind eyes are seeing and undimmed. He stands more upright, and that pleading air, which he has always detested in himself, is gone – as if he had not spent his time dwelling on what was taken away. He walks naturally, like the other people on the street, as if there were no reason he should not be here. He resembles one of those men, perhaps, who has just emerged from a theatre – for it is night – or from a jazz club, and who wanders, satisfied with what he has seen.

He comes in under the marvellous light, and stops to watch. Dazzling screens wrap polyp towers, which spire against the orange sky. His white hair reflects the logos, and turns harlequin.

His attention is captured by the familiar features of Albert Einstein playing on a vast video display. Einstein's face is the size of a large house, and it lights up the damp ground. The screen dims, and text appears: *The highest form of musicality in the sphere of thought* – and Ulrich smiles possessively, for these are words he had once written on his wall: Einstein's opinion of Niels Bohr's theory of atomic structure. The text dissolves and converts to plasma. The advertisement ends with the logo of a mobile phone company.

It is late and he grows tired. He looks around to orient himself, and sets off into the dark streets. The wind is cool and he puts his hands in his pockets, which are heavy with marbles.

Boris's signature on the contract is a work of art. Still, the lawyer asks him to do it again.

'In English, please. Our people can't read Cyrillic.'

The document is fifty-nine pages long, and there are three copies. Boris has to initial every page. *Hereinafter called 'the Artist'*. He is bemused by their heavy-handed ways.

The CEO of Universal Music has stepped into the room to give the moment some razzle-dazzle.

'We're really excited to have you on board,' he says, shaking Boris by the hand. 'You're a great musician, and you've come to the right place. You'll see what we do here when we pull out all the stops.'

Boris nods appreciatively.

It is eleven in the morning, and the ceremony does not last long. People turn away to discuss work, even over champagne.

The CEO is left one-on-one with Boris.

'I want you to think of this place as your home. Universal is like your family, and the only thing we care about is helping you make great music.'

Boris does not reply. The CEO says,

'It's nice to get a bit of good news from Bulgaria. All I usually get from that part of the world is piracy. I guess you must have seen it on the streets.'

He shudders. He looks at his watch and says,

'It's an uphill battle. Consumers don't pay for music anymore because they think it's free. They don't respect the work we do, you and me.'

Plastic puts an arm around Boris's shoulders.

'I need to steal this man away,' he says to the CEO.

'I've been telling him about piracy,' says the CEO. 'But you have nothing to worry about, Boris. You're with the biggest music company in the world. You have a lot of muscle on your side.'

'I'm taking him to buy a new violin,' says Plastic. 'Look at that old thing he uses.'

Boris is holding the violin that Slavo gave him years ago. It's somewhat knocked on the corners, and the varnish is dulled, but he doesn't understand why these men look at it with such derision. It has new strings, and the sound is good.

Plastic makes a quick exit with Universal's new star, and they get into his limousine, which is waiting outside the building.

By now, Boris has been in New York for a while. He has settled down with a small group of musicians: a piano player, a bandoneon player and a DJ. He is writing a lot of music.

Boris is staying in a company apartment, but he also has the keys to Plastic's home. Plastic wants every kind of resource to be available to Boris while he composes. There is a full-time butler in Plastic's apartment who takes care of meals, and it has a sound-proof music room with a miraculous stereo system. Boris spends many days there, working through Plastic's enormous record collection. He has taken to writing music at his Blüthner piano.

When he wants to think about other things, he sits in Plastic's living room. He reads his books and watches his TV.

Today, Plastic is in a rush to buy the violin. The driver takes them to a violin dealer's studio, which is open to a little courtyard and invisible from the street. Mr Stern, the owner, has half-moon glasses hanging on a string of coloured beads around his neck, and is standing outside plucking a pomegranate from one of the trees in the courtyard. He is expecting Plastic, and leads them inside.

Boris gasps at the riches held there, and Mr Stern shows him violins from every place and time. He can recite the list of owners over centuries, though the names mean little to Boris. He has a lute and a viola da gamba, and curiosity instruments with ten strings.

He has made a shortlist for Boris, who begins to try them out. With each trial, Mr Stern identifies the precise cause of his dissatisfaction and offers him another instrument, nearer to perfection.

The ageing Mr Stern eyes Plastic as Boris frowns over each violin. His look says, *Who* is *this boy?*

Boris is absorbed by the sounds he is making with these instruments. He is already at work, testing ideas. It is impressive to see how he thinks, but Plastic is due to give a speech at a charity lunch, and he cannot stay long. Two violins are lying on the counter, and he pushes Boris towards a decision. Boris plays the same phrase on each, and Mr Stern smiles.

'Now it's obvious,' he says, and he laughs delightedly when Boris indicates his choice. He picks up the violin himself, and caresses it.

'Italian,' he says. 'Not such an old instrument, but extremely fine.'

'And by far the most expensive,' says Plastic. He looks at Boris. 'You'll have to pay me back when your album comes out.'

Mr Stern says,

'Take it home, live with it a few days. If you don't like it, you can come back and try again.'

He lays the violin in its case.

Boris is looking at the battered fiddle he came in with. He turns it over and strokes it mournfully. Plastic picks up the new violin, trying to hurry things up.

They go outside. Prophets in tall hats are relating visions on street corners and drawing obstructive crowds. Plastic is trying to get away fast, and he's zigzagging angrily. It takes him a while to realise Boris has not kept up. Exasperated, he turns around. To his consternation, he sees that Boris is crouching over his old violin, which is already in flames on the sidewalk.

'What the hell are you doing?' demands Plastic, running back. 'You can't light fires on the street!'

Boris does not look up. He is completely absorbed in the burning violin. He has a can of lighter fluid in his hand. The wood is already turning black.

Plastic says,

'You'll get yourself arrested!'

Plastic is about to stamp out the flames when he sees a young woman standing by, taking video of the burning violin with her cell phone.

The young woman is Khatuna. She is fascinated by the sacrificial fire, and she feels a wave of relaxation pass through her as she watches. Through the flames, she notices a streak of green where a metal string is burning, and she thinks this is the most beautiful thing she has seen for a long time. Boris turns and looks at her. She says,

'Why are you burning your violin?'

She says it in Russian – she does not know why.

The flames die down.

Boris stands up and looks at Plastic. He holds out his hand for the new violin. Plastic hands over the case, wary after what he has just seen. But he is distracted by Khatuna.

'You like fire?' he asks her.

Plastic knows something about names, and when she tells him hers he says *Georgian?* and thinks he sees her interest awaken. He takes an invitation from his pocket and gives it to her.

'This man is a great musician. Come to his show. I'm his producer. Plastic Munari.'

Boris's first performance in New York is only a week away.

'Will you come?' Plastic asks.

'Maybe,' she says. She looks him over. She likes his suit.

Plastic is running very late, and can stay no more. He says *See you next Saturday* and walks away. Khatuna watches him get into his limousine and disappear.

Boris prods the charred violin with his foot, and it scrapes on the concrete. He smiles at Khatuna and she begins to walk with him. He leads her through anonymous streets of warehouses and old factories. He opens a faceless entrance and takes her into a hallway of garish tiles. They go up aged wooden stairs, the stairwell cavernous around them. She follows him, thinking to herself *This is not me who is doing this, this is not Khatuna.*

The apartment is huge, and built in an old factory. It has Persian rugs on the floor and antique maps on the walls. In one corner is a huddle of chairs, and Khatuna sits down on the sofa. Boris brings two glasses and a bottle of vodka. He pours for both of them.

I have a meeting in an hour, thinks Khatuna. *What am I doing here?*

There are pipes from floor to ceiling and the bricks show through the paint. There are windows instead of walls, and the great expanse of concrete floor ripples in the light, for it is not exactly flat. There are paintings stacked against the walls, and objects on the shelves that are worn with age.

Boris does not speak at all. When the silence becomes too big, Khatuna says, 'What star sign are you?'

Boris does not know about such things.

'When is your birthday?'

He tells her. She says,

'The same day as my brother!' She is strangely exhilarated. She asks what year he was born, and says,

'You're one year older than him. To the day.'

She tells him all about Irakli.

'He's an artist too. He writes poetry. He sits all day in our apartment, writing.'

She doesn't know why she feels so happy with Boris, for he remains silent throughout. She feels something significant will happen because of him.

He gets up and leaves the room, and she waits for him to come back. She hears him playing the violin somewhere else in the apartment.

She takes out her phone. She puts on the video camera and turns it in slow circles, sweeping the clocks and paintings of this large and doleful room and coming back to herself, expressionless on the sofa. She wants to capture herself at this moment, sitting in this place, with this music in the background.

The music finishes, but Boris does not return. Khatuna waits for several minutes. Then she gets up and looks for him in every room of the apartment. She cannot find him and finally, incredulous, she lets herself out.

13

KHATUNA AND IRAKLI EMERGED from the elevator and crossed the lobby. The doorman wished them a good night as they passed through the open door.

Outside, it was dark and cold.

'You're not wearing enough clothes,' said Khatuna. 'Where's that jacket I bought you last week?'

She stood on the edge of the sidewalk, the lights of the ziggurat terraced above her. She held out her glove; a taxi swooped.

She let Irakli in ahead of her. He had an old umbrella, which he'd bought at a flea market and took with him everywhere.

Khatuna had dyed her hair blonde for this evening, and she checked the effect in the cab's rear-view mirror. She turned her head to both sides.

'I look so sexy,' she said. 'I am jealous of myself.'

She put in sixteen-hour days at Struction Enterprises, and she had lost the habit of going out at night. She had taken pleasure in dressing up tonight. Normally, she thought only about work.

She was now head of security systems at Struction. It was a role for which she was superbly qualified. New York boardrooms had never heard anyone speak so nonchalantly about snipers, chemical weapons and truck bombs, and on her lips this breezy militarism seemed not retrograde but futuristic – even profound. Everyone wanted a piece of her advice.

Her early estrangement from Charles Hahn had done nothing to hamper her advancement in his company, and within a year she had gained a seat on the board.

The taxi drew up in front of the club.

Inside, there was neon darkness. They stopped in front of a little wooden hatch to buy tickets. It seemed they were early. There was no queue in the lobby, and the old woman inside was playing solitaire on a computer. She stopped her game to write out their tickets.

'That's forty-four dollars, please.'

Khatuna paid and stopped to leave her fur in the coat-check. Irakli handed her his umbrella. He murmured amusedly,

'Did you see that woman?'

'What woman?'

Khatuna looked at herself in the mirror.

'The woman who sold us the tickets. She added twenty-two and twenty-two on a calculator.'

Through the doors, the music was louder. A man played piano onstage, and sang a duet with a woman in a top hat. There were only a few people as yet, and the atmosphere was like someone's house. People shouted jokes at the performers.

Khatuna chose a place near the front. She looked around at the battered furniture and said,

'I thought it would be a fancier place.'

Irakli put his head close to hers. He was still thinking about the ticket seller.

'She added the total on a calculator. Then she wrote out the tickets by hand.'

The singer hit a high note and lifted her bare leg onto the piano, and both performers dissolved into laughter. People clapped, and another act came onto the stage.

'So what's her computer for?' said Irakli. He was full of glee. 'It's just for her to play solitaire. It's just a two-thousand-dollar pack of cards.'

Plastic was backstage with his entourage. The editor of a big magazine was there, and a movie director, and a princess from the deposed Bulgarian royal family.

'It's absolutely true,' he said sotto voce. 'He grew up in a totally empty town. There was no one else except his grandmother. He grew crops and raised pigs – he made candles from pig lard to light his house, for God's sake. When he first got here he didn't know – you know – *anything*. But he's a genius. He's just a pure natural fucking genius. When you hear him you'll understand. I haven't been this excited about an artist in years.'

The room was small, and the photographer kept flashing. Boris had turned his back and was warming up in the corner. He had on a green military uniform. Plastic introduced his guests to the owner of the club.

'Isn't this place great, though?'

They gushed compliments. Someone mentioned the antique chemical bottles so artfully laid out in the men's room. A conversation began about a fabulous little store in the Village where you could pick up the most eccentric things. They drank champagne and chatted happily.

'I'm allergic to sulphites, you see.'

'Once in his life, a man should buy a pair of leather pants.'

'I saw him play in Carnegie Hall just two months before he died.'

'*Africa?* I said. There's nothing to *do* in Africa!'

Noise was building in the club. The owner said it was getting full out there. The bandoneon player took off his jacket and warmed up with a tango. The magazine editor said,

'Plastic has probably done more than anyone else—'

A cell phone rang. The movie director took the call and got into an argument with someone on the other end.

'He didn't mean it in a negative way? Can someone please explain to me—'

'Boris needs water. Get some water over here. And keep the volume down!'

'—more than anyone else I can think of to dictate cultural taste in the world today.'

The Bulgarian princess lit a cigar. Her hair was shorn. Boris had a melody he was trying out, again and again. The movie director was indignant on the phone:

'I'd like to know how someone can say *genocide* in a positive way.'

'His influence goes beyond music, because it's not just about music. It's an aesthetic *attitude* to globalisation.'

The CEO of Universal stopped by with another bottle of champagne and they drank a toast. Boris autographed a couple of invitations, and the CEO did a mock benediction.

'OK', said Plastic, 'OK, everybody out!'

'If he'd stayed in the States, he would have been as big as Duke Ellington,' said the movie director to the princess. 'But no one's heard of him because he spent the whole of the thirties in Europe. He played Carnegie Hall right before he died. There were maybe forty people in the audience.'

'Let's have some quiet back here!'

'He was playing in Berlin and Paris. He was playing in Latin America.'

Everyone filed out, still talking, and Plastic was left alone with the band. He shook hands with each of them.

'You don't need any advice from me,' he said. 'Go make music.'

From the moment Boris appeared onstage, Irakli was transfixed: he had never heard anything as magnificent as this. Boris played four pieces, back to back, and the music came to Irakli like poetry.

She plane? She solstice?
She sixty forecast of seven breezes, the anticyclone miniature,
a mossy-flooring wading girl!
Was cirrus not she, nor tremor nor breakfast? She fair was timely –
but storm wind loafs impatient.
The whale is averse on a New England beach.

She bitter squints the squat-eye fool
and mirthly mock entire the mull:
My dearly friend, so faithful-word,
does your deliquesce recur?
Is your senescence waking up?

He not fuss the morphosis, his lugubrious style:
This is radium love, do not litter the arm.
They don't count the corpses that sink to the deep.

Boris shone as he played, and all the people in that room were filled with new kinds of desire. They wanted to follow him through his hole in the sky. They tugged at him with infantile dependence. They coveted the perfection of his body's sway. They applauded him, reached out their hands, and sucked at him with clammy eyes. They became wet with their own saliva, for he was unattainable, and his absence crept into their mouths.

The music ended, the lights went up, and the crowd screamed and clapped. They were sitting under Boris's feet, for the stage was small, and everywhere was free champagne.

Irakli said to Khatuna, raising his voice over the outcry,

'He is amazing! Amazing!'

His face glowed with excitement.

Khatuna raised her eyebrow. She said,

'I'd like him to *rebuke* me.'

The DJ and the bandoneon player filed offstage, leaving Boris alone with the pianist. Boris said,

'I will play the second violin sonata by Alfred Schnittke, written in 1968.'

It was a piece he had learned from Plastic's CD collection, but Plastic was aghast.

'What the hell is he doing?' he whispered. 'He's supposed to play his own music!'

The sonata was dissonant and excruciating, and the faces in the audience went blank. Irakli heard it like an endless struggle –

radium cholera bitumen patriot
albatross desiccate fungicide pyramid
chemical Africa national accident
multiply hurricane industry motivate

– the violin not played but wrestled, the piano pummelled like a broken gun.

terminal citizen management piracy
digital contribute parasite northerly
democrat corporate marketing ministry
generate synchronise quality property
Pakistan automate cellular weaponry
bullet hole Heisenberg certify history

Plastic wanted to stop it. He said,
'This is suicide'

alcohol medicine embassy recognise
dentistry personal hospital circumcise

It was interminable, and there was no refusal. The piano crashed the same chord a hundred senseless times.

document educate financing bellicose
structural legalise radical standardise
borderline distribute rational wintertime

The audience was racked across silence. The music ended, and there was no relief.

Boris bowed, and people clapped with dull recognition. The hall was wrung out: they wondered why they had deserved it.

He said,

'Now I will play music of my own.'

The violin began alone, the stirring of future love. The other musicians quietly returned to the stage. Plastic's heart was grinding. The bandoneon trembled, the chords were poised.

The ptarmigan ruff, the mastodon mouth, an emerald cotyledon…

In a blink, *embark rebellious!*, the band explodes with a riot-dance and Boris stamps exultant like a seven-foot Gypsy, vaulting in a circle, a Cossack caper, shouting the spirit for all he is worth, *Hey! Hey! Hey!* he cries like seven giant peasants, and in a slow-motion second the trussed audience unfurls euphoric, it opens like a canyon, *proclaim the tsunami klaxon after flesh!*, and they all stand like the glorious mountain-bud, they thank the journey, what relief, what exaltation, what—

Beautiful beautiful beautiful I am speechless before your song
Liquid is flowing again in the dry conduits
I cannot tell, I cannot tell, I cannot say the way it fell

The music has merged with tumult, and Irakli sees a passage open up before him. He is on the stage already, his Georgian dance erupting, his Caucasian footwork a-flicker. He jumps and reels and the crowd watches in delight, the band drawing round. This audience will rip down the building, it will howl and fornicate. Irakli leaps high in the air and lands flat on his back with the end chords, laughing unheard in the impossible roar. There are people standing on tables, weeping openly.

Boris gives Irakli a hand and pulls him up. The band goes offstage.

The crowd is on its feet, and Plastic has to shield his way through the corks they are throwing at the stage, which is empty with its piano and silent chairs. They shout for Boris but he is in the black-and-white backstage, the light bulbs burning and shadows under his cheekbones. Around him are the other musicians, who have no words for what has happened. The pianist smokes a cigarette, trying to piece it together.

Plastic beckons to Khatuna and takes her hand in the crush. With her other hand she reaches for Irakli so as not to lose him. Plastic leads her out of the bellowing mass, he hauls her backstage to Boris's dressing room – and she likes the strength of his grip. The doorway is so thronged there is no space to see what is happening inside. There are men trying to get in with video cameras and tripods. Plastic tells them to clear the entrance and pushes through with Khatuna and Irakli. In the full light he notices Irakli for the first time.

'Aren't you the guy who danced onstage?'

A well-known novelist is drinking champagne from the bottle. The ones who have tricked and lied their way in here stand wide-eyed, trying to look as if they belong. Boris is taking hungry bites of a hamburger.

A cameraman puts a microphone in Plastic's face and asks him to comment on the show. Plastic serves up some simple but effective phrases over the noise. But the journalist is angling for something profound:

'It's a very tragic place, isn't it? The Balkans? Would you say that came through in his music?'

Plastic wants to get out of here; he calls his people to evict the media. He gives everyone the address of the restaurant for dinner and takes his people out through the back door.

Khatuna and Irakli do not go with him. They have to get their stuff from the coat check.

They weave back through the crowd in the club. They are high on alcohol and sensation when they make it to the lobby. The attendant hands over the coat and umbrella to Khatuna. Irakli looks inside the little wooden ticket hatch. The old woman has gone home, and the office is dark except for the glowing fishes drifting restfully across the computer screen. Slack-faced, he watches them for a while and, such is his altered mind, he has the feeling, when he walks out to the street, that the wet splashes on his face are dripping from those fish. Khatuna puts up his umbrella and he realises it is rain.

They walk towards the address Plastic has given them, and at the end of the first block they find Boris standing alone.

'What are you doing here?' asks Khatuna.

'I wanted to walk on my own,' says Boris. 'But I don't know which way from here.'

Khatuna holds the umbrella over him and they set off, the three of them huddled close, happy and optimistic, three ordinary kids in the night.

'It's just down there,' Khatuna says lightly.

At that moment, the umbrella flies out of her hand and catches in some railings down the street. She runs after it in her heels, racing her brother, laughing at the rain on her dyed-blonde hair, her fur coat flaring on the wind.

Plastic had booked a private room in a Vietnamese restaurant. The table was already laid with hors d'oeuvres, and the music critics waited for him to seat them. Two waitresses walked the length of the room, ceremonially releasing disinfectant spray above their heads, like in an aircraft.

People applauded as Boris entered, and took photographs of him with their phones. There were crystal drops down the back of his jacket and his hair was damp. The Bulgarian princess shook her head with emotion and put her arms reverentially around him. The journalists gathered close.

'What do you call your music? Is it jazz? Is it Gypsy?'

'You've been described as a feral child. Do you know what that means?'

The novelist shook Irakli by the hand.

'Your dancing was spellbinding,' he said. 'I would have done the same if I knew how.'

They sat down in groups. There were orchids on the table, and starters of tofu and soft-shell turtle. Everyone was seized by hunger. The room was full of steam and aroma, and they began to eat greedily. One of the critics said through his noodle soup,

'Let's not forget it was also the best performance of the Schnittke sonata we've ever heard!'

The movie director sat next to Khatuna and asked her about her work. She told him about advances in architectural security. She said,

'We don't make our buildings here anymore. We bring them on a ship from China. They make everything there. If you want you can buy yourself a jail for next to nothing. It's precast in concrete. You just tell them how many cells you want and they ship it over.'

There was roast duck, and beef with lemon grass. If you could have tuned out all the other sounds you would have heard a great cacophony of mastication.

The movie director was sweating a lot. He had taken it upon himself to explain to Khatuna a word she did not know.

'It means what you've just written is wrong, and you know it's wrong.'

He had a bit of coriander leaf caught in his teeth.

'If you know it's wrong, why would you write it?'

'Maybe because you're quoting someone else who wrote it wrong? So you put *sic* after it to show it wasn't you.'

Khatuna thought he must be the most boring film director in the world. She said,

'You get to sit next to someone like me, and this is all you can find to talk about?'

She wanted to know Boris. He had unbuttoned his military jacket but still cradled his violin, even at the dinner table. She got out of her seat and went to him. She whispered in his ear,

'You left me alone the other day! Where did you go?'

Her cheek had touched his forehead. Boris said,

'I didn't want to stay there any more.'

'Why didn't you take me?'

Boris did not reply. She said,

'Will you come out with me now? We can find somewhere to be alone.'

Boris looked up into her eyes. He studied her, and then he said,

'No.'

People began to change places around the table, and the bamboo room became jumbled. Clear-thinking waiters removed empty bowls and laid on full ones: stir-fried eel, shrimp with sugarcane, sautéed frog, cuttlefish salad, lobster wrapped in rice and banana leaves. The meal was a riot for the tongue, and people slurped their wine loudly for the extra sensation.

Boris was trying out his chopsticks on the roasted suckling pig. He asked the Bulgarian princess whether they raised pigs in America.

'Of course they do.'

He contemplated the meat. He said,

'How much milk do you get from an American pig?'

The princess said,

'I don't know. I live in Spain.'

She put the question to the table, provoking lively debate.

'Do pigs give milk? I suppose they must.'

'Pigs give bacon.'

'*Suckling* pig.'

'We're educated people and we don't know this?'

'Pigs are mammals, for Christ's sake!'

'*Suckling pig!*'

The waiters brought more steaming plates, and looked for gaps in which to put them. Cooked snakes were coiled up in bowls, and the party examined them with ghoulish delight. There was a discussion about outlandish things people had eaten. Dog and alligator.

'I once ate monkey brain,' said a soft-spoken actress.

The group embarked upon a compilation of things eaten in China. There was a list of places where people supposedly ate insects.

'In Papua New Guinea they eat the dugong.'

Haloed with alcohol, the conversation seemed brilliant. It carried on for a long time, and no one noticed when Boris slipped away, taking Irakli with him.

Irakli could not stop talking about Boris's music.

The rain fell harder than ever, and the wind was extreme. Irakli spoke breathlessly as they ran through the streets:

'This is what I thought of while you were playing. I saw joyful barbarians dancing in a stormed palace. They were hanging up their flags, tossing cigarettes on the priceless carpets, and posing for photos in gold bathtubs. Chandeliers were smashed on the ground, and they were stashing paintings in suitcases. They were inventing ministries for themselves, and choosing imperial bedrooms for their offices.'

'You speak well,' said Boris. 'I could never say it like that.'

They were drenched when they arrived at his apartment. Boris brought Irakli a towel and a fresh shirt.

The apartment was on the forty-fifth floor, and there was almost nothing in it. An enormous window looked over the Hudson River to New Jersey.

Irakli was rubbing his head with the towel. He said,

'I want you to read my poetry. When I was listening to your music I was thinking, *He has felt the same things! He's had the same intimations I've had all my life*. I'm trying to put them into words, like you put them into music.'

Boris poured brown liquid from a bottle with no label. Irakli continued,

'When I saw how easily your music came, I thought maybe the task is just too difficult for me. It's beyond me.'

'You're just young,' said Boris. 'It will take you another twenty years.'

'You're barely older than me. But look how you play!'

Boris grinned.

'Don't judge me by what you heard tonight. Wait a few years and you'll hear what I can do!'

They drank avidly, filled with the rare elation that two people sometimes feel on finding each other. They wanted to know everything about each other. They told the story of their lives until that point. Irakli told Boris about Khatuna, and what had happened to her.

'That was her?' asked Boris. 'Who was there tonight?'

'She doesn't usually look like that. She's dyed her hair.'

'I didn't like her,' said Boris.

He held his violin in his lap, and his left hand fluttered on the strings. Irakli was taken aback.

'Men usually enjoy meeting her,' he said.

The night passed, but the weather did not let up. The wind whistled around the building, and the window was lashed with rain. They talked about coming to America. Boris talked about the startling new sounds of New York: the stricken alarm of reversing trucks, the industrial growl of electronic shutters, the hydraulic sigh of brakes. He talked about the way that strangers passing on the sidewalks looked you boldly in the eye.

Boris and Irakli sat facing the window, and they could see blades of lightning as they talked, and the hypnotic stream of car lights leaking into New Jersey from the Lincoln Tunnel. And then they saw a concrete water tower collapse on the other side of the river.

The tower stood next to the highway, and it was brightly lit. First they saw the column sway unnaturally. With the enormous weight of the bulb on top, it could not right itself and, majestically, the entire structure slowly toppled over. Irakli started as it crashed, but from this distance all was silence.

The tower fell away from the highway onto unlit grassland where nothing could be seen. A moment later, a raging wave emerged from the blackness and smashed over the highway, sweeping cars away to make a semicircular lake, blazing in the floodlights. Car collisions spread up and down the lanes in a chain reaction.

'Did you see that?' asked Irakli.

'I know!' said Boris, incredulous.

The traffic tails, red and white, hardened in each direction. The water reached its greatest extent over the highway and began to subside. Silent sirens converged on the zone.

'I wonder if anyone died down there,' Irakli said dreamily.

Boris reached for his violin and began to play. The storm wound down.

Irakli had been drinking for hours, and wanted to close his eyes. The sofa felt so warm. He let Boris's music flood over him.

Nothing can be wrong – the fancy? the corruption, the border?
Every one a flagrance, a fragrance that he made:
he made a delicate amethyst out of winter,
a crystal dodecahedron through a pinhole peephole –
he snowflake he malleus he
cochlea he
eyelid.

14

When Khatuna awoke there was no one next to her. The room was strange, and her dress was snagged on a post at the foot of the bed. She rescued it, slipped it on, and walked out of the room.

Plastic was already in his gym clothes. He had muffins and coffee on a tray.

'I was about to get you up,' he said, and kissed her.

He was handsome, which made up for a lot.

She sat down.

'Wait a minute,' she said. 'I've been in this room before.'

'No,' he said, smiling.

'I came here with Boris. I sat on this sofa.'

She took out her phone and showed Plastic the video she had shot in that very place. There was this room, and Khatuna's face, stolid and foreign in the image, and the sound of Boris's music in the background.

'He brought you *here?*' he said.

'I assumed it was his apartment,' Khatuna said.

She got up and walked around, curious again. There was an ancient French tapestry on the wall, and a large Venetian mirror whose silvering had curdled like diesel oil in the rain. There was a set of old engravings of Vienna. There was a carved wooden statue on a pedestal, a Buddha with an arm missing.

She said,

'Why is your place like this? You're a rich man but all your things are falling apart.'

Plastic said,

'Those antiques cost more money than you'll see in your whole life.'

'You like old things,' she replied. 'That's not good.'

He kissed her on the ear.

'I like young things too,' he said.

She stood very still as he nibbled her earlobe, trying to work out whether she liked it. She said,

'Do you have a gun?'

'No,' he said. 'Why?'

'Nothing.'

'I like that tattoo in the small of your back. I feel I'm being watched.'

'That eye is not watching *you*.'

He looked at her curiously, and drained his coffee. He said,

'I have to get to the gym.'

'You're leaving?'

'I work out every Sunday morning.'

'Do you have a beautiful young woman in your house every Sunday morning?'

'I get grumpy if I don't work out.'

Khatuna curled her lip with distaste.

'You don't love women,' she said.

'We'll see each other again, won't we?'

'I don't know,' she said.

After he left, she wanted only to get out of his house. She collected her clothes and took a taxi home. She was unhappy to find that Irakli was not there. She fretted, and paced between rooms. He refused to carry a mobile, so she could not call him.

The only life in the house was the parrot in the kitchen. Khatuna had bought it as a present for Irakli so he would have company while she was at work. She took the cover off the cage, and the parrot scratched animatedly at the mesh, reciting all its phrases. Khatuna interrogated the bird, asking where Irakli could be.

Bye-bye, it said. *Good morning Baghdad.*

She shushed in exasperation and kicked off her high heels. She called Plastic to see whether he would know how to contact Boris, but he did not answer his phone.

His fucking gym.

She put on her slippers and lit a cigarette. She slid open the balcony door and sat on the chair she kept there. The storm had left a damp, cool morning, but Khatuna felt claustrophobic in sealed-up American homes, and liked to have access to the sky. The balcony was the most satisfying thing about this house, with its arabesque decoration and ferns hanging down from the terrace above.

She sat with her eyes fixed on the front door, imagining the catastrophic things that could have happened to her brother while she was away with a strange man. She kicked one leg nervously and watched her slipper bounce on her foot. Suddenly she had the feeling that she looked exactly like her mother, and this made her even more anxious.

The door opened, eventually, and Irakli walked in with his umbrella.

'Where have you *been?*' she shouted.

He looked her up and down. He said,

'You're still wearing the same dress.'

'So what?'

'Who were you with?'

'I went home with that producer. He's very rich.'

She felt like punishing Irakli. She said,

'He made that guy Boris out of nothing.'

Irakli went out on to the balcony and looked out across town. A couple of blocks away, the Empire State Building sparkled after its recent restoration. Khatuna said,

'Where were you?'

'I slept at Boris's house.'

'What's wrong with him?' she demanded. 'Why did he want to go home with you?'

Irakli shrugged wanly.

'What did he want from you?' she asked.

'We talked all night,' said Irakli, still high with it. 'I had an amazing time. It was like running into an unknown brother by mistake.'

'Did he want to have sex with you?'

'Don't be ridiculous.'

Khatuna inspected her brother suspiciously. She said,

'His smile was like a gay man's.'

'All you can think of is sex,' said Irakli. 'Can't you think of anything else that people can do together?'

Khatuna smirked.

'If I want advice about sex, I'll ask someone with a bit of first-hand knowledge.'

Irakli leaned on the rail and looked at the clouds, hanging like white rocks in the sky. Sirens whined in every part of town. A sign on the side of the Empire State Building said in massive letters, *For RENT.*

15

How many times has Ulrich imagined himself knocking at an American door, and finding behind it a young man with a resemblance to himself?

All those imaginings accompany him now as he enters Boris's building and takes the elevator to the forty-fifth floor. Everything has the echo of presentiment.

He rings the bell at Boris's door. His heart is throbbing. He has put on good clothes, but he is old and does not resemble a father. The words have gone out of his head.

Boris answers brusquely, keeping his hand on the door handle.

He is taller than Ulrich expected. He is not wearing a shirt, and he carries his violin in his hand. Round his neck he wears a pendant on a string; it is made of gnarled pig skin, and looks vaguely obscene. There is a broad scar on his torso, which makes Ulrich mourn.

They stare at each other for a time. Ulrich feels ashamed that he has reached such an age while Boris is still so young, and he is all too aware of how he must appear. This morning, with unsteady hand, he shaved the top off a pimple, which now bleeds periodically over his chin.

He looks past Boris into the apartment. It is full of cardboard boxes, each neatly stacked and labelled with a skull-and-crossbones. On the floor are polystyrene balls, duct tape and other packing paraphernalia.

Ulrich would love to go inside, to sit for a while. He begins,

'I am—'

It is absurd to say it like this. He does not know this boy. It would be an offence to say what he wants to say. He swallows several times to regain control of his larynx.

'Will you play for me?' he asks in Bulgarian. 'I would like it so much.'

He studies the stubble on Boris's face. He sees his badly cut hair, his violin bow twitching in his hand, his youthful eyes shining with suspicion, the impatient muscles in his bare arms.

Boris relaxes his grip on the door handle, and for a moment Ulrich thinks he is going to let him in. But at the last minute, the young face turns wary, and Boris shuts the door. Ulrich's tense shoulders slump, and he lets out his breath.

I was too eager, he says to himself in the corridor. *He could see it. He doesn't want some stranger making claims on him.*

But he smiles to himself, because even this unsuccessful contact has made him happy.

I have to be patient, he thinks.

He writes a polite note to Boris, telling him how he can contact him, and slips it under the door.

Boris and Plastic work late nights on the album. They are light-headed with it, and need little sleep. Something wonderful is emerging, unlike any music they have ever heard.

Plastic has unexpected insights, and Boris gains respect for a kind of knowledge he has not encountered before. Plastic knows how to *finish* things: to push and polish until they slot into perfection.

Boris has bought recording equipment and sometimes turns up with sounds he wants to use on the album. He's written a duet for violin and the rhythmic near-far moan of an industrial vacuum cleaner. Plastic doesn't think it belongs here.

'In my home town,' explains Boris, 'sounds lasted a long time. Here there's so much other noise, they're stifled immediately. I want to get that feeling in. The sounds desperate for space, all dying young.'

Plastic tries to set him right.

'You're at the beginning of your career,' he says. 'You don't have to say everything in one go.'

Boris doesn't look at him while he speaks. Plastic continues,

'I'm not thinking about one album. I'm thinking about how we can make the next five albums. Ten. I'm thinking how we can sustain you as a great artist until you're seventy years old.'

Boris grins. Plastic says,

'You can smile now because you don't know anything, and your talent is screaming to be let out. It won't be the same forever. Most people of your generation lose their way when they hit thirty-five. While they sit in their jacuzzis wondering how they ever did what they did, the system spits them out.'

He adds,

'You should have heard me play piano when I was your age.'

Irakli opens the door of the parrot cage. The bird steps off the parapet and flutters across the kitchen, alighting on a chair.

'*Good morning*,' it says, though the day is quite over. It looks Irakli over with avuncular concern.

He has sat all day with his pen and notebook, but he has not a single word to show for it.

Irakli has always lived among visions, which come to him just like memories of the womb return before sleep. Under their influence, he feels his hands as big as planets in the absolute night, and hears the postponed echo of ancient sea monsters. Khatuna looms there, unseparated from him, and the horrors of the world are turned inside out. Beyond his nose, and impossibly remote, great spheres pass through each other, weightless and incandescent.

Since he met Boris, these visions have departed, and Irakli has become listless and depressed. He sits in the house day after day doing nothing. He tries to unstop himself with alcohol, but it does not help.

Khatuna is getting irritated with him.

'It's like living with a corpse,' she says. 'You used to make me laugh. Now you're always morose. I get depressed just seeing you.'

She tells him it's time to give up this writing. *Your fucking poetry!* she says every day. She tells him how he should improve himself, and buys him presents – a biography of a famous CEO, a gold case for business cards – that are designed to draw him out of his slump. Irakli does not pretend to be grateful. She gives him a silver pen holder for his desk, and he fills it with vodka and empties it down his throat. He says,

'I was born for one thing. When I'm on my deathbed there is only one thing I will look back on and feel proud of.'

He does not know how to speak to Khatuna anymore. She is cynical, and takes pleasure in humiliating everyone around her. She says things like *retooling*, *benchmarking* and *value-add*. She meets many people at parties with Plastic and all she can say about them is how many dollars they are worth.

It is late, and Khatuna is still not home. Irakli proffers some seeds to the parrot, which it eats messily, dropping husks on the floor. It sings some lines from a Russian pop song that Khatuna likes and rounds off with the *beep beep* of the microwave. The parrot says *Come to Irakli!* and *Make a cup of tea!* – which is a phrase it learned before it arrived in this house.

Irakli sits down to write a letter to his mother. The worse he feels, the brighter and more effusive his letters become. He tells her his book is going well. The parrot dribbles on the paper. Irakli writes more often to his mother than she to him. Her letters are brief. She has stopped drinking and is cutting hair in a salon. He has sometimes found bits of her customers' hair between her pages.

Irakli addresses the envelope and puts the parrot back in its cage. It says *Good night!* again and again, alternating between Khatuna's voice and his own. Its imitation of voices is uncanny, and Irakli and Khatuna are each surprised now and then by ventriloquist visitations of the other.

Irakli picks up his umbrella and leaves the house. As he walks he sees the new zombies let loose in the street: the radio-wave imbeciles with wires in their ears, talking to the beyond. He sees the curving aerial highways, braided in concrete, and smooth-moving at this hour. He sees bars on street corners, and crowds outside packed into the electric glow. He sees helicopters overhead, and night markets. He sees the messages on fluorescent paper on the walls. *UNDER THE WEATHER? If you're fading, call us now. A friendly voice changes everything.*

Irakli has begun to feel despondent in this city. He talks wistfully about Tbilisi, but Khatuna cuts off this line of thought.

'There is still danger for us there,' she says.

But he is not sure whether she really believes it.

He arrives at the recording studio and waits outside until Boris comes down. He fills in the time with a can of Coke, and makes notes of things around him. He sees an old man checking the slots in the phone booths for any coins left behind. He sees a woman sprinting past him in high heels, holding her breasts against the jolts.

Boris comes down the steps and puts his arm around his friend.

'We just finished a track,' he says excitedly as they walk down the street. 'It sounds really good.'

He ducks into a store to buy a chocolate bar and proposes they go to a late movie. The cinema is his favourite place to talk. They walk quickly to get there in time, cutting the corners of the blocks to try to force a diagonal through the right-angle city. Boris has become formidable while recording this album, and people look at him as they walk. Some of them he greets and shakes by the hand: Irakli is always amazed how many people he knows.

'Some Russian sailors I met once,' explains Boris.

They buy tickets for the movie and settle down with a tray of nachos. Boris eats loudly and tells stories. He tells Irakli about the book he is reading. He has found gems he never dreamed of in Plastic's library, and he is reading a new book every day. Today's title is *Robinson Crusoe*, and Boris has found incredible revelations in it.

'You have to read this book! He describes thoughts exactly as they are, thoughts you didn't know there could be words for.'

He is full of his reading. He quotes entire paragraphs by heart so Irakli can admire them. He asks about Irakli's poetry. Irakli tells him he is not writing anything right now. When Boris asks what he has done with his day, he makes up a story of idleness – though this is belied by the exhaustion in his face.

The movie begins, a staccato symphony of grunts and gunshots. They are blanched in its glow. Boris says,

'Will you write something for me? The tracks on my CD need titles. You're the only one who can put my music into words.'

'I don't know if I can.'

Boris is irritated.

'Why are you always so dismissive of yourself? I've read your poetry. I know how you write. Come on. You're the only one who really understands what I do. Remember how you danced that night? Write like that.'

At that moment their conversation is shushed by a woman who is trying to record the movie off the screen with a video camera.

'I'm getting your voices on the audio track,' she complains.

They apologise, get up and leave the cinema. They buy some vodka and go back to Boris's apartment.

These days, Boris's energy is irrepressible, and he refuses to sleep. He gets out his violin and plays to Irakli every phrase from the day's recording, asking him what he thinks. His head is coursing with music, and it keeps Irakli up all night, so he is useless the next day.

Khatuna thinks it's funny that Plastic's leather shoes creak as he walks. *How can you stand it?* she exclaims.

She crouches by his chair, undoes his laces and takes the shoes off his feet. She finds she can fit into them with her own shoes still on.

'Your feet are so big!' she says.

She marches up and down the concrete floor of his loft, his shoes clunking on her feet. He is irritated.

'You'll spoil them, for God's sake. Those are fifteen-hundred-dollar shoes.'

She takes out her phone and starts to video her feet walking noisily in his shoes.

He says,

'Bring them back! And stop constantly filming yourself.'

She drags her man-size feet over to him and sits on his lap. Her camera is still running and she turns it on his face.

'A woman is supposed to love how beautiful and sexy she is,' she says.

She turns off the camera.

'In this country you don't know anything about love,' she says pityingly. 'You import Asian women to love the men, and Mexican women to love the children. So how could you know?'

She laughs at his dour expression.

'You're good-looking and rich. That much you have going for you, Plastic.' She ruffles his hair. 'What's your real name, anyway?'

'No one calls me that anymore.'

Khatuna takes his shoes off, kneels on the floor and puts them on his feet. She proceeds to tie the most symmetrical of knots.

Plastic considers the focus she brings to the tying of shoelaces and wonders why he was so annoyed a moment ago. He wants spontaneity in his days; he wants a woman who is still young enough to know her own feelings, who will put him skin to skin with life. But when he finds her, his instinct is to stifle her and run away.

'Come here,' he says, and they kiss, her hand in his ample hair. 'Let's go away together. Let's go to Paris. I'll take you for the best food you've ever had.'

'Let's go now. Tonight!'

'Let me finish Boris's album. Then we'll go.'

He kisses her again and carries her towards the bed.

'Fuck me where I can watch you with my other eye,' she says. 'The one on my back.'

Boris's album is soon to be released, and Plastic sets up preview concerts for the inner circle. He wants the journalists and critics talking about Boris even before the music hits the market. He sets up gigs in Chicago, D.C. and L.A. Boris takes Irakli along for the ride.

The concerts create a furore, and Boris wants to go out all the time. People like to have him at their parties. They want to touch him, to see how he drinks, how he sits in a chair – and Boris is developing a style for dealing with it. He lets himself be taken here and there.

Irakli loses track. Most nights he ends up cutting loose early and going back to their suite to sleep.

One morning in L.A., Irakli is watching TV alone in the hotel when Boris comes back there with a girl named Lara. She is beautiful and unslept. She carries a single yellow rose, which she stands tenderly in a glass of water. She puts her bare feet up on the table and lights a joint. Boris is in high spirits and sings. He says to Lara,

'This is Irakli. He's my muse. He's my mentor.'

Boris walks around the room in a goblin dance.

'Just look at this hotel room,' he says. 'A herd of cows could live in here!'

His violin is never far away, and now he plays a rustic jig. Lara passes the joint to Irakli, and it tastes fantastic. He draws from it several times and feels the armchair fold like warm wax.

'Lara can sing,' says Boris.

Lara's blonde hair is in braids and she has a pretty voice. She sings an old jazz song that Boris tresses with his violin.

He says,

'Lara and I played all night at a party. Some guy had a bass and we hit it with him. It came together out of nothing.'

'It was fucked up,' says Lara dreamily.

Boris takes a drag of the joint too, but it does nothing to still him. He is so full of energy he cannot sit down. He looks out of the window and says,

'Who wants to swim?'

'I do,' says Lara.

Irakli does not respond. He can feel the vibrations of the world rising through the feet of the armchair, and he does not want to disturb them.

Boris uproots him unmercifully and carries him out of the door. They get in the elevator, Lara chanting the descending numbers of the floors and drumming them on Boris's head. Boris still holds Irakli in his arms, and when the doors open on the ground floor he marches him out into the lobby, speeds along the corridors under the arrows saying *Swimming Pool*, manoeuvres through the narrow exit into the hot L.A. morning and, breathless, lays him down on a recliner.

'Now get your clothes off,' he says, pulling off his own.

Boris and Lara jump into the pool. Boris splashes exuberantly while Lara glides underwater like a stretched white seal. She comes up laughing.

'The water's beautiful!' shouts Boris to Irakli, who is not moving from the chair. The heat is blazing, and he shields his eyes against the force field of the sun. There are parakeets screeching in the palm trees. The grain of his own skin is like a mesh of glistening ravines, and he can smell the sweat gathering in the crook of his elbow.

Through the heat haze, Irakli sees Lara climb on Boris's shoulders. Boris makes like an angry bull, roaring and snorting and trying to unseat her, but she digs her feet into his flanks and has an arm locked around his head. She is high above the water in her translucent bra and panties, singing defiantly, and she swings a rodeo arm round and round in the air. They struggle against each other until Boris tips her crashing into the water, and for a moment she is lost below a whirlpool. Two parakeets swoop low over the pool, their shining bellies reflecting turquoise. Lara bursts through the water's surface, puts her arms round Boris's neck and kisses him. Irakli closes his eyes to a crack, until he sees only the curved horizon of his own cheeks.

'What are you doing?' Boris shouts to him. Irakli does not answer, and Boris comes to get him, wet-stepping over the hot stone. His shadow flashes across Irakli's face, who flinches. Boris starts to undo Irakli's clothes. Dripping water from his hair on to Irakli's burning face and arms, Boris strips him down to his underpants, picks him up and carries him into the pool. His torso feels clean and cool.

'How can you be this heavy?' Boris says.

As Irakli's body touches the water, it turns to loam. Boris lays him with infinite gentleness on the surface, he holds him there for a long while and draws his arms away so slowly that Irakli does not know the instant when he is floating alone. Boris paddles away to intercept Lara, who is submarining from end to end.

Irakli looks up at the hot plate of the sky, the sun lighting rainbows in his eyelashes. Around him, the white water is duned with lapping blue, and it closes in a creeping tickle over his still-dry stomach. His ears are submerged and all the sounds are deep. He hears the protest of liquid as Lara and Boris fall over each other again, and the altered sound of their distant cries. With washed eyeballs he has new focus, and sees eagles circling in the remote sky – but then the surface floods over, and the palm trees turn molten. He closes his eyes and feels himself drift, his limbs outstretched, and eternity just around the corner. The water removes the impact from things, extracts their sound and colour, and soothes them all.

There's something amazing about this kind of sleep. There is nothing so calm as the muffled deep.

Suddenly he is uprooted again.

'Breathe!' shouts Boris in terror, dragging him out with adrenaline strength and laying him on the side of the pool. He slaps his face first one way then the other.

Irakli opens his eyes. He wants to say *I'm fine*, but he is seized with coughing, and chlorine water pours out of him.

'What were you thinking?' demands Boris.

They go back into the hotel, where the air conditioning is cold on their wet skin. Irakli's eyes will not adjust to the light inside, and he is in darkness; his ears are full of water, and he hears only the caverns of his head. They take the elevator to the room. Irakli lies down on the sofa. He feels drunk and exhausted.

Boris and Lara are kissing on the floor. They have thrown off their wet clothes and they lie naked in the rectangle of sunlight pouring in through the window. Their hair is still wet and their eight limbs move over one another like the lingering tentacles of sea creatures. Lara's back shines in the sunlight, dappled by the protruding curve of her vertebrae. The hairs on Boris's calves still hold the wavy pattern of pool water running away. Irakli watches the kneading route of their hands and it is as if he can feel responsive flesh under his own.

Boris turns to him.

'Come here.'

Irakli's ears are completely blocked with the water, and he cannot hear what Boris says, but he understands the gesture. Lara looks round at him too, her breasts small and perfect, and they are both open to him, waiting. But Irakli closes his eyes and, as their lovemaking resumes, he succumbs to his own great desire: to sleep. He has a glorious dream.

He wakes up with regret. He does not know how long it has been. The rectangle of light has moved, and Boris and Lara are lying in the dark shadow, passed out in each other's arms. Irakli tilts his head to better see them lying there.

At that moment the water shifts in his inner ear. There are tremors as it pools together and begins to move; it thunders over the eardrum, and courses through the ear canal, his whole body shivering with the arousal of tiny hairs. It oozes around the curves, unblocking him and letting in the sound – and when it spills out, wet and final, on the cushion, Irakli lets forth an involuntary moan.

16

Boris left on tour, and Irakli did not know exactly where he was. He was playing in Montreal and Seattle. He was in Madrid and Berlin. He played in Bulgaria. He played in Moscow and Vienna.

Irakli did not hear from him. He saw him only on TV.

Khatuna was always travelling too. She was working on buildings in São Paolo and Dubai. She spent weekends with Plastic in exclusive Caribbean resorts.

Irakli was left alone, trying to write. He composed phrases in his head, and sometimes they seemed good, but when he saw them on paper he realised they were stupid. He wondered whether he would ever write anything worthwhile again.

He received his copy of Boris's album in the mail. It came wrapped in cellophane and sealed inside with hologram stickers. He cut it open carefully. Inside was the list of track titles, which Irakli had composed himself. They were the only thing he had managed to write for a long time.

The Delight of the Barbarians

1. It was after you understood everything perfectly that you realised she was speaking an unknown language

2. What disappointment, when you see a landscape from on high and realise that a map is true

3. It is thanks to moths' exacting sense of smell that night flowers are so fragrant

4. You assumed his fingernails were yellow from the nicotine until you noticed his toenails were yellow too

5. Modern life only seems safe because the ones it cuts down never survive to tell the tale

6. Before demolishing the walls of my childhood, they should have taken care to remove the shadows I left there

Inside the CD was a black-and-white photograph of Boris sitting with his violin on a desolate mountainside against a thunderous sky. The caption read, 'Genius of the Balkans', but Irakli knew the picture had been shot in Colorado.

Irakli prised the disk out of the holder and put it in his stereo. He drew the curtains, pressed Play and sat down to listen.

When the CD was over he sat for some time in silence. Then he opened a bottle of whisky and turned on the television.

He watched moguls on chat shows explaining why they were rich and everyone else was poor. *Because I dared to dream.* He watched music videos and men wrestling with crocodiles. He enjoyed the endless cacophony of flicking channels. He saw infomercials for cosmetic surgery, fireplaces and phone sex. Water ballet. Horoscopes. Folk dancing. He watched documentaries on Jesus Christ, Stalin, Alexander the Great, Hitler and the Crusades.

Irakli let himself sink in television. Days floated past, and he did not clutch at them. He realised he could drink entire bottles of liquor, and he would find a blankness there that released him from the irrelevance of his thoughts.

When Khatuna returned home she found him twisted and immobile on his bed. He was unconscious with drink and had saliva crust across his cheek.

She shook him until he came to. He opened his eyes and, seeing her, smiled in bliss. As if still in a dream, he called her by her secret name. She brought water for him to sip, and he came back to life.

She thought of the night, many years before, when she had discovered him wrung out with fever in their freezing room in Tbilisi. She realised that the same scene had recurred many times in her life – coming upon her brother after a separation to find that he had settled down, in her absence, only just this side of death. This accounted for her background of panic whenever they were apart.

'Why do you do this to me?' she asked, stroking him. 'Why do you cause me so much pain?'

He closed his eyes with the pleasure of her fingers in his hair. She said,

'You were always so happy when you were a child. You were the one who kept me happy. What's happened to you? Now we have a nice life.'

He said nothing. She wet a finger in her mouth and wiped at the residue on his cheek.

'Tell me if there's something wrong,' she said, 'and I'll try to understand.'

She lay next to him on the bed, and her smell was intoxicating. She had that primordial smell of flesh to which one has once been joined. He said,

'Sometimes this thing descends on me. It's not like a curtain or a mist. It's like a bridge falling, or a building, pinning me down. The only way to escape is to give in.'

Khatuna looked stricken.

'What is this thing with Boris? Are you in love with him? Are you lovers?'

'You don't understand,' said Irakli. 'It's nothing like what you think.'

'I don't like him,' said Khatuna. 'I don't care how great people think he is: I don't like the way you are when you're around him. I think you'd feel a lot better if you didn't see him anymore.'

'Can we go to Tbilisi?'

'Don't ask that,' she said. 'You know it's impossible.'

'I need to get away for a bit. I can't write here, I can't think.'

Irakli's eyes were still closed. He said,

'I feel bad when I think of mother all alone.'

'We'll go one day,' Khatuna replied. 'Just not yet.'

'Where's Boris now?' asked the CEO.

Plastic was in the Universal boardroom, answering questions.

'He's supposed to be playing in London tonight,' he said.

'Do we know if he's arrived?'

'The band's there, waiting in the hotel. But they haven't seen him since Amsterdam.'

'So he's missing in action. He disappears for four days and you just sit here hoping he'll show up. He's our hundred-million-dollar property, and you're telling me you don't know where he is.'

'He's probably spending our cheque,' said the head of Decca, trying to lighten the mood. 'He's a Bulgarian peasant: give him that much money and he'll be off at the Ritz doing coke with a couple of hookers.'

The CEO ignored him.

'What's the latest on our situation?'

'Without knowing all the facts,' said the lawyer, 'it's very clear that Boris is in multiple breach of contract. He seems to be willing to record with anyone who turns up with a microphone. Four other labels have issued original music by him. Some small pieces, one full-length seventy-two-minute album. Available for download on the internet.'

'Maybe Boris didn't know,' Plastic said. 'Maybe they recorded this stuff without him knowing?'

'It's possible,' said the lawyer. 'That's why I say I don't know all the facts.'

'His album's only been out two months and already it's through the roof,' said the CEO. 'What more does he want? The kid should be promoting it with every cell in his body. Instead he's screwing around like an amateur.'

'I'm dealing with it,' said Plastic. 'I've left him a hundred messages.'

'Oh, you've left *messages*,' said the CEO savagely. 'I'm *sorry*, I didn't realise you'd left *messages*. So what am I getting concerned about?'

There was silence in the room. Under the table, the head of Verve Records typed a message on his phone. The CEO said,

'I don't need convincing about this guy's music. His album's one of the great achievements of this company. It proves why big music companies like us are still relevant. It shows we can still pull genius out of our ass. This kid's like Piaf or Armstrong or Elvis – people will always pay money for him. He's got a long career ahead – a solid revenue stream with no end in sight, which you'll all agree is a ray of hope in today's bullshit market. So you'll forgive me if I'm a little sensitive when things go awry. I'm hearing a lot of weird things about this guy: unscheduled concerts, unauthorised recordings, trips to Morocco no one tells us about. Someone has to tell him how we do things.'

He looked around the circle of music mavens. He said,

'If you have to get on a plane, Plastic, and hold his hand the entire tour, then that's what you have to do.'

Plastic left the meeting cursing his colleagues and cursing Boris.

Outside, there was sleet in the street lights: it was one of those dark January five o'clocks that made him loathe New York. He buttoned his coat as he walked. The aerial highways seemed empty, and when sometimes an engine strained overhead, its Doppler fall was like a dirge.

Plastic got home and his phone rang. He leapt for it, but it was Khatuna, not Boris. She was coming over. He almost told her not to, but didn't have the energy to invent an excuse.

They went down for a meal in a small Italian restaurant. The place was full of rich foreign tourists, and did nothing to improve Plastic's mood. When they went back up, Khatuna lit a cigarette, which he'd told her not to do in his house. She said vacantly,

'What do you want to do?'

He had no conversation. They went into the bedroom. They undressed and lay on the bed. But Plastic was unable to make love.

'You're disgusting,' she said, rolling over. 'You sleep with a beautiful young woman, trying to get your youth back, and still it's not enough.'

His phone rang again, fallen out on the bed. She grabbed it and turned it off. Plastic said angrily,

'That might have been Boris.'

'Boris, Boris!' she cried. 'Everyone is fucking obsessed!'

She threw his phone across the room.

'I hate your little phone. It makes you look like a woman.'

'I thought phones were supposed to be small,' he said.

'That's so old,' she said contemptuously. 'Kakha's phone was huge like a fucking BMW. With diamonds.'

'Shut the fuck up,' said Plastic.

Khatuna picked up her jacket, and reached inside for another cigarette.

'Don't smoke in my house,' said Plastic.

'I want to smoke,' she said.

She started to put her clothes on.

When the door slammed behind her, Plastic picked up his phone and went to sit on the toilet. He dialled Boris's number again and again. He called the other members of the band. Looking at himself in the bathroom mirror, yellow and naked, he listened to the phone ringing endlessly in another country. Then he sent a grim torpedo into the underworld.

Boris returned from his tour, but he didn't come to see Irakli. Irakli did not hear from him, nor could he get an answer on his phone. Eventually he decided to go to his apartment.

Boris wanted to get out, and they walked together. Boris told a story from Prague.

'This guy came to meet me at the airport when I arrived, said he wanted me to do the music for his film. I discovered he was a famous director. He took me to a restaurant and told me the story of the film and how he wanted the music to be. There was no time at all, I was only there for three days, but he said, *I know you can do it.* I sketched some things out with the band, and on the last night after the gig he screened the film without audio and we improvised to the images. It started at three A.M. There were just ten or twelve people in the room; the actors were all there, absolutely silent. We played through in one take and went straight to the airport.'

He played the melodies to Irakli on his violin as they walked. They came to the gates of an old cemetery, and Irakli led them in.

'You have no idea how much money he paid me,' Boris continued. 'I came back with a suitcase of money from this trip. People paid me to do anything. They paid me to record a piece for four minutes. They paid me to come to their restaurant. I have so much money I can buy you anything you want.'

They sat down on a bench. Boris said,

'Where's your umbrella?'

'It was stolen,' said Irakli. 'Some bastard picked it up in a café and walked away with it.'

Boris studied him.

'You don't look well.'

'Why didn't you call me?' Irakli burst out. 'You've been back for days. I'm having a terrible time.'

Boris stared in surprise.

'I needed a few days to rest,' he said.

Irakli tried to contain himself. He said,

'I can't eat, I can't sleep. My skin's peeling off. I walk around the city and everything makes me angry. I can't write at all. I hate you because it's no effort for you. I struggle with every single word. I wish I'd never met you. I wish you'd get out of my head and leave me alone.'

A funeral was going on in a far corner of the graveyard. Mourners huddled around the grave, and snatches of the priest's voice carried in the air. Boris said,

'Look, I've been playing concerts non-stop for three months. I've been with people all the time. That's all. I needed a few days on my own.'

Irakli studied him. He hung his head in his hands.

'I'm sorry,' he said. 'Something's happening to me I don't understand, and I can't talk to my sister anymore. I don't want to see anyone except you, and you're never here.'

The sun was dropping, and the shadows were long behind the headstones. In the distance, the mourners stepped back for the filling in of earth, and Boris and Irakli watched.

Irakli said,

'It's strange: it's like I can taste soil in my mouth.'

Boris played a funeral march quietly on his violin. Irakli inhaled the graveyard air. There was the faintest scent of flowers.

Boris remembered something. He put down his bow, reached in his pocket and pulled out a book.

'I forgot: I picked this up in a bookshop and thought of you. It's poetry. She's very famous in Ireland.'

Irakli opened the book and read one poem, then he closed the book and put his hand on the cover. He looked up into the trees, which had lost all their leaves. It was cold, and the wind blew in gusts.

He pointed and said,

'Look at that.'

A piece of videotape was unspooled in the branches. It was looped across the cemetery, passing from tree to tree. It shook in the wind and glinted with the evening sun, and the untrapped lengths leaped and fluttered with inner life, like the ribbons of Russian gymnasts.

17

IT IS A GREY DAY when Ulrich goes to see the Woolworth Building. A long time ago, when he was in Berlin, he bought a postcard of this building – *Tallest Man-made Structure in the World!* – and he has always wanted to see the real thing. But today the summit is swathed in cloud, and the building does not have the anticipated effect.

He stands for some time, hoping for the clouds to lift. He has waited a lifetime, after all, and a few more minutes will not hurt. He looks at the gold script over the entrance – *Woolworth Building* – and the grand Gothic arches above. He hums a tune he used to know.

As he stands there, motionless amid the Broadway swarm, he becomes aware of someone else waiting next to him. He looks round and sees it is Clara Blum. She is old and quite stooped, but he recognises her at once.

'Clara!' he cries.

She smiles radiantly, and he stoops to kiss her cheek. He is amazed to see her again after so long.

'What are you doing here?' he asks.

'I've come to see the Woolworth Building,' she says, and he remembers the charm of her Czech accent.

'You've never seen it before?'

'This is the first time.'

Ulrich is astonished at this coincidence of time and place. There are so many things to ask, he does not know where to start.

'I recognised you immediately,' he says. 'You're still beautiful.'

She smiles at his gallantry. He says,

'How are you, Clara? What have you been doing? You became a chemist – I heard that. I heard you got married, too.'

'True,' she says.

'I thought of you very often,' he says, 'after I left Berlin.'

She says nothing in response. She does not seem eager to speak of personal things. He says,

'I lost touch with science after I left Berlin, and I never understood what it became. It was so far away from Sofia. What happened to everything we knew?'

The day is brightening, and all at once the sun breaks through. They both look up to see the top of the Woolworth Building. For a while they gaze at the ornate tower. Ulrich says hesitantly,

'It's big—'

'But it's not *that* big,' finishes Clara, and suddenly they laugh with merry complicity. They look up again, and the building is quite ordinary, and this seems hilarious.

'I imagined something far more,' says Ulrich.

'I don't know what we were expecting,' replies Clara. 'It's quite unimpressive!'

Ulrich feels relieved. It is wonderful to be together like this.

'Shall we walk?' he asks.

She leans on his arm and they wander slowly into the park, where businessmen are sitting around the fountain eating lunchtime sandwiches. They find a bench and sit down.

'You always loved Einstein,' says Clara. 'Did you ever hear the story of his children?'

Ulrich wants to hear it. Clara says,

'When Einstein was studying in Zurich, he fell in love with a brilliant Serbian student called Mileva. They were penniless: they lived together in a cramped apartment and worked on physics problems – and before long she was pregnant. You know what things were like in those days: Einstein was worried that a scandal might harm his career, and he sent Mileva away to the Balkans. While she was away, of course, he got his job in the Swiss Patent Office, and his fortunes were transformed.

'Mileva had a little girl and she called her Lieserl. Einstein was excited to be a father, but he couldn't tell anyone. When Mileva came back to Zurich, she was forced to leave their daughter behind.

'And that's the last anyone knows about Lieserl. Can you believe it, Ulrich? No one knows where she ended up, or whether she lived or died. Einstein was embarking on the greatest work of his life, and he was determined to keep his daughter a secret. And he did. The only trace of her was the melancholy she left behind in Mileva, who always spoke to her friends about the unhappiness of having no daughter.'

As Ulrich listens to the story, he thinks that he and Clara might have had children if events had been different. He wonders whether she ever had children of her own. He wonders whether she is speaking to him about the things that did not happen. He watches pigeons bobbing for crumbs.

'Einstein and Mileva had two sons after their marriage, but over time their love turned bitter, and when he moved from Zurich to Berlin he left her behind. When you and I were in Berlin he was the most famous scientist in the world, but he suffered from an irrational fear that Mileva might bring him down. He agreed to give her the money from his Nobel Prize as a settlement in their divorce, but he could never bring himself to hand it over. He lost it in the Wall Street crash, and Mileva ended her days in poverty.

'Poor Mileva had to take care of their musician son, Eduard, who was schizophrenic. He had to be committed to an asylum, which she could hardly afford. Einstein only visited his son once, and he was horrified at what he saw. He didn't want his scientific legacy to be tainted by it. He told everyone that Mileva was from degenerate stock, and had caused this madness all on her own. Einstein would have nothing to do with Eduard, and refused to respond to his letters.

'Eduard was given insulin and electric shocks, and he attempted suicide several times. When his mother died, all the money for his care ran out, and he was placed in a pauper's cell. When visitors came to see him, he said he wished he could play the piano, but he had been told his playing disturbed the other inmates. He said he wanted to sink into absolute sleep, but the doctors had said it wasn't sensible.'

'Meanwhile, Einstein was a celebrity in America,' says Ulrich.

'Quite,' says Clara.

Clara's story holds a revelation for Ulrich about his own life, but he needs some time before he can understand precisely what it is. For the moment, he is too moved by what is happening.

'Your story is making me sad,' says Ulrich. 'Let's not be sad. It's good to think of those old days. It's good to find someone who knew me then. So much has happened since.'

Clara seems to agree, though she is strangely distant.

Smiling, he says,

'I was never very good at chemistry, was I?'

'No,' she agrees.

'I wanted so much to be good at it.'

'You must have found other things to do with your life. You were always full of ideas.'

Ulrich looks up at the sky. He sees an arrow of geese flying overhead, and though they are inconceivably high, he fancies he can hear their cries. He says,

'I'm sorry I failed you, Clara. You cannot have regretted it as much as I did.'

Clara does not respond, and Ulrich says,

'I didn't know how to hold everything together. I had to go and save my parents; it was the only thing to do. But I loved you, and I couldn't live up to my love. I always wondered what would have happened if I had stayed with you in Berlin.'

Clara's hair is tied up, but a slight breeze plays among the grey wisps at her temples. The strands are iridescent, for by now the clouds have all gone. It is a beautiful day.

'You know this is all a dream,' Clara says.

'What do you mean?'

'You and me, together in New York?' She cuffs him playfully with the back of her hand. 'You must know I died long ago – a Jewish woman in Berlin in those days, married to a Jewish professor. In your heart you know that, yes? You know we're not really here, and it's only a dream?'

'Yes, I know.'

But Ulrich cannot leave it there.

'It's a dream, Clara, but it's not *only* a dream. There is far more to us than what we live.'

He speaks with unusual passion.

'Life happens in a certain place for a certain time. But there is a great surplus left over, and where will we stow it but in our dreams?'

Clara stares into her lap. She says,

'Those children of yours are imaginary.'

'I have a real son, who is even more imaginary. These ones stay with me, and make me proud.'

A butterfly alights for a time on Clara's floral dress, and then takes flight again.

'When I die,' says Ulrich, 'they will put me under the ground, and I will lie with an eternity of dreamers, breeding visions that will flicker on the surface – and the children of my daydreams will roam free.'

18

ULRICH SITS ON A DOORSTEP opposite the entrance to Boris's apartment block. He has tried repeatedly to gain entrance, but Boris is famous now, and security has tightened. Still, when he finally emerges, he is accompanied only by his violin, and for this Ulrich is grateful. He walks fast to catch up with him.

To his relief, Boris is not hostile. When he sees Ulrich he stops in his tracks and says,

'Is it you, old man?'

Ulrich leans against a wall to regain his breath. Nothing about Boris's appearance reveals his new-found success and prosperity. Ulrich would like to take him in his arms. But now is not the time. He says,

'I wanted to say something about your friend, Irakli. I've seen him, wandering in the streets on his own. He's not himself.'

Boris is surprised at this intervention. But he does not dismiss it.

'I've been worried about him myself,' he says.

'He needs something to set him back on track,' Ulrich says. 'And it's best if it comes from you.'

Boris thinks for a moment.

'There's one thing I could do,' he says.

'Don't neglect him,' says Ulrich. 'He's more delicate than you.'

He reaches into his pocket and takes out two marbles. Looking into Boris's eyes, he puts the marbles into his hand, like two glass tokens of solemnity.

Boris arrives at Irakli's apartment with an animal wrapped in a sack.

'I thought this would cheer you up,' he says.

He opens the sack and lets out a little pig. It's pink with two grey patches on its flanks. It feels exposed in the spacious room, and runs away squealing, keeping close to the walls, trotters clicking on the wooden floor.

'You have this big balcony where he can live,' says Boris. 'Pigs are very intelligent and they fill your head with wild ideas. He'll be good for your poetry.'

'I already have a parrot.'

'The parrot is nice, but you need something biologically closer. You'll write much better with a pig around.'

Boris goes to get nails, wood and roofing, and he builds a shelter for the pig on the balcony. They drink beer and laugh while he works. Irakli is impressed by how fast Boris can build, and makes no attempt to get involved. The pig sniffs at the planks of wood and eats an apple from Irakli's hand. Its ears are enormous for its small size.

Boris saws and hammers, his breath clouding in the air, and before long he has built a sty into the crook of the building, big enough for a man to stoop into. He lays down straw and newspaper inside, and the pig goes in of its own accord to look around. Boris says,

'After everyone left my town, I grew up with pigs. I slept between them.'

'Thank you,' says Irakli. 'Thank you.'

Afterwards, they go out to a bar. Irakli is suddenly animated and cannot stop talking. He tells stories, and finishes his drinks so fast that Boris tells him to calm down.

'Are you trying to empty the bar?' he asks.

'I'm thirsty,' Irakli says.

He tells Boris about things he has seen in New York.

'There's a tower where ten thousand Africans live. It's not far from here. People from Senegal on one floor, Nigerians on the next. Some are legal, some are illegal; they've come to satisfy the city's craving for luxury handbags and DVDs. Can you imagine the stories in a tower like that – the friendships, the conflicts, the journeys people have taken just to get there? I tell you: no one is writing the real novels of our age. There must be more in that tower than in the whole of Tolstoy.'

Boris listens quietly, happy to see him spirited. Music throbs in the background.

'Writers have a lot of work to do,' finishes Irakli.

The music is calling out to him and he says,

'Do you want to dance?'

Boris shakes his head, smiling, and Irakli goes on his own. He stands next to a large speaker and begins to move. His steps, once again, are Georgian. His legs scissor, slicing beats in half, and soon there are people gathered around him, who have never seen feet move so fast to keep a torso so still. He dances for several songs, transforming himself completely with every new mood. Now his heels stamp and he slices the air with his hands, his eyes gleaming with masculine seduction; now he beckons to the earth like a woman. He puts a bottle on his head and spins on his knees, finding a corridor through the crowd, and there seem to be no limits on his body – for now he is leaping close to the ceiling and there is gasping and cheering in the bar.

When he finishes they call for more, but Irakli is spent. He bows elegantly, heaving breathlessly, and he goes back to the table. He is happy and sweating. Boris puts an arm round him.

'I love to see you dance,' he says.

A stranger is sitting in Irakli's place; he has come to ask Boris for an autograph. Irakli stands by, waiting for the man to leave. He has another drink to cool down. He suddenly feels tired and rests his head on the table.

He does not feel well.

He looks out of the window, trying to steady his stomach. The street is quiet, but he can see a figure he recognises. He goes to the door and calls out to his sister, who is walking with Plastic. They turn back when they hear him; they come into the bar and stand by the table.

'Hello, Boris,' Plastic says emphatically.

'This is my brother, Irakli,' says Khatuna to Plastic.

'Yes, I remember,' says Plastic, reaching out for Irakli's hand. Irakli fails to register it.

'Are you drunk?' Khatuna asks him.

Irakli denies it, but he cannot focus properly on her face.

Khatuna sees Boris chatting to the autograph-seeking stranger, while Irakli does not even have a seat at the table and is drinking himself stupid in the corner. She is seized with hatred for Boris, in whose company her brother is so diminished. She would like to erase this musician from their lives.

Plastic says,

'I must have called you a hundred times, Boris. Everyone in the company has been trying to get hold of you. You've been back a long time. Why can't you answer your damn phone?'

'I don't like the phone,' says Boris breezily.

'We even went to your apartment,' Plastic is beside himself. 'It was full of people, but you were never there. Who were all those people?'

'Friends.'

'That's a company apartment. You can't use it for just anything you like.'

His lips are tight as he speaks. He is trying to keep himself under control.

'I've stood by you, but you're making me look like an idiot.'

Boris says,

'Would you like a drink?'

'No, I *don't* want a drink. I want to know what's going on. Do you realise I have hundreds of thousands of dollars of your personal money that I can't give you because you are in serious breach of contract? There are articles all over the press about it. And there's everything else I don't even want to go into, rumours I don't even understand.'

Boris is not enjoying this conversation.

'I can't do everything the way you want,' he says.

Plastic calms a little, now he's let the head off his anger. He says,

'You're a great musician. But there are ways of doing things. There are rules.'

Khatuna is annoyed by Plastic's approach. She wants to see him drag Boris into the street and beat him into oblivion. She says to Boris,

'Isn't it time you paid him back for your violin?' She places her hand dynastically over Plastic's. Her voice is caustic. 'You're making so much money and you can't even pay your debts. Everything you have, you owe to us.'

Boris finds the gesture absurd, and laughs in her face.

'Everything I have,' he says, 'I had long before you knew me.'

A young woman approaches and asks Boris to sign a napkin. Khatuna tells her to fuck off. There is silence around the table.

Irakli is suffering with all this. He says,

'Boris bought me a pig.'

'What?' says Khatuna.

'He bought me a pig.'

'What are you going to do with a pig?'

'He built a house for it on the balcony.'

'He's been building on our balcony?'

Khatuna's instinct tells her Boris is trying to sabotage her life at its very core.

'You better get rid of it right away,' she says.

Boris has had enough. He gets up to leave, and Irakli gets up with him.

'You're drunk,' Khatuna says to her brother. 'I want you to come home with me.'

'I'll be OK,' Irakli says.

Plastic says to Boris,

'Come to the office tomorrow morning. We have a lot of things to discuss. Do you understand?'

Boris's grunt is ambiguous. He and Irakli walk outside and disappear from sight. Khatuna stares after them.

She and Plastic wander in the streets. It's a Sunday night, and the city is empty. The helicopters droning overhead are the only sign of life. They come to a corner that Khatuna knows well.

'This is one of the blocks we're developing,' she says. 'We're going to pull down the whole thing and convert it into high-security housing for high-net-worth individuals.'

They walk the length of the block, Khatuna pointing out its features.

'Businessmen need a secure environment, which you can't get in Manhattan. Manhattan buildings open directly onto the street. So we're pulling this whole area down, making a private road with barricades. It will be a totally secure block, as good as you can find in any modern city.'

High above, advertisements flash on and off, signalling to each other. Khatuna's heels echo in the street. They pass an empty square where a three-storey-high inflatable puppet is cavorting with the night, flapping and flailing with the air blowing inside, and no one there to see. Khatuna says abruptly,

'I want to kill Boris.'

'What are you talking about?' says Plastic.

Khatuna goes silent, and Plastic can feel her harden towards him. They are walking under old bridges where the bricks are black and the rivets are mighty. There is scrawled graffiti, and people are sleeping here and there.

Passing under a bridge, they see a young man standing by a fire that he feeds every now and then with a squirt of kerosene. She and Plastic stop and watch. She calls out,

'Why don't you pour the whole bottle?'

The young man looks at her, wide-eyed.

'Why?'

'I want to see it.'

She is suddenly flirtatious. The man unscrews the lid of his bottle and upends it over the fire. The blaze roars – at their distance Khatuna and Plastic feel the heat on their faces – and the man is engulfed in flames. He backs away, yelping and beating his head. The fire dies down quickly.

He is dazed, and his hair is singed.

'Idiot!' shouts Khatuna.

'You told me to do it!' he wails.

'Next time I'll tell you to jump off the bridge.'

Plastic feels estranged by everything he has just witnessed, and he and Khatuna continue on in silence. There are no cars in the streets. They turn onto Fifth Avenue, where the mannequins are vibrant in the store windows, but there are no people. They wander down the empty avenue and find a man who has fallen asleep while walking his dog.

'I wish I was in Shanghai,' remarks Khatuna bleakly, 'where everything is new.'

They walk all the way to her building. She goes up the steps to the front door and Plastic stays below. She shuts the door behind her without looking back.

Upstairs, the apartment is in darkness. She puts the light on in Irakli's room and contemplates his empty bed. Then she opens the balcony doors and goes out to see what has happened there.

There is Boris's sty, nailed to the outside wall. She can see his footprints in the sawdust, and everything smells of pig shit. She picks up a discarded hammer gives a few angry blows to the construction, but it is not as flimsy as it looks. She peers inside and sees the pig huddled in a corner, trying to keep warm.

Disgusting creature, she thinks.

She goes back into the apartment and sits down. She thinks about Boris, who has dared to take hammer and nails to her house. She smokes several cigarettes. She taunts herself with unhappy thoughts. She thinks of her mother, living alone, her poor mother who was beautiful once. She thinks of all the things she bought Irakli, and how he scorned all of them, only to be delighted by Boris's pig.

She knows Irakli will not come home tonight, and she goes to bed.

She has been lying there only a few minutes when her phone rings. The call is from a hospital, where Irakli is recovering after being hit by a car.

The hospital is nearby, and she runs there. Irakli is lying in bed with his arm in plaster, and he is still drunk. She says,

'How could you get hit by a car tonight? There were no cars on the streets.'

'I don't know what happened,' he says.

She looks him over with concern.

'Where's Boris?' she says. 'Didn't he stay with you?'

'He was here. He just left.'

Khatuna sighs with contempt.

'He's a fucking coward.'

She touches the tips of her brother's fingers poking out of the plaster.

'I was clearly lit up in the headlights,' says Irakli, 'and still it drove into me.'

His eyes are closed, and his forehead wrinkles.

'I think I'm becoming transparent,' he says.

19

Item

Perhaps Boris would not have achieved such extraordinary fame if he had cropped up in another age. But these were unusual times. It was noticeable, for instance, that children knew less than their parents, who themselves preserved a mere fraction of what they had been taught. People no longer felt they could rely on the future, and they fell upon Boris's musical prophecies as if they were sparkling ponds in the desert.

Item

Khatuna employed a private detective to collect information about Boris.

'Anything suspicious, I want to know it. Anything at all. Anything that can be made to *look* suspicious. There are a lot of stories circulating about him, so it shouldn't be hard.'

The detective blew air both ways through his lips.

'He's a public figure, a famous musician. It'll cost a lot to keep tabs on him.'

'Don't give me that bullshit. I'm in security. I know what I'm talking about. He has no protection; he goes everywhere normal people go. He's an easy target. Just do what I tell you.'

Item

Irakli went out to gather food. Near the apartment was a cage of bins where a local supermarket threw out expired produce, and that was where Irakli got his supplies. He climbed the fence and began to sift. His arm was mended now, and he felt light without his plaster.

In recent weeks, his poetry had returned. Now the remote feelings of his heart broke out of him in words, and poems arrived, fully formed, without any urging. His book was nearly finished.

He picked out cheese, meat, vegetables, and a couple of loaves of olive bread. He found a packet of macaroons he thought Khatuna might like, though he would not tell her where they came from. He took a bag of apples for his pig.

He returned home and let the pig in from the balcony. It had grown since Boris first brought it. It had developed the habit of staring unceasingly into Irakli's eyes.

Item

Plastic flipped back through the article in consternation. He no longer knew what to believe.

The CEO had called him at 7.15 on a Sunday morning.

'You get the *Times*?'

'Yes.'

'Read the magazine cover story and then call me back.'

The photo on the cover showed a simple stone room, with a wood stove in the middle where two men stood to keep warm. They had guns slung over their shoulders, and they watched two other men at a game of chess. One of these chess players sat amply, like their leader.

The journalist had managed to secure an interview with a fugitive Serbian general wanted for war crimes committed during the conflict in Yugoslavia. He had been blindfolded when he was taken to and from the hideout, which he surmised was in Montenegro. He had spent two days with the voluble Serb, who lived in a house in the mountains with only four bodyguards for company. A priest of the Serbian Orthodox Church stayed in the evenings to lead them in chanting and prayer.

The journalist was informed that a world-famous musician was coming to play a concert in the house. 'Do not think we are sad people', said the guard. 'Do not think we are poor.' That evening, to the journalist's astonishment, Boris was brought in by helicopter. This was during his European tour, and he came with a Hungarian accordion player he had met on his travels. The two of them played the whole night. The general wept for hours, drinking to Boris and his genius, and kissing his hands. In the morning, Boris got back in the helicopter to resume his concert schedule.

'The beauty of music,' said the war criminal, shaking his head as the helicopter receded above the fir trees. 'Whatever happens, no one can take that away from you.'

Item

Khatuna put her business card on the table. The man had heard of her company. He nodded at her title, Vice-President, Security Systems.

'You've been referred to me,' he said, 'because of the nature of your information. But so far I don't have a real detailed … I only have a basic outline of what it concerns.'

Khatuna had a folder of papers and photographs. She placed it in front of him.

'This is a file about an organised crime network operating between New York and a number of eastern European countries. Boris is a key player in these operations. His musical activities provide a front.'

'Interesting,' said the agent. He flicked through the folder, lingering on the photographs. 'These things happen all the time, of course, but you don't expect it to happen with … When it happens with someone so well known it's a bit of a surprise.'

He took out a sheet of paper and began to read.

Khatuna looked at the FBI crest on the wall behind him. It showed a pair of scales surrounded by a wreath. She was disappointed by it. What harm could you do to someone with a pair of scales? She had thought it would show a gun at least, or maybe a missile.

In America, the strength lay with the government, and if you wanted to destroy someone you had to get the government to do it. But there was little gratification in that. People in the government looked like bus drivers and chewed their nails. Considering this man's ugly suit and tie, Khatuna mentally jabbed her fingers twice down her throat.

Item

A song was released on the internet: a duet featuring Boris and a female singer, recorded live. There was no documentation of the performance, and it was never clear who had written it.

Everything that was difficult or obscure in Boris's other music fell away for that song, and what was left was the simplest, most heart-rending beauty. The song became a worldwide sensation. For a time, people played it everywhere, and it was the greatest moment of Boris's fame.

Item

Boris never went back to his apartment, and Plastic did not know how to find him any more.

People called Plastic every five minutes to get hold of Boris. They wanted him on TV. They wanted to hear him speak. They wanted to know what he thought about every possible subject.

Plastic read about him in the newspapers, like everyone else. He read about him getting kicked out of restaurants and beaten up by angry film stars. He read about the drugs he took, and his excessive sexual tastes.

Boris appeared on the covers of all the big music magazines. He was the future of jazz and the future of folk. He had raw good looks. He said crazy things that looked great in print.

Boris had ceased to be a single person. There were too many stories about him for them all to be true.

Plastic read that Boris was a sadist and a fake. He read that he hated the U.S. government and gave his money to terror. He read that he performed in Baghdad and Kabul. That he was a laundry machine for eastern European crime money. That he liked prostitutes and sometimes conducted rehearsals without clothes on.

Boris's music began to torment Plastic. He stopped his ears in the streets, trying to shut out the radio play, the endless replays of bars and restaurants. They had turned his music into a public neurosis. As if they could absorb it only by beating it to death.

Item

The newspapers reported that two eastern European men who had entered the United States as part of Boris's road crew had been arrested for drug trafficking. Pavel Alexandru, twenty-eight, from Constanta in Romania, and Vladislav Penkov, twenty-four, from Plovdiv in Bulgaria, were accused of bringing substantial quantities of MDMA into the country from the Netherlands. One journalist wrote:

> *Organised crime is the fastest-growing sector of our economy. Hyper-violent criminal gangs from the Caribbean, eastern Europe and Latin America are taking over our cities, while international criminal organisations, as wealthy as the very largest corporations, are buying off our politicians and judges. We should not doubt the power of these organisations to infiltrate the glitz and glamour of our entertainment industry. Major celebrities move easily around the world without attracting the attention of security men, and they are a natural vehicle for international crime.*

In their official statements, however, the police emphasised that Boris himself was not involved with these activities.

Item

The CEO of Universal said,

'Are we going to let him attend or not?'

'He's the brightest star this company has,' said Plastic. 'Not sending him would be suicide.'

The CEO had lost interest in Plastic's opinions, and did not reply.

'I agree with Plastic,' said somebody else. 'We can't pull an artist like that out of the Grammy Awards. He's nominated in every category there is. We'd look like idiots.'

'The song that made this guy most famous,' said the CEO, 'we had no hand in. We don't own it, and we're not making money from it. So you tell me: how can we put him forward as *our guy* in the awards?'

'I know we all wish that song had never happened. But let's just admit it is a *gorgeous* piece of music. You can't take that away. Everybody loves it. We put that guy up in the Grammys and it knocks everyone else out of the park.'

'How did that song get away from us?' asked the CEO. 'Can someone remind me how the *fuck* that one got away?'

Item

When Irakli came home, the radio was on in Khatuna's room and her door was open. She was standing naked in front of her mirror. Her dark hair fell tousled down her back, and above the curve of her buttocks was tattooed a terrible black eye.

She was shooting video of herself with her phone.

Irakli stopped short in confusion. He crept out of the front door, walking backwards, undoing his steps. When he returned later, he was careful to make a lot of noise.

By then Khatuna was dressed. She was putting on make-up. There was welding going on outside, and shadows kept flashing on the ceiling.

'Where are you going?' asked Irakli.

'We're going to a casino,' said Khatuna. 'I want to gamble. Tonight I want to drink and gamble like a falling empress.'

'People never win in casinos. They win once, and then they give it away.'

'I'm not going there to win,' said Khatuna. 'I'm going to lose. I'll take Plastic's money and bleed it out on the tables.'

'What has he done?'

'Nothing! Plastic is not capable of doing a fucking thing.'

She had drawn Cleopatra flourishes on her eyes, and her lipstick was wild. She turned away from the mirror.

'No man will ever be Kakha,' she said. 'All my life I will be in mourning.'

Irakli said her secret name, silently and to himself. He thought she looked like a whore.

Item

Irakli finished writing the last line of his book. He piled the sheaf of papers on the table. He did it with some ceremony, and the parrot said *Dinner is ready!*

'*Androgyne*,' proclaimed Irakli, reading out the title. For his book began with lost bliss: when creatures were whole before they were separated into yearning halves of men and women. On the title page was a quotation from Plato:

> *When a person meets with his other half, the actual half of himself, he is lost in an amazement of love and friendship and intimacy. The two don't want to spend any time apart from each other. These are the people who pass their whole lives together; yet they could not explain what they desire of one another. No one can think it is only sexual intercourse that they want, that this is the reason why they find such joy in each other's company. It appears to be something else which the soul evidently desires and cannot tell, and of which it has only a dark and doubtful presentiment.*

For a moment, Irakli was distracted by the pig, which was sitting by his chair, staring at him. Sometimes the animal was uncanny. Irakli stared back at it. He thought, *You're the oldest creature I know. You're only a few months old, but everything about you is ancient.*

He turned over the title page and began to recite the book aloud. He read from beginning to end. Somewhere along the way he fell silent, and read in his head.

It became dim in the room as he went through, and when he had finished he rubbed his eyes from the strain.

Waves of nausea flowed over his skin, like an oil spill in a mustard field. He tossed the manuscript on the floor and covered his eyes with his hands.

His book was completely worthless.

20

Boris stops off to buy a car. It is impossible to get anywhere in Los Angeles without one, and they are going to be there for several days. He chooses a blue convertible, and puts it on his credit card.

Irakli sits in the passenger seat. Boris says,

'I used to drive a tractor on the land, and sometimes an old Lada, while we still had gasoline. But never on roads like this.'

He is wearing sunglasses to cover up a black eye.

There are poor people all around. There's an old man singing in a baby carriage, and scabby children passed out on air-conditioning vents. Skeletal women with bulging eyes are motioning to the traffic, trying in vain to sell themselves.

'Khatuna's going insane, knowing I'm out here with you,' says Irakli.

'Your sister doesn't know what friendship is,' says Boris. 'She's never experienced it, so it makes her insecure.'

They drive for a long time in silence. Irakli looks drained, and has little to say. Gas stations announce themselves with fluttering pennants, like fairgrounds. There are palm trees, and the largest houses they have ever seen, and pale people staring out. They imagine they will chance upon some inviting destination. They imagine they will see places to stop. But they find nothing of the sort, and finally they drive back to the hotel.

When Boris's first award is announced, Plastic seizes him with unfeigned delight. Enmity is forgotten, for Plastic never stopped believing in the music. He relieves Boris of his violin and pushes him into a funnel of smiling, clapping people.

Boris's own music plays at excruciating volume through the speakers, but it has become unrecognisable. It has become military. He is passed from usher to usher and propelled onto the stage. A tall woman hands him a trophy, a gold gramophone player, and puts a mike to his mouth. He looks at the audience head-on, so many, the sweeping spotlights brown through his sunglasses.

The woman's teeth are like beacons.

'Boris, you have such an amazing story.'

Her voice does not come from her. There is the impress of a million eyes, and his name is sprinting on the screens over his head.

He forces words into the microphone, and his own voice is stolen too.

'I spent a decade in an abandoned town, alone with the animals. Everyone should try it.'

The audience laughs, and he is stupefied by the scale, cameras spinning over his head. The many images of Boris turn their eyes upon the multitude.

'I'm not joking,' he says.

The cackling gallery gives way to clapping, and his music thunders again. He is led off stage, and with all the video screens it is like finding his way through a hall of mirrors.

'No! Come back! We *must* have Boris!'

The man and woman who stand for the cameras either side of Boris possess two of the most well-known faces in the world, but he does not recognise them. He is bent over, laughing in the flashes, the woman's bare arm brushing his cheek, the journalists shouting.

'Boris! Take off your glasses!'

Irakli stands by, watching. He has become invisible. He stands under the blazing lamps, and still people try to walk through him.

Plastic and Khatuna are standing nearby. Khatuna wears dark make-up and has drawn silver lightning flashes on her cheeks. A journalist wants a comment from Plastic.

'Is it true the American music industry is being taken over by eastern European gangs?'

Plastic is smiling for the cameras. He says,

'That's an insane question. Who gave you an idea like that?'

Security men are trying to protect the demigods who walk here so close to mortals. The love they inspire is so consuming that ordinary people cannot keep from throwing themselves at them and ruining their hair. As they pass through the doors into the evening, humans line up along the immortal corridor and wail with the pain of adoration. Khatuna walks down the carpet on Plastic's arm, looking at the goggling, afflicted faces, and wonders again how American youths can get so fat.

Boris leaves a cosmic shower behind him, as the camera flashes fade.

'Where's your girlfriend, Boris?' shouts a photographer.

Boris is full of witty remarks. His hands are full of trophies. He is irresistibly magnetic, and Irakli is inconspicuous by his side. He looks at the way Boris holds himself and realises there are parts of his friend he will never know.

The four of them get into the same limo. The car doors shut and they can hear their voices again. Boris seizes the champagne with relish, and pours four glasses. Khatuna drinks hers straight down and grabs the bottle.

'Are you OK, Irakli?' asks Boris. 'You're very quiet.'

Irakli nods, and forces a smile.

Plastic's face radiates gladness. He locks an elbow around Boris's neck and kisses the top of his head.

'That's my boy!' he shouts. 'My genius boy!'

Plastic and Boris exchange tributes, and Khatuna gets increasingly impatient. A line of limousines is blocking the street, and theirs has hardly moved.

'How far is this party?' she asks irritated.

'It's in that building.' Plastic points about a hundred metres down the road.

They are motionless in the traffic. Irakli's face is turned towards the crowds outside, and Boris plays a snatch of music on his violin, though there is hardly space to move a bow. It's a tune from his album, and he hams it up, crossing his eyes and playing like an idiot. Khatuna can't stand it, and she shouts over the music at him,

'Is it true you're dating that actress?'

She manages to make it sound like an insult. Boris says,

'I hate that word. Am I a calendar?'

'Jerk,' she says.

Boris puts his window down and hangs his arm outside the car. His violin is in his lap.

Khatuna says,

'You're losing your hair. I can see it in this light. You'll be bald by the time you're thirty.'

Plastic glares, trying to rein her in.

Suddenly Khatuna seizes the violin from Boris's lap and begins to whack it against the window ledge. Plastic tries to save the instrument, but she roars like an animal and her strength is unexpected. She smashes the violin three times, and it is entirely destroyed, only the strings holding the pieces together. She tosses the carcass through the open window.

It is Plastic who turns on her, hits her in the mouth and shouts obscenities. She laughs in his face, and touches her finger to her bleeding lip. A glass is broken, and there is champagne running down Plastic's suit.

Boris turns up at the party with nothing in his hands. Smiling moguls put their arms around him and lead him to the right people.

Irakli stands on his own, watching. The room is full of faces he has seen every day on television. Pop stars and movie stars are serving up smiles, and using gestures they have prepared beforehand. They are stealing glances at each other's clothes. They fawn and are fawned upon: everyone loves everyone, but it is not the love of humans.

The most famous woman in the world is here, a woman so impossibly celebrated and beautiful that she must sit in her own private corner behind a velvet rope, surrounded by young men selected for their looks and their ability to keep talking.

Previously, at home, Irakli has watched some of these people with rapt attention, his pupils wide. If he has ever speculated about being in a room with them, he has probably imagined his emotions in a heightened state. But here he is excessively bored. Waiters are passing with cocktails and he takes them two at a time, and still he is unable to lose himself. The banality is strangely devastating.

Plastic and Khatuna are off among the crowds, sparking with their rancour. A bruise is blooming on Khatuna's cheek, and she seems to be showing it off. Plastic is trying to be charming, but the strain is showing, and it's noticeable that people walk away from his conversation.

The most famous woman in the world sends a message to Boris, inviting him to join her in her private corner, for she is not above the fascination of ordinary people. Boris sits down next to her and she asks him questions about himself. She says,

'You're quite a normal size. I imagined you would be big.'

Boris laughs. 'People are getting smaller. Haven't you noticed?'

He becomes restless during their conversation. He does not want to talk. While she is asking how he feels about the great number of his awards, he takes her cool hand under the table and positions it firmly on his penis.

The most famous woman in the world does not remove her hand. She looks him in the eye and says,

'You'll have to excuse me. I'm a vegetarian.'

Boris matches her gaze. He is enjoying himself. He says,

'I've heard of vegetarians. Don't they lose their talents young?'

Irakli is on his own. He listens to conversations about the sensational hookers who have come into town for this night. He cannot get close to his friend, who is cocooned in the corner, and he decides to get up and dance. He spills his drink over his clothes, and curses. He starts to move to the music, and he knows it is all wrong: he cannot hear the rhythm or master his body. He bumps into somebody, who turns round, complaining and indignant. Eventually Irakli leaves. A camera flashes as he emerges into the fresh air, the photographer like a jumpy sniper realising too late that the figure coming out is no one.

Irakli walks back to the hotel and takes the elevator to the twenty-first floor. His room has been altered in his absence, the signs of his existence removed. The bedcovers have been straightened, his stray clothing folded away. There is a promotional package from Universal on the table. He takes out the CD and looks at it again.

He looks at himself in the mirror. Turquoise half-moons are buried under his eyes. It is true that he has become difficult to see.

He unwraps the cellophane from Boris's CD, and puts it into the player. He pours himself a drink from the minibar and lies down on the bed. Water has seeped into the corner of the ceiling of this expensive hotel, yellowing it and making stale bubbles. Irakli presses Play on the remote.

Boris plays the *crepuscule encounter* and the *eighty leagues of sleep*. The *fulminating spiral-hair*, the *pale glow in the deep*. It is beautiful and poisonous. Irakli lets himself be swallowed by the hungry ear. He bleeds blindness and weaves a mattress of vertigo; he wishes he could sacrifice himself to this loveliness. Boris plays *the Arab shirt she saw and loved, the wart-faced Tetrarch and the falcon on his glove*. Irakli weeps in the dark room, for this is needlessly perfect. Above his stone head, a congregation of wild scintillas spend themselves in the night.

Through the music, Irakli hears Khatuna and Plastic come back to the room next door. They too have left the party early, and Irakli hears the inarticulate bark of their discord. While Boris plays the insect mother, while he thanks the steamy air, Irakli can hear irate sounds through the wall, which ebb and flow, gather and evolve. The noises become rhythmic.

The CD comes to an end.

Irakli lies in the darkness, listening. Plastic and Khatuna stab each other with obscenities, and Irakli coils up in a whorl.

At length he gets up, sits down at the desk and writes on the hotel notepaper.

The dream of the embryo on the night before birth

The dream
Held prisoner in my dark head
Wants to escape and prove its innocence to everyone outside.

I hear its impatient voice,
See its gestures, its furious
Menacing state.

It doesn't know that I too am only someone's dream.
If I were its jailor
I'd have set it free.

Irakli reads it back to himself, stands up, and tidies his belongings. He takes Boris's CD out of the player and puts it back in its case. He looks around to check that everything is just so. He opens the sliding door to the balcony. He climbs onto the rail and sits for a moment, his feet swinging above twenty-one floors of void. Then he lets himself go.

Manatee

21

When Boris arrived at Khatuna's New York apartment, he found the front door standing open.

Khatuna had a scarf around her head and was packing up the house. She looked up when Boris came in, but she did not greet him. She was shrouding things in bubble wrap. Paintings and vases, and many other objects whose shapes had been obscured in the wrapping. She was gagging their mouths with plastic.

The air stank of cigarettes.

Boris looked over the piles of clothes arranged in rows across the wooden floor.

'Are you leaving?' he asked.

She nodded.

Boris could see things of Irakli's that he recognised. The shirt that was drenched in the rain on the night they had met. A pen he used to carry. On top of a pile of books he saw the volume of poetry he had given to Irakli after returning from his tour.

Boris listened to the slight noises in the room: the hum of glass, the collision of dust, the echo of before. There was nothing here that did not whisper of Irakli.

He imagined Khatuna returning to this place after the horror of LA. He imagined how she would have staggered, walking in, when she saw everything so unchanged. He saw her fingering Irakli's imprint upon the rooms: his food half eaten in the fridge, his pocket coins spilled on the sofa. He saw the devastation of a book half read, and an unwashed shirt. He saw her following the source of her brother's radiation, looking at the parrot and the hollows in his half-made bed, and coming, eventually, to the pile of papers on his desk, where she stopped and placed her hand.

He could see all this vividly – as if it had been left behind in the room, too barbed for time to swallow away.

She had put Irakli's manuscript in the middle of the dining table, and Boris could read the title. *Androgyne.*

He saw that the shelter he had built out on the balcony had been removed, and there was no sign of the pig. Everything had been fixed and cleaned.

The parrot was perched on the table. It had lost its feathers, and its scaly skin was unpleasantly exposed.

'What happened to the parrot?'

'It pulled out all its feathers,' said Khatuna.

She lit a cigarette. Boris stroked the parrot's bald head.

'I came to read Irakli's poems,' he said. He gestured to the manuscript on the table.

'Don't say his name,' she said. 'I don't want you to say a word about him.'

But she didn't stop him when he picked up the manuscript.

He took it out to the balcony and slid the door closed behind him. He read the book from beginning to end. When he had finished, he stood with his hand on the rail of the balcony.

His eyes were red when he went inside. He said,

'It's a wonderful book. It's a wonderful, wonderful book.'

He waited for Khatuna to say something, but she was intent on her packing. He said,

'What will you do with it?'

'I'll publish it. Even if I have to sew the fucking pages together myself. The whole world is going to know my brother was a poet.'

Boris put the manuscript back on the table. He picked up a button from the floor. He said,

'I know you don't like me. But I loved Irakli too.'

Khatuna looked at him for the first time. There were hollows around her eyes. She said,

'Don't think just because Irakli is gone that you and I are friends.'

'I've never—'

'You have no idea what I've been through in the last few weeks. You have no idea what an effort it was just to pull myself out of L.A., when I only wanted to stay with him and die. You have no idea. He was the one thing I *couldn't lose*; he was the one thing that was absolutely necessary to me. I've lost everything many times, and I can get through that, but I *cannot* lose my brother.'

Khatuna's grief suddenly took her over. She fell to her knees, crying. Her face was terrible, and between her sobs she sucked loudly for breath. Boris went to her and took her in his arms, absorbing the spasms of her body.

She calmed down. She pushed him away and lit another cigarette.

'I'm not ashamed of crying,' she said, sitting on the floor.

He took one of her cigarettes too, though he never smoked. For a time there was only the sound of the two of them inhaling and exhaling.

Boris said,

'Are you going back to Tbilisi?'

'I'm going to Baghdad,' she said. 'I'm going to design new security compounds. Renovate the abandoned palaces.'

She took a drag of her cigarette.

'I have to go on living. *I'm* not dead. I have to put myself some*where* and do some*thing*. I want to see a city at war. I'm fed up with this boring place. I want a place where real things happen, a place with real men.'

Boris did not know what to say. He stubbed out his cigarette, which tasted awful. He tried to conjure Irakli back into the room, picturing him on the sofa, where he had seen him many times. It was strangely hard, and he felt his memories, too, were being slowly taken from him.

Khatuna said,

'Let me tell you something, because it doesn't matter anymore. I made reports about you to the FBI. I implicated you in all sorts of crimes. You've done some weird things, and it wasn't difficult to exaggerate them a bit. I know a lot about crime. Those guys aren't very complex; I know how to get inside their heads. It's only a matter of time before they come down on you.'

She stood up and dusted cigarette ash off her knee.

'It doesn't matter now. I wanted you to go to jail and suffer. But now I don't give a shit. All I want to do is smoke cigarettes in this apartment until I've inhaled everything he's left behind.'

Boris walked over to the door.

'Bye-bye, Khatuna,' he said.

'Wait!' she said, suddenly running out of the room.

He heard her opening doors in the kitchen, and the icy scrape of the freezer. She came back weighed down, her arms laden with a ruddy frozen mass.

'Here,' she said 'Take this away.'

She put it into Boris's arms and he realised in horror that it was Irakli's pig. Its throat had been slit.

'How could you do this?' he cried.

The pig was solid against Boris's chest, and turned it numb. He began to weep.

'How could you do it?' he said. 'This pig was part of Irakli. It's like killing him again.'

'No,' said Khatuna. She had ice crystals on her T-shirt, and she was rubbing her hands to warm them up. 'It was like killing you.'

22

THE CEO CALLED PLASTIC into his office. Plastic was in his gym suit. He hadn't shaved for a couple of days. The CEO massaged a pile of business cards, aligning the edges. He said,

'I'm sorry to have to do this, Plastic, but you're fired.'

'You're kidding.'

'I'm not happy about it, but you haven't left me any choice.'

'What?'

The CEO put his neat pile of business cards into a golden box. He straightened the keyboard of his computer. He was in a mood for tidying up.

'Look, I don't know what you're mixed up in. But it's got to a stage where this company's looking questionable, and I can't have that.'

'You can't really believe all this! I thought you were on my side!'

'I've just been interviewed by the FBI,' said the CEO. 'I didn't appreciate it.'

'Take a look at me. Look at the state I'm in. They've taken over my apartment: I can't go home. I slept in the office – I haven't had a shower for two days. They've taken my paintings, my papers, my laptop, they've had me in a room for two days, asking questions. They want to know where Boris is – how the hell do I know where he is? They're asking me what are *my* links to organised crime. They arrived with piles of my bank statements and asked me to explain cheques I wrote ten years ago.'

The CEO did not feel obliged to comment. Plastic raised his voice

'That guy who committed suicide – I hardly knew him! I didn't exchange ten words with the guy. He was my girlfriend's brother, that's all. My *ex*-girlfriend, I should say – she hasn't spoken to me since it happened. Look, he was a depressed poet, and he committed suicide. End of story. They're manufacturing a crime around it because he was a friend of Boris, who has disappeared off the face of the planet. Because he was from Georgia and his sister was involved with a gangster – and they think the only thing that comes out of that part of the world is crime. Well, I have nothing to do with any of it!'

He seemed short of breath.

'You're an idiot if you fire me!' he said.

The CEO exhaled into the mask of his hands.

'I'm sorry, Plastic. It's not what it is, but what it seems that matters. Suicides? Artists disappearing? It's all gone too far. All the newspapers can talk about is America's new criminal underworld. And Boris is the poster boy. Boris is the Pied Piper, leading us all into the shit.'

'He's more famous than he ever was,' said Plastic. 'Universal has a legend on its hands.'

'Do I have to remind you that we *don't own his music?* It floats free, remember, in some very cool, post-industrial sort of way, and all the lawsuits in the world are not going to bring it back. That's how my differences with you began, remember?'

'Do you remember who you're talking to? I'm not one of your managers, sitting on my suited ass. I'm Plastic Munari, for Christ's sake! You can't do this to me!'

'You were great,' said the CEO. 'I'm not denying it.'

After this conversation, Plastic was not allowed to go back to his office. He was escorted down to the lobby. Security men put their hands on him and he lost his cool.

'I need to get my stuff from my office. I'm not letting anyone else do that. I've worked fifteen years in this company – at least let me pick up my fucking things!'

Above the lobby, people had come out onto the landings to see Plastic evicted. The whole company was there, murmuring.

'We'll get everything sent to your home,' said a security guard.

'I can't get into my home!' shouted Plastic. 'The FBI has taken over my home. Does no one understand anything I say? Just give me half an hour in my office to pick up my personal things. I have antique paintings. I have two eighteenth-century globes in there – do you think I trust you people to pack them up?'

Eventually, the security team forced Plastic out onto the sidewalk, where all New York was around him and there was no point shouting anymore.

He got a taxi and checked into a hotel. He had a shower and changed back into the same clothes. He went out for a walk. He had to buy some deodorant. He had to calm down.

Offices and lively restaurants surrounded him, and he tried to get out of their way. The cacophony of clothes boutiques and hairdressers grated on him. He looked for emptier streets. He turned a few corners and found his way out of the crowds.

He passed a red-light district, peaceful at this time of day. He saw a naked arm stretched out of a window, and a woman reaching on tiptoe, trying to put a sandwich into the hand.

He walked for a long time, not really knowing where he was going. He passed liquor stores and warehouses, and the roads became cracked. He saw two men labouring under the bonnet of a car, a crushed can of oil on the road beside them. He saw a cat sleeping in a doorway, and a young girl crying in an alley – and then no one at all. He reached a part of town where entire skyscrapers stood vacant. He walked aimlessly, and ran his hands along a wall.

Evidently, few people ever came here, and the thistles that grew between the paving slabs came up to his thigh. The cars parked here were old models, and they had merged with the tarmac and the trees. There were clocks on buildings, stopped at different times. The area was abandoned.

Plastic was surprised, therefore, to see an open music shop. The lights were on, and the windows had sparkling displays. Above the entrance was a wooden sign carved with lyres and decorated with gold script. Plastic pushed at the door, and a bell tinkled inside.

'Good afternoon,' said the owner. He was busy polishing the keys of a clarinet, and spoke to him in the mirror.

'Hello,' said Plastic, looking around the shop. What a beautiful place it was. How amazing he had never seen it before.

'May I have a look around?'

'Be my guest!' said the man, engrossed in his work.

They had old gramophone players on sale here, and hundreds of records. They had shelves and shelves of music scores. An entire case was devoted to metronomes. Plastic looked at the rows of flutes and oboes in the glass cases; he looked at the harps and organs laid out.

Finally he sat down at a piano and, hesitantly, he began to play.

23

ULRICH IS WAITING ON THE CORNER of Hudson and Canal. Boris pulls up in a brand new car, and opens the passenger door. He leaves the engine running.

'Don't you want to stop for a bit?' Ulrich asks. 'I'd like to buy you a drink.'

'I have to go,' says Boris. 'I have to meet someone soon.'

Ulrich lowers himself into the car and settles in the seat. He shuts the door, and Boris sets off. The car turns a corner and heads down a slope, and now they are driving underground. There's hardly anyone else in sight, and driving through the Holland Tunnel is like swimming in a yellow dream.

Boris is accustomed, now, to American roads.

When they emerge on the New Jersey side, Ulrich takes a last look back at the Manhattan skyline. He doesn't think he will see it again.

Boris finds that Ulrich has introduced a new smell into the car: a smell of old candles and much-worn wool. It's a familial smell, and Boris is drawn to this strange old man. He feels bad that he shut the door in his face the first time he saw him.

The evening is pure sapphire light, and the empty road is broad and peaceful. There are green banks of grass along both sides of the highway, blocking out the view, but when they reach the crest of a hill they get a panorama over the rolling green of New Jersey. There is a sheepdog bringing in the flock at the end of the day, the sheep running in waves among the factories.

'I look at the beauty of an evening like this,' says Boris, 'and the fact Irakli is in the ground and cannot see it is the most terrible thing in the world.'

The car moves so smoothly there is hardly any noise from the engine. Ulrich turns so he is facing Boris, and the new leather creaks.

'I found that note again,' Boris continues, 'the one you slipped under my door with your phone number – and I wanted to see you one more time. I keep thinking back to what you said about Irakli when I met you in the street. As if you already knew.'

Ulrich says,

'I didn't think it would go so far.'

They pass a fairground in the distance, the big wheel glinting in the sun.

'He was like the other half of myself,' says Boris.

He looks desolate and strung out. Ulrich says to him,

'You haven't lost Irakli, you know. I don't know if it helps to say that. I lost a friend once myself, and I know how it goes.

'He'll find his way inside you, and you'll carry him onward. Behind your heartbeat, you'll hear another one, faint and out of step. People will say you are speaking his opinions, or your hair has turned like his.

'There are no more facts about him – that part is over. Now is the time for essential things. You'll see visions of him wherever you go. You'll see his eyes so moist, his intention so blinding, you'll think he is more alive than you. You'll look around and wonder if it was you who died.

'Gradually you'll grow older than him, and love him as your son.

'You'll live astride the line separating life from death. You'll become experienced in the wisdom of grief. You won't wait until people die to grieve for them; you'll give them their grief while they are still alive, for then judgement falls away, and there remains only the miracle of being.'

Boris drives on. His exterior is as thin as a meniscus, and Ulrich can see through to the grinding inside. He watches the play of thoughts on his face, and the swallow in his throat. This son of his daydreams has already done things that Ulrich could not do in a hundred years. But he is still so young, and he is tossed around by feelings he cannot understand. It will be difficult to leave him, knowing he will be alone.

Ulrich thinks of Khatuna and Irakli too. *None of them is the child I thought I'd have*, he reflects. *But what else could I expect? A confounded man like me, living through such a mess, I couldn't hope to father well. They'll have a better life than I did and things will smoothen out. Their children will be better than they and in a couple of generations they'll give birth to angels – and nothing will be left to show what bad times we sprang from.*

By now the highway is delivering prophecies of sea. Seabirds careen overhead, and there's a maritime smell in the air. When the gaps line up in the landscape, it is possible to spy the continent's end.

Ulrich tells Boris that he's been holding on to a story for him and now he wants to let it out.

'Back in my day,' he says, 'there was a scientist named Albert Einstein. I had a passion for science when I was young and I thought Albert Einstein was the greatest man alive. I even studied at his university in Berlin, where I used to see him in the flesh.

'One day I was walking behind him in a corridor and he dropped a sheaf of papers. He didn't notice he'd lost them, so I picked them up and raced after him. I handed them over and he looked at me, smiled and said, *I would be nothing without you*.'

The old man gives Boris a look.

'What did he mean, he would be nothing without me? It seemed so personal, the way he said it. It seemed like a divine verdict. In those days, I had such an opinion of the man that there had to be greatness in his words even if he was only talking about a few missing papers. *I would be nothing without you*. I had a hopeful ego in those days: I tried to think of something I had done that could have contributed to Einstein's achievement. I assumed that a great success such as his must be fed by many smaller successes all around. Perhaps I was part of this blessed orbit, I thought, perhaps I would grow to unfold exploits and discoveries of my own.'

Boris's eyes are fixed on the road ahead. He has to be in a certain place at a certain time, so he has those thoughts in his head. He overtakes a solitary truck.

'Later on,' says Ulrich. 'I heard new stories about Albert Einstein that altered my thinking.'

He tells Boris the story of Einstein's pitiable wife, Mileva. He tells him about the Nobel Prize money lost in the Wall Street crash. He tells him about the daughter mislaid somewhere in Serbia, and the son abandoned in an insane asylum. He tells him all these stories and he says,

'I'd imagined that Einstein would live in a realm of uninterrupted success. Fulfilment as far as the eye could see: happy people bursting with rich conversation and achievements. But it wasn't true. He was surrounded by failure. The people close to him were blocked up and cut off. Their lives were subdued, and they were prevented from doing what they hoped to do.

'And that is exactly the point. That's how he could make such unnatural breakthroughs. Do you see? How could one man do what he did otherwise? He could not summon such earth-shattering energy on his own!'

Ulrich is speaking heatedly.

'How many stopped-up men and women does it take to produce one Einstein? Ten? A thousand? A hundred thousand? We can't answer questions like that; they are simply too mysterious. But we know that if we are to feel the thrill of progress and achievement, there have to be sacrifices elsewhere.'

Ulrich raises his eyebrows at Boris.

'So this is what Einstein meant when he looked me in the eye that day and said, *I would be nothing without you*. It was not success he saw written in my face. He saw, rather, that I would never accomplish anything at all.'

At this point in the old man's speech, Boris spies a gap in the railings and he drives the car off the road. It jerks violently over the edge, and Ulrich is forced to grab onto his door handle. The crest of the grassy bank bounces in the frame of the windscreen and the unevenness of the slope shakes them from side to side. They climb the slope and still juddering, they reach the summit. The horizon opens, they see the great ocean glittering beyond, and the car comes to a halt.

Boris turns off the engine, and there is silence. They can see the containers stacked high in the port, and the cranes, and the trucks queued up for cargo.

Ulrich says,

'I have a lot of failure to give away. Look at my music: a fantastic failure. A triumphant failure. I nurtured it for a lifetime!'

The sun is setting, over the land, and the ships on the water are aflame in its final rays.

'My failed music, Boris, that's my gift to you. That's the legacy I leave behind.

'If I could make an Einstein with my failed science, think what will come of my music!'

Boris is fully attentive, but Ulrich is not sure he understands everything he is saying. Ulrich has the impression, not for the first time during this ride, that Boris has become more absent than before. He is acting strangely, as if he is worried about waking someone: his voice has become soft and he takes care to avoid sudden movements.

Boris opens the door and gets out of the car, leaving the keys in the ignition. The wind is strong off the sea, and his hair is swept back. He takes Ulrich's arm and helps him down the slope to the highway. The air smells of salt and kelp and manatee.

Ulrich says,

'I'm happy I had this time with you.'

Boris is watching the highway, waiting for something, and before long a grey van appears in the distance. He steps into the road and waves to attract its attention. Ulrich realises that time is short and there are still so many things he has not asked. As the van draws up he says,

'Where are you going?'

Boris puts his face close to Ulrich.

'I have a new music in my head,' he says. 'Since Irakli died I've been hearing something new. But it's so remote I can't grasp it. There's too much noise here. I need somewhere quiet. I need to be alone.'

Ulrich treats this information as if it is an amazing revelation. He breathes it in and it sets him nodding for a while. *A new music*, he mutters to himself.

The van door opens from inside, and there are several men crowded there who haul Boris in, laughing and clapping him on the back. They greet him in Russian. Boris reaches for the open door.

'These men are my friends,' he says to Ulrich. 'They're sailors. They're going to hide me in their ship.'

He grasps Ulrich's hand, and Ulrich holds on tight. It is all happening so fast.

'Thank you!' Boris calls, but the van is already pulling away. Boris let's go of Ulrich's hand and slams the door. He waves from inside the moving vehicle.

Ulrich shouts,

'Wait!'

He runs as best he can, banging on the van's metal rear with the flat of his hand until it slows again, and stops. He catches up finally, holding his chest.

'That nearly killed me,' he says breathlessly, supporting himself against the van. His face is radiant. He says,

'I forgot. This is for you.'

He shows him the gold watch on his wrist.

'Can you take it off me? I have trouble doing it myself.'

Boris can see the glow in Ulrich's face, and it has an inviting authority. He steps out of the van to undo the watchstrap. He takes the watch off and puts it on his own wrist. Ulrich smiles, seeing it there. He puts his arms around Boris's bigger frame and embraces him. Boris returns his affection, holding him like a vice while the air is whipped by passing cars and the sailors call out from the van. Boris turns and gets back in.

'Goodbye,' he says.

'Goodbye,' Ulrich replies, smiling. He has lived this parting before, and this time it is joy.

A tinnitus starts up in his ears. He still has the force of Boris in his arms, and from the depths of his memory an ancient word floats into his throat, speaking itself through his involuntary mouth. *So-i-né.*

He has been trying to think of that word for – what? – decades and decades. It is a Japanese word he heard about long ago. It speaks of a feeling that is not named in the old man's own language. *The unique sensuality of holding an infant. Not erotic, but indecent, nevertheless, in its fervour.*

The engine roars, the van pulls out, and Ulrich watches it drive away. The sun is bursting on the horizon, and gulls cry overhead, infinite and plaintive. At last the van turns into the port, and Ulrich can see it no more.

ACKNOWLEDGEMENTS

For conversations and stories: Irina Aristarkhova, Nadeem Aslam, Rossitsa Draganova, Elena Filipovic, Graham Harwood, Robert Hutchinson, Claire Levy, Boris Katzunov, Nikoloz Kenchosvili, Christina Madjour, Vakhtang Maisaia, Siddhartha Mukherjee, Tim Parks, Lisl Ponger, Shveta Sarda, Alexis Schwarzenbach, Shuddhabrata Sengupta, Tristram Stuart, Jeet Thayil, Matsuko Yokokoji, and the members of Riyaz.

Thanks to Valery Katzunov for unforgettable walks through Sofia, and to Alexander Kiossev, who, when I related the story I was about to write, said, *You have just told me the life of my father*. Thanks to Natalia Kajaia, who led me through the remarkable worlds of her Tbilisi. And to Paul Fennell, who explained how to make barium chloride.

Thanks to my agent, Toby Eady, for bewildering insights whose brilliance unfurled over time. To Laetitia Rutherford for getting me drunk and making everything clear. To Tib Eckardt and Nicholas Pearson, who set me straight and reined me in.

In writing this novel I have enjoyed the immense privilege of a number of dedicated and exhilarating allies. All words fall short of the affections and insights offered by Jeebesh Bagchi, Sofia Blake, Marlene Nichols, Bhrigupati Singh, Prerna Singh and Phil Taffs.

Alas, one of these allies, Shakti Bhatt (1980–2007), did not live to see the end. These pages bear her trace, and my gratitude to her is, I suppose, eternal.

Monica Narula has lived in delicious complicity with this novel. She has inspired it, reasoned it and loved it – and dedicating it to her is like throwing a wave back into the sea.

NOTES

The folksong heard by Ulrich and Boris on pages 61–3 is adapted from a song described by Tim Rice in his account of Bulgarian music, *May It Fill Your Soul* (University of Chicago Press, 1994), page 154.

The opening of Alexander Pushkin's *Eugene Onegin* on page 121–2 is adapted from a translation by Vladimir Nabokov (Princeton University Press, 1991, page viii) and the translation by James E. Falen (Oxford World's Classics, 1998, page 5).

The jokes on page 122–3 are adapted from *Russia Dies Laughing: Jokes from Soviet Russia* by Zhanna Dolgopolova (Unwin, 1983).

The lines on page 223 are from Anna Akhmatova's poem 'Requiem' as translated by Judith Hemschmeyer in *Selected Poems of Anna Akhmatova* (Zephyr Press, 2000).

The extract from Plato's *Symposium* on page 334 is adapted from the translation by Christopher Gill (Penguin Classics, 2003) and the translation by Benjamin Jowett (Dover Thrift, 1994).

Irakli's poem, 'The dream of the embryo on the night before birth', on page 334, is adapted from Eliot Weinberger's translation of 'Nocturno Preso' by Xavier Villaurrutia in *Nostalgia for Death* (Copper Canyon Press, 1993), page 23.

For information on Einstein's life I was particularly indebted to *Das Verschmahte Genie: Albert Einstein Und Die Schweiz* by Alexis Schwarzenbach (Deutsche Verlags-Anstalt, 2005).